FOREIGN INFLUENCE

Scot Harvath, a former Navy SEAL, is now a field operative in a secret and uncompromising new spy agency. He is summoned when a bombing in Rome kills a group of American college students. Evidence points to a dangerous colleague from Harvath's past and a plan for further attacks on an unimaginable scale. Harvath must re-establish contact with the man, lure him out of hiding and kill him on the spot. But what if it is the wrong man? Simultaneously, a young woman is struck by a taxi in a hit-and-run incident in Chicago. But eventually the police give up on their investigation. Then the family's attorney uncovers a shocking connection to the bombing in Rome and the perpetrators' plans for America and Europe . . .

BRAD THOR

FOREIGN INFLUENCE

Complete and Unabridged

CHARNWOOD
Leicester

First published in Great Britain in 2010 by
Hodder & Stoughton, London

First Charnwood Edition
published 2012
by arrangement with
Hodder & Stoughton
An Hachette UK company, London

The moral right of the author has been asserted

British Library CIP Data

Thor, Brad.
  Foreign influence.
  1. Harvath, Scot (Fictitious character)- -Fiction.
  2. Intelligence officers- -United States- -Fiction.
  3. Terrorism- -Prevention- -Fiction.
  4. Suspense fiction. 5. Large type books.
  I. Title
  813.6–dc23

  ISBN 978–1–4448–0981–7

Published by
F. A. Thorpe (Publishing)
Anstey, Leicestershire

Set by Words & Graphics Ltd.
Anstey, Leicestershire
Printed and bound in Great Britain by
T. J. International Ltd., Padstow, Cornwall

This book is printed on acid-free paper

For Mark and Ellen LaRue,
two of the most dedicated patriots I know —
Thank you for everything you do for our
great nation.

He who does not punish evil commands it to be done.

— *Leonardo DaVinci*

Prologue

The strategic military outpost was such a closely guarded secret it didn't even have a name, only a number — site 243.

It sat in a rugged, windswept valley far away from cities and centers of industry. Its architecture was minimalist; a cross between a high-end refugee camp and a low-rent university. Tents, trailers, and a handful of cheap concrete buildings made up its 'campus.' The only outward signs of modernity were the Pizza Hut, Burger King, and Subway mobile restaurant trailers which made up the outpost's 'food court.'

It was just after three a.m. when the attack began. Lightweight Predator SRAW missile systems took out the fortified entry control point along with the watchtowers. Mortar rounds blanketed the campus, obliterating key infrastructure and force protection targets. When the heavily armed assault teams breached the perimeter, the outpost was in complete chaos.

The well-trained soldiers tasked with 243's security were no match for the men who now overran their positions.

Dressed in black, with specialized night vision goggles and suppressed weapons, the professional

1

combatants appeared only long enough to engage each soldier with an economy of surgically placed rounds before slipping back into the darkness, often before their victims' lifeless bodies had even hit the ground.

At the main concrete structure, a detachment from the assault team used a shaped charge to blow open the fortified door. As they rushed in, they heard the high-pitched whine followed by the thump of a limited EMP device being detonated. It was part of 243's emergency protocol meant to destroy the facility's data. The men in black, though, didn't care. Their superiors already had a copy.

With night vision goggles impervious to electromagnetic pulse, the men swept through the rest of the building, making sure they killed every occupant. From there, they moved on and cleared two more buildings while their team-mates took care of the remaining tents, trailers, and concrete structures.

Fifteen minutes later, three helicopters landed and the team was extracted. As they lifted off and disappeared back into the ink-black sky, not a single member of military outpost 243 had been left alive.

LONDON

A man in a blue linen blazer pushed away the hand of his subordinate. 'I know how it works,' he said, placing the tiny bud into his ear and activating the video on the smart phone.

His liver-spotted hands cradled the chrome device in his lap as he watched the scenes from Mongolia. It had been the most expensive and dangerous undertaking of his life. Though his club was actually a haven for members of the espionage community, he also sensed the presence of some of history's greatest sociopolitical figures around him at this moment. Had he looked up to see the smiling ghosts of Lenin, Stalin, Marx, or Mao, he wouldn't have been surprised. Great men who change the world shared a bond that transcended time, and he was on the verge of becoming just that, a great man who would change the world.

Though they were alone in the club's library, he kept his voice low. 'We're confident that all of their data was destroyed?'

The subordinate nodded. 'We have the only copy that remains.'

'And the personnel?'

'Everyone associated with the program has been terminated. The Chinese have gone berserk trying to figure out what happened. They have no idea who hit them.'

'Excellent,' said the man in the linen blazer. 'Let's keep it that way. Now, what about our network?'

'The network is fully intact and ready to go operational.'

This was an incredible moment, the man thought as he plucked the bud from his ear.

He removed the SIM card from the phone and handed the device back to the subordinate. 'I want you to initiate stage one as soon as possible.'

'So I have your permission to activate the network then?'

'You do. And whatever happens, don't lose sight of the bigger picture.'

CHICAGO

Alison Taylor hadn't planned on going out drinking after work, but it was a gorgeous summer night, the sales presentation was pretty much complete, and everybody else in her department was going.

It was supposed to be only one drink at RL, but as things often go, one drink led to another and then another. The party worked its way south hitting Pops, Shaw's, the Roof bar atop the Wit Hotel, and finally some seedy dive bar just west of the Loop. Before any of them knew it, it was four a.m. and their presentation was in less than five hours.

To counteract the heavy volume of alcohol they had consumed, someone had suggested the nearby 24/7 pharmacy for charcoal tablets and caffeinated beverages, but the idea was put on the back burner when they noticed that the tiny burger joint across the street was still serving. 'There's nothing like grease to absorb the alcohol molecules in your system,' one of them said.

After cheeseburgers and fries, they conducted an unsuccessful search of the pharmacy for charcoal pills, loaded up on energy drinks, and then headed for the subway.

Since two of the women lived in the suburbs, Alison invited them to stay at her apartment where they could borrow clothes and head into work with her in a few hours. The fact that one of the women was five inches shorter and the other seventy-five pounds heavier was lost on all of them in their drunken state.

They spent the subway ride cursing the bright lights of the train compartment, downing Red Bull, and wondering how much sleep they could grab at Alison's before having to leave for the office.

At Division Street, they stumbled up the steps from the Blue Line platform and out onto the sidewalk where they began to head east. It was in the crosswalk at Milwaukee Avenue that the unthinkable happened.

A taxicab came flying around the corner and slammed into Alison. Her friends watched in horror as she was tossed into the air and then landed, headfirst, fifteen feet away.

All of it had happened so suddenly. Everyone was in shock. As the taxicab sped away into the night, neither of Alison's friends had even gotten its number. The only thing they would be able to remember was the color of the vehicle, and that its driver appeared to be Middle Eastern.

1

BASQUE PYRENEES SPAIN
SIX DAYS LATER

In a sixteenth-century farmhouse, a dwarf known to intelligence agencies across the globe only as 'The Troll' lay bleeding to death as his house burned down around him.

He had made a very serious mistake, but it wasn't until he had pulled his hands away from his throat and had seen the blood that he had realized just how serious. There was no excuse. He *should* have known better.

The woman had been too attractive, too perfect, *too much* his type. She had described herself as an 'erotic gourmand,' with predilections ranging from troilism to chrematistophilia. But it was her fetish for peculiar body shapes, particularly dwarfism — known as morphophilia — that had convinced him they were perfect for each other and that he had to have her.

Precisely because she had seemed too good to be true, he had checked her out thoroughly. When satisfied that she was legitimate (and after having admonished the director of the Academy, as it was referred to, for not having brought her to his attention sooner), he arranged for her to be flown first class to Bilbao. There, he had a car meet her at the airport and take her to the train station where she traveled southeast into the Pyrenees. From the moment her feet touched the ground in Spain, he had had her watched. The nature of his business demanded that he be extremely cautious.

She had been advised to bring nothing but her passport and the clothes on her back. He had requested her sizes in advance and assured the Academy that he would provide everything that she would need.

When her train arrived in the sleepy mountain village, another car was waiting. The driver was professional and kept to himself as he made his way to the next transit point. Occasionally, though, the driver's eyes wandered to the rearview mirror to steal glimpses of her incredible beauty.

After dropping her off at a nondescript trailhead, the car retreated down the rutted, dirt road and disappeared. Two large men on horseback appeared from the thick forest of trees leading another horse behind them. They each carried knives in their boots and sawed-off shotguns in short, leather scabbards forward of their saddles.

After checking the woman for weapons, they helped her atop her mount, and led her up into the mountains.

The party rode for almost two hours and not much was said. The men had been instructed not to make small talk with their charge. Finally, they arrived at the farmhouse.

The men galloped off with the horses, and she

was left alone outside the little stone structure. Pushing open the front door, she saw a long wooden table covered with a fine linen tablecloth. Upon it was set a myriad of gourmet dishes. Champagne sat in a sterling silver bucket, a riot of exotic flowers exploded from a large crystal vase, and sitting at the head of the table was the Troll.

He was flanked by his two ever-present companions — a pair of white Caucasian Ovcharkas named Argos and Draco. Standing over forty-one inches at the shoulder and weighing over two hundred pounds each, the giant animals had been the dogs of choice for the Russian military and former East German border patrol. They were exceedingly fast, possessed a powerful urge to defend, and could be absolutely vicious when the situation called for it. They made perfect guardians for a man who stood just under three feet tall and had very powerful enemies — many of whom were also his clients.

What the man lacked in height, he more than made up for in charm and intelligence. He had a sweet face with deep, warm eyes. He proved himself to be a perfect gentleman, and his guest was more than happy to provide what he was paying for.

Through intense carnal rituals such as the *Etruscan Butterfly* and *Erotic Entrainment*, she took him to new heights of ecstasy.

They engaged in acts of sexual pursuit forbidden by even the most permissive of ancient societies. For the two of them, nothing was off-limits. In fact, the more outrageous or dangerous the act, the more willing she was to indulge in it.

She surrendered herself completely, infusing him with the greatest aphrodisiac of all (and the antidote to his greatest insecurity), power. A devotee of erotophonophilia, he twice pushed her right up to the very brink of death itself, only to bring her back at the last possible second. Holding her life in his hands was an incredible feeling. It made him feel like a god. Little did he know that she was slowly disarming him.

When they weren't having sex, they engaged in conversations of such intellectual depth that he felt he had finally met his equal. Though he knew he shouldn't, he fantasized that their relationship might lead to something more. He knew it was foolish, but no woman had ever stirred such deep emotion inside him.

He tried to remind himself that this was nothing more than a business relationship, but in his heart he still hoped. Gradually he was overcome. When he realized that there was little, if anything at all, this woman could ask of him that he wouldn't do, he knew she had conquered him. And she knew it too.

Her first request concerned his dogs, the same two dogs that were never away from his side, not even when he took her to his bed.

There was no need for her to make up excuses as to why she wanted the dogs removed. The more rough their sex, the more agitated the dogs became. Even the dwarf had to admit that his dogs were ruining the mood, so into the hallway they went.

With the dogs safely at bay, the woman didn't attack; not right away. She was an artist and true artists never rush their craft. For her masterpiece to be complete she needed his total trust, and so, she led him on a bit longer.

After two nights of making love without the dogs in the room, the time was finally right and the woman was ready. She had saved her most erotic, sexually charged game for last.

The little man wore a neatly kept beard. He was fastidious about it and trimmed it with a pair of scissors daily. To maintain the beard at his neck and cheeks, he used an old-fashioned straight razor.

It was highly polished with an ivory handle. She enjoyed watching him use it. It reminded her of being a little girl and watching her father, and she told him so. It was the only truth about herself that she ever revealed.

This time, she held out her hand for the razor. He was hesitant. It only lasted a fraction of a second, but it was long enough for her to notice.

'I want you to shave me,' she purred, opening the razor and handing it back to him as she stroked herself.

As the dwarf obliged her, the woman writhed in ecstasy atop his crisp, white sheets. Despite the size of his hands, they were surprisingly strong, as was the rest of him. He performed the delicate act with surgical precision.

When it became his turn, he propped two pillows against the headboard and leaned back.

Unlike some of the more unusual games she had instigated, he had heard of this one before, but had never trusted anyone enough to do it. Of course the game could be played with a disposable razor, but that would have defeated the purpose. The excitement came from the danger.

Withdrawing the polished blade from the bowl of warm water, she struck a coy smile as she began to hum the 'Largo al factotum' aria from *The Barber of Seville* and ran the razor back and forth along a towel as if it were a strop.

Sweeping her long, chestnut hair behind her neck, she bent down and kissed him on the mouth, allowing her heavy, bare breasts to briefly brush against his chest. Then she began to shave him.

The pleasure was indescribable. His senses were on fire as waves of sexual electricity pulsed through his body.

He licked his lips as he closed his eyes and arched his back. That was when she struck.

2

Professor Tony Carafano smiled as the last of his students, two sophomores from the University of Texas, shuffled into the breakfast room of the two-star Hotel Romano and sat down.

'Good morning, ladies,' he said as he removed his glasses and placed them next to his cappuccino.

Carafano was a charming man in his early fifties. He had gray hair and a large, aquiline nose, a feature, he enjoyed pointing out, which was not only the Pre-Raphaelite ideal of male beauty, but which also placed him above the other summer abroad professors because he really had been born with a 'nose for art.'

From Assisi, Perugia, and Cortona to Orvieto, Siena, and the hilltop town of Coricano, Tony Carafano had used his sense of humor to baptize his students in Italian art history. He believed that when they were having a good time, they learned more. He also believed that if you were traveling throughout the country by bus with twenty strangers for six weeks, the quicker you could get them all laughing the more enjoyable the trip would be.

13

He only had one rule: no matter how late the students stayed out the night before, they all had to be back by breakfast. They were good kids, sweet kids — the kind of kids that parents had a right to be proud of. None of them had broken his one and only rule. The fact that they hadn't showed respect, and it was mutual. This was the best summer group he had ever had the pleasure of teaching. And as much as his colleagues complained about the 'future of America,' these young men and women proved that America's future was bright, quite bright indeed.

Checking his watch, Carafano addressed the students. 'I can see that some of you are moving a bit slower than normal this morning and I'm not going to inquire as to the reason. I think I know why.'

A wave of polite laughter swept the breakfast room. When it died down, he continued. 'You've got ten minutes to load up on caffeine, aspirin, whatever it is that helps make you human, and then I want to see everyone in the lobby, checked out, with their bags ready to go. Okay?'

Heads nodded and with the scrape of chair legs across the tile floor, the students rose to get more coffee and return to their rooms to finish packing.

Depending on traffic, the professor knew that the drive south from Rome to Pompei would take a little over two and a half hours. Halfway there was a church with amazing mosaics that he wanted them to have plenty of time to study and sketch. After that, they had reservations for lunch at one of his favorite trattorias overlooking the Bay of Naples.

Half an hour later, the tiny hotel lobby was awash in a sea of suitcases and backpacks. As a handful of students made one last dash to the breakfast room for coffee, others helped the program's bus driver, Angelo, load the bags into the belly of the bright yellow motor coach. In the chaos of everyone checking out, none of them noticed that one of the bags didn't belong to their group.

After a final head count to make sure everyone was on board, Tony Carafano gave Angelo the okay to depart.

As the Italian maneuvered the coach through Roman traffic, the professor distributed the day's itinerary. Walking down the aisle, he found his students engaged in their morning ritual of texting friends back home, checking e-mail, and listening to their iPods. Few were bothering to take in their last glimpses of one of the most beautiful and historically significant cities in the world.

With one of Rome's most popular landmarks drawing near, Carafano called his students' attention to it. 'If anyone's interested, we're about to pass the Colosseum on our left.'

Some of them looked up. Many, though, were too busy. It was a shame that even though they had all seen it before, a thing of such wondrous beauty should go ignored. Especially considering what was about to happen.

As the bus pulled even with the ancient arena, a spotter on a rooftop half a mile away removed a cell phone from his pocket and dialed the number he had been given.

Six seconds later, an enormous explosion rocked the city as the motor coach erupted in a billowing fireball.

3

As his Russian GAZ sped down the dusty road, Omar-Hakim was fuming. The local Iraqi National Guard commander had been engaged in plenty of blackmail schemes, but always as the *perpetrator* — never the victim.

Next to him sat the man who had ensnared him and who had broken his hand when he had gone for his gun. He never should have agreed to meet with him. In fact, he should have shot him on sight. But now it was too late. He was trapped and there was nothing he could do.

The man in question was a forty-year-old American who spoke Arabic as well as Omar-Hakim spoke English. He was five-foot-ten with light brown hair, blue eyes, and a well-built physique. A Navy SEAL who had been recruited to the White House to help bolster the Secret Service's counterterrorism expertise, the man had become a previous president's favorite weapon in the war on terror. But when that president had left office, the man's tenure had expired. Now, he was working for a private organization.

His employer was a legend in the intelligence

17

world and had spent the last year polishing and honing the skills of the man who, always deadly serious about his work, now approached his life with a renewed sense of vigor.

He had a sense that somewhere a clock was ticking down. It was due, in part, to a realization that his own time on the playing field was winding down, but there was something more to it. There was a sense of foreboding; a sense that a storm was gathering and picking up strength as it sped toward shore — his shore — America.

There wasn't a specific act or event he could pin his sense of foreboding on. It was everything; the movements and chatter and unending determination by America's enemies to hit again and again and again. He and others like him believed that something else, something different was on the way, and they constantly reminded each other to keep their 'powder dry.'

There were only two things any of them could do about it — hunker down and wait for it to happen, or get out there, locate the threat, and take the fight to the enemy head-on. Scot Harvath wasn't the hunker-down-and-wait-for-it-to-happen type.

Looking at his GPS device, he activated his radio and said, 'Two minutes. Stand by.'

'Roger that,' replied a voice from the neighborhood up ahead. 'Standing by.' The snipers had been in place for hours. It was now nearing four a.m.

Even though he couldn't see it, he knew the drone was still above them on station. Via the Combined Air and Space Operations Center, he

18

radioed for a final situation report from the drone pilots back at Creech Air Force base northwest of Las Vegas. 'Press box, are we still good to go?'

'That is affirmative,' came the reply. 'Tangos one through four are still in place. Thermals show that the heat signatures inside the target have not changed.'

Harvath didn't bother asking about the hostages. He knew why there were no longer any heat signatures from them.

As they turned the corner, the outline of their target could be seen silhouetted against the night sky. It was time to go to the next phase of their operation. 'This is it,' he said over his radio as he set the GPS down on the seat next to him and adjusted his beret. 'We're going to sterile comms,' which meant from this point forward they would communicate only via a series of prearranged clicks.

In the two trucks following his, the rest of the team made ready. After checking their weapons, they straightened the uniforms Omar-Hakim had provided and donned their Iraqi helmets.

Power outages were a common occurrence in Iraq. Per Harvath's request, the power to this neighborhood had been cut earlier in the evening. The streets were completely dark. At this hour, even families with their own generators were sleeping.

'Remember what we discussed,' Harvath said to Omar-Hakim when the vehicles pulled up in front of the target.

'I remember,' said the man.

Harvath then motioned for him to get out.

In front of them was a house surrounded by a thick mud wall. Its entrance was a set of wide double doors fabricated from sheet metal and scrap wood. A fist-sized hole had been punched through each side. A heavy chain padlocked from the inside kept them securely closed.

There wasn't a sound to be heard.

Omar-Hakim sucked in his gut and attempted to ignore the throbbing pain from his broken hand. Harvath had warned him to leave it by his side and not draw attention to it.

The commander walked up to the gate and whispering, so as not to awaken anyone, addressed the sentry inside. 'Abdullah. Open up.'

'Who is it?' replied a voice in Arabic.

The Iraqi bent his face down to the hole and spoke over the chain. 'Commander Hakim, you idiot.'

'What do you want?'

Omar-Hakim came from a large, powerful Fallujah family. He was accustomed to being respected. The insolence of the al-Qaeda sentry grated on him. 'Open these doors right now or I'll tell Assad you're the one who betrayed him to the Americans.'

'The Americans?'

'Yes, you idiot. The Americans. They know you're here. Now open up so I can speak with Assad before they arrive.'

The sentry bent down and looked through the hole. He studied the Iraqi National Guard vehicles.

'I've brought extra uniforms and men to help

you,' added the Iraqi. 'Hurry up.'

Slowly, the sentry removed a key from his pocket and placed it in the lock. As he removed the chain, Harvath toggled the transmit button of his radio and sent two distinct clicks.

When the al-Qaeda man designated as 'Tango One' pulled back the gate, the snipers engaged their targets.

Muffled spits raced through the air. The sentry on the roof was killed instantly, as was the covert sentry positioned a block away. A burst of radio clicks over the team's earpieces served as confirmation.

With his suppressed Russian Makarov, Harvath stepped from behind Omar-Hakim and placed two rounds into the gatekeeper's head.

The corrupt Iraqi commander was no stranger to killing, but the suddenness and violence of the act froze him in place. He had no idea that this was part of the plan, though he should have expected a raid on an al-Qaeda safe house to result in a bit more than hurt feelings.

While Omar-Hakim was staring at the dead man, Harvath struck him in the head with the butt of his weapon. The overweight Iraqi collapsed to the ground as the rest of the team exited their trucks.

Two men from the lead vehicle bound the commander with zip ties, gagged him, and threw him in the back. They then took up lookout positions.

The rest of the team fanned out into the compound.

Based on their intelligence, there was only one

obstacle remaining. He was inside the rear of the house near the back door.

Harvath had conducted raids like this so many times before that he could picture exactly what was going on inside.

All of the men, save the remaining sentry, would be gathered in the large room at the front of the house. They would be sleeping on heavy fleece blankets purchased at the local market. One or two might be up having tea. If the power had been on, a few more might have been watching jihadi videos. More than likely, a couple of them were having sex with each other. Homosexuality was so rampant among the jihadists that catching them in the act had stopped surprising Harvath a long time ago. As a matter of fact, very little surprised him anymore; even less shocked him.

A colleague of his in Fallujah named Mike Dent had told him the story of a six-year-old boy named Khidir. Khidir was the son of a local police officer. Two years ago while his father was at work, members of an Iraqi al-Qaeda cell had burst into his home and savagely torn him from where he was hiding behind his grandmother, desperately clinging to her skirt.

The kidnappers wanted Khidir's father, Shafi, to help free several al-Qaeda members being held in his jail. Shafi knew how dangerous the prisoners were and refused to set them loose upon the citizens of Fallujah. He knew full well they would conduct more killings and put more families through the same horror he was experiencing. The kidnappers promised to slit his little boy's throat if he didn't comply, but Shafi refused to give in to their demands. Khidir had not been seen since.

Dent had been so moved by Khidir's story that he had made it his goal to help find out what had happened to the little boy. As a civilian trainer for the Fallujah police, he spent a lot of time building a network of informants. After a while, he started to wonder if it had all been a waste of time when one day a contact passed along a rumor that a group of al-Qaeda members was holding several children hostage on a small farm outside the city. With no funds to pay for any more intelligence, Dent had reached out to Harvath. He knew how Harvath felt about children, and to cement his assistance had e-mailed him a picture of a bright-eyed, smiling Khidir taken before the little boy's nightmare had begun.

Three days later, Harvath landed in Baghdad with his new boss's blessing, an expense account, and permission to do whatever necessary to bring the al-Qaeda cell to justice.

It took Harvath, Dent, and the team of contractors they had assembled $20,000 in bribes and ten days to find the location of the terrorists.

Pure hate for what they had done fueled Harvath as he cobbled together the operation. Like Dent, since hearing the little boy's story, he had been living for this very moment. Each of the men would be the first through his respective entry point.

They moved quickly and quietly across the

cracked, brown earth of the courtyard. Harvath's team went to the front door while Dent took the other half of the men to the back.

Harvath's team put on their night vision goggles and when they all flashed him the thumbs-up, he signaled for the battering ram to come forward.

With his team in place, he 'clicked' Dent's team in back and gave them the go-ahead. Moments later, there was the sound of splintering wood as the rear door was battered open and the remaining sentry was taken out.

Harvath counted down from fifteen. He could hear the shouts of the al-Qaeda operatives in the front room as they leapt from their beds and scrambled into the hallway that led to the back door.

Harvath reached the end of his countdown and motioned for the assaulter with the ram to hit the front door.

The entry tool knocked the door completely off its hinges and Harvath charged through, followed by the rest of his team.

Bottlenecked in the hallway, the AQ operatives were mown down with bullets from both sides.

The air was thick with the smell of blood and gun smoke. When Harvath called cease fire, Dent's team moved up from the back of the house to secure the hallway while Harvath and his team cleared the rest of the house.

They found the entrance to the 'spider hole' beneath a stained rug in the main room. One of the men said it reminded him of the hole Delta Force operatives had pulled Saddam out of.

Harvath looked down into the pit. It smelled atrocious. Six sets of hollow, half-dead eyes stared up at him. 'Everything is okay,' he said in Arabic as he removed his night vision goggles. 'We're Americans. We're going to take you home to your families.'

In the beam of his flashlight, he could see a shaft six feet deep that opened into a pit five feet square by three feet high. For their bodily functions, the al-Qaeda animals had left their child hostages only a rusted coffee can. Disgusting didn't even begin to describe the scene.

Harvath sent one of his men outside to find a ladder and when he returned, they lowered it into the pit.

The children were all male, between four and eleven years old, and were all sons of Iraqi police officers in Fallujah.

They had another thing in common. All of them had been brutally tortured. The oldest boy took charge and sent the others slowly up the ladder. As they emerged, they were assessed by the men of the team, medically treated as necessary, and wrapped in blankets.

As the oldest boy came into view, he was quite upset and explained that there was still one child left behind, badly in need of help.

'Is it Khidir?' Harvath asked hopefully.

The boy nodded.

Gently moving him away from the shaft, Harvath climbed down into the pit. What he discovered wrenched his heart out.

Khidir was now eight years old and severely

malnourished. His eyes were set deep in their sockets and surrounded by black circles. His once thick head of black hair had fallen out in clumps and he looked as if he had probably soiled himself repeatedly.

As Harvath triaged the little boy, he discerned that both his arms and legs were broken. His left knee had a large iron nail driven through it, and all the teeth in his mouth had been pulled out, leaving behind infected gum tissue.

His breathing was shallow and came in rapid gasps. Harvath noted his elevated temperature and pulse. The boy was shocky.

Dosing a child for a morphine injection was a tricky gamble. Getting him up the ladder and out of the pit was going to be extremely painful. Harvath removed a preloaded syringe and injected half.

'Prep an IV!' he yelled up the shaft.

Khidir was becoming unresponsive. He needed to move him now.

Cradling the child to his chest, Harvath shifted to the ladder and climbed using one arm. At the top, the medic gently took the little boy from him, laid him down, and began an IV.

'Assad's dead, but we've got two survivors from the hallway,' said one of the men from the team. 'What do you want to do?'

'Where's Dent?'

'He's processing them outside.'

'Are they stable enough for transport?' asked Harvath.

The man nodded.

'Cuff 'em and stuff 'em with Omar.'

'You got it.'

The medic looked up from Khidir and said to Harvath, 'In addition to four broken limbs and septic shock, he has a collapsed lung. I can give him some more morphine so he'll be comfortable, but he's not going to make it.'

That was unacceptable. The little boy didn't deserve to die. Being the son of a policeman should be an honor, not a death sentence. 'Can we get him to the hospital in Fallujah?'

'Even if we could, it will be too late.'

Harvath knew both Camp Slayer and the Green Zone were too far. 'What about the Norwegian facility near the airbase at Ramadi? They've got a fully staffed MSF clinic there.'

The medic shook his head.

Harvath looked down as Khidir started guppy breathing.

'It's your call,' said the medic. 'What do you want to do?'

Harvath couldn't take his eyes off the boy. 'Can I hold him?'

The medic thought about it a minute. 'Of course,' he said as he prepped a second syringe of morphine.

Once Harvath had the boy cradled in his lap, the medic piggybacked the drug into the IV.

'His breathing is probably going to stop soon, but I promise he won't feel any pain.'

Harvath wanted to say *Thank you*, but the words didn't come.

'These people are savages,' said the medic as he stood.

Harvath nodded. 'Have Dent bring the two

27

survivors from the hallway back in here. I want them to see this.'

The medic nodded. Moments later, Dent and one of his men brought the al-Qaeda operatives back into the room. Harvath nodded at the opposite wall and Dent shoved them down into a sitting position. He told the team member who had helped him bring the prisoners in to go wait outside. Once he was sure the entire house was empty, he came back into the room and nodded to Harvath. He had a feeling he knew what was going to happen next.

One of the al-Qaeda operatives turned his head away. Harvath yelled at him in Arabic to watch. The man reluctantly complied.

The other sat there with a smile on his face and Harvath bored holes into the man's head with his stare.

Harvath wished the little boy could live, though he knew it wasn't going to happen. The extra morphine had sealed the deal.

Unable to do anything else for him, he did something he hadn't done in a long time; he prayed for a painless exit.

The little boy was fast losing his fight. His little chest rose and fell so infrequently that Harvath went for tens of seconds at a time wondering if the child had already expired.

He knew it was only a matter of time. He held the boy tighter and rocked him. The terrorist with the smile laughed at Harvath and called him a pussy.

Harvath ignored him as he tried to figure out how many seconds had passed since the little boy had last breathed.

Placing two fingers on the little boy's neck, Harvath felt for the carotid artery. There was no pulse. Khidir had passed.

The al-Qaeda operative who had been laughing realized what had happened and now fell silent.

Harvath adjusted the boy in his arms and reached for his lifeless hand. Khidir's fingers were rough and blistered. Into the boy's hand he placed his Makarov and wrapped one tiny finger around the trigger.

He raised the boy's arm. Steadying his aim, he pulled Khidir's finger twice; firing into the laughing terrorist's stomach.

The al-Qaeda operative screamed in pain. He began rocking back and forth, unable to reach out and clasp his wounds with his hands zip-tied behind his back.

Standing up, Harvath carried the boy outside and placed him in the truck next to Omar-Hakim.

Once everyone was loaded, the drive to Fallujah's main police station took under half an hour.

It was almost morning, and while it would be a day of thanksgiving for five of the families, for Khidir's it would be a day of incredible sadness.

As for Omar-Hakim and the two surviving al-Qaeda operatives, their ordeal was only beginning. They would probably never see the inside of a courtroom. Justice for them would be meted out in a different fashion. For what they had done, and what Omar-Hakim had allowed to be done to those little boys, no torture could be too painful or too horrific.

Harvath took little pleasure in what he did, but it had to be done. America was engaged in all-out war with the Islamists. And as America became more aggressive in taking the fight to them, he knew that they were going to become more aggressive in taking the fight to America.

He also knew that the loss of life wouldn't end with Khidir. Things were going to get much, much worse before they ever got better.

4

Harvath changed into shorts, grabbed two six-packs from the fridge, and walked down to his dock. He had wanted to get good and drunk in Iraq, but there hadn't been time. He had to debrief and clean up a bunch of loose ends before flying home. Now, he had all the time he wanted.

The dock's wooden planks were hot beneath his feet. Without the throng of weekend boaters, the Potomac was quiet. A light breeze stirred the surface of the water. *It was good to be home.*

In addition to tying one on, what he needed to do was put the things he'd seen and heard — things he'd known from the outset he'd probably not be able to forget — in an iron box and bury it as deep as possible in one of the farthest corners of his mind. The practice was unhealthy, but he didn't care. It was the only way he could do his job.

Sitting down at the end of the dock, Harvath leaned against one of the pier posts, opened his first beer, and tipped it back.

His fiancée, Tracy, was up at her grandfather's

31

cottage in Maine, and he was grateful for the solitude. He didn't want to see her right away. He needed to decompress and come back to reality. Or at least what he liked to call reality; that world beyond kicking in doors and shooting Islamic fanatics in the face.

The biggest reason he needed time, though, was that he knew he couldn't talk to Tracy about what he had seen. Children had become one of those topics that they no longer discussed.

Harvath closed his eyes and lifted his face toward the sun. He had given up trying to change her mind. Because of the persistent headaches she suffered, she said she couldn't even consider becoming a mother. At the same time, she knew that he wanted a family and she had tried to convince him to start over again with someone else. But he wouldn't leave her, no matter how many times she worked to push him away.

She had been the victim of a vendetta launched by a sick terrorist who wanted to torture him by targeting the people around him. There were days when the pain Tracy suffered was so severe that she wished out loud that the bullet that had struck her in the head had done its intended job. It was agonizing for Harvath to hear her talk like that.

For Tracy, some days she couldn't tell what was worse, the physical pain from the attack, or the emotional pain from watching one of the most decent men she had ever known forgo the family he desired in order to stay by her side.

His father had also been a Navy man — a

32

SEAL and then a SEAL instructor. When he died, father and son were barely on speaking terms. Harvath had forgone college for a career as an amateur athlete, something the elder Harvath had zealously disapproved of.

After his father's death in a training accident, Harvath had found it impossible to return to competitive sports. Worried about what might become of him without any sense of purpose and direction in his life, Harvath's mother had encouraged him to enroll in college.

He graduated from the University of Southern California in three years cum laude with a double major in political science and military history. By the time he finished, he knew exactly what he wanted to do.

Following in his father's footsteps, he joined the Navy and was eventually accepted to Basic Underwater Demolition SEAL school (BUD/S) and a specialized program known as SQT or SEAL Qualification Training. Though the process was grueling beyond measure, his mental and physical conditioning as a world-class athlete, his stubborn refusal to ever give up on anything, and the belief that he had finally found his true calling in life propelled him forward and earned him the honor of being counted as one of the world's most elite warriors — a U.S. Navy SEAL.

He served with SEAL Team Two and then Team Six, where he assisted a presidential security detail and caught the eye of the Secret Service. Wanting to bolster their anti-terrorism expertise at the White House, they eventually succeeded in wooing him away from the Navy and up to D.C. Harvath soon distinguished himself even further and after a short time was recommended for an above-top-secret program at the Department of Homeland Security called the Apex Project.

The project's raison d'être was to level the playing field against America's enemies. The belief was that if the terrorists weren't playing by any rules, then neither should the United States, especially when it came to defending its citizens and interests at home and abroad.

But with a new administration had come a new approach to dealing with terrorism, and the Apex Project was dismantled. Harvath had found himself out of a job.

With a unique skill set and a desire to continue serving the interests of his country, he accepted a private sector position with a company specializing in intelligence gathering and highly advanced special operations training near Telluride, Colorado.

In the words of a former CIA director, Harvath knew that intelligence was at the nexus of every major security challenge facing the United States. It didn't matter if it was al-Qaeda or Hugo Chavez, the need for timely, accurate, comprehensive information was unprecedented.

Harvath and the former CIA director weren't the only people to recognize that the drive for quality intelligence was paramount in the post-9/11 world. A well-funded group of high-level former military and intelligence operatives had seen the need as well. Deeply concerned with the entrenched bureaucracy at the CIA and the political hobbling of the nation's defense apparatus, they sought to create an organization that would boldly do what the country's politically correct, vote-chasing politicians and constantly-covering-their-cowering-asses bureaucrats were too timid and too inept to attempt.

Named after its founder, Reed Carlton — a retired thirty-year veteran of the CIA and one of the nation's most revered spymasters — the Carlton Group was based upon the Office of Strategic Services, or OSS, the wartime intelligence agency that had been the predecessor to the CIA. The Carlton Group was composed of patriots who wanted one thing and one thing only: to keep Americans safe no matter what the cost.

Its modus operandi was quite similar to that of the Apex Project, except for one thing — it didn't fall under the auspices of any politicians or bureaucrats. The Carlton Group was an obscure, private organization funded completely from Department of Defense black budgets. Only a handful of high-level career military DOD personnel knew of its existence, and it represented a major shift in counterterrorism's center of gravity. The only thing it was missing was a reliable private intelligence branch. To use existing government intelligence apparatus like DOD, DIA, NSA, or CIA risked exposure and was out of the question. Therefore, they had to seek something in the private sector.

When the Carlton Group purchased the

company Harvath had been working for in Colorado, he received a phone call. The new powers that be were restructuring and they wanted to move Harvath out of simply gathering intelligence and building human networks and into something much more interesting.

Carlton, or the 'Old Man' as he was affectionately known by those who worked for him, had personally invited Harvath to his home in northern Virginia to discuss a new position. He had assembled a small group of operatives with military and intelligence experience to carry out 'immediate action' assignments. Using the popular Pentagon catch-phrase, 'Find, fix, finish, and follow up,' he explained that Harvath would be responsible for identifying terrorist leadership, tracking them to a specific location, capturing or killing them as necessary, and using the information gleaned from the assignment to plan the next operation. The goal was to apply constant pressure to terrorist networks and pound them so hard and so relentlessly that they were permanently rocked back on their heels, if not ground into the dust.

In addition to immediate-action assignments, Carlton planned clever psychological operations to eat away at the terrorist networks from within, sowing doubt, fear, distrust, and paranoia throughout their ranks like a cancer. It was everything the United States government should have been doing, but wasn't.

Serving under a man like Carlton was an honor in and of itself. The scope and intensity of the operations were icing on the cake. Harvath was sold.

For twelve months, the Old Man had put him through the most comprehensive intelligence training he had ever experienced. In essence, Carlton distilled what he had learned over his thirty years in the espionage world and drilled it as deeply as possible into Harvath.

On top of the intelligence training, Harvath was required to keep his counterterrorism skills sharp. He took additional courses in Israeli hand-to-hand combatives and the Russian martial art known as Systema. There were driving classes, language classes, and tens of thousands of rounds of ammunition fired on the range and in shoot houses with a host of high-end private instructors.

He made excellent progress and, despite his recent milestone birthday, felt that he was in better shape and better equipped than he had ever been before. Even so, he'd recently begun to notice that it was taking him slightly longer to bounce back from injuries. The job was a dream come true, but he knew he couldn't keep doing it forever. At some point, maybe ten years from now, maybe fifteen, things were going to change. He couldn't spend the rest of his life kicking in doors and shooting bad guys in the head.

Carlton had been ready to put Harvath in the field, but before he could begin, Harvath had asked for permission to conduct the Iraq operation. The Old Man had agreed and through the DOD had greased Harvath's passage into

37

Iraq, seeing to it that he had everything he needed.

With the Iraq operation complete, the Old Man had given him a couple of days off before the real work was to begin. He had suggested time with Tracy. Harvath had told him he'd think about it.

He was on his second beer, still thinking about it and gazing absent-mindedly across the water when his phone vibrated. He took it out and checked the display. It was an international call, but the country code was 34 — Spain. Figuring it had to be one of his guys who was using a Spanish cell phone company to get better calling rates out of Iraq, he took the call.

The minute he heard the heavily accented voice on the other end, he realized he had been wrong. 'Mr. Harvath?' said the voice.

'Who's this?'

'I'm a friend of Nicholas.'

'*Nicholas?*' repeated Harvath. '*Nicholas* who? How'd you get this number?'

The man ignored the question. 'He says you share an affinity for the same breed of dog.'

Immediately, Harvath's mind was drawn to his dog, Bullet. A Caucasian Ovcharka, or Caucasian sheepdog as the name translated, Bullet was named after an old friend of his, Bullet Bob, who had been killed during a terrorist attack on New York City. Ovcharkas were exceedingly fast, fiercely loyal, and absolutely vicious when it came to guarding those closest to them, which was why Bullet

38

was with Tracy up in Maine.

The name *Nicholas* now registered. Harvath's dog had been left on his doorstep as a thank-you *cum* peace offering from a dwarf who dealt in the purchase and sale of highly sensitive and often highly classified information. Though commonly referred to as the Troll, the little man had told Harvath he preferred his friends to call him Nicholas.

Harvath had reached a certain détente with Nicholas, but describing it as friendship would have been stretching the definition of their relationship. In fact, if he never saw or heard from the little man again it would be fine by him.

'What do you want?' asked Harvath.

'Someone tried to kill Nicholas,' said the voice.

'You reap what you sow. He probably deserved it.'

The man pushed forward undeterred. 'The bombing in Rome two days ago — '

'Does he know something?' interrupted Harvath. He had heard about the bus explosion and the horrible loss of lives before leaving Iraq. It was all over the news.

'He says he needs to talk to you about it.'

'Does he know who was behind the attack?'

There was a pause as the man seemed to gather his thoughts.

'I want to speak with Nicholas,' Harvath said finally.

'He's not in a condition to talk. Not right now.'

'Well, when he is, tell him to call me back.'

Harvath was about to hang up when the man stated, 'He needs to see you in person.'

'I'm not comfortable with that.'

'Mr. Harvath, you're going to be presented with evidence, false evidence, implicating Nicholas in the attacks. In fact, two black SUVs have just pulled into your driveway.'

Harvath looked up toward his house. 'Why should I believe you?'

'I'm just the messenger,' replied the voice. 'Nicholas is the one you need to speak to. He can help you track down who did this, but he needs you to come to him, and to come alone.'

Harvath didn't like it. It felt wrong, and that little voice in the back of his mind that never lied and had always helped to keep him alive was telling him to be very, very careful. 'The only thing this offer's missing is a dark alley,' he said.

'Someone wants your government to believe Nicholas was involved. Ask yourself *why*. Review the evidence, and if you decide you want the truth, be in the old town of Bilbao the day after tomorrow. Behind the Cathedral in the Calle de la Tendería is a tobacconist. Ask the man there for cigarettes named after Nicholas's dogs and you'll receive instructions on what to do next.

'And Mr. Harvath? Please hurry. Nicolas believes there may be more attacks in the works.'

Harvath was about to interject when the call was disconnected. From up near the house, he could just make out the sound of several car doors slamming.

40

5

Burt Taylor had just come back from the hospital cafeteria, and his wife, Angela, was next to their daughter's hospital bed when trauma surgeon, Dr. Dennis Stern, walked into the room.

It had been ten days since the hit-and-run. Alison Taylor had suffered severe brain damage, as well as multiple broken bones, severe lacerations, and internal bleeding.

Her parents had driven in from Minnesota as soon as they'd received the news. For the first few days, neither of them had left the hospital. Now, they spent the days together with Alison and took turns spending the night by her bed.

'Have the Chicago Police come up with anything?' asked Stern as he finished his examination.

Mr. Taylor had trouble keeping his anger in check. 'Not a damn thing.'

Normally, Mrs. Taylor would have called him on his cursing, but in this case she agreed with his choice of words. The police had been less than satisfactory.

'It's like they aren't even interested in finding the guy,' continued Taylor. 'They quote stats for annual hit-and-runs as if we're supposed to just

41

accept what happened to Alison as a consequence of living in Chicago. It's ridiculous.'

'I agree with you,' said Stern. 'Most cops mean well, but the CPD is overworked. This city's deficit is like a black hole. It just keeps sucking more and more into it, and it leaves the cops with less and less to work with.' He could see the anger building in Burt Taylor's eyes. 'But that doesn't mean that they shouldn't be doing everything they can to find the person who did this to your daughter.'

'You're damn right.'

'I think you should have someone working this for you from the inside.'

'*Working this from the inside?*' repeated Taylor incredulously. 'Isn't that what the detectives assigned to Alison's case are *supposed* to be doing?'

'Technically, yes. But like any big-city police force, the CPD has a large bureaucracy. That doesn't excuse how your daughter's case is or isn't being handled. It's just a fact. Again, the majority of cops at the CPD are good people. They're just swamped with murders and rapes and shootings and all of it.'

Angela Taylor brought the trauma surgeon back to the matter at hand. 'What do you mean by someone working for us from the inside?'

'Lots of cops moonlight,' replied Stern. 'Many do security. But they also do other things. I've done a lot of tactical medicine with the SWAT team and have a friend who is now over in the department's Organized Crime Division. He

42

happens to be a lawyer and he moonlights taking cases.'

Burt Taylor looked at him. 'So you're telling me that if we want our daughter's case to get the attention it deserves, we've got to pay someone off? What the hell kind of police department is your city running?'

The surgeon put up his hands. 'Absolutely not. What I am suggesting is that you meet with him, talk about what happened, and share your frustration over the lack of progress by the CPD. He might be able to help you.'

'I'm afraid I'm confused as well,' added Mrs. Taylor. 'Once the police find who did this, the city or district attorney will bring charges, won't they?'

'Correct. It'll be the state's attorney,' said Stern. 'But I want you to understand, I'm not trying to sell you anything. You're either going to like John and want to work with him or you're not. He wouldn't be acting as a Chicago police officer; he'd be acting as an advocate for Alison and your family. He'd be your attorney, and his role would be to push the CPD's investigation. He'd also launch his own investigation so that you can not only nail the person who did this and have the state's attorney bring him up on criminal charges, but you'll also have a person you can sue in civil court for damages.

'That's what I mean by having someone working for you on the inside. He knows how the CPD works. Even though he'll be wearing his lawyer hat, the fact that he's also a cop will bring a lot of pressure to bear on the investigation.'

43

Burt Taylor thought about it for several moments. After looking at his wife, he turned back to Dennis Stern and said, 'How do we get in touch with him?'

★ ★ ★

They met at an out-of-the-way restaurant not far from the hospital in the city's Little Italy neighborhood along Taylor Street.

Sergeant John Vaughan was sitting at a table in the corner, his back to the wall, with a view of the front door. It was just after eleven a.m., and the restaurant was empty. He noticed Burt Taylor through the window before he even entered.

The hostess showed him to the table and John stood to shake his hand. 'I'm very sorry about what happened to your daughter.'

'Thank you,' said Taylor as he released the man's hand and took a seat. Vaughan was in his late thirties. He wore a brown suit with a green tie. His dark hair was cut short and he had eyes that moved around the room. 'Are you expecting someone else?'

'I'm sorry,' said Vaughan. 'I don't come to this neighborhood a lot. It's nothing personal.'

Taylor didn't know what to make of him. So far, he wasn't very impressed. 'Dr. Stern thinks you may be able to help us.'

'Dennis is a good man.'

It was an odd reply. 'You're a police officer, but not a detective, correct?'

'That's right.'

'But you *are* a lawyer.'

'I am,' he responded.

Taylor paused, waiting for some sort of a sales pitch as to why he should hire him, but nothing came. Whatever this man was, he was definitely no salesman. 'Setting aside your relationship with Dr. Stern, why should I consider hiring you?'

'Well, it depends on what you want.'

'We *want* to find the driver of the taxi who ran down our daughter.'

'Good, because that's what I want too.'

Finally, Taylor saw a spark in the man.

Vaughan continued. 'Are you familiar with Maslow's hierarchy of needs? You know, categories of needs that have to be met before a person can start focusing on achieving the needs of the next category?'

'I am.'

'Well, when it comes to cops, detectives in particular, that's pretty much BS. There are two types of cases that will always get solved — the easy ones and the ones where there is so much pressure grinding down on the investigators that they absolutely have to climb out of the ring with a victory.'

'So which one is Alison's?'

'Unfortunately, neither. There are more than five thousand Yellow Cabs in this city and the only witnesses to the crime were so inebriated, their testimony is worthless. So that scratches your daughter's case from the easy category. And let's face it, if this was an easy case, you and I wouldn't be sitting here.

'As far as crushing the investigators with pressure, unless you have a very close relationship with the mayor, our police superintendent, or your daughter is some sort of notable personality, there's just not going to be enough pressure to make this case a priority and get it solved.'

Taylor was confused. 'Then where does that leave us?'

John Vaughan smiled. 'It leaves you with me.'

'And what would you do differently?'

'For starters, I'd do the job the detectives were supposed to. I'd investigate the entire incident from front to back.'

'Then what?'

'I'd follow up on any leads and see where they take me.'

'That's it?'

'That's how it's done,' said Vaughan.

'Officer, how many hit-and-run cases have you ever investigated?'

'To be honest with you, none.'

'How many violent crimes?'

There was a pause, so Taylor added, 'Give or take.'

'Two or three,' responded Vaughan.

Taylor was beginning to feel that this had all been a waste of time. 'How old are you?'

'Thirty-five.'

'And exactly how long have you been an attorney?'

'Six months, sir.'

'*Six months?* When the heck did you get out of law school, yesterday?'

'Actually, four years ago.'

Taylor was now completely convinced that he had wasted his time. 'It took you that long to pass the bar?'

'No. I took a four-year leave to fight in Iraq.'

Taylor wondered if maybe he had the man. 'What branch of the service?'

'The Marine Corps.'

'You're a *Marine*?'

'Yes, sir. I worked in intelligence and helped shape our counterinsurgency strategy.'

After several moments of silence Taylor said, 'Do you believe you can help with my daughter's case?'

'I wouldn't waste your time, sir, if I believed otherwise.'

Waving the waiter over, he replied, 'Then let's order some lunch and talk about what you can do for my family.'

6

Coming up from the dock, Harvath decided to stay out of sight until he knew what was going on.

He cut across his neighbor's property and used a stand of trees for cover. Peering toward his house, he saw two blacked-out Suburbans parked in his driveway. Either Nicholas had someone watching his house, or he had access to real-time satellite imagery. Knowing the little man's skills, he suspected it was the latter.

A small contingent of hard men in crisp suits with earpieces stood near the vehicles, their heads on swivels. They definitely hadn't come to sell Girl Scout cookies. Harvath wished he'd taken his .45 down to the dock with him.

As he watched, one of the men spoke into a microphone at his sleeve. When the passenger door of the second vehicle opened, Reed Carlton stepped out and Harvath relaxed.

He was a tall, fit man in his mid-sixties with a prominent chin and silver hair.

'You really should call first, Reed,' said Harvath as he slipped from behind the tree line and took Carlton's security team by surprise.

'Sorry about that,' said the Old Man as

48

Harvath met him in the driveway and the two shook hands. 'Something has come up. Can we talk inside?'

'As long as you're okay with casual Monday,' replied Harvath, referring to his shorts-and-no-shirt look.

The older man nodded and followed him inside. After pulling a shirt from the hall closet and putting it on, Harvath directed his new boss to the kitchen.

'Coffee?' he asked.

'Please,' said Reed as he sat down at the kitchen table and placed his briefcase next to him. 'I understand Iraq was a success.'

'Not for the little boy who died.'

'I was sorry to hear about that.'

Harvath didn't reply. He kept his back to the man, pulled two large mugs out of the cupboard, and set them on the counter.

'I haven't read your full debrief yet,' continued Carlton. 'Did you go through with the whole thing?'

There was silence, and the Old Man waited. Finally, Harvath said, 'All of it.'

While Carlton was a master at psychological operations, this assignment had been Harvath's from start to finish. He had dubbed it *Paradise Lost*. The idea was to shake any other al-Qaeda cells who might be considering the kidnapping and torture of children. Upon each terrorist body at the safe house was left a black envelope. Inside the envelope was a detailed account, in Arabic, of horrible things supposedly done to the men before they had been killed. Placed into the mouth of each terrorist had been a pickled pig's foot from a jar that Harvath had brought with him from the U.S.

The idea of the notes in the black envelopes was to send a message to all of the other terrorists preying on children in Iraq. They would not die martyrs' deaths. They would not go to Paradise. They would be defiled before their god. They would be unclean and unworthy. And to make sure the point was driven home, the pickled pigs' feet were placed into the mouth of each of the corpses.

It was a derivative of the Colombian necktie, and Harvath was confident word of it would spread quickly, its meaning clear.

Carlton changed the subject. 'You heard about Rome?'

Harvath filled the coffee cups and brought them to the table where he sat down. 'I did. Twenty American college students.'

'Plus their teacher, the bus driver, and eleven others who had the misfortune of being near that bus when it detonated at the Colosseum. Current count has over forty wounded.'

He shook his head. 'Do we have any leads?'

Reaching into his briefcase Carlton withdrew a folder. 'The Italians are investigating a rumor about four Muslim men trying to purchase military-grade explosives in Sicily. The same kind used in the attack in Rome.'

Sicily could mean only one thing. 'They think the Mafia's involved?'

'That's what they thought at first. And considering the fact that the Cosa Nostra did over two billion dollars in illicit-weapons trafficking last year, it makes sense to start with them.'

'So there's a connection?'

Carlton shook his head. 'From what they've uncovered, the Mafia was happy to sell the suspects guns, but they drew the line at explosives, fearing correctly that they might be used on Italian soil.'

'Then where did the terrorists get the explosives?'

'According to the Italians, the explosives came in through another channel. A man mentioned in chatter before and after the attack — Moscerino.'

'Who is *Moscerino*?' asked Harvath.

'It's not a *who* exactly, it's a *what*,' replied Carlton, as he slid the file across the table. '*Moscerino* is Italian for 'dwarf.''

Harvath hesitated as he reached for the file. It was only a fraction of a second, but the old man noticed.

'Based on a tip they received, the Italians located a private airfield in the north of Sicily where the exchange supposedly took place. Sifting through air traffic control records, they traced the plane to a charter company in Naples. After being served with a court order, the company handed over its records and made the pilot available for questioning.'

'And let me guess. He admitted to flying a dwarf in and out of Sicily?'

'Along with two very large dogs.'

Harvath didn't like it. 'Did the pilot see anything?' he asked as he flipped through the folder. 'Did he see any Muslim men or any alleged transaction take place?'

'No. Whatever happened, it took place inside a closed hangar. The passenger and his dogs deplaned with a large Storm case on wheels, entered the hangar, and then about ten minutes later returned without the case, reboarded the plane, and instructed the pilot to take him back to Naples.'

'What? No aluminum briefcase full of cash handcuffed to his wrist?'

Carlton looked at Harvath. 'I'm not going to beat around the bush with you, Scot. We both know who this is.'

'I know who *you* think it is.'

'You're telling me this isn't the Troll?'

Harvath closed the file. 'That's exactly what I'm telling you.'

'And how can you be sure?'

'First of all, he sells information, not military-grade explosives. And secondly, he'd never conduct an operation like this himself. He'd use an intermediary; a cutout. Somebody is obviously trying to set him up.'

Carlton thought for a moment. 'I know he helped you track down the man who shot Tracy.'

'Only after I'd erased all of his data and emptied out all of his bank accounts.'

'So there are no underlying loyalties I need to worry about between you?'

On the surface, it was a fair question. The Troll was all about money. He lacked integrity and often worked with terrorist organizations. He had taken advantage of an al-Qaeda attack on New York, which killed thousands of Americans, including one of Harvath's best friends, to steal information from a top-secret, U.S. data-mining operation.

At the same time, though, Harvath felt sorry for him. Not only had he been born a midget, but his parents had abandoned him as a child; selling him to a brothel in Russia where he'd been starved, beaten, and forced to perform unutterable sex acts. It was difficult for Harvath to admit that he felt pity for the little man.

The pair had worked together, and Harvath had respected the Troll's love for animals, particularly his dogs. He also respected his ability to glean information. Though he should have seen him as reprehensible, no different from the many men who operated on the wrong side of the law whom he'd been tasked with tracking down and killing over the years, he couldn't. Despite his flaws, Harvath had come to like him.

'What I want to know,' said the Old Man, keying in again on Harvath's hesitancy, 'is if I assign you to find him, can you carry it out?'

Harvath studied the file folder, knowing what his answer should be, but instead of answering he asked a question of his own. 'Is there an order for him to be terminated?'

'Would that make a difference?'

'Maybe.'

'Then maybe you shouldn't take this assignment.'

'So they *do* want him dead,' stated Harvath.

'Actually, they'd prefer captured, but they'll accept dead. Considering your history together, I

53

thought you'd want to be the one to make the choice.'

Which option did his boss think Harvath would exercise? He studied the man's face, but couldn't tell.

'Why isn't the CIA spearheading this?' he finally asked.

'Ever since the Agency snatched that radical cleric in Milan, they've been persona non grata in Italy.'

Like everyone else in the intelligence world, Harvath knew the story. Though the Italians denied ever giving their blessing to the operation, the CIA claimed that all of the appropriate authorities had been filled in on the plan. According to the Agency, they had been granted permission to grab the al-Qaeda-aligned cleric in Milan. As part of their extraordinary rendition program, he was then flown to Egypt where, after being released two years later, he went public with stories of how he had been tortured by Egyptian interrogators.

While it wasn't exactly great PR, what was unforgivable was that the fifteen CIA operatives involved had used their *real* names during the operation to rack up hotel loyalty points. To make matters worse, they had also used their personal cell phones. It was beyond embarrassing.

'Do we have anyone in Italy working the bombing?'

'Besides a nonofficial cover operative or two the Agency secretly still has over there, the Bureau continues to have a decent relationship with the Italians and had a couple of teams wheels up within an hour of the attack.'

Harvath liked the people at the FBI, but he knew that outside the forensics specialists they'd have working the bombing, any other agents would take a backseat to their Italian counterparts. The attack had happened on Italian soil, and despite the high number of American casualties this would remain an Italian investigation.

'I still don't buy that the Troll was involved in something like this.'

'Maybe you put too much of a dent in his business. Maybe he needed to branch out and start dealing in explosives. It doesn't matter. We've been tasked with bringing him in. If you don't want the assignment, I can give it to somebody else.'

'No,' replied Harvath, removing the file from the table. 'This is mine.'

Carlton nodded. 'We have an apartment in Rome you can use, unless you want to begin in Naples, in which case we'll arrange something for you there.'

'He's not in Italy. He's in Spain.'

'How do you know?'

Harvath had a lot to do. Standing, he picked up his coffee mug and said, 'Because he just called me to set up a meeting.'

7

After landing in Madrid, Harvath passed through immigration and customs, then took the metro into the city. It was packed with tourists.

Near the boisterous Puerta del Sol, he entered a nondescript building, rode the aging elevator to the fourth floor, and used the key he had been given to gain access to the Carlton Group's Madrid safe house.

He located the capabilities kit that had been left for him and cataloged its contents. While capabilities kits could be tailored to the specific assignment, as a rule they contained all of the hard-to-acquire items an operative might need in a foreign country.

Kits were Spook 101 and normally included cash, sterile SIM cards, cell phones, lock-picking tools, a condensed trauma kit, tracking bugs, Tuff Ties, a Taser, folding knife, multitool, IR laser designator, infrared strobe, night vision monocular, and a compact weapon with high-end ammunition. In Harvath's case, the compact weapon was a Glock 19 with two spare magazines of 9mm +P ammunition.

The contents of the kit fit neatly into the

3-Day pack he had brought along with him.

Following a quick shower and shave, he gathered up his belongings and returned to the metro. At Chamartín station, he boarded a train headed north.

Though Carlton could have arranged for the gear to be dead-dropped in Bilbao, Harvath preferred doing it this way. There was no telling who or what would be waiting for him when he arrived. It was a city he didn't know and didn't have any allies in. Too much could go wrong. It was better to arrive prepared.

As the high-speed train raced across the Spanish countryside, he closed his eyes. He thought about Tracy and the good-bye call he had placed before leaving. He also thought about the family he was never going to have with her.

★ ★ ★

Shortly past nine o'clock in the evening, the train arrived at Abando Station. Mixing in with other passengers, Harvath kept his eyes open as he headed toward the escalators beneath the magnificent wall of stained glass at the end of the terminal.

He took the Bilbao metro and got off two stops before his hotel. Moving through the neighborhood, he conducted a series of surveillance detection routes, or SDRs, to make sure he wasn't being followed. The evening air was cool and carried a hint of rain.

At a small café across from the hotel, Harvath ordered a coffee and watched the ebb and flow of the sidewalk traffic. He studied the cars parked up and down the street and when he was confident that he hadn't been followed and that the hotel wasn't under surveillance, he paid his bill, crossed the street, and checked in.

In his room, he changed into a pair of dark jeans and a sweater. He tucked his Glock into a leather holster near the small of his back. He put on a comfortable pair of low-profile hiking boots and a leather jacket with deep pockets.

Exiting the hotel through the service entrance, he struck out for the city's medieval neighborhood known as the Casco Viejo.

It was a fifteen-minute walk. Most of the restaurants and bars were still empty, save for the few that catered to tourists not yet in sync with the Spanish custom of dining later in the evening.

Oblivious to the cars and the hour, children kicked soccer balls in the street as older people walked small dogs and young mothers pushed babies in cheap strollers.

Bilbao was a featureless city like Milan, but with a Spanish twist. Bland buildings roofed in red tiles were wedged cheek-by-jowl, fronted by concrete sidewalks. There were very few trees and even less grass. Every single inch of space that could be used, had been used.

Nearer the old town the streets narrowed and the architecture became more interesting. Harvath removed a map he had picked up in the hotel lobby and studied it as he walked. He strolled up and down the *Siete Calles*, or seven streets as they were known, and got a feel for the neighborhood. It was full of shops, bars, and restaurants.

Behind the cathedral in the Calle de la Tendería he found a Basque restaurant within sight of the street's only tobacconist. He took a seat inside, two tables back from the window, withdrew a guidebook from his pocket, and made himself comfortable.

Over the next three hours, he pretended to linger over his food and his guidebook as he watched the traffic patterns at the tiny tobacco shop. He even tipped the busboy to go buy cigarettes for him.

As he watched the young man cross the street, he debated finding a stand-in to do the exact same thing for him tomorrow. He was concerned that the meeting could be a setup. But if he conned some unsuspecting person into going into the shop on his behalf and something happened, the person could very well be killed. That wasn't a risk he was comfortable with.

He knew he had to walk into that store himself tomorrow if he wanted the truth about the Troll. He didn't like it, but there was no way of getting around it. All he could do was be as prepared as possible.

8

John Vaughan had accepted Burt Taylor's handshake and a promise that a check would be forthcoming. They'd get to the paperwork later. Too much time had already gotten away from them. As it was, it took him a full twenty-four hours before he could unravel himself from his police work and start on the Taylor investigation.

Tuesday afternoon, he stopped in a tiny sundries shop, bought a small spiral notebook, and walked back to his car. Inside, he wrote Alison Taylor's name and the pertinent details he knew thus far of the case. He then focused on his next step.

The city of Chicago was divided into five policing 'areas,' each with its own headquarters. Alison's hit-and-run had happened in Area Five.

The detective division of each area was broken into three sections — Special Victims Unit, Robbery/Burglary/Theft, and Homicide/Gang Crimes/Sex. To streamline operations, the city no longer maintained a major accident investigation division. Instead, cases like Alison Taylor's were now handled by HGS — Homicide/Gang Crimes/Sex.

Vaughan understood the rationale behind it, but collapsing vehicular crimes into HGS had never seemed like the best fit to him. Homicide detectives are used to pursuing linear crimes; A shot B, this is why A shot B, we've captured A, case closed. There is often malice involved, and that helps them track down and apprehend offenders.

Hit-and-runs, on the other hand, are atypical. They are not very sexy, and that was why, without even having seen Alison Taylor's file, he knew the HGS detectives probably hadn't put a lot of effort into pursuing it. It wasn't because they were bad cops or because they were lazy, it was simply because with all of the cases they had, human nature was such that you pursued those you felt best equipped to handle and which you saw yourself having the greatest chance of solving.

The only people who took on loser cases were the young idealists who felt it was a personal failing if they didn't solve every case that crossed their desk. A year of overwhelming detective work in a city like Chicago helped grind that idealism out of most detectives. Vaughan made a call to an Area Five HGS cop he knew and within ten minutes one of the detectives from Alison's case called him back.

'You're welcome to see the file,' said the detective. 'But we didn't make a lot of progress. Her coworkers were blitzed. Even if we had located the cabbie, their testimony would have been worthless in court.'

'I'm sure you guys did the best you could. I

just want to be able to tell the family we didn't leave any stones unturned.'

'I hear you. When can you get down here?'

Vaughan looked at his watch. 'How's a half hour?'

'I probably won't be here, but — ' There were a couple of seconds of silence while the detective muffled the mouthpiece before coming back on the line. 'Ask for Detective Ramirez. I'll leave the file with her.'

Vaughan wrote down the name and was about to thank the man, but he didn't get the chance. The detective had hung up.

★ ★ ★

The half-hour drive, thanks to Chicago traffic, took almost an hour. When he arrived at Area Five and found Detective Ramirez, she told him, 'You're late,' as she handed him the file and offered to let him join her at her desk.

He hung his suit coat over the back of the metal chair, removed his notebook and pen, and opened the file. The detective he had spoken with had been right. They hadn't made a lot of progress.

There was an incident report, pictures from the scene, and witness statements. In addition to the statements taken right after the hit-and-run, the detectives had gone back to interview Alison Taylor's friends when they were sober.

A piece of black plastic had been recovered from the scene and was believed to have come from one of those triangular, rooftop advertising setups popular on taxis throughout the city.

The neighborhood had been canvassed for further witnesses and phone calls had been made to all of the cab companies. None of it resulted in any additional leads.

Vaughan arrived at the end of the file. Flipping the last page over he said, 'Where's the blue light camera footage from the intersection?'

Ramirez didn't even bother looking up from the report she was reading. Reaching into her desk drawer, she withdrew the DVD the detective had given her for Vaughan to look at.

'Is this a copy for me to keep?'

'No. That's our copy. There's a DVD player in the conference room,' she said pointing across the sea of desks to a door on the other side of the room.

Vaughan took the disc and walked over to the conference room. He was back fifteen minutes later.

'God, I hate our blue light cams.'

Ramirez was still working on her report and not very interested in Vaughan's problems. 'Let me guess. The footage was blurry, and the camera automatically panned right at the minute you needed to see something.'

'Exactly.'

'Those cameras aren't for solving crimes,' she said, looking up. 'They're for deterring crimes. I'm surprised they record any footage at all.'

Vaughan shook his head. They had footage of the cab speeding through the intersection, but it had happened so fast it was all blurry. And just like she had said, the camera panned away at the crucial moment where the cab number could have been identified. 'There has to be another camera that caught this accident.'

'Are you done with that?' she asked as Vaughan began tapping his thigh with the folder.

'Yeah, I'm done,' he said, handing it back to her. Standing up, he removed his jacket from the back of the chair and pulled out his business card. 'In case anything comes up.'

She dropped it into the file and offered him a piece of advice. 'Because you're a lawyer probably getting paid by the hour, I'm not going to tell you you're wasting your time, but there are a lot of cabs in the city. Don't get too emotionally involved.'

Vaughan understood where she was coming from. Detachment was the key to staying sane in their line of work. He still shook his head. 'Lawyer, cop, it doesn't matter. I'm a human being, and so was the woman who got run down in that intersection. I want to find the guy who did this.'

Ramirez held his gaze for a moment and then dropped her eyes back to the report she'd been using as an excuse to ignore him. 'Have a nice evening, counselor.'

9

Harvath spent a good portion of the morning doing additional reconnaissance on the tobacco shop. Just after ten a.m., he stepped away from the tour group he was shadowing and with both his Glock and Taser handy, entered the shop.

The old man behind the counter didn't even bother looking up.

'Do you have Argos and Draco brand cigarettes?' he asked in Spanish, using the names of the Troll's two dogs.

'Three Euros,' the old man replied, reaching under the counter and producing a pack of Fortuna Lites.

Harvath gave him the cash, pocketed the cigarettes, and exited the store. He conducted what felt like his hundredth SDR of the day and when he was confident he wasn't being followed, walked into a small hotel he had identified earlier and headed into its café. Taking a table near the back, he ordered coffee. Once the waiter had walked away, he pulled out the pack of cigarettes and examined it.

It had a plastic wrapper, but had been opened from the bottom and resealed. Harvath peeled

65

off the plastic and opened the package at the top. It was stuffed with tissue paper. After removing the paper, he withdrew a car key rubber-banded to a prepaid parking receipt. In addition to the name and address of the parking facility, someone had written *C-11*.

Harvath remembered having joked that the only thing the Troll's offer was missing was a dark alley. It would seem that he hadn't been creative enough. A dark parking structure was much more apropos.

The underground garage was on the other side of the river. It took Harvath about fifteen minutes to walk there, fifteen minutes for reconnaissance, and another five to locate the car. So far, so good.

He found a structural column and used it for cover as he depressed the button on the remote. The lights flashed. The door unlocked.

After thoroughly checking the vehicle for explosives, he tossed in his backpack, climbed into the driver's seat, and started the car. He reversed out of the space, drove up two levels, and after using the prepaid receipt, exited the facility.

He drove through several neighborhoods before finally pulling over and looking for a clue as to where he was supposed to go next.

Inside the glove compartment were a portable GPS device, a window mount, and cigarette adaptor. After powering up the GPS, he toggled to the screen with pre-loaded routes and saw it contained one destination labeled 'Nicholas.'

It appeared to be a village in the Basque

Pyrenees. According to the GPS, the drive was five hours and forty-three minutes. Harvath kept his gun where he could get to it.

Incredibly, he found a radio station playing the American funk classic 'Pass the Peas' by Fred Wesley, and turning up the volume, he pointed the car toward the Autopista and stepped on the accelerator.

Fifteen kilometers outside of Bilbao, he noticed he was being followed.

10

The immediate exits outside the city offered only bad neighborhoods, and the shoulder of the highway was equally dangerous. Harvath decided to wait.

As long as they weren't trying to overtake him and run him off the road, he was fine. The problem lay in whether or not there was an ambush waiting somewhere up along the route; somewhere he could be forced off the road and everything could be made to look like an accident.

It seemed a bit over the top, especially when they could have arranged for something to have happened to him in Bilbao, but maybe they had another scenario in mind. All Harvath knew was that he didn't like being followed. He needed to find out who these people were and what they wanted. Fifty kilometers later, an opportunity presented itself.

Gunning the car, he sped off the Autopista and raced down the exit road to the service area. The parking lot was crowded and Spaniards coming or going from their cars gesticulated wildly and cursed him for his excessive rate of speed.

He slowed down as he neared the restaurant and parked in one of the handicapped spaces up front. Grabbing his backpack, he unplugged the GPS device, tucked it in his pocket, and left the keys in the ignition. He wouldn't be coming back for the car.

The lot was peppered with cars and long-haul trucks. Inside the café cum restaurant, most of the business was gathered around the beer taps at the counter. There were two families having a late lunch and Harvath noted four police officers drinking coffee at a nearby table, but that was it.

He stepped to the far end of the crowded counter and ordered a beer. Seconds later, he saw the car that had been following him since Bilbao, a black Peugeot, roll through the parking lot. When it came upon his vehicle parked in one of the handicapped spaces up front, it slowed down and then moved on. If Harvath had needed any further proof that they were following him, that was it.

The Peugeot had been moving slowly enough that Harvath could make out a large man at the wheel with a thick neck, a sloping forehead, and eyebrows so thick they were like Brillo pads. Then, the car disappeared from sight.

Harvath had a good vantage point. Not only could he look out the windows onto the parking lot, he could also see straight through the building's front door.

As he continued to watch, he ordered a sandwich. He didn't have to see them to know they were outside waiting for him. The same questions that had been plaguing him since he'd first seen them in his rearview mirror continued. *Who were they, and why were they following him?*

Asking the police for help was out of the

question. The men outside would say they had no idea what he was talking about and that they had pulled in simply to rest and get something to eat. Naturally, they would then have plenty of questions for Harvath, who was carrying a firearm, a stack of cash, and had no idea exactly where he was going. He would have to pull this off on his own.

Removing the GPS device from his pocket, he powered it up and copied the directions down on the back of his paper placemat. Then he requested the device plan an alternate route for him, but because he was indoors and out of range of the satellites, the device was unable to complete the task.

Frustrated, Harvath turned the device off and slid it back into his pocket. Using his limited Spanish, he asked for the check, paid it, and then waited for the right moment to walk back to the men's room.

The man at the urinal was about twenty years old and Harvath ignored him as he walked over to the sink and turned on the water. He splashed some on his face and then leaned heavily on the edge of the bowl.

When the young man approached, Harvath pretended to lose his balance before righting himself.

'Se siente bien, señor?' the young man asked. Are you feeling okay?

He feigned difficulty focusing. 'Do you speak English?'

'I do. Are you okay?'

'I left my pills in the car,' Harvath said,

gesturing toward the door.

'Do you want me to get them for you?'

He took a deep, labored breath. 'I would really appreciate it. Thank you.'

'Give me your keys and tell me where your car is.'

'It's a blue Opel,' he said. 'It is in a handicapped spot just outside the front door. The keys are in it. It's unlocked. I think I left the pills in the glove box or they may be in the pocket behind the passenger seat.'

'Wait here,' replied the Good Samaritan. 'I'll be right back.'

Harvath thanked him, and once he left the men's room, followed him at a safe distance. He cut through the gift shop and exited the structure via a side door at the far end.

Since no one from the black Peugeot had come in looking for him, there was only a handful of places they could be. Either they had given up and left, which he highly doubted; they had driven off to another point where they would wait to pick up his trail again, virtually impossible to do without being seen; or they were sitting out in the parking lot somewhere. And if they were out in the parking lot, they would be positioned so that they could keep an eye on his car while they waited for him to come back out. It was the answer that made the most sense and therefore the one he went with.

It didn't take Harvath long to find them. The young man from the men's room was politely ransacking the Opel, looking for a nonexistent bottle of pills while the two men in the Peugeot watched in silence, trying to figure out what was going on.

The Peugeot was three rows back and they never saw Harvath coming. Using the butt of his Glock, he smashed the rear passenger window. Popping the lock, he opened the door and sat down upon the spill of broken glass.

'Nobody move,' he said, holding his pistol so that both of the startled men could see it.

Next to Eyebrows was the driver, an equally beefy and thick-necked mouth breather with a thin scar on his right cheek. Whoever these two were, they were not operators. They were muscle. And poorly dressed muscle at that.

'Why have you been following me?' asked Harvath.

'*No hablamos ingles,*' said Eyebrows.

'Bullshit. Why have you been following me?'

'*No hablam —* '

'Shut up. Do you have any weapons on you?'

'*Qué?*'

'*Dónde estan las armas?*' he said, pulling Eyebrows' shirt up so he could check his waistband. '*Las pistolas? Dónde estan?*'

'*No pistolas. No armas.*'

Harvath put the gun against Scarface's temple and patted him down. He was clean.

He used his pack to brush off some of the glass on the seat and settled back. These two needed to be dealt with, but not here. '*Vamonos,*' he said.

'*A dónde vamos?*' replied Scarface nervously.

Leaning forward Harvath put his Glock against the man's head and slowly repeated,

72

'Va-mo-nos. Got it? Now quit jerking around and get moving.'

The Spaniard started the engine, put the car in gear, and pulled out of the rest area and onto the motorway. Two exits later, Harvath signaled for him to turn off.

They followed a small country road and he instructed Scarface to pull behind a thick copse of trees. He then told him to turn off the engine.

Climbing out, he instructed them to exit the vehicle one at a time. *'Afuera.'* His Spanish was lousy, but the pistol was a wonderful interpretive aid that seemed to help get his points across.

He motioned for the men to put their hands on their heads and get down on their knees. It was obvious from their faces that they believed he was going to execute them.

He walked around to the back of the vehicle and popped the trunk.

Pulling back an old blanket, he discovered two sawed-off shotguns. 'No *pistolas. No armas,* huh?'

Eyebrows began to speak, but Harvath cut him off. 'Shut up.'

He searched the rest of the trunk, but didn't find much. There was an empty gas can, some road flares, snow chains, a spare, and a jack. What he really would have loved was some duct tape, but there wasn't any. The plastic Tuff Ties from his kit would have to do.

Walking around to the front of the car, he tucked his Glock in the back of his jeans and after making sure it was loaded, set one of the sawed-off shotguns on the hood of the car. With his eyes on Scarface and Eyebrows, he fished through his backpack and removed the plastic ties.

He walked over to Eyebrows and demonstrated how he wanted him to secure his friend. When Scarface was zipped up, Harvath had Eyebrows lie facedown in the dirt and he returned the favor.

With their ankles zipped together and wrists bound behind their backs, Harvath had them hop over to the car and helped load them in the trunk facedown. Once they were in, he chained a couple more Tuff Ties together so he could hog-tie the men. It was cramped quarters in the trunk and neither of them was going to be able to move until they were cut loose.

After gagging the men, he slammed the lid shut and climbed into the driver's seat. He removed the GPS unit, fired it back up, and once it had acquired the satellites, planned an alternate route to the destination, which he quickly memorized.

The reason he had been able to ID Eyebrows and Scarface coming out of Bilbao was that they had been following close enough to be seen. If the GPS unit or the Opel he had been driving contained some sort of a tracking device, they should have been able to stay back and out of sight. Nevertheless, he didn't want to gamble that the GPS device might give him away to whoever had sent the two geniuses in the trunk, and so as he pulled back out onto the country road and headed for the motorway, he dropped the unit out the window.

He had no idea that the car he was now driving was the biggest giveaway of all.

11

After leaving Area Five headquarters, Sergeant John Vaughan drove to the intersection where Alison Taylor had been struck. He parked his vehicle and surveyed the entire area on foot.

Beyond the lone Chicago Police Department blue light camera used to discourage street crime, Vaughan located five other privately owned security cameras that might have footage of the hit-and-run.

The first belonged to Alison Taylor's apartment building. Vaughan scared up the resident manager, who had 'already' spoken to the Area Five detectives. John mollified the man and explained that he was simply following up.

The manager told him exactly what he had told the detectives. The building's exterior camera provided a 24/7 feed so that residents could see who was buzzing them from the front door. Unfortunately, the feed wasn't recorded.

Was it possible that a resident could have had their TV switched to the video loop when the accident occurred? Yes, but at three o'clock on a weekday morning, he doubted it. The majority of his renters were young professionals like Ms. Taylor. What's more, he assumed that if anyone

76

had seen something, they would have alerted the police.

The manager agreed to send an e-mail to his residents asking if they had seen anything and took Vaughan's card.

The next three cameras belonged to merchants near the intersection, all of whom had previously spoken with the detectives. Of the businesses, one's camera had not been turned on that evening, another stated that her camera was a fake and only there to deter crime, and the third merchant replied that unless he'd been broken into during the night, he automatically erased the footage every morning when he came in and started anew.

The fifth camera was from a bank ATM, and they still had their footage from the night in question. Though the Area Five detectives had already screened the footage, the bank manager was happy to let Vaughan see it.

Considering the camera's field of view, it should have been perfect. In fact, it would have been perfect if not for a large delivery truck that had parked on the street just in front of the ATM that evening. All of the bank's customers had been recorded perfectly, but seeing beyond the truck to the intersection was impossible.

Vaughan had figured it was a long shot, but sometimes those were the ones that paid off. His hopes of catching the act on tape now were all but gone.

After dinner at home with his family, homework, and baths for the kids, Vaughan returned to the intersection and went into the subway station. He wanted to re-create the scene for himself as closely as possible to the way it had happened.

Coming out of the subway, he turned to the right, exactly as Alison and her friends would have, and retraced their steps along the sidewalk.

He spent hours studying the intersection and its flow of pedestrians and traffic. He watched the timing of the lights and how many vehicles rushed the reds. He charted the vehicles that turned into the crosswalk where Alison had been struck and noted their rates of speed.

For most people it would have been mind-numbing tedium, but for Vaughan it was a challenge; a puzzle. He was convinced that he could find the answers he was looking for here. He just needed to keep looking.

At 5:30 in the morning, he went home in time to shower and change into a new suit before the children were up and wanting breakfast. Thirty minutes, four kisses, and one family hug later, his wife took their son off in one direction to his school, while he took their daughter to hers.

As a Marine who had seen hundreds of firefights in Iraq, he was no stranger to sleep deprivation. In fact, he'd often joked that he could handle sleep deprivation in combat. It was the sleep deprivation of parenthood that was the real killer.

Because there was no Dunkin' Donuts near his daughter's school, he broke one of his hardest and fastest rules and stepped into a Starbucks. The minute he did, he could hear the giant sucking sound of money being vacuumed out of customers' pockets. Starbucks had good coffee, and as a capitalist, he didn't fault them for getting the most they could for their product. He just disliked the whole vente/grande, mocha-frappu-B.S.-cino, coffee-as-art shtick. Hot, black, and in a cup — that's the complete extent of the relationship he wanted with the beverage.

Instead of taking his large cup of house blend back to the car, he found a table and took a seat. His eyes were glazed over as he stared absently out the window and there were probably multiple customers who found the sight of a man with a pistol on his hip and a thousand-yard stare more than a little disturbing.

If people were looking, he didn't notice. The weapon was so much a part of who he was that he never really thought about it. It was just one of several tools necessary for doing his job.

As his mind wandered, he watched a Yellow taxi drive by outside. He watched as it neared the corner and slowed to a stop. A uniformed crossing guard directed the cab to stay where it was while she crossed a group of kids with backpacks and skateboards.

He had never liked cabbies very much. The fact that they were predominantly immigrants wasn't what bothered him. As long as they had come in the front door like everybody else, he was okay with it. What bothered him was what lousy drivers they tended to be.

It didn't make any sense. A rational person would be correct in thinking that the more one performed a task, the better one would become at it. But that didn't seem to apply to cab drivers.

He seriously doubted the cab would have even stopped for the kids if the guard hadn't been there.

At that moment, he got an idea. Pulling out his notebook, he turned to a fresh page and clicked his pen. He removed his cell phone and dialed the main number for the CPD. When the operator answered, he asked to be connected to the Public Vehicles Division.

'Public Vehicles. Officer Brennan,' said the voice who answered.

'Good morning, Officer Brennan. This is Sergeant John Vaughan from Organized Crime.'

'It was all my wife and mother-in-law's idea. I had nothing to do with it. Put me in the witness protection program and I'd be happy to testify.'

Vaughan loved working with cops. No matter what, they all had a pretty good sense of humor. 'I'll send someone down to take your statement, officer. In the meantime, I'm wondering if you could help me out with something I'm working on.'

'For the sergeant who's going to relocate me to Florida or Arizona, you name it.'

'Part of your responsibility is keeping an eye on the cab companies, right? You make sure the licensing and the medallions are all in line, follow up on criminal complaints involving drivers; that sort of stuff, correct?'

'That's us. *Miami Vice* without Miami or the vice.'

'I'm looking into a hit-and-run that involved a

Chicago Yellow Cab.'

'Do you have a number?'

'Case number or cab number?'

'I'll take whatever you've got,' said the officer.

Vaughan read off the case number. 'That's all we have. We are trying to track down the cab.'

There was the sound of keys clicking as Brennan pulled up the report on his computer. 'It looks like Yellow Cab was contacted by our division, but we were unable to get any further information. Yellow claims it doesn't have any knowledge of any of its drivers being involved in hitting a pedestrian on the evening in question.'

'What about damage to a vehicle consistent with a hit-and-run on the night in question?'

Once again, the keys clicked away. As the officer searched, Vaughan added, 'Or maybe there was a driver who failed to return his vehicle.'

Finally, Brennan said, 'Sorry, Sergeant. It doesn't look like we've got anything here that can help you. This doesn't mean you're going to back out of your promise to get me into the witness relocation program, does it?'

Vaughan chuckled and then was all business. 'If your wife was struck by a cab and the driver fled the scene,' he began and then corrected himself. 'Strike that. If your mother was struck by a cab and the driver fled the scene, who in your division would you want on the case?'

'Paul Davidson. No question.'

The officer hadn't even hesitated. 'He's that good?' said Vaughan.

'You asked me who I'd want. I'd want Paul

Davidson. Now, if the guy had struck my mother-in-law, that would be completely different.'

'I'm sure it would. Can you pass me over to Officer Davidson, please?'

'He's up in Wisconsin, fishing.'

'Can you give me his cell number?'

Vaughan absorbed a couple more jokes about the man's wife and mother-in-law, and after getting his promise to put in the word for him with the witness relocation program, Brennan gave him the number.

Thirty seconds later, a cell tower had located Paul Davidson on Wisconsin's Lake Geneva. 'You have reached the cell phone of vacationing Chicago police officer Paul Davidson,' said the forty-five-year-old cop pretending to be his own outgoing message. 'If this is an emergency please hang up and dial 911. For all other matters, hang up and call me when I'm back in my office two days from now.'

Someone in the background then happily yelled, 'Hey! Look at that! Hurry, get the net!'

Vaughan was getting the distinct impression that the Department of Public Vehicles didn't hire people unless they were certified wiseasses. There was the sound of line being pulled from a reel as he said, 'Officer Davidson, this is Sergeant John Vaughan from the Organized Crime Division.'

'I didn't have anything to do with it. It was my wife and mother-in-law's idea.'

'Brennan already used that one.'

'What a thief. I leave the office for three days

and he steals all my material.'

'Is this a bad time, officer?'

'Let me see,' said Davidson as he took stock of his surroundings. 'Six-packs, sandwiches, Chamber of Commerce weather, and the last day of my vacation. No, now's perfect.'

'I can call back.'

'If you let that line snap again,' he said over his shoulder to his fishing companion, 'I swear to God I'll drown you right here.'

'Got your mother-in-law with you?' asked Vaughan.

'No, my priest. Now, what can I spend the last day of my vacation doing for you, Sergeant?'

'I'm working on a hit-and-run. Not a lot of leads. A Yellow Cab hit a young woman about two weeks ago. We know where it happened and approximately what time it happened, but that's all.'

'Do you have a description of the driver?'

'The two witnesses we have are friends of the victim and were intoxicated at the time.'

'Is the victim still alive?'

'Yes, but she's got serious trauma and some bad brain damage.'

'I've never heard of good brain damage,' said Davidson.

'Touché.'

'So were the witnesses too drunk to give you a description of the driver?'

'They think he was Middle Eastern,' replied Vaughan.

'Okay. Iranian? Iraqi? Jordanian? Palestinian?'

'I have no idea. All I know is that Officer

Brennan said that if his mother had been the victim of a hit-and-run like this, you're the one he'd want on the case.'

'First of all, Brennan doesn't even have a mother. He was a foundling and there's lots of times I think he should have stayed lost. But setting aside his penchant for Irish bullshit, he does occasionally get some things right.'

'Then you can help?'

'What's the Organized Crime angle here?'

'I'm also an attorney. In this case, I'm representing the family, trying to help track down the driver.'

'So you're getting paid for this?'

'Yes,' said Vaughan. 'But when I find the guy, then my lawyer hat comes off and I'm going to arrest him myself.'

'Seeing as how you're supposed to pursue this as a lawyer and not a cop, I assume you've got a licensed private investigator working with you?'

Vaughan hadn't gotten that far. In fact, he really hadn't thought about it until now. Normally, he worked his cases alone. 'Actually, I don't have one.'

'You do now. I charge two hundred bucks an hour plus expenses, nonnegotiable.'

'Two hundred dollars an hour? That's more than what I'm charging as the attorney.'

'The difference between you and me, though, is that it'll only take two hours of my time to get this guy. And, unlike a lawyer, I don't charge for simply thinking about cases. I only charge when I am working on them.'

This guy has been drinking in the sun too

long, thought Vaughan. 'If you can find this guy in two hours, you've got a deal.'

'I said two hours of my time. It might take me forty-eight overall to get a name and a cab number for you, but I'm only going to charge for the two hours I work. Plus expenses, of course.'

'What kind of expenses?' asked Vaughan.

'Don't worry, Sergeant. I'll keep it under a hundred bucks. So do we have a deal?'

Vaughan didn't need to negotiate with him. If Davidson could deliver, and do it that quickly, it would be worth ten times the amount. 'You've got a deal.'

He gave him the rest of his contact details and asked, 'When can you start?'

'How about right now?'

'Are you serious?'

'Of course not,' said Davidson. 'I'm on vacation. I'll call you when I get back to the city.'

Vaughan said good-bye and set the phone down on the table. Davidson reminded him of a cocksure young Marine he'd gone into Tikrit with. Everything was a joke and he never broke a sweat. Twelve hours later, when the Marine went in to clear an insurgent safe house, he zigged when he should have zagged and died on the spot.

12

BASQUE PYRENEES
SPAIN

The out-of-the-way route Harvath had chosen meant that it was well after midnight when he drove into the village of Ezkutatu. Like many of the villages he had driven through since entering the Pyrenees Mountain Range, Ezkutatu was composed of rugged, squat buildings made of stone. Its highest point was the steeple of the local Catholic church.

With its tiny, storybook-like railway station, it was as if he had driven back in time. Clear the cars from the streets, and the village would look no different now than it had over a hundred years ago.

Pushing further into the heart of Ezkutatu he came upon its cobble-stoned, communal square. According to the route that had been planned for him on the GPS, this was his final destination. He would have liked to have done some reconnaissance, but the village was built along the side of a mountain with only one road in and one road out.

Against the lights illuminating the church façade he saw the silhouette of a man in a long, dark coat. As he slowed the Peugeot, the man began walking toward him. Harvath balanced the sawed-off shotgun on his lap; his finger on the trigger. He had no idea who the man was and didn't like that he had apparently been waiting for him.

When he got within forty yards of the church, he realized that the figure was not dressed in a long coat, but rather the vestments, or *soutane*, of a Catholic priest.

Harvath brought the Peugeot to a stop on an angle, powered down the passenger window, and raising the sawed-off said, 'That's far enough, Father. Let me see your hands, please.'

The figure lifted his hands into the air, but kept walking forward. Harvath gripped the weapon tighter and aimed for center mass. Though they couldn't have looked more dissimilar, the man's flowing garb reminded him of the robes worn by many Muslim imams and he had learned the hard way how well the costume lent itself to secreting weapons and psychologically disarming opponents.

'That's far enough,' he repeated. The man was within ten feet of the vehicle and Harvath could now make him out. He looked to be about the same age as him, with dark hair and a clean-shaven face. He held himself ramrod straight, almost military-like, as if he were undergoing an inspection. And while he projected a serene countenance, he was not like any priest Harvath had ever seen before. Something about his eyes put him on edge.

'You seem to be carrying a lot of weight in your trunk,' said the priest. 'Should I be preparing to hold funerals tomorrow, or can we release those two men and let them return to their warm beds and families?'

Harvath recognized the man's voice from the phone call two days ago in Virginia. 'That depends. Why were they following me?'

'To protect you.'

'To protect *me*? From whom?'

'From whoever tried to kill Nicholas,' said the priest.

'These are Nicholas's men?'

'No, I sent them.'

'Funny, they didn't strike me as altar boy types.'

'Mr. Harvath, it's late. I'm tired, and because you changed the route those men are long overdue at home.'

'Hold it a second,' replied Harvath. 'How do you know what route I took?'

'You're driving a vehicle that belongs to the Basque Separatist organization, ETA. I have been receiving updates on your progress ever since you entered the foothills from the opposite direction from the one I programmed into the GPS device we left for you.

'Now, in the trunk of your vehicle you have the cousin and brother-in-law of one of the district commanders. For your sake and mine, I hope that they're still alive.'

'They are.'

'Good. The sooner you let them go, the sooner they can report in and the sooner the men of this district can stand down and we all can get some sleep.'

Harvath lowered the shotgun and stepped out of the car. He scanned the buildings around the square and wondered how many pairs of eyes they had on them at the moment.

'So this is ETA country?' he said as he met the priest at the trunk.

'Practically the epicenter,' replied the man. 'Once we take care of this, I have a bed and food waiting for you.'

'I'd like to see Nicholas first.'

'I'm afraid that's not possible. It's too dangerous. We'll leave in the morning.'

'Where is he?'

The man smiled. 'You expected us to keep him here in the village? Please, Mr. Harvath. You may not find us very sophisticated, but we're not amateurs.'

'That's good to know,' said Harvath as he lifted the lid of the trunk and revealed the two Basque men hog-tied inside. 'Because if you had sent amateurs, I would have been insulted.'

13

The embarrassed priest produced a Basque Yatagan and cut the men loose. Both glared at Harvath as they climbed out of the trunk and massaged their stiff limbs. Though he didn't speak Basque, he had no problem interpreting the priest's remarks as he chastised the men and sent them home.

Once they had driven off, the priest formally introduced himself. 'I am Padre Peio.'

Harvath shook his outstretched hand. The man had an unusually strong grip.

'I have a car nearby if you're ready.'

Harvath nodded and quietly followed the priest down a small street to a battered Land Cruiser. 'Would you like to place your bag in the back?' the man asked as he opened Harvath's door for him.

'No thank you, Padre. I think I'll keep it with me.'

The priest gave a slight nod as he walked around to the driver's side and climbed in. Though it was an older vehicle, the inside was meticulously kept and the engine instantly sprang to life. Harvath closed his door, and Padre Peio pulled away from the curb and piloted the Land Cruiser out of the village.

'I'm sure you have many questions,' said the priest.

'One or two,' admitted Harvath.

'Well, when I take you to Nicholas in the morning, I'm sure he'll be happy to answer them for you.'

'Who are you? If you don't mind me asking.'

'I don't mind. I'm just a priest. A friend of Nicholas.'

Harvath doubted that was the long and the short of it, but changed the subject anyway. 'Does he know who attacked him?'

The priest took a moment to find his words. 'It is a delicate matter, Mr. Harvath, and I think it would be better if he explained it to you himself.'

It was obvious he knew the answer to the question, but he wasn't going to give it up. 'Let me rephrase my question. Is the person who attacked Nicholas still alive?'

'No, dead.'

'Who killed him?'

'It wasn't a he, it was a she, and the dogs killed her.'

'Nicholas was attacked by a woman?'

The priest downshifted as the road began to climb. 'According to what he told me, she was a very patient assassin. She bided her time; worked on gaining his trust. She even got him to remove the dogs to another room. That is when she struck.'

'Then how did the dogs kill her?'

'They heard his screaming and broke through the heavy oak door of his bedroom. She was mauled to death and they tore her throat out. There was blood everywhere.'

'Didn't Nicholas have any security?'

'No one was supposed to know he was here.'

It was a subtle, disapproving tone that Harvath picked up on. 'He invited her, didn't he?'

'Mr. Harvath,' said the priest, returning to his previous posture, 'I think it's best if you discuss these things with Nicholas.'

Harvath watched as the headlights bounced off of large rocks and thick-trunked trees. He wanted more answers. 'Are you a priest, or is that just a cover?'

'No, I am actually a priest.'

'Have you *always* been a priest?'

'I have been many things,' the man replied, his eyes focused on the road.

Harvath could only imagine.

As they gained altitude it grew colder. Peio reached over and adjusted the temperature knob, trying to coax a little more heat from the Land Cruiser's vents. 'How do you know Nicholas?' he asked.

'You could say we met through work,' replied Harvath. 'How about you?'

'I also met Nicholas through work.'

'Don't tell me. You were in the seminary together.'

'I take it you don't think much of him.'

'In all honesty, Padre, I don't know what to think of him. He has done a lot of bad things in his life.'

'Haven't we all?' asked the priest.

Harvath didn't reply.

Peio maneuvered the Land Cruiser around a small slide of rocks and once they were back on the road stated, 'I know very little of who

Nicholas is and what he has done. He has not taken confession with me.'

'Be careful what you wish for, Father.'

The priest looked at him. 'No one is beyond God's love and mercy. Not you. Not Nicholas. Not anyone. Despite what you may think of him, Nicholas has a very good heart. There is incredible decency in him. As do all men, he has his failings, but he has a desire to do good in the world.'

'You'll forgive me for asking, but how long have you known him?'

'Many years now.'

'And you say you met through *work?* What kind of work?'

Peio removed a pack of cigarettes from the dashboard and offered one to Harvath. When he refused, the priest removed one for himself, lit it from the vehicle's cigarette lighter, and cracked the window. He took a long, deep drag, and then exhaled. 'Have you ever heard of the children of Chernobyl?'

Harvath, like everyone else, had heard of the Chernobyl nuclear disaster. It happened in the Ukraine in 1986 and was the worst nuclear power plant disaster in history. The only level-seven event to ever occur on the International Nuclear Event Scale, it distributed four hundred times more fallout than the atomic bombing of Hiroshima. Fifty-six people were killed directly, with about 4,000 more being stricken with various forms of cancer. Nuclear rain fell as far north as Ireland and over three hundred thousand people had to be resettled across huge swaths of area far beyond the Chernobyl Exclusion Zone.

He had never heard any reference, though, to the children of Chernobyl. 'I assume these were children somehow adversely affected by the disaster?'

Peio took another drag on his cigarette. 'Sixty percent of the fallout landed upon Belarus. You can imagine the consequences. One of the most disturbing has been the increase in birth defects. Parents in the affected areas are usually poor, scared, and lacking in hope. If they have children born with mental or physical impairments, they often abandon them at state orphanages. It is such a common occurrence that a word for them has entered the lexicon, *Podkidysh: one who is left at the door*.

'Early in my priesthood, I did missionary work at one of the orphanages in Belarus. That's where I met Nicholas.'

Harvath knew that when Nicholas stopped growing because of his dwarfism, his Russian parents hadn't even bothered to try to find a suitable home for him. Nor did they even have the kindness to place him in an orphanage. Instead, they had sold him to a brothel near the Black Sea. That troubling aspect of his past, and the man's obvious love for his dogs, had been two of the biggest reasons Harvath could not completely harden his heart toward Nicholas. Knowing his history made it easy to understand why he might be involved with an orphanage dedicated to the children of Chernobyl.

'He was very generous to the orphanage, as

94

well as the children, with both his time and his money,' said Peio. 'In exchange, he was accepted. I would even say loved by many of the people there.'

'What happened?'

'As Nicholas put it, the only way one can outrun his past is to keep running.'

'But his past caught up with him in Belarus, at the orphanage?'

'We never knew,' replied the priest. 'One day, he just disappeared.'

'How did he end up here?'

'We remained in touch. I told him that when the day came that he got tired of running, he could come here.'

'And when exactly did he arrive?'

Either Peio hadn't heard him or he had chosen not to respond. He quietly turned off onto a smaller road bordered by high rock walls. Three hundred meters later, a locked livestock gate prevented them from going any further.

The priest flashed his brights — *long, long, short, short, short* — and from behind a large boulder off to the side of the road a man appeared. He reminded Harvath of the two Basque from the Peugeot. He was about the same size and was cradling a similar sawed-off shotgun. He peered into the Land Cruiser and, after acknowledging Peio, unwound the chain from around the gate and swung it open for the vehicle to pass.

As they drove through, Harvath saw three more men through the open door of a wooden guardhouse that had been obscured by the large boulder. They sat around a propane heater, but instead of sawed-off shot-guns, were armed with high-end tactical rifles and night vision optics.

'Where are we?' asked Harvath.

'Someplace safe.'

14

Harvath was given four hours to rest in a small apartment above the stables. Judging by the heavily armed guards and all of the other security precautions he had seen on their drive in, they were at some sort of fortified ranch compound that probably belonged to ETA.

In the apartment, a single place had been set at a wooden table in the kitchen. Next to it was a chipped glass and a half bottle of wine. On the stove was a traditional dish of Basque beans flavored with ham and Basque chorizo.

After eating, Harvath slept fitfully with his hand wrapped around his Glock.

Just before sunrise, Padre Peio knocked at the door. 'Good morning,' he said, handing Harvath a thermos of hot coffee. Gone was the soutane. In its place, the priest was wearing blue jeans, boots, and a dark green fleece. He had a small bag slung over one shoulder. 'Were you able to sleep?'

'A little,' replied Harvath.

'Good. You'll need your strength. It's a tough journey. Ready to go?'

Harvath put on his jacket and grabbed his pack. 'Will we be coming back?'

'No. And just so we understand each other, we were never here.'

'Understood,' replied Harvath as he followed

the man into the hall and down a flight of wooden stairs.

When they stepped outside, two horses were saddled and waiting for them. It was cold and their breath rose into the air.

Peio offered him a pair of leather gloves. 'I assume you are comfortable around horses.'

Harvath walked up to one of the animals and patted it on the neck. 'I like all animals, Padre. It's people I usually have problems with.'

'Is Nicholas one of those people?'

'Nicholas is a thief.'

'And yet you have come halfway around the world to help him.'

'I've come for answers.'

'We're all searching for answers.'

'I think you and I have different questions, Father.'

'You'd be surprised, Mr. Harvath.'

After a cup of coffee, Harvath tucked the thermos into his pack, swung into the saddle, and fell in behind the priest as he led the way further up into the mountains.

The trail was narrow and didn't allow for them to ride abreast, so they rode in single file. It made conversation difficult, which was fine by Harvath. There was still something about the priest that didn't fit. Until he had him better figured out, he preferred not to get too chummy with him.

Harvath's mount followed the horse in front and didn't need much guidance. Either the animal was used to following the priest's, or it had made this journey before. He suspected both answers were probably correct.

The trail was covered in scree and large rocks that had tumbled down from above. They passed precipitous drop-offs where he had serious concerns about the narrowness of the eroded trail combined with the weight of his horse. Twice, the animal lost its footing and scrambled nervously.

Two hours into their journey, the trail widened and they emerged from a high mountain pass. Beneath them was a lush valley bisected by a wide stream. Near the stream was a burned-out stone farmhouse.

'That was where Nicholas was staying when he was attacked,' said Peio as Harvath drew alongside him.

'Was the fire set on purpose?'

'I don't think so. His bedroom had apparently been filled with candles. In the struggle, one fell over and ignited the draperies.'

Perched upon a steep cliff across the valley was a small hermitage or priory of some sort. 'And that?'

'That is where Nicholas is now,' said the priest. 'The monastery of Saint Francis Xavier.'

They descended into the valley and rode past the charred farmhouse. Harvath noticed the remnants of a diesel generator as well as multiple solar panel fragments. There were also cables coming from the stream and he assumed that they led to some sort of hydro-electric turbine.

They crossed the stream and rode to the other side of the valley where they were met by one of the monks, who saw to their horses. Peio then led Harvath up a lengthy switchback on foot to the monastery itself.

Though the architecture was simple, Harvath marveled at the amount of work it must have taken to construct this refuge in this hidden valley deep in the Pyrenees. All of the materials looked as if they probably came from the valley itself.

The interior had a solidity and a solemnity to it. It was like being inside a vault. The only sound came from their footfalls. The air of the little monastery smelled of wood smoke and spices.

At the end of a short hallway, Peio came to a closed door and softly knocked. When dogs began growling on the other side, Harvath knew he had arrived at their destination.

The door was opened by a young monk, whom the priest conversed with briefly in Basque and then excused. After the monk exited the room, Peio stood back and held the door open so Harvath could step inside.

The two enormous dogs immediately got to their feet and came to Peio. They then recognized Harvath and came to him. He scratched both of the Caucasian sheepdogs behind their ears and crossed the threshold.

The little man was lying in bed beneath an old wool blanket and looked like he had run face-first into an airplane propeller. Someone had sewn him up, but the stitches were thick and uneven.

'Cut yourself shaving?' asked Harvath as he drew a chair alongside the bed.

100

Nicholas looked up at his visitor and smiled. 'I assume I won't be winning any beauty pageants.'

'No, but you weren't exactly a stunner to begin with now, were you?'

'Too true,' said the little man with a laugh. 'Thank you for coming.'

'Don't thank me. Thank the United States government. Which reminds me. You have the right to remain silent. Anything you say can and will be used against you in a court of law. You have the right to an — '

'Are you actually Mirandizing me?'

Harvath shrugged. 'It's a service we provide everyone now.'

'Even suspected terrorists?'

'You've been living in the mountains too long, my friend. We declared defeat in the war on terror about two years ago. We don't even use the word terror anymore. There's only 'man-made disasters' caused by disenfranchised groups who are really just 'misunderstood.'

'In fact, I've undergone intense training so that I can better relate to your feelings. If, and I'm not promising we'll get there, but *if* you can assure me you will repent of your evil ways, I'll be able to let you go with only a warning.'

Nicholas studied him. 'You don't believe I had anything to do with the bombing in Rome, do you?'

'Hell, no,' said Harvath, who turned and apologized. 'I'm sorry, Father.'

'Don't worry. He's heard much worse than that. Haven't you?'

The priest bowed his head slightly and backed

out of the doorway. 'I think I'll give you two some time to catch up. If you need anything, please let me or one of the brothers know.'

'Thank you,' replied Harvath.

'How about some more bandwidth?' said the Troll as he tapped the laptop lying on the bed next to him.

'Patience, Nicholas. The brothers are doing the best they can with what they were able to salvage from the farmhouse.'

The little man threw his hands in the air as the priest left the room. They were covered in bandages and wrapped with gauze. 'We're in the middle of fucking nowhere and I'm all but cut off. Before the fire, I had a halfway decent uplink. Now I'm lucky to have any signal at all. Secretly, I think they prefer me cut off. I think they're worried that if I connect back with the outside world something else might happen to me.'

'So what *did* happen to you?'

'A woman tried to kill me.'

'You do have an unusual proficiency for pissing people off.'

Nicholas's face was like stone. 'She was not just some woman, she was a professional. She knew exactly what she was doing.'

'She couldn't have been that professional. You're still alive.'

'Call it a higher power, but at the very last minute I sensed something and moved as she swung at my throat. But the real credit goes to the dogs. If they hadn't broken through the door, I'd be dead. They're the ones who stopped her and dragged me outside, away from the fire.'

Harvath examined the wounds a bit closer. 'What did she use? A knife?'

'Straight razor.'

'Why would you let anyone near you with a straight razor?'

'I thought I could trust her. I was wrong.'

'So who was she?' asked Harvath as he pulled the thermos from his pack and offered Nicholas a cup of coffee.

'She was a courtesan,' he said, declining the coffee.

'You mean a prostitute.'

'We're splitting hairs here. Call it what you want. She was a very expensive woman for hire, an escort.'

'How did you find her?'

'Through an agency.'

'What's the name of this agency?' asked Harvath as he took a sip of coffee.

'I don't know what it says on their bank statements, but to its clients it's known as the Academy.'

'And how does it work?'

'They have an online password-protected catalog. When you see something you're interested in, you send them a query. The director speaks with the courtesan in question and if she agrees, you set up a Skype visit as a sort of get-to-know-you session, then the price is set and the details are worked out.'

'And you're convinced she was a professional, not just some whack job?'

The Troll shook his head. 'No, she was

definitely a professional.'

'What does this have to do with the bus bombing in Rome?'

'You've been shown the evidence of my supposed involvement?'

'I have,' said Harvath. 'What can you tell me about it?'

'Someone obviously wanted to frame me. They chartered a private jet to Sicily and sent a little person with two dogs and a suitcase into a hangar. Ten minutes later, he comes out and the plane takes off. The pilots never see the meeting, but plenty of grist has been thrown into the rumor mill and a scenario starts to emerge. Add to that some Muslim men who make contact with the Cosa Nostra looking to buy explosives and why wouldn't the authorities believe what they're being told? The only thing is, I'm not in the arms business. I didn't sell any explosives to some Muslim terror cell. That's cheap and beneath me.'

It was the same thing Harvath had told the Old Man. 'So the idea was to frame you and then kill you to make the frame job stick?'

'Dead or alive, as long as they could convincingly pin it on me, I assume that it meant nobody would be looking for them.'

Harvath raised his eyebrows. 'And who are they?'

'I don't know. What I do know is that whoever this person is, they began building their attempt to frame me for the bus bombing before it even happened. That means they had advance knowledge of it.'

'I agree,' said Harvath. 'Did you buy or purchase any information leading up to the bombing that could be connected?'

'As far as I can tell, no. There was nothing I was involved with that indicated this attack was coming. I don't like when children are targeted. I never would have gone along with something like this.

'I might have taken money from animals who wanted to target children, but I would have found a way to either sell them incomplete intelligence, or leak their plans to the authorities so that I didn't get implicated but the attack would have been stopped.'

Harvath was good at telling when he was being lied to. Right now, he wasn't. 'So you believe the woman who tried to kill you was placed at the Academy as bait?'

'I'm sure of it.'

'Who knows that you're a client?'

Nicholas thought for a moment. 'It's not something I advertise. There's the women themselves and the director. Other than that, nobody.'

Harvath knew the list had to be longer than that. He was also certain Nicholas knew it as well. In the sex trade, everything was for sale, even the identity of valued customers. It all came down to how much someone was willing to pay.

'Whoever placed the woman there knew enough to build a profile that I would find irresistible. I should have known better.'

'You should have, but right now that's not my problem. When Padre Peio called me, he said you believed there would be more attacks. I want to know when and where.'

The Troll began to shrug but abandoned the gesture due to the pain. 'I'm only picking up bits and pieces. There has been chatter. The handful of sources I have communicated with are talking about attacks in multiple European cities against Americans.'

'Like the one in Rome or something different?'

'I don't know.'

'C'mon, Nicholas,' said Harvath. 'If we're going to stop these attacks, I have to know more.'

'Nothing would make me happier than to give you more information, but everything has gone quiet. You know what that means.'

Harvath did know what that meant. Terror networks often went dark before a big attack.

'Our best hope for stopping these people is for you to uncover who placed my attacker at the Academy.'

He was right.

'The director's name is Dominique Fournier. She's based in Provence. Nothing happens at the Academy without her knowledge. She's an absolute bitch, and I promise that she will not willingly cooperate with you.'

'We'll see,' said Harvath. 'What kind of security does she have?'

'Better than most. I've already discussed my plan with Peio.'

'He isn't a priest, is he?'

Nicholas smiled. 'Father Peio is definitely a priest, but it's what he did before his calling that makes him so interesting.'

'I'm going to assume he didn't run a petting zoo.'

'No,' said Nicholas with a laugh. 'He didn't run a petting zoo.'

'He was an ETA operative, wasn't he? What happened? He got tired of planting bombs and found religion?'

'You've got Peio completely wrong. He wasn't a terrorist. He was actually an intelligence agent.'

'Peio was a spook?'

Nicholas nodded. 'With the Centro Nacional de Inteligencia.'

Harvath was familiar with Spain's official intelligence agency, also known as the CNI. 'How did he end up making that kind of career change?'

'You can ask him on the way.'

'On the way where?'

'France. He's offered to make sure you get across the border. I just hope you can get to Fournier in time.'

15

When John Vaughan met Paul Davidson at a health food restaurant under the 'L' tracks in Chicago's River North neighborhood, he thought he had the wrong guy. Davidson was a barrel-chested man in his late forties who looked more like a narcotics officer or a Hell's Angel than a cop from Public Vehicles. He had long hair pulled back in a ponytail, a goatee, and even an earring.

Vaughan, who had dropped off his daughter at school and bypassed the Starbucks in order to get to this meeting on time, hadn't been expecting this.

'We've only got one type of coffee,' said the waitress after he had joined Davidson at the table. 'But I've got tons of teas. I can bring over the box if you want to choose.'

'No thanks,' said Vaughan. 'Just coffee, please.'

'Anything to eat?'

'Their turkey sausage is off the hook,' replied Davidson.

Vaughan shook his head. He hated health food.

Davidson rattled off an order that sounded

like it was straight from a craft services table for some Hollywood movie. Vegan this and tofu that. It was disgusting.

'Why do you eat that stuff?' asked Vaughan.

'Because I'm too stubborn to go on Lipitor.'

'I'd rather take a bullet.'

'No you wouldn't. Trust me. It's not fun.'

'You've been shot?' asked Vaughan.

'I didn't move to the Public Vehicles Division for the action.'

'When did it happen?'

'Four years ago. I was a patrol officer. My partner and I were doing a traffic stop. Some thug pulled a gun, and my partner and I both got capped. I took it through the shoulder and my partner got a round in the leg. I shot the offender in the head and killed him.'

'So you decided to hang it up being a patrol officer?'

'No. My wife decided. *No mas* patrol.'

'How did you wind up at Public Vehicles?' asked Vaughan.

'Due to my *heroism* and *valor*, blah, blah, blah, the department let me have my pick. There was a slot at Public Vehicles and the rest is home-by-six-every-night history.'

Vaughan was amazed by how the man downplayed what had happened. 'Is your partner still a patrol officer?'

Davidson laughed. 'He is and he's been shot two more times since then. I'm glad I got away from him. The guy's a bullet magnet.'

Vaughan laughed. 'Listen, I'm sorry again for bothering you on vacation.'

'Don't worry about it. I'll let you pay for breakfast and we'll call it even.'

'I was going to offer to pay anyway.'

'In that case, I'll think of something else.'

Wiseass, thought Vaughan. 'You've already got something for me?'

'You sound surprised.'

'I only called you the day before yesterday.'

'I can hold on to it for a day or two if it'd make you appreciate it more.'

'No. What have you got?'

Davidson pulled a blue notebook from his jacket pocket and set it on the table. 'Are you familiar with how the cab system works in Chicago? I don't want to bore you with a bunch of stuff you already know.'

'I know the basics. You've got the actual cab owner who purchases a license to operate from the city office of Consumer Services. It's also called a medallion. You can't legally operate a cab without one. Usually, the medallions are worth more than the cabs themselves.'

'Correct.'

'Each cab is required to have a meter. The meter is turned on when a fare gets in. The meter has set rates, et cetera.'

'Exactly. Drivers then lease the cab for a short period of time from the owner. The most common lease is for a week for about six hundred bucks. Owners, whether it's a small-time guy with a handful of cabs or a big conglomerate like Yellow, also do weekend leases for about two hundred bucks if they've got extra vehicles sitting around not making them any money. That's the surface material. When it starts to get interesting is when you get beneath that.

'Like gas stations and mini-marts, cabs are a popular entry job for immigrants. In Chicago, the taxi subculture is composed of three predominant cartels: the Middle Easterners, the Pakistanis, and the East Africans.'

'What about the Russians?' asked Vaughan.

'The Russians and Eastern Europeans own a lot of cabs, but I'm talking about drivers. The Eastern Europeans are more into the limo business.'

'You know all of this from being in Public Vehicles?'

'I know it because I have initiative. Public Vehicles may be a safe place to work, but it's frickin' boring. After a year of wanting to put a gun in my mouth, and I'm kidding by the way, I decided to get out on the street. I got my sergeant to approve a sting operation I wanted to run on gypsy cabs at the airport. I was busting these guys left, right, and center. You should have seen it. I'd pop the glove box and they'd have ten grand in cash and a stack of food stamps. It really pissed me off.

'I wanted to learn more, so I started building a network of informants. When I caught a guy I thought could be useful, I'd let him go.'

'Which meant he owed you.'

'That's right,' said Davidson. 'I started visiting the pool parking lot where they all wait and got to know as many drivers as I could. I became friendly with a lot of them and learned what

111

restaurants they hung out at and started eating in those places and so on and so forth. What really surprised me was that nobody was doing this. Not the CPD, not the FBI, nobody. I mean before 9/11 I could understand them overlooking these guys, but not doing it afterward was nuts. Nevertheless, that's the way it was and still is. I'm it.'

'How does this play into Alison Taylor's case?'

'I put the word out to all of my informants. I wanted to know if they'd heard of anything that fit with our case. Was anyone suddenly out sick? Was anyone suddenly remorseful or guilty? That kind of stuff.

'I pumped my contacts at the cab restaurants, the roach coaches, the hummus stands, the hookah bars; everywhere. I even spent the last two nights cruising the neighborhoods most of these guys live in, looking for cabs with damage.'

'How'd you do?'

'I struck out,' replied Davidson. 'I didn't get anything.'

'So?'

'So I reached out to another driver I know. He's not a regular informant, but I let him slide on something a ways back and he owed me.

'I wanted to put myself in the shoes of the guy we're looking for, so I called him up and laid out the scenario for him. I asked if he had been involved in a hit-and-run, what would be going through his mind.'

'I would assume, getting caught by the cops,' said Vaughan.

Davidson shook his head. 'Not quite. According to this driver, he'd be more afraid of his owner learning that the cab had been in an accident.'

'Seriously?'

'Yup. And to prevent the owner from finding out, the guy we're looking for would need to get the cab repaired as quickly as possible. Enter the Triple P.'

'What's the *Triple P*?'

'Piss, paint, and pray,' replied Davidson, as the waitress set his breakfast down on the table. 'It's an under-the-radar taxicab mechanic and body shop. They're all over the city and fix damaged cabs while drivers wait. And they're fast too. The Muslim ones have little prayer rooms in them and the joke is that as soon as you've taken a piss and said your prayers, the paint on your cab would be just about dry.'

Vaughan was fascinated.

'If you're a Middle Eastern driver, you go to one of the Triple P's owned and run by a Middle Easterner. If you're Pakistani, you go to a Pakistani operation. If you're East African, you go to an East African one, yada, yada, yada.'

'How come I haven't heard about these places before?'

'Like I said, they're under the radar. They operate around the clock, only deal in cash, and don't advertise. They do business only within their own ethnic group.'

'And you think the driver who hit Alison Taylor used one of these body shops to repair the damage to his cab?'

113

'According to my source, there was a Pakistani driver who brought his vehicle into a particular shop on the night in question. He was shaken up and was dumb enough to blab about clipping some woman. He wanted to get his cab repaired as soon as possible and was willing to pay extra for it.'

'This is fantastic,' said Vaughan. 'When can we pay a visit to the shop?'

'Right after we're done with breakfast.'

16

They left Vaughan's Crown Vic at the restaurant and drove Davidson's Bronco to the Crescent Garage and Body Shop. Outside, several cabs were double-parked along the street. Men dressed in the traditional *salwar kameez* — long, cotton tunics over loose-fitting trousers that stop just above the ankles — stood in front talking. Many had long beards without mustaches and almost all of them were wearing sandals. Vaughan couldn't tell if he was in Chicago or Karachi.

As the two police officers walked up, the men ceased their conversations and stared at them. Davidson had purposely left his jacket in his truck and all eyes fell to the shield clipped to his belt and the large pistol he wore on his hip. For his part, Vaughan didn't flash anything. He didn't need to. They all could tell he was also a cop.

With the overhead door down, they accessed the garage via a standard entrance next to it. There were four hydraulic lifts: two on each side. In the far corner was a makeshift painting bay. Tool chests lined the walls and there were fenders, bumpers, mirrors, body panels, and other parts stacked everywhere. At the far end, another overhead door led to a small lot crammed with beat-up taxis out back. The garage was lit with sputtering fluorescents hung from the ceiling.

The first thing Davidson noticed when he walked in was a man attaching a medallion to the hood of a freshly painted taxicab. 'What the hell do you think you're doing?' he demanded.

If there was one thing Davidson had learned from dealing with the cab communities it was that their cultures only respected strength. If you showed any weakness whatsoever, you were screwed. You had to get in their face from the get-go, project power, and never let them forget who was in charge.

All of them came from countries where the police were famous for abusing their power. They carried with them a deeply ingrained fear of law enforcement that Davidson used to his advantage. It wasn't any different from how he handled the inner-city thugs he'd been dealing with his whole career as a cop.

'Are you deaf?' he said. 'I asked you what you're doing with that medallion?'

'Nothing,' replied the mechanic as he stepped away from the cab and set his drill down.

'It doesn't look like nothing to me.' Turning to Vaughan he said, 'Get his name, his ID, all of his information.'

'Why?' asked the mechanic.

'Why? You know damn well that only the office of Consumer Services can touch a taxi medallion. You're in a lot of trouble.'

The mechanic was about to speak when an old man with a long gray beard came out of the office yelling in Urdu. He was followed by another man who looked to be in his late twenties.

'Who's in charge here?' demanded Davidson.

The old man walked up to him, still yelling in Urdu until the younger man put a hand on his arm and pulled him back.

'My father doesn't speak English,' said the younger Pakistani man.

'That's okay,' replied Davidson. 'I'm sure the court will provide an interpreter for him.'

'The court? What are you talking about?'

'What's your name?'

'I am Jamal and this is my father, Fahad Bashir. I still don't understand what you are talking about, though.'

'I'm talking about four cabs double-parked outside,' said Davidson as he wrote down the two men's names. 'I'm talking about your mechanic over here affixing a city of Chicago medallion to the hood of that cab. And that's just for starters. Tell your father he can send all of his employees home. He can tell the customers to beat it too. You're going to be closed down.'

'Closed down? Sir, please. There must be something we can do. We can't afford to be closed down.'

'Well, you should have thought of that before you helped cover up a hit-and-run accident.'

'Cover up?'

Jamal's English was perfect, and Davidson figured he was probably first-generation American. 'When you help destroy evidence of a crime, we call that a cover-up.'

'What crime? Sir, please. I don't know what you are talking about.'

Though he had all of the details committed to memory, Davidson flipped back several pages in his notebook and recounted the facts. 'On Friday, June 9, in the early morning hours, a Yellow taxicab was involved in a hit-and-run accident. Shortly thereafter, the cab was brought here for repairs. You fixed it.'

'We fix many cabs that have been in accidents. That's what we do.' The young man stopped and translated for his father, who was demanding to be filled in.

After communicating briefly with his father, Jamal turned back to Davidson. 'We don't ask our customers how their damage happened. We simply repair the vehicles. Even if a customer told us how the damage had been committed, why would we suspect that they had not done the right thing and alerted the police?'

'I don't like being messed with,' said Davidson, bypassing the young man's excellent point. 'We'll hash this out in court. In the meantime, you're going to be shut down.'

The older Pakistani man said something to his son and gestured toward the office area.

Vaughan came back from collecting the mechanic's personal information and stood next to Davidson.

'We keep very good records,' stated Jamal. 'My father doesn't want any trouble. If you come to the office with me, we'll see what we can do.'

The old man bowed his head and gestured

toward the office, encouraging the policemen to follow his son.

The office reminded Vaughan of many he had seen while in Iraq. There were prayer rugs in the corner and the walls were relatively unadorned save for a Pakistani airline calendar that looked as if it was ten years out of date. He looked up at the stained acoustic ceiling tiles above the room's three desks and figured it had to suck being in here when it rained. In fact it probably sucked being here at any time. He could only imagine the toxic mold that was growing up in the ceiling.

Jamal was looking through a filing cabinet when his father returned with three mugs and a small dish of sweets. Vaughan didn't have to look inside the cups to know what was being served — tea.

The old man gestured to a threadbare couch fronted by a nicked-up coffee table and two mismatched chairs. Davidson nodded for Vaughan to sit down. Both of the officers knew that nothing got done in the Muslim world without tea.

As Jamal continued to look through his files, the other men sat and took tea.

Finally, the young man said, 'I can't find it.'

'Can't find what?' replied Davidson, the tone of his voice indicating that he wasn't happy.

'Our logbook. We keep one with all of the details of the repairs we do. I can't find it.'

'Bullshit.'

'I'm serious,' said Jamal, who then spoke several words to his father. Once the old man responded, Jamal pointed at one of the desks and

119

said, 'The other man who works here. He keeps the logbook.'

'What's his name?'

'Ali Masud.'

Davidson wrote it down. 'Where is he now?'

Jamal shrugged.

'Do you have a phone number for him?'

'Yes.'

'Call him.'

The young man removed his cell phone and dialed. Moments later, he began speaking. He chatted for less than a minute and then hung up.

Davidson looked at him. 'So? Does he have the logbook?'

Jamal put his palms up and smiled. His head bobbed as if he had just been given the answer to a profound riddle. 'Ali Masud took the logbook home with him last night.'

'And?'

'And he's coming in to work in about three hours and will bring the book back.'

Davidson stood and said, 'Then we'll be back in two, and if that book isn't here, I'm not only going to have you closed down, I'm going to arrest you and your father for obstruction of justice. Is that clear?'

Jamal nodded as Vaughan stood, and the two officers left the garage.

Out on the sidewalk Davidson asked, 'What do you think?'

'I think he's lying.'

'I do too.'

'So what do we do?'

Davidson fished his keys out of his pocket as

they approached the Bronco. 'We give him the two hours and if he dicks us around, we go to plan B.'

'What's plan B?'

'I'll let you know when I figure it out.'

17

At the appointed hour, Vaughan and Davidson returned to the Crescent Garage and Body Shop and were shown into the office. Jamal sat behind one of the desks with a red spiral notebook in front of him. Sitting on the couch were his father and another Pakistani man who they assumed was Ali Masud. Jamal never bothered to introduce him.

'Is that it?' said Davidson as he approached the desk.

'As promised.'

Davidson flipped open the cover to the first page and noticed that it was damp. 'What happened?'

'Ali Masud regrettably spilled some tea on it. You can still read all the information.'

Davidson's BS detector was fast approaching the red zone. Quietly, he turned the moist pages. The handwriting was meticulous and listed each cab number, the date, what work was done, and the dollar amount. 'This is your handwriting?' he asked the man sitting next to the old man on the couch.

'It's his,' answered Jamal.

'Am I talking to you?' asked Davidson.

'No.'

'Then be quiet.'

Davidson asked the question again.

'Is this your handwriting?'

The man on the couch nodded.

Davidson stopped when he got to the entries for July 9, the date of Alison Taylor's hit-and-run. 'Do you recall a cab coming in here on or around the ninth of July with damage from a hit-and-run?'

The man shook his head.

'What's your name?'

'Ali Masud.'

'Mr. Masud, do you recall anyone talking about a hit-and-run accident recently?'

'No, sir,' replied Masud. 'I do not.'

Davidson studied all of the entries for July 9 and wrote down the cab numbers and then did the same for the next seven days. 'Can you make a copy of this for me?' he asked Jamal.

'I would be happy to, sir,' said Jamal as he gathered up the book and walked over to a small Xerox machine.

Davidson turned his attention back to Masud. 'Have you ever had a customer who needed repairs due to hitting a pedestrian?'

The Pakistani shrugged. 'I would have to look back through the files.'

'I can't expect you to remember something like that,' Davidson cracked.

Ali Masud didn't respond.

Jamal returned with the copies and handed them to Davidson. 'I'm sorry we couldn't be more helpful.'

'Me too,' said Davidson as he removed a pair of handcuffs.

While he was sure all three of the men were lying, Vaughan had not witnessed anything that constituted an arrestable offense. The last thing he wanted was to get dragged into a false-arrest claim with Davidson. Leaning in, he said quietly, 'What are you doing?'

'Time for plan B,' answered Davidson as he walked out of the office and onto the garage floor.

Vaughan followed him and was just in time to see him point to the mechanic from earlier and, holding the handcuffs at his side, say, 'You. Put your tools down and come over here. You are under arrest.'

'Me?' said the mechanic.

'You.'

Davidson had only taken two steps toward him when the mechanic dropped his tools and bolted for the door.

Looking at Vaughan he yelled, 'Get him! I'll get the car.'

* * *

Vaughan made it out the door just in time to see the mechanic turn right at the corner. Chasing suspects was one of his least favorite parts about the job, but he took off after him.

Turning right at the corner, he saw the mechanic cross the street and turn into the alley. If there was one place you didn't want to chase someone, it was into an alley. The problem was that these guys seldom ran across open, flower-strewn meadows.

The mechanic cut in between two buildings, leapt up onto a Dumpster, and flipped over a

124

chain-link fence into a vacant lot. Vaughan was fifty yards behind him and closing.

At the far side of the lot, the mechanic hit the pavement and turned left. Vaughan had not chased a lot of Pakistanis, but if this was what he could expect the next time, he made a mental note to just take out his gun and shoot the guy.

'Stop running!' he yelled, but the Pakistani man wasn't interested in following orders. Instead, he picked up his pace even further. This guy was running like his life was on the line.

Vaughan was pissed. *Where the hell was Davidson?*

They came to the next intersection and the mechanic didn't even slow down. He ran right through traffic and almost got nailed. Horns were still blaring as Vaughan, who was tightening the gap, raced across the street after him.

Up ahead, the Pakistani began to slow down. Whatever reserves he had, he must have burned through them.

Nearing the middle of the block, he stopped and risked a glance backward.

'That's right,' Vaughan yelled. 'You fucking stop right there.'

The mechanic must have judged the distance and figured he had enough energy left to outrun the police officer, because something flickered over his face ever so briefly. It looked like a smile. He wasn't stopping. He was just catching his breath.

That did it. Now Vaughan was really pissed. Not only was he going to catch this dirtbag, he was going to beat him full of courtesy with either an Emily Post guide or the Chicago phone book, whichever was thicker. *Go ahead. Start running again, asshole*, he thought to himself.

It was almost as if the Pakistani man could read his mind. With his eyes still glued to Vaughan, he sucked in a huge breath of air and took off once again.

He had only made it three steps when he stepped off the curb into the area where the alley met the street and Paul Davidson hit him with his Bronco.

The mechanic tumbled across the ground like a human lint roller, picking up shards of glass and loose gravel as he went. It wasn't the worst road rash ever suffered by man, but for a guy that hadn't been pitched off a bike or a motorcycle, it was pretty impressive.

By the time Vaughan reached them, Davidson had already leapt out of his truck and had the suspect's arms pinned behind his back.

'They teach you that move in Public Vehicles?' asked Vaughan as he leaned against the building at the mouth of the alley and tried to catch his breath.

'My doctor says I shouldn't exert myself,' replied Davidson as he snapped a pair of cuffs on the mechanic and yanked him to his feet.

'I am in pain,' complained the Pakistani.

'The party is just starting, my friend,' said Davidson as he led him into the alley and propped him up behind his truck.

His breathing slowly coming back under control, Vaughan walked back and joined them.

'I told you not to run.'

'I am sorry, sir,' replied the mechanic.

'It's a little late for that.'

'Please, sir, I cannot go to the jail.'

Davidson laughed. 'Oh, yes you can, my friend. And it is not a happy place.'

The Pakistani looked away from him and for some reason seemed to decide that Vaughan was the more rational and reasonable of the pair and focused on him. 'Sir, please, no jail.'

'You should have thought of that before you started running.'

'Actually,' injected Davidson, 'you should have thought of that before you started playing with cab medallions like they were refrigerator magnets.'

'I can pay you,' said the man. 'I have money. Please.'

'Don't do that,' said Vaughan. 'Bribing a police officer is a very serious offense, and you are already in enough trouble as it is. What's your name?'

'Javed Miraj.'

Davidson removed his notebook and wrote the man's name down.

'Where do you live?'

The man answered and, after a few more questions about his background, Vaughan asked, 'Why did you run?'

'I told you, sir,' said Miraj, 'I do not wish to go to the jail.'

'I got that part. What I want to know is *why* you ran?'

The mechanic was quiet for several moments before responding. 'If I go to the jail, I will be sent back to Pakistan.'

'You're illegal.'

Javed Miraj hung his head and nodded.

Vaughan whistled. 'Not good, Javed. Not good at all, my friend.'

'Unless you can convince a judge you're from Mexico, you're definitely going to be on the next plane out of here. Can you *habla Español?*'

Miraj looked up at Davidson and then turned his tearful eyes to Vaughan. 'Please, sir. There are no jobs in my village in Pakistan. I send money to my family so they can buy food. If you send me home, we will all starve.'

'But look at it this way,' replied Davidson, placing an arm around his shoulder and steering him toward the passenger door. 'At least you'll all be together.'

'No,' implored the mechanic. 'Please, sir, no. Do not send me back.'

'There's nothing we can do. We have to follow the law. Besides, you should see what you did to the hood of my Bronco.'

'I can fix your Bronco, sir.'

'Wait a second,' said Vaughan, who had figured out Davidson's plan B the moment he stepped out of the Crescent office waving a pair of handcuffs at the mechanic. 'Maybe there is something we can do. Maybe, if Mr. Miraj can help us, we can help him.'

'Javed can't help us. He's going back to Pakistan.'

Vaughan looked at the man and shrugged. 'Sorry, Javed.'

Miraj hung his head as Davidson opened the

128

passenger door of his Bronco. Just as Davidson was about to place him inside, he took a deep breath and asked, 'If I help you, you *will* help me?'

Davidson stopped and leaned him against the side of the truck.

'It's your decision,' said Vaughan. 'You either help us or you go to jail and get sent back to Pakistan.'

The mechanic winced and Vaughan saw another flash of what he had previously thought had been a smile.

'I must go to the toilet,' said the man. 'My stomach is very bad. You chasing me has made it worse.'

'No,' corrected Davidson. 'You *running* from us made it worse. Now, if you'll pardon the pun, shit or get off the pot.'

The Pakistani was confused.

'He means, give us something we can use, or you are going to jail. Right now.'

'The logbook they showed you is false. It is not real.'

'How do you know?'

'I heard them,' replied Javed. 'They told Ali Masud to make up a new book.'

Davidson knew it. They'd even spilled tea on it to age it and disguise the fact that it was brand new. 'So we were right,' he said. 'The cab from that night had been there.'

'Yes.'

'Who worked on it?' asked Vaughan.

Javed looked at him. 'I did.'

18

Forty-five kilometers east of the border, Padre Peio pulled into a tiny French village and parked behind a four-year-old blue Citroën. He had taken a circuitous route through the mountains and down into France. Much of what they had driven on could hardly have been called roads at all. In fact, Harvath suspected that they were very likely Basque smuggling routes, but he didn't ask. He was more interested in listening to Peio.

As they drove, the priest had opened up about his past. The information came slowly at first, but built from there. Harvath wondered how many people the priest had ever shared his story with. He doubted his fellow priests would fully understand. Harvath wondered if, because of their similar backgrounds, Peio felt more comfortable with him; that somehow Harvath was better equipped to understand it.

He began by talking about his family. They were Basque, and his father had worked for the government. When Peio was in his first year of high school, his family had moved to Madrid.

130

With so many members of the family involved in the separatist movement, they were worried about him and his older brother becoming involved with ETA too.

The fear wasn't unfounded. Within a year of graduating from high school, Peio's older brother had returned to the Basque country and joined. Three months later, he was killed in a shoot-out with police. The family was devastated.

Peio did his compulsory military service and proved himself quite proficient in military intelligence. He extended his tour, completed his college degree on nights and weekends, and eventually transferred into the Spanish Intelligence service, where he met his wife.

They deeply loved their jobs and each other. They had a plan to work five more years in the intelligence field and then transition into something steady and less dangerous so that they could begin a family. They were six months shy of that goal when, on a cold March morning in 2004, Peio's wife, Alicia, boarded a rush hour commuter train for Madrid.

At 7:38 a.m., just as the train was pulling out of the station, an improvised explosive device planted by Muslim terrorists detonated, killing her instantly.

It was the Spanish 9/11 and Spain was in shock. Peio was beyond devastated. As an intelligence operative who specialized in Muslim extremism, he felt that he had not only failed his country, but that somehow he should have been able to prevent the attack. Because he hadn't, he had gotten Alicia killed.

None of what was going through his mind could have been further from the truth, but Peio had slipped into a very dangerous mental and emotional state.

He came into work the very next day, demanding to be allowed on the investigation. His superiors rightly refused his request and sent him home, placing him on a leave of absence. Friends from work took turns staying with him over the next two days until the third day when he disappeared. His colleagues assumed he had gone up to the Basque country to get away from Madrid and the scene of his wife's murder. They had no idea how wrong they were.

Over the next thirty-six hours, Peio hunted down and brutally interrogated several Muslim extremists, severely hampering the Spanish investigation. No matter what direction the authorities chose to follow, Peio, like some all-knowing deity, had already been there.

He captured two members of the terror cell and tortured them for three days before executing them. After drawing out all the money in his bank account, he left Madrid for the island of Cabrera, where he drank himself nearly to death and became hooked on heroin. When he ran out of money, he attempted suicide.

It was a priest on the tiny island who found him and helped bring him back from the dead. When it became time for Peio to decide whether or not to return to Madrid and put the pieces of his previous life back together, he felt that God had another plan for him.

As Harvath now sat waiting for Dominique Fournier, it was Peio's last statement that made him wish the priest had kept his past to himself. The biggest regret Peio said he had was not the brutal interrogations, the tortures, or the executions of the terrorists he had captured. For those acts, he had repented, atoned, and would ultimately have to answer to God. What he regretted the most was not having had children with his wife. If they'd had children, even just one, those days and months after Alicia's death would have been different.

Harvath doubted it. Any real man, especially someone with Peio's background, would have tried to hunt down his wife's killers. It was the six-month bender, heroin addiction, and suicide attempt that were troubling. Maybe a child would have prevented Peio from sinking so far into despair, but maybe not. There was no telling. For all he knew, Peio's circuits weren't exactly wired properly. The way his past life still seemed to pull at him, he had serious doubts about whether or not the man could or would remain a priest.

What bothered Harvath was the whole thing about not having kids. He didn't mind Peio unloading on him. It was a long drive and maybe he really did see something in Harvath that made him feel he could confide in him. But that his biggest regret, even after God had supposedly called him to a life in the church, was never having had kids really stuck with Harvath. If this man, a priest, couldn't get over it, how would he? There were parallels between Peio's loyalty to the church and his loyalty to Tracy that he didn't want to even begin exploring. He had some very serious things to consider, but for now they would have to wait. Dominique Fournier was almost within his grasp.

Nicholas had been right about her security measures. They were indeed better than most, but they weren't perfect. With limited band-width, his satellite phone, and a small wire transfer from one of his many bank accounts, finding Fournier's Achilles' heel had not proven difficult. The woman had made more than a few enemies in her lifetime.

The terraced hills near Fournier's estate were fronted by stone walls and planted with grapevines and olive trees. The fields beyond were an undulating sea of lavender. It was definitely one of the more picturesque places Harvath had ever conducted an ambush.

After confirming that Fournier had left the house, he returned to the Citroën, tossed his binoculars into his pack, popped the hood, and waited. Fifteen minutes later, she and her bodyguard came jogging up the road.

Leaning against the front of the car, he put on his most charming smile.

Fournier was a stunning woman. She was in her late forties, stood almost six feet tall, and had been a print and runway model until the business had finished chewing her up and had spit her out. She had long red hair drawn back in a ponytail and green eyes, and there wasn't an ounce of fat on her extremely athletic body, which Harvath had a more than ample view of as she was wearing one of the skimpiest jogging outfits he had ever seen.

Her bodyguard looked hard as nails. He was about the same age, but stood two inches shorter. He wore a fanny pack, which is where Harvath assumed he carried his weapon. He was clean-cut and intelligent looking. This guy wasn't just hired muscle. He was experienced and professional. Harvath noticed his demeanor change the minute he spotted him. He stiffened up and gave his protectee a subtle signal to drop back.

As they drew closer, Harvath stood up straighter and waved. The bodyguard was in front of Fournier by several feet and cautiously approached.

In addition to jogging the same road every day with only one bodyguard, Dominique Fournier had another weak spot, her vanity. 'If this is what roadside assistance looks like in France, I'm going to have to make sure I break down more often.'

Though Harvath spoke very good French, he wanted to put the pair at ease with him as quickly as possible. He figured the best way was to play the role of American tourist. He wasn't ready for what came next.

'What's wrong with your car?' said the bodyguard in perfect English. His accent sounded like he came from somewhere around Baltimore.

'Are you American?' asked Harvath, his smile growing even broader.

'Yes,' replied the bodyguard, who continued to

remain professional. 'What's wrong with your car?'

'I don't know. I think Citroën is French for piece of shit.'

The bodyguard cracked a smile. 'When we get to a phone, we'll call a wrecker for you.'

'Why don't you see if you can help him, Richard,' said Fournier as she stepped up and introduced herself. 'My name is Dominique.'

'Bonjour, Dominique,' said Harvath. 'My name's Russ.'

'It's nice to meet you, Russ. Are you here for the summer, or just passing through?'

She had an incredibly sexy accent and Harvath could have stood there all day and listened to her speak. 'I'm here for the summer actually.'

'Really? How nice. Did you bring your wife, or maybe your girlfriend?'

'Nope. Just me.'

'That's even nicer.' The sex appeal just oozed from this woman. It was obvious that she was interested in Harvath.

He turned his attention to the bodyguard. 'I appreciate your help. I'm not really a car guy.'

'Richard is very good with all things mechanical,' said Fournier.

'I'll see what I can do. Why don't you hop in and try to start it?'

While the man was being polite, Harvath could see that he hadn't let his guard down one bit. He really was a professional. The only reason he was helping a stranded motorist was that his employer had asked him to. He knew better than most how often this kind of ploy was used to facilitate an attack.

'Okay,' said Harvath as he opened the door and slid into the driver's seat. 'Here goes.'

He turned the key. 'Anything?'

The bodyguard looked under the hood and laughed. 'Turn it off for a second and try it again.'

Harvath did and the engine roared to life. 'That's fantastic. Thank you. What did you do?'

'The ignition control module was loose. I tightened it up, but you should get it checked out.'

'I will. Thank you,' said Harvath, who then looked at Fournier and added, 'And thank you.'

'Do you have a pen?' she asked.

Harvath fished around in the glove box until he found one and then handed it to her.

'Give me your hand,' she said.

He obeyed, sticking his left hand out the window, palm up. Fournier leaned into it and allowed it to rub against her upper thigh for a moment. Harvath felt a jolt of electricity rush through him.

She then cupped his hand and wrote her cell phone number on his palm. 'I suggest you call me before it rubs off.'

Before Harvath could respond, Fournier tilted her head and she and the bodyguard began jogging once again.

Harvath took a breath and noted that his heart was actually beating faster. Fournier had gotten to him.

Tossing the pen on the floor he shook it off

137

and put the car in gear.

He drove slowly, allowing them to pull a bit ahead of him. It was a tactical decision meant to disarm the bodyguard. That said, it also provided an excellent opportunity to check out Dominique Fournier from behind. She was gorgeous.

Not only that, she had been very charming. He couldn't tell why Nicholas thought she was such a bitch.

Harvath began to increase his speed until he pulled right up alongside the runners. 'Thanks again for the help,' he said.

The bodyguard smiled back. 'Anytime,' he replied.

That was when Harvath lifted the Taser and fired.

19

Harvath slammed on the brakes as the bodyguard's muscles seized up and he fell over into the road. He had to act fast.

He threw the Taser on the dash, its long wires running through the window to the two barbed probes embedded in the bodyguard's chest.

He had figured that Dominique Fournier would take off on her long legs like a gazelle, but he had figured wrong. He wasn't even halfway out of the car when she was on top of him. Immediately, his original opinion of her shifted as she kicked him in the groin harder than he could ever remember being kicked.

His vision dimmed, the wind whooshed from his lungs, and his knees buckled. He fell to the ground and realized how badly he had misjudged this woman.

He looked up just in time to see her considerably sized fist come sailing through the air at his head. He was on his knees between the car and its open door, powerless to do anything to stop her. He had no choice but to absorb the blow.

The problem was that it wasn't just one blow; it was several, a combination. Two punches followed, and Harvath's ear began to ring as a trickle of blood started to run from his nose. Whether this woman had taken martial arts training or had just attended one too many Tae

Bo classes made no difference. He was getting his ass kicked and if she kept this up, he was going to end up being knocked unconscious.

And to make matters worse, it was only a matter of seconds before the bodyguard would be up and around. Once that happened, the game would be over.

Even though the woman had kicked his eggs so far up into the henhouse he thought his beak was going to snap off, he needed to do something. He needed to push aside the pain and get control of the situation, now.

Before he could do anything, though, Fournier grabbed the open car door and slammed it into his side. Harvath had a rule about striking women, but was about ready to tear that page from his book.

The whole right-hand side of his body was on fire and five feet away, the bodyguard was struggling to stand.

Planting his left foot, Harvath exploded into the door with his shoulder and knocked Fournier backward with it. She lost her footing as she tripped over the bodyguard, and fell on top of him.

Harvath lunged for the Taser atop the dash and pulled the trigger. Because Fournier's skin was in physical contact with her bodyguard's, the electricity was transmitted to both of them and they got to 'ride the bull,' as it was known, together.

The minute Fournier was incapacitated, Harvath removed a handful of Tuff Ties from his pocket and trussed her up tight. He did the same thing to the bodyguard. After removing the man's fanny pack, he slapped pieces of duct tape over each of their mouths and placed hoods over each of their heads. Then he had to get them into the car.

Fournier had done a real number on him, and it was a lot harder moving the two of them than it normally would have been. The bodyguard was a pretty solid fellow and even though she didn't have an ounce of fat on her, six feet of woman was a hell of a lot of sugar and spice to be moving right after the beating he had taken.

The bodyguard got dumped in the trunk and he laid Fournier down on the backseat and covered her with a blanket. He didn't have far to go, but even out here in the middle of the countryside there was always the possibility someone would see them. The last thing he wanted was to drive past some bicycling tour of Provence with the red-headed Amazon queen in plain sight, bound and gagged across the backseat.

For their destination, he had searched for something close that would allow him to work without being disturbed. After driving around yesterday, he had found it. The abandoned barn was only a few kilometers away from the ambush site. Though part of the roof was missing, all of the sides were still intact. It was well off the road and hadn't been touched in decades. It was perfect.

He drove the Citroën directly into the barn, turned off the ignition, and then got out and closed the barn doors.

Leaving her hood on, he pulled Fournier off the backseat and then took her to a stool in the middle of the barn. He sat her down and gently dragged his knife blade across her midriff before placing it against her throat and telling her not to move.

With that, he walked back to the car and fished some gauze out of the first aid kit and shoved it into his nose to stop the bleeding.

After he'd had enough time to assess the rest of his injuries, he tuned in the Citroën's radio and turned up the volume. The bodyguard didn't need to hear what he and Fournier were about to talk about.

Next to the stool upon which she sat was a rickety old table. Upon it, Harvath had assembled several pictures Nicholas had e-mailed him. It was his hope that they would be all that was necessary to secure Fournier's cooperation.

Removing the gauze from his nose, Harvath walked up behind the woman and snatched off her hood.

She was frightened and her eyes swept the barn as she tried to figure out where she was and what was going on. Harvath stepped into her field of view so that she could see him. When she did, the look of fear in her eyes turned to one of pure hate. She tried to say something but the duct tape made it impossible. Whatever it was, she was very animated about it and Harvath could imagine what it was she was saying.

'Shut up,' he replied.

Fournier ignored him.

Harvath walked back over to her, grabbed a

fistful of her ponytail, and jerked her head backward as he played the tip of his knife along her cheek just under her eye. 'Don't say another word,' he cautioned. 'Look.'

Still holding her hair, he directed her attention to the photos laid out along the table. They were partially illuminated by a shaft of sunlight filtering in from the damaged roof above.

Harvath himself had trouble looking at the pictures. They had been chosen because of Fournier's vanity. He had no desire to physically harm her. That said, he had no reservations about threatening the use of harm and leaning on her as hard as he could psychologically. He also knew that if it came to it, and he was left with no other choice, he would use violence against her if it meant preventing more Americans from being killed. But the person who would decide what ultimately came to pass was Fournier herself.

'Ms. Fournier, you are in the position you are right now because you tried to kill the wrong person,' he said.

Instantly, Fournier protested through the duct tape and began to shake her head.

'There's no use denying it. The man you tried to kill has sent me to exact his revenge. Now, in front of you, you see the pictures of five women. The man who sent me suffered serious facial trauma because of your botched attack.

'He is not unreasonable and though I suggested he kill you and be done with it, he has decided to keep things fair. Each of the women you see on the table before you was disfigured in

143

a very specific manner. Each attack was painful and caused grotesque disfigurement.

'My employer is willing to allow you to select the means by which you will be disfigured.'

Fournier began screaming behind the duct tape and shaking her head wildly. Tears streamed down her face as she looked at the photos depicting the results of torture by acid, knives, hammers, and other terrifying instruments.

'You need to make peace with it, Ms. Fournier. Undoubtedly your looks have served you very well in life. Shortly, you will become a monster and will have no choice but to hide your face from the world. I'm going to remove the tape from your mouth. Please choose your method.'

The moment Harvath pulled off the tape, Fournier began to negotiate with him. 'Please,' she begged. 'Don't do this. I have money. I will pay you. I also have girls; lots of *beautiful* girls. They can all be yours.'

Harvath wasn't finding her very attractive anymore.

'I could tell you liked me back on the road. I like you too. I can be yours if you want me.'

'I don't want you,' he said. 'I want payback for the man you tried to kill.'

'But I didn't try to kill anyone!'

He smiled. 'Yes, you did. Maybe not directly, but you used his trust in you, his loyalty, to place an assassin in his bed.'

A flash of recognition raced across Fournier's face. It only lasted for a fraction of a second before it was gone. Harvath had seen it. It was called a microexpression and he had been taught to spot them years ago by the Secret Service.

'You know who I'm talking about, don't you?'

'No,' she replied, and the tell was visible again.

'Ms. Fournier, I have lunch in Nice and a flight back to Paris. Choose or I will choose for you,' he said, tapping the table with the edge of his knife.

'You don't want money. You don't want sex,' she sobbed. 'What do you want?'

Harvath looked at her. 'I told you, I want revenge. Revenge for the man you disfigured.'

'I had no choice!' she stated. 'Besides, how was I supposed to know she would try to kill him?'

'Ms. Fournier, I'm giving you thirty seconds to choose.'

'I was forced to take her. I was told not to place her in the general catalog; only the one that was made available to him.'

Harvath walked several feet away and with his back to her asked, 'Who are we talking about?'

'The dwarf, of course. It's the little man who sent you, isn't it?'

Harvath didn't respond. 'Who forced you?' he demanded as he turned back to face her.

'I can't tell you.'

'Fine. First we'll use the acid and then I will go to work on you with the knife.'

'No!' Fournier screamed. 'No!'

'Then tell me,' he shouted. 'Tell me right now who forced you. I will not ask you again.'

Fournier was silent and Harvath removed a

bottle from his pocket and began unscrewing the top.

'Leveque! Gaston Leveque!' she cried.

'How did he force you?'

'One of my girls had been involved in smuggling a substantial amount of drugs into France. He was going to implicate me. I would have lost everything.'

She was lying. Harvath could see it in her face. 'You're not telling me the truth,' he said.

Fournier hung her head and was quiet again. Finally, she said, 'I have a child, a little boy. His name is David. He's eight years old. He was in a private boarding school outside Paris.'

'*Was?*'

'Leveque found him and kidnapped him. He told me I would never see my boy again unless I did what he asked. He said if I told anyone he would kill me and David both.'

Fournier then broke down sobbing.

'Where is your son now?'

'Back with my mother in Toulouse.'

'And this Leveque?'

Fournier tried to stop crying. 'Antibes.'

20

HOTEL DU CAP-EDEN-ROC
ANTIBES

The only thing Harvath disliked more than Russian Communists was the Russian mafia, and the Côte d'Azur was lousy with them. What once was a tasteful European summer playground was now choked with bulletproof Hummers, women overinjected with silicone, and men wearing so much gold jewelry that no matter what direction they faced when sitting down in the cafés, they always ended up pointing magnetic north.

They were as gaudy as the Saudis and had bought up much of this stretch of the French coast. Even the Russian president was rumored to have a villa here. They did what they pleased and even handled crime in their own special way. To wit, when the home of a rich Russian gangster had been burgled, he sent his own leg breakers in every direction to crack heads until they found the perpetrators.

Once the Mafioso's goods had been recovered, he loaded the two thieves into his helicopter, flew it out over the Mediterranean, and shoved them out. The French police never even lifted a finger.

For years, the center of Russian gravity was the exclusive Hotel du Cap-Eden-Roc. Its owners were more than happy to suck up the Russians' ill-gotten gains, and once they found themselves to be the hotel of choice, they began ratcheting up their prices. Not only was it a license to print money, they found that the more expensive they were, the more popular they became. As their clientele rarely used credit cards, they abolished their use at the hotel completely. Instead, armored cars came three times a day to carry away the money to the bank.

Finally, a big-time Russian billionaire purchased the hotel. A subtle sign that the economy was catching up even with the Russians came when the hotel quietly reinstituted credit cards.

Despite the global economic hardships affecting the hotel's clientele, it was still comfortably booked throughout the summer months. Harvath was less than ten minutes away when Nicholas called to inform him that he had finally managed a reservation.

When he pulled the black Porsche Panamera Turbo he had rented in Cannes up to the hotel's front doors, his $135,000 sports car was the least expensive vehicle by far. He counted three Maybach Landaulets, two Bugatti Veyrons, an SSC Ultimate Aero, a Leblanc Mirabeau, a Pagani Zonda Cinque Roadster, a Lamborghini Reventon, and a Koenigsegg CCXR. It was easily twenty million dollars of exotic cars right there. Knowing the Russians, they all probably belonged to one man.

Harvath tipped the valet and followed the bellman inside. The lobby was full of fresh-cut flowers and potted palms. It was bright and elegantly furnished. Its high ceilings and soaring white columns bounced back the sunlight that streamed in through the porticos and open French doors. It wasn't at all garish and Harvath put a check in the billionaire owner's column for having the good sense not to mess with a good thing.

After the front-desk clerk had checked him in, Harvath sent the bellman on to his room with his bag. He had a stop to make before going upstairs.

Behind the concierge desk was an average-looking man of medium height and thin build in his late fifties. He had a long Gaelic nose upon which were perched a pair of trendy designer glasses. Affixed to his perfectly pressed uniform was the prestigious *clefs d'or*, or crossed keys of gold, marking him as a member of the top concierge society in the world. Beneath the *clefs d'or* was a name tag which read 'Leveque.'

'May I help you, sir?' the concierge asked as he saw Harvath approach.

Harvath smiled. 'I hope so,' he said, removing a stack of bills, counting off a thousand dollars, and sliding it across the counter to the man. 'I'm going to need some dinner reservations while I'm here, and I also would like to charter a yacht.'

'Absolutely, sir. Where would you like to eat?'

It was all Harvath could do not to reach out and throttle the man right there. If only half of what Dominique Fournier had told him about Leveque was true, it would be too much. He was a fixer for the Russians. Whatever they wanted,

149

he got for them: drugs, underage children for sex, you name it. Fournier used to arrange liaisons for the wealthy guests of the Hotel du Cap, but had stopped. She claimed the Russians drank too heavily and when they did they beat her girls mercilessly. Add to that the fact that Leveque trafficked in children for prostitution and Fournier had severed all ties with him — at least until he had orchestrated the kidnapping of her son.

Harvath brought his mind back to the business at hand and answered the man's question. 'A colleague of mine is supposed to e-mail me some suggestions. Can I get back to you on that?'

'Certainly,' said Leveque. 'What about your yacht charter? If you can tell me which day you would like to go out, how many people, how long you'd like to go, and what kind of a vessel you are interested in, I can get started on that right away.'

'I'd like to go tomorrow for a half day. There will just be four of us, and I'd like to have lunch served. As far as the vessel, I'd like a motor yacht at least seventy meters in length. Oh, and we'd like to swim.'

'Of course. Tomorrow should be a beautiful day for swimming. I'll get started right away on this for you.'

Harvath gave Leveque his room number and headed upstairs. After tipping the bellman, he put the stopper in the tub, turned on the tap, and called room service.

Fifteen minutes later a waiter knocked on the

door and was shown in. Harvath tipped him and told him he could leave the table on wheels in the middle of the room.

Next, he called down to the valet and asked to have his car brought around. He then began filling the tub the rest of the way with the ice the waiter had brought.

He tossed the buckets into the closet, moved the table out of the way and, once everything else was ready, called down to Leveque. The concierge was only too happy to personally bring Harvath an Ethernet cable for his laptop and help him retrieve the e-mail his colleague had sent with restaurant suggestions in Antibes.

When Leveque's knock fell upon his door, Harvath was ready. He opened it with a smile and showed the concierge in. Once the door had closed behind him, Harvath sprang.

The punch took the Frenchman completely by surprise and he staggered backward, knocking over a lamp and hitting his head on the coffee table as he fell to the floor.

Grabbing him by the back of his collar, Harvath dragged him into the bathroom and dropped him next to the tub. He wrapped one hand around the concierge's throat and used the other to pull the Glock from underneath his shirt.

'Make one noise and I will kill you. Do you understand me?' he asked, the barrel of the weapon pressed against Leveque's head.

The man nodded slowly, the terror evident in his eyes.

'Good,' replied Harvath. He pulled the pistol

151

away and then slammed it into the side of his face, breaking the man's jaw. 'That was for Dominique Fournier's son.'

Leveque wanted to cry out in pain, but Harvath squeezed his throat so hard no sound was able to escape. 'Now we're going to go ice fishing. Let me know if you see anything.'

With that, Harvath raised the concierge up and over the side of the tub backward so that his head went into the water upside down.

Filling the tub with ice and submerging the victim in this fashion intensified the psychological trauma. A spinoff of waterboarding, it was known colloquially as iceboarding and was based on a concept called 'cold calorics' that could manipulate and irritate brainstem reflexes.

The sensation of being drowned was bad enough, but the layer of ice and the intense cold of the water compounded the experience. It also succeeded in better muffling any screams the victim might make. The only drawback was that if you weren't wearing gloves, which Harvath wasn't, your hand got cold very quickly.

Leveque's legs thrashed wildly and Harvath brought the butt of his pistol down hard into the man's crotch before pulling his torso back out.

The concierge vomited out both his mouth and nose and Harvath shoved him back over the side of the tub and under the water once more.

The thrashing started all over again and Harvath held him under for what must have seemed like an eternity to Leveque.

Finally, he pulled him out of the water again and asked one question. 'Who hired you to kidnap Dominique Fournier's son?'

'I don't understand what you are talking about.'

'Wrong answer,' said Harvath as he plunged the man back into the water. This time he let Leveque stay down a long time.

The Frenchman flailed wildly until Harvath pulled him back up. Once out, he vomited again and his body heaved for air.

'Listen to me, Leveque,' said Harvath. 'Scumbags who target children don't deserve to live. I want to kill you so bad I can taste it. The only way you're going to walk out of this bathroom alive is if you tell me who hired you to kidnap Dominique Fournier's son right now.

'As a matter of fact, screw that,' he added as he tipped the man backward again. 'I'm going to give you some more time underwater to think about it.'

'No,' croaked the concierge. 'Please. His name is Tony Tsui.'

'I've never heard of him. Who was the girl you forced Fournier to place inside her operation?'

'Tony set all that up. I was just a middleman.'

Harvath had figured as much. 'What was her name?'

'I don't know. I was just the go-between. Tony handled everything. I just passed the information to Dominique.'

Harvath was about to ask another question when he felt the cell phone he was carrying vibrate. It was one of the clean SIM card phones from the safe house in Madrid, the one he was using to communicate with Nicholas.

'I've got a name,' he said as he connected the call and raised the phone to his ear.

'You've got to get out of there,' said the Troll. 'I just learned the entire hotel is wired. The new owner is a blackmailer. He's got mics and cameras in every room.'

'But I swept the room when I got in,' said Harvath.

'As does every guest who knows even a little bit about security. This is all new equipment they're using. You've been blown. There is a security team about to kick down your door. Get out of there now!'

21

Harvath heard the soft click of his door being opened and tightened his grip around Leveque's throat. Quietly, he pulled the concierge to his feet. He then got behind him and, placing his pistol in the small of the man's back, clamped his left hand down around Leveque's mouth.

If the luxurious lobby was an indication of the 'money is no object' approach of the hotel's billionaire owner, Harvath had to assume his security team was going to be top-notch as well. Any hope that they might be nothing more than sides of beef in dark suits was dashed when they chose to enter his room quietly instead of breaking down the door.

Harvath assumed the men now entering his room were very well trained, either former FSB operatives, or Spetsnaz — Russian special operations soldiers.

He had his answer the minute they stepped all the way into his room. Their weapons were drawn, but they weren't in any tactical formation. At worst, these were FSB. At best, they actually were slabs of beef in dark suits. In the end, it didn't matter. Harvath was the only person with any cover. Whether he'd agree or not, the concierge was earning his $1,000 tip.

The only weapon Harvath had was his Glock. The three security operatives facing him all had ear pieces and he assumed they were getting a play-by-play from someone somewhere in the hotel who was watching via their hidden-camera system.

'Put the gun down,' said the lead security agent in heavily accented English. 'Now.'

Harvath kept Leveque between him and the three Russians at all times as he shuffled toward his backpack. If he could get to it, he might have a chance of getting out of this.

'Stop moving and put gun down!,' the same man yelled.

Harvath talked as he moved, careful to remain hidden behind Leveque. He doubted any of these apes could get him with a headshot, but he didn't want today to be the day one of them got lucky. 'Listen, I don't want any trouble.'

'Stop and put gun down now or we shoot.'

That made three warnings. Harvath doubted there would be a fourth. Tucking his Glock in the back of Leveque's waistband, he removed his cell phone, flipped it open, and held it up so the security men could see it. 'I have a bomb.'

The lead security man laughed. 'There is no bomb.'

Lowering the phone, Harvath slid it back into his pocket. As he drew his Glock he shoved Leveque at the security team and said, 'You're right.'

His first two shots kneecapped the lead security agent. Hitting the floor, he rolled to the right and drilled the second agent in the hand and the third in the shoulder. With Leveque in their way, none of the Russians were able to fire. Harvath gave a small prayer of thanks that they

156

were professional. Had they been strictly gangster muscle, they would have filled the room with lead and sorted out the dead once the smoke cleared.

Grabbing his pack, Harvath charged for the door. He fished a Guardian Protective Devices pop-and-drop pepper fog canister and activated it in the hallway before running to the stairs.

He knew that his every move was being watched and that the rest of the security team was being activated. They would know exactly where he was and, because this was their home turf, exactly how to get to him. The only thing he could do was put as many obstacles in their path as possible. And the best way to do that was to activate the fire alarm.

As it began blaring, he charged for the lobby. He encountered a security team of two. He fired close enough to scare the hell out of them, but not anywhere near enough to hurt them. They retreated momentarily back in the direction they had come.

The next team was waiting just beyond the chaos of the lobby. With the fire alarm and shots fired, guests ran in every direction. There were four security men between Harvath and the cars outside.

He saw a young woman hiding behind one of the couches in the lobby and he grabbed her. She screamed as he pushed her forward and tried to lash out at him. As soon as he had his pistol up underneath her chin she stopped.

'I promise I won't hurt you, but you've got to cut that out and cooperate.'

He had no idea if she spoke English or not, but she seemed to understand. Shoving her toward the door, he encountered no resistance.

Harvath hoped that the security men outside were as professional as the ones upstairs had been. As he stepped through the doors with his hostage, the men exchanged quick remarks and lowered their weapons as they backed away.

Looking for his car, Harvath saw that it was blocked in by two large Bentleys. Idling in the drive was a Saleen S7. While the paint job was a little flashy for his taste, beggars couldn't be choosers.

Pushing his hostage through the driver's side into the cramped cockpit, he pulled down the gull wing door and took off.

Even though he didn't need to look in his rearview mirror to see what was going on, he did so anyway. Commands were being shouted as the security team scrambled for their vehicles.

'You've made a big mistake,' said the woman sitting next to him. She had a thick accent.

'It probably won't be my last.'

'Don't be so sure. You've stolen something very valuable.'

Harvath gripped the steering wheel and turned hard onto the street at the end of the drive. 'At $400,000, you'd think this car would corner a bit better.'

'I'm not talking about the car,' said the attractive blonde as she buckled her seatbelt. 'I'm talking about me.'

'And who are you?'

'My name is Eva, but it's my husband's name

you should be concerned with.'

Downshifting, Harvath took another tight turn and accelerated. Knowing the Russians, they wouldn't call the police. Just like the thieves infamously dropped from the helicopter out in the ocean, they'd want to handle him personally. The thing was, Harvath was in no mood to go swimming.

The security men were going to come after him hard. But *fast* was going to be a little tough for them. They were creatures of habit, trained to follow orders. It wouldn't occur to them to grab several of the guests' sports cars. Instead, they'd pile into their heavily armored SUVs and wend through the narrow streets of Antibes as fast as their enormous tanks would allow.

Hitting the Boulevard du Littoral south toward Cannes, Harvath tried to focus on the traffic and not the tanned, toned legs projecting from the woman's exceptionally short skirt next to him. 'I don't even want to know your husband's name,' he said as he overtook the car in front of them. 'As soon as we've put enough distance between us and the men from the hotel, I'll let you out.'

'That's going to be difficult,' said Eva as she produced what looked like an iPod Nano.

'Your husband monitors you with a tracking device?'

'He's very jealous,' she said. 'And very insecure.'

'Okay, I've changed my mind. Who's your husband?'

'Nikolai Nekrasov.'

'Never heard of him.'

'The Russian billionaire? Owner of the Hotel du Cap.'

Now he knew why the guards had been so quick to lower their weapons. 'Sorry,' he replied. 'Doesn't ring a bell, but in all fairness to your husband, I've fallen behind on my *Forbes* lately.'

Eva smiled. 'So this isn't a kidnapping?'

'No.'

'That's too bad.' Rolling down the window, she tossed out the device. 'That should buy us a little time. If you're hungry, I have a friend who runs a wonderful restaurant in Cavalaire-sur-Mer.'

Either this woman was extremely unhappy with her husband or this was the world's quickest case of Stockholm Syndrome on record. 'Maybe I can take a rain check,' he said, looking into his rearview mirror. He could see the Russian security team weaving in and out of traffic behind him. They had to be insane to be driving like that in those kinds of trucks. They were going to get people killed.

'That's too bad,' the woman said. 'Nikolai hates Cavalaire-sur-Mer, but I think it's very romantic. Something tells me you would enjoy it.'

Harvath didn't doubt it. 'Maybe another time,' he said as he pulled into the oncoming lane and accelerated. The closer they got to Cannes, the heavier the Saturday-evening traffic became.

Drivers honked and flashed their brights, but he kept going before a truck forced him back onto his side.

He glanced in the rearview mirror again and couldn't see the security men. Not yet, at least. The momentary satisfaction he felt evaporated when his passenger said, 'It looks like Nikolai is taking you very seriously.'

Harvath looked to his left and saw a red EC135 Eurocopter tracking parallel with them over the water.

'Your husband is very persistent, isn't he?'

'He doesn't like sharing his things,' she said, placing her hand on the inside of his thigh.

She quickly pulled it back and gripped the edges of her seat as Harvath slid between two cars with just inches to spare.

Now that there was a helicopter involved, there was only one way he could disappear and to do it, he'd need cover.

Turning to Eva, he said, 'I need a favor.'

'That depends,' she replied.

★ ★ ★

When Nikolai Nekrasov's armored Denalis thundered into Cannes, they came to a screeching halt at a café on the Avenue du Petit Juas. As the hotel helicopter hovered above, Mrs. Nekrasov recovered from her ordeal over a glass of Montrachet. The American who had tortured the hotel's concierge and shot three of its security staff was nowhere to be seen.

22

Javed Miraj, the Pakistani mechanic from the Crescent Garage, turned out to be an excellent source of information.

He explained in detail how Ali Masud, the shop's bookkeeper, had been instructed to create a new logbook and to leave out the vehicle the police were searching for.

When asked why, the mechanic's response was very simple. Not only were Fahad Bashir, the Crescent's owner, and Ali Masud from the same village in Pakistan, but so was the driver who had run down Alison Taylor.

In Pakistan, loyalty followed a very strict hierarchy: family first, then village, and then tribe. The rules were even stricter abroad. It was a firmly held *us against them* mind-set.

Davidson asked the mechanic if he knew where the original logbook was. Miraj had no idea, but strongly suspected it had been disposed of. Fahad Bashir and his son, Jamal, were smart. Once they were committed to doctoring the logbook, he was certain they wouldn't leave behind any information that could incriminate them.

Vaughan was more concerned with nailing the

driver than the men of the Crescent Garage, but this was where Javed Miraj's usefulness as an informant started to break down.

Yes, he had worked on the cab in question. He even ID'd the piece of black plastic that had been recovered at the scene which turned out to be part of the plastic header from above the radiator. He described how he had replaced the hood and a side mirror and had pulled a new windshield, complete with a Chicago City sticker, from one of the damaged cabs in the lot behind the garage.

The driver had been nervous and upset. He had offered to pay double to get the work done right away. The mechanic had been pulled off another taxi to work on the Yellow Cab. It was a small shop and he couldn't help but hear how the man had sustained the damage. At that point, though, the information flow from the mechanic practically dried up.

Understandably, he couldn't remember the cab number. He saw lots of cabs every day. Cataloging the numbers was Ali Masud's job. All he could remember was that it was a four-digit number with a three in it.

He was able to provide a description of the driver and even coughed up a first name, but a dark-skinned Pakistani named Mohammed in a city like Chicago probably wouldn't do much to winnow down the haystack.

As the mechanic had no Chicago family that would be looking for him, Vaughan and Davidson decided to let his coworkers think he'd been arrested. After cleaning up his road rash they drove him down to the Department of Revenue and searched every four-digit cab license with a three in it until their eyes were bleeding and they had come up with their man, Mohammed Nasiri.

With Nasiri's full name and cab number, they approached the owner of his cab, Yellow Cab Company.

Because of his position with Public Vehicles, Paul Davidson was fairly well known by the cab operators. He was also, because of his no-BS, take-no-prisoners style, fairly disliked.

He wasted no time in going straight to the top at Yellow, calling the director of operations at his home and waking him up. After Davidson threatened to enact a crackdown of epic proportions on Yellow Cabs across the city, the director agreed to meet him the next morning at their corporate offices.

When Davidson and Vaughan showed up, the director was there, along with the company's corporate counsel, who quickly and repeatedly pointed out that their cooperation was in no way an indication of liability on their part. Rather, in the interest of being a good corporate citizen, Yellow want to help in the investigation in any way it could.

Davidson gave them a list of things he wanted, and within the hour he and Vaughan left Yellow Cab not only with Nasiri's personnel file, but also with the dispatch logs and GPS coordinates that placed his cab right in the vicinity of the accident that evening.

They were golden. Now all they needed to do

was collar Nasiri. Vaughan didn't need to subpoena the phone records of the three stooges at the Crescent Garage, as he had taken to referring to Fahad, Jamal, and Ali Masud, to know that Nasiri had already been tipped off. If they were willing to fabricate a new logbook to protect him, there was no question that they would call and warm him that the police were closing in.

The question at this point was whether Nasiri was still in Chicago. For all they knew, he had hotfooted it back to Pakistan. And if that was the case, their investigation was as good as dead.

With his address in hand, they drove to Nasiri's heavily Pakistani Devon Avenue neighborhood on Chicago's north side. As it was Saturday, the sidewalks and streets were crowded with people doing their shopping. Cars were double-parked and those that were moving were committing so many traffic violations, Vaughan and Davidson could have handed out tickets all day long.

As a car blew a stop sign and almost hit them, Davidson commented, 'Some day, I'm going to read the Qur'an. But if I've learned anything in the Public Vehicles Division it's that it doesn't contain anything about the proper operation of a motor vehicle.'

Vaughan chuckled and kept his eyes peeled for Nasiri's cab. The neighborhood looked like any other immigrant neighborhood in the city. People dressed differently and he couldn't read any of the signs. He didn't feel here the way he did in other immigrant neighborhoods. He was an obvious outsider. He could read that in the people's faces and it was more than just about being a cop. This world was alien to him, much the way Iraq had been. The culture couldn't have been any more different from his own. It wasn't like driving through Chicago's Polish or Mexican neighborhoods. This one put him on edge and he didn't like it. It was how he had felt when they operated outside the wire in Iraq. He wasn't supposed to feel like that here in America. The little voice inside his head, the same one that had told him something wasn't right on that assignment in Tikrit, was trying to tell him something again. But it wasn't clear enough for him to understand. He wondered if maybe he was just being stupid. This wasn't Iraq, after all. This was Chicago.

Shaking it off, he refocused on the search for Nasiri's vehicle. Two blocks later, they found it.

'This means he's gotta be close, right?' said Davidson as he pulled over to the curb. 'Should we hit the apartment now?'

'First things first,' replied Vaughan as he reached into the bag he'd brought along and removed two black triangles about five inches long and three inches high.

'What are those?'

'SWAT chocks,' he said, pulling back the tented part to show the Public Vehicles officer the spikes underneath. 'If we miss him or he tries to run, he won't get very far with a flat tire.'

Davidson laughed. 'Did they teach you that little trick in the organized Crime Division?'

'I was on SWAT before I landed at OC.'

'I heard you did intel work in Iraq. Why aren't you in the Intelligence Division here?'

Vaughan shrugged. 'You know how things work. A, there's got to be a slot and B, you have to have impressed someone enough that they'll go to bat for you.'

'So in other words, ass-kissing isn't your forte?'

'Not exactly. No.'

'You just don't try hard enough. All you have to do is put your lips together and — '

Davidson closed his eyes to demonstrate and Vaughan held up his hand to stop him. 'I get it,' he said as he zipped up his bag and reached for the door handle.

'I'll keep the car running. Just in case he comes out before you're done and you have to chase him.'

Vaughan was tempted to flip the man the finger, but he didn't think he knew him well enough yet. 'Let's get a patrol car to back us up on the arrest.'

Davidson nodded and picked up his radio.

'I also want to impound the cab, so let's get a flatbed too. Once we have it impounded, we can have forensics go to work on it.'

'Aye, aye, Captain.'

Vaughan walked back to the cab and did a slow loop around it. The bodywork was pristine, right down to the shiny new rivet holding the medallion in place on the hood. The interior was clean and contained no items of any personal nature other than a beaded seat cover. He placed his chocks. One went in front of the rear passenger tire and another behind the front passenger tire. This way, whether Nasiri pulled straight out or backed out of his space, they'd be covered.

The chocks set, he walked back up to Davidson's Bronco and got back in. 'What's the ETA on the patrol unit?'

'They're about two blocks away,' replied the Public Vehicles officer. 'Where do you want them?'

'Somewhere in front of the building, but not directly in front. Let's not tip our hand until we have to.'

Davidson radioed the instructions to the patrol unit.

'He's in the third-floor rear apartment,' said Vaughan as he checked the file once more. 'We'll go through the alley.'

Davidson moved his truck to a better spot and then the two men climbed out. They were both wearing plain clothes and tried to act natural, but they stood out like a couple of sore thumbs in Chicago's de facto Little Pakistan.

'Man, I must look really good today,' quipped Davidson as he noticed people staring at him. 'What do you think? Do I have my mojo working or what? This has got to be what it's like for Brad Pitt when he goes out, huh?'

Vaughan wasn't paying attention to his colleague. As a cop, he was always careful, always aware of his surroundings, but there was something about Nasiri and this neighborhood that put him on edge. He knew these were Pakistanis and not Iraqis, but nevertheless, he had clicked into his Iraq mode. It was a heightened sense of awareness and almost hypervigilance. It bordered on paralyzing.

He moved slower than he normally would. Davidson noticed and shortened up his stride to keep next to him. 'You all right?' he asked.

Vaughan nodded. He scanned apartment windows for spotters and checked the rooftops for kids who might give away their approach via cell phones. He looked for the LOPs — the little old people who were always used as watchdogs. Thank goodness there were no shops along this street. Shopkeepers in Iraq were notorious spies.

It was all stupid and he knew it, yet he couldn't stop himself. Every day in Iraq he had honed the skills that had kept him alive while other men had been killed and had come home in boxes. Once developed, those instincts don't disappear. But why were they flooding back now? *My God*, he thought. *I've got PTSD.*

'You still want to do this?' asked Davidson as they reached the alley and Vaughan stood still on the sidewalk.

He coughed and shook it off. 'I'm good to go. Let's do it.'

The men entered the alley and came up behind Nasiri's residence. It was a four-story brick building with a wooden set of stairs. There was a chain-link fence separating the property from the alley. Its gate was unlocked.

'So far so good,' said Davidson as he pushed it open and walked down the narrow gangway toward the stairs.

As they climbed, Vaughan had an inexplicable

urge to pull out his gun. He didn't. Nasiri was the driver responsible for a hit-and-run accident. They weren't about to pop Osama bin Laden. Nevertheless, his hands were sweaty and his heart was pumping harder than it should have been. PTSD, anxiety attack, or whatever this feeling was, he didn't like it.

The open-air, third-floor landing outside Nasiri's apartment contained a couple of rusting lawn chairs and some empty cardboard boxes. Vaughan looked out across the alley with its asphalt-shingled garages at the apartment buildings on the other side. In one of them, he could see someone watching them. Somewhere close by Pakistani music was playing.

A large window with its drapes drawn stood next to Nasiri's back door. 'I guess we knock,' offered Davidson.

'Of course we knock. The only time you don't knock is when you have a no-knock warrant. Besides, I think we may have an audience.'

'Lawyers,' said Davidson, rolling his eyes. 'No wonder you haven't impressed anyone in the Intelligence Division.'

'There's someone watching us from the building across the alley.'

Davidson turned, but didn't see anything. 'Don't worry. You're just paranoid.'

This time, Vaughan didn't hesitate to give the man the finger.

The Public Vehicles officer knocked. There was no answer. He knocked again. 'Police. Open up.' There was still no response.

Davidson tried the door handle, but it was

locked. 'You're right,' he said, glancing over his shoulder and gesturing across the alley with his chin. 'We are being watched. I think it's a Scumbagasaurus.'

'A what?'

'You know what those are,' he said as he bent closer to the door handle and slipped something from his pocket. 'They suck blood and feed on bribes. Normally you don't see them this far from a government building. *Politicus assholus* is the correct Latin term, I believe.'

Vaughan knew what the man was doing, but before he could stop him, the lock was picked and the door was open. 'That's breaking and entering.'

'The door was open. In fact, I think I hear someone calling for help,' he replied, closing his mouth and trying to throw his voice like a ventriloquist. 'Help me. Help me.'

The Organized Crime cop wasn't impressed.

'Allah akabar?' Davidson asked.

Vaughan still wasn't buying it.

'Allah snack bar?'

'Paul, we're not authorized to — ' Vaughan began, when he saw Davidson raise his radio to his mouth, announce his intent to the patrol officers outside, and step into the apartment.

'Are you coming?' he asked.

This wasn't the first time Vaughan had broken the law, and it probably wouldn't be the last. Nevertheless, he wasn't proud of himself. Shaking his head, he followed the other cop inside.

23

It was a dump. They entered through the door into the kitchen. A plate of food sat half-eaten on a folding table covered with a vinyl table cloth.

'Somebody left in a hurry,' said Vaughan. He touched the food to test its temperature and then walked over to the stove and reached for the teapot. Both were cold. He shook his head at Davidson.

The fridge contained very little. There was nothing in the freezer. As they made their way further into the apartment, Davidson pulled his weapon and Vaughan followed suit.

They cleared the bedroom, living room, and bathroom. No one was there. Davidson reholstered his weapon. 'Well, seeing as how we've already crossed the Rubicon, do you want to take a more in-depth look around?'

Neither the cop nor the lawyer in him wanted to make an already bad, and unquestionably illegal, situation worse by turning Nasiri's apartment inside out. But it wasn't the cop or the lawyer inside him that won out.

There was no question that what he was doing was wrong. He couldn't moralize it, rationalize it, or loophole his way out of it. But he didn't feel guilty about it.

Mohammed Nasiri had run down a woman and had fled the scene. People from his village then tried to cover up for him. Whether he asked them to or not made no difference. Judging from what he saw in the apartment and what his gut had told him, Nasiri had been tipped that the police were on his trail.

Cops were not bad people. In fact for the most part, cops were one of the best classes of people Vaughan had ever known. They were the good guys. They stood on the side of law and order and civilization. They manned the wall that protected everyday, good, hard-working Americans. They were the sheepdogs, and beyond that wall there were the wolves.

At times, the wolves could be smart; very smart. A few knew just how much rope the people had given their sheepdogs and they operated just beyond it. They were constantly coming up with new ways to stay one step ahead of the law. Luckily enough for the people, the majority of the wolves were stupid. When they were caught, it was not always because of great police work, but because of some colossally stupid mistake.

It bothered John Vaughan that while the wolves were constantly evolving and finding new ways to commit crimes and horrible acts of violence, the sheepdogs remained bound by the same rules of engagement. The courts seemed more disposed to protect the criminals before their victims and that was wrong. But so was breaking into an apartment and searching it without a warrant. Vaughan knew that, but he didn't care; not right now. In fact, he had been slowly caring less and less the longer he stayed on the job. Did that make him a bad person?

Maybe, maybe not. What he knew was that if he had to bend, and sometimes break, the rules to bring the guilty to justice, he was willing to consider it. He'd seen far too much suffering and far too many bad guys escape answering for their crimes to completely ignore the fact that sometimes the ends do justify the means.

'Which room do you want?' asked Davidson, halfway into the bedroom already.

'All of them.'

'*All of them?*'

'That's right,' said Vaughan as he pushed past him into the bedroom. 'Now watch the back door and make sure we don't get ambushed.'

He worked quickly and methodically. Nasiri had a lot of books and not much else. Almost all of them were in Urdu, the national language of Pakistan. It was a language Vaughan couldn't read, so he took a picture of the books with his camera phone. He had a friend in Marine Intelligence he could send it to for translation, though he had a feeling he wasn't going to like what he heard back.

His feeling was based on Nasiri's other books, the ones he had in English. They had all been penned by the same author, Sayyid Qutb. Qutb was the intellectual father of Islamic fundamentalism, and his teachings were at the very core of Muslim justification for violence and jihad in the name of Islam. Two of his biggest fans were Osama bin Laden and his deputy, Ayman al-Zawahiri.

Vaughan had read an interesting compendium of Qutb's work while he was in Iraq called *The*

Sayyid Qutb Reader by Albert Bergesen. It was his gateway into the mind of Islamic terrorism, and the fact that Mohammed Nasiri had several titles by Qutb only reinforced the unease he was feeling.

He continued to search the apartment, hoping to find something that would tell him where Nasiri had gone or what he was planning to do. There was nothing. No personal letters, no laptop, no cell phone. The man didn't even have a landline, but those were growing less and less popular these days.

In short, he and Davidson had taken a huge risk, had broken several laws, and had come up with nothing. Even Nasiri's shirts, trousers, and jackets were clean. What pocket litter there was, wasn't helpful. The whole place looked more like a movie set than the apartment of an actual human being.

Vaughan walked back into the kitchen. Davidson was sitting at the table and looked up. 'Anything?'

'Nothing,' replied Vaughan.

'Do you mind if I take a look around now that you're done?'

Vaughan grabbed a towel off the counter and threw it to him. 'Go ahead. Just make sure you wipe everything down. I don't want to leave any prints behind.'

'Cautious motherfucker, aren't you?'

'Ten minutes,' he replied, 'and then we're out of here.'

Davidson nodded and headed toward the bedroom.

Opening up the double doors beneath the sink with the toe of his shoe, Vaughan bent down and looked for another towel or a rag of his own. There were certain places you didn't want to be linked to. An apartment you broke into without a warrant was definitely one of them, followed closely by a residence belonging to a Muslim cab driver who had a fondness for Sayyid Qutb. Nothing but trouble could come from being connected to this place.

Under the sink, he found a white plastic grocery bag stuffed with more of the same white plastic bags. In the center was what looked like a pink towel. He emptied the lot of them onto the kitchen floor only to realize that the pink mass in the center wasn't a towel but a folded shopping bag from a beauty supply store.

It was an odd item for Nasiri to have. Maybe someone had left it in his cab. Or maybe Nasiri had a girlfriend. If they could locate a girlfriend, they might be able to locate him.

Vaughan unfolded the bag. There was a silhouette of a woman with perfectly coifed hair and the name, address, and phone number of the store. Vaughan opened the bag and looked inside. He found a receipt dated two days before the accident. Nasiri had purchased only one item, but multiple bottles of it.

Vaughan began going through the other bags looking for receipts. He didn't find a ton, but he found enough and they were very interesting.

In addition to purchasing hydrogen peroxide at the beauty supply store, he had also bought more of the same, along with drain cleaner, at grocery stores and pharmacies. He included other odds and ends to try to mask what he was doing, but Vaughan knew what he was up to. Nasiri wasn't giving out dye jobs and throwing drain-cleaning parties for his friends.

Davidson stepped back into the kitchen and saw Vaughan with the plastic bags. 'What'd you find?'

'Do you know what the mother of Satan is?'

'No idea,' said Davidson.

'Triacetone triperoxide. TATP,' said Vaughan, holding up the receipts.

'Should I know what that is?'

'It's also called acetone peroxide. It is an explosive popular with terrorists. Its ingredients are very easy to get. The two most important things you need to make it are hydrogen peroxide and sulfuric acid.'

'Where do you get sulfuric acid?'

'Drain cleaner,' said Vaughan, holding up the receipts. 'It looks like every time he goes to the store, he picks up a bottle or two, or sometimes even three. He appears to have been doing it in small batches so as not to raise suspicion.'

'And fly right beneath the radar.'

Vaughan nodded. 'Exactly. It's called the mother of Satan because it is so volatile. One of the ways we could spot bomb makers when I was in Iraq was because the best ones were missing fingers, sometimes even hands.'

'The *best ones* were missing fingers or hands? That doesn't make sense.'

'They were the ones who learned to respect their craft. Lose a finger, or two, or three and

177

you become incredibly conscientious. Lose a hand and you'll probably end up being an instructor.'

'Is that the stuff that was used in the London bombings?' asked Davidson.

'Yup. It was also part of the shoe bomber plot, the 2006 transatlantic plane bombing plot, the underwear bomber plot, and what that Afghan named Zazi they busted in Denver was working on.'

'So Nasiri is a bomb maker?'

'That, or he was acquiring the ingredients for someone else,' said Vaughan. 'Either way, this is probably the real reason he took off after hitting Alison Taylor.'

'So what do we do now? I'm no *lawyer*,' Davidson stated, drawing the word out, 'but that evidence is definitely fruit of the poisonous tree.'

Even though his metaphor was a bit mixed up, he was right. Evidence obtained through an illegal search, seizure, or interrogation was known as a poisonous tree. Any evidence later discovered because of knowledge gained from the first illegal search, seizure, or interrogation was known as the *fruit* of the poisonous tree. None of it would be admissible in a court.

It would also be impossible to get any warrants based on it. This put the officers in a very difficult position. Nasiri was up to no good, but legally their hands were tied. They couldn't share what they knew about the bomb-making ingredients.

While the mechanic's information had been

given under duress, they probably could get a warrant with it and come back, but someone across the alley had already seen them enter the apartment. As far as the apartment was concerned, they were dead in the water.

'We're definitely impounding the cab. Somehow, there's got to be a way to get it tested for bomb residue. If we get a hit, then everyone is going to climb on board this case.'

'Let's say you do figure out a way to bury our poisonous fruit and get them to test the cab. What if there's no residue?'

'It doesn't matter. We can't give up. We've got to stay on this guy. We legally obtained his name and photograph. We can put those out across the PD and I'll reach out to a guy I know on the Joint Terrorism Task Force. I'll have him pull all the flight records and see if Nasiri has tried to board any aircraft.'

'And if he hasn't?' asked Davidson.

'Then we should assume he's still in the city and that he's not planning on taking his bombs back to Pakistan with him.'

Davidson looked down at the half-eaten plate of food. 'We should also assume he's not coming back here.'

'Agreed. So if you were him, where would you go now?'

'Someplace safe.'

Vaughan nodded. 'Someplace with people you could trust.'

'Like members of your terror cell?'

'Bombers tend to need support, so I'm willing to bet there's a cell.'

'But how do you track it down?' asked Davidson.

'We may not have to,' replied Vaughan. 'Let's finish up here and get back to your truck. I want to see if Nasiri will lead us to it all by himself.'

24

Abdul Rashid's cell phone vibrated again. He held it up so the man sitting across from him could see it.

Rashid was in his mid-twenties with dark hair and a handsome, angular face. He was lean and stood about six feet tall. He had green eyes, an unusual feature that marked his mixed Arab descent. 'The longer we ignore him, the more dangerous this gets.'

The man gave a dismissive, backhanded wave.

'That's your answer?' asked Rashid. 'Are you serious? You know what? Fuck you, Marwan.'

Rashid stood up from his cushion and threw his cell phone at the man.

Marwan Jarrah, a man in his late fifties with gray hair and a neatly trimmed salt-and-pepper beard, dodged the phone and smiled. He loved the younger man's passion. Rashid had more than earned the right to be so outspoken. He was one of the very few true believers who could effortlessly stroll among the infidels without raising their suspicion. His methods of waging jihad were often unorthodox, but they were also brilliant. It was why Jarrah kept him close. It was also why Jarrah tolerated Rashid's impulsiveness and foul language.

Blessed with a Caucasian father and an Egyptian mother, Abdul Rashid possessed a mixed set of features. Those features were such that Westerners never saw him as an Arab, or as being distinctly Muslim. To them he appeared perfectly American, while to Muslims he looked Arab. Such was the magic gift of his parents' combined DNA.

With family scattered across the Muslim world, he had a backstopped cover for the extensive trips abroad where he studied in some of the most rigorous and extensive mujahideen camps. Marwan had personally witnessed him gun down two Jordanians who had tried to double-cross them in Iraq. Though they had known each other for only a couple of years, he was proud to call Rashid his brother, even though he was more like a son. The man's experience and skills were beyond question. So talented was he, and so beloved, that he was referred to in Arabic as *Shahab* — a bright star that illuminates the heavens.

As talented as he was, though, he often could be obsessive about details and got angered when others didn't listen to him or follow his plans. Marwan attempted to calm him down. 'The man doesn't know enough to be a danger.'

'Give me my phone back so I can throw it at you again.'

'You worry too much, Shahab.'

'It's my job to worry,' said Rashid as he walked behind his boss's desk, parted the blinds, and looked out the office window over the showroom floor. 'You should worry too.'

'Why?' said the older man with another wave of his hand. 'You worry enough for both of us. Everything will be fine. We are in no danger. We

182

will send Mohammed Nasiri back to Pakistan.'

'We can't send him back to Pakistan now. The police are looking for him. His name is going to be on the no-fly list.'

'Then we'll kill him.'

It was a choice made as casually as someone ordering off a menu.

'Wow, Marwan. You really wrestled with that decision, didn't you?'

'Mohammed Nasiri will be a martyr for the cause of Allah. That is all that matters.'

'Did you ever stop to think,' asked Rashid, 'that maybe Allah values success more than martyrdom?'

Jarrah smiled again. 'Are you about to give me another lecture on our duties to Islam?'

'Consider it a lesson in management economics. We have a project to complete. This project must be completed on time. We have limited resources. If we remove Nasiri from the production line, we will miss our deadline.'

'Not if you take his place.'

Rashid was shocked and didn't even try to hide it. 'I can't believe it. You want me to be a Shahid? After all that we have been through, you're asking me to martyr myself?'

'It would put to rest all of the questions about whether or not we can really trust you.'

'Yeah, *permanently*. I'd rather you continue to doubt my loyalty.'

Jarrah laughed. 'We both know you're much too valuable to become a martyr. Besides, I'd be lost without your company.'

'What you'd be lost without is my ability to

move amongst our enemies.'

'You have been a great blessing to us,' the older man said as he raised a finger in caution, 'but never underestimate our opponents. You must never believe yourself completely beyond their grasp. When that happens, you will get careless. And when you get careless, that is when you will start making mistakes.'

'Which brings us right back to Nasiri.'

Jarrah sighed. 'What do you want to do?'

'I want to bring him in; protect him. He made a mistake, but I don't want the rest of us to suffer because of it.'

The older man began to speak, but Rashid held up his hand. 'Wait, Marwan. Hear me out. Nasiri has been loyal to the cause. He will do whatever we tell him to do. He can still be useful. In fact, we may even find a completely different use for him.'

That remark piqued Jarrah's interest. 'A *different* use? What are you thinking of?'

'The police want him for his hit-and-run accident. Maybe we can use that to our advantage. We may be able to use him as a decoy of some sort.'

'That is interesting.'

'I haven't figured the whole thing out, but I know that we can't use him for anything if he's dead.'

'You're too soft,' said the older man, baiting him.

This time, Rashid laughed. 'Listen, if I can't figure out a use for him, I'll kill him myself.'

'Fine. Next issue. Where are we going to keep him?'

'Give me my phone back first.'

'Why?' asked Jarrah. 'Are you going to throw it at me again?'

'No. I don't want *you* to throw it at *me*.'

25

Samir Ressam took another drag on his cigarette and tried to look bored as he walked down the Boulevard Saint-Michel toward the Seine. He had made his martyrdom video and knew that within the next half-hour it would be uploaded to the Internet along with the videos of seven other martyrs.

The setting for his had been particularly brazen. A graduate student at the International Film School of Paris, Ressam had eschewed the traditional backdrop of a black Islamic flag. This was to be his final film. It would be seen all over the world and he wanted it to be special. Therefore, it had to grab people, move them.

The introduction was shot in a park across the street from the U.S. Embassy and contained a raging diatribe about America's imperialism as well as its moral and cultural decline.

The film transitioned to a montage of American tourists at different attractions across the city, focusing on the heaviest and most unattractive ones he could find. He conducted man-on-the-street interviews, asking Americans their opinions about Islam and the involvement of their country in the affairs of various Muslim

186

nations. All of the responses were then edited to make America look as evil as possible.

In what would become a chilling reminder from beyond the grave, he spliced together a series of shots of unattended bags in churches, parks, sidewalk cafés, metro stations, and department stores.

It ended with Ressam reading several passages from the Qur'an set to a popular jihadist tune from his ancestral home in Algeria. The picture then faded to black, and the music was replaced with the sound of French revelers counting down the final ten seconds to midnight on New Year's Eve. At zero, there was the audio and visual of a large, Hollywood explosion. Scenes of the 2005 Bali bombings were juxtaposed against scenes of supposed American atrocities against Muslim civilians and set to the music of the American national anthem.

Finally, the word *fin* appeared and the video was finished. There was a reason Ressam had never been able to find any work in the French film industry.

At this moment, though, it made no difference. As Ressam crossed the Boulevard Saint-Germain, he had no misgivings, no second thoughts. He was about to launch his greatest production ever. It was all in the name of Allah the most merciful, the most compassionate.

Had he been struck with a change of heart, there would have been nothing he could do about it and he knew it. He understood why the cell phone had been wired to the vest he wore beneath his clothes. If he tried to back out, his handler would complete the job for him — from a distance of course.

Twice he thought he caught sight of the man, but each time he looked back, the figure was gone. The sensation was somewhat disquieting. Why that would bother him considering what he was about to do didn't make much sense, and the ridiculousness of the emotion made him laugh nervously to himself.

Ressam crushed out his cigarette on the sidewalk and lit another. He held the smoke deep in his lungs and thought about his family. As he exhaled, he banished all worldly emotion from his heart. Like the tendrils of smoke, the last vestiges of humanity within his soul were banished from his body and whisked skyward into the warm Parisian night.

The crowd of tourists thickened as he wound his way deeper into the warren of narrow, twisting streets around the Rue Saint-Séverin. Predominantly off-limits to cars, it was one of the greatest concentrations of restaurants in all of Paris. It had almost every cuisine imaginable. Being in the shadow of Notre Dame guaranteed its popularity with tourists, particularly with Americans.

He had wanted to detonate inside one of the city's many McDonald's restaurants and had argued with his handler about it at great length. While the man agreed that it would have been wonderfully symbolic, the idea was to create the largest death toll possible and to make the Americans realize that there was no place they would ever be safe.

Firm in his belief that Islam could only prevail by slaughtering as many nonbelievers as possible, Ressam strode down the middle of the street to the busiest section of restaurants. All of the outdoor areas were packed. He checked his watch. He was right on time.

He unslung the backpack from his shoulder and casually carried it with one hand. Near the entrance to a Greek restaurant was a large sandwich board. It had a picture of a Greek fisherman holding a blackboard upon which the evening's specials had been scrawled. Setting the bag on the ground near the opening of the tent-like sign he read the menu from top to bottom. Then he peered around to see what was written on the other side. As he did, he used his foot to nudge his bag underneath.

'May I help you?' asked the restaurant's owner in a haughty tone.

'Do you serve couscous?' Ressam asked.

The owner dropped his voice, grabbed Ressam by the arm, and guided him off the curb and into the street. 'Does this look like a fucking couscous restaurant to you, asshole? Go find someplace else to pick pockets. Get lost.'

The owner turned back to his guests and smiled. 'No problem, no problem,' he said with a laugh. 'Gypsies. Very bad.'

Ressam kept his temper in check and walked to the end of the block. Turning the corner, he stepped into a doorway, lit a cigarette, and watched the final seconds tick down on his watch.

The explosion was deafening. From his

189

vantage point, he saw a cloud of smoke belched from the end of the street and watched as debris from his primary device rained down from above. As soon as the ringing in his ears started to abate, he could hear the sound of people screaming.

Leaving the security of the doorway, he walked back around the corner. His handler had been very specific about this part. He was so very close now. He needed to fight his urge to rush right in. *Let it happen*, he had been told. *Be patient*. It was much easier said than done.

Ressam was certain that at any moment someone would point him out and yell, 'That's him! He's the one who placed the bag at the Greek restaurant.'

It was a foolish fear. Nobody was looking at him at all. Everyone was rushing to the scene of the blast. All of the other restaurants were emptying out as people ran to see what had happened. They were like moths, drawn to the flame. In the distance, he could already hear sirens.

As he neared the restaurant, he could see the carnage firsthand. Tables were overturned, windows were blown out, bodies were everywhere. And there was blood. *Oh, so much blood!* Blood that had been shed for Allah and all of the world's Muslims. God was indeed great. So great indeed. *Allahuakbar*, he thought. *Allahuakbar*.

And then he began saying it. Quietly at first, but raising his voice as he moved closer to the crowd that now numbered at least two hundred people.

'Allahuakbar!' he yelled at the top of his lungs. People heard the Islamic war cry and screamed, but it was too late. Samir Ressam took his finger off the detonator and completed his masterpiece.

26

Harvath had wanted to put as much distance between himself and Cannes as possible. Despite playing dumb with the man's wife, he knew who Nikolai Nekrasov was. Considering all of his ties to organized crime, it didn't surprise him one bit that he had a lowlife like Gaston Leveque working for him.

At the Palais des Festivals, Harvath had pulled into the underground parking garage where he had earlier left his Citroën. After having wiped his prints from the Saleen, he had grabbed his pack, turned over the keys, and had said good-bye to Eva Nekrasova.

At the ticket booth, she had blown him a kiss and had roared away toward the center of town. Harvath had let two cars pull out after her and had then exited the structure. Looking up, he had seen no sign of Nekrasov's helicopter and so had pointed his Citroën toward Marseille.

He made the drive in under two hours and took a room at the Sofitel near the Vieux Port. The valets seemed distracted as did the front desk staff when he checked in.

'What's going on?' he asked.

'There has been a series of suicide bombings in Paris,' the clerk replied.

The minute he got into his room, he turned on the TV. There had been bombings at major tourist attractions across the city. Footage was being played of the devastation at the Eiffel Tower, along the Champs Élysées, at Montmartre, and near Notre Dame. The facts were still sketchy, but there was talk of primary and secondary detonations. It was a favorite tactic of Islamic terrorists to detonate a primary device in order to draw in further victims and first responders, and to then detonate a second, more powerful blast.

French news services were speculating whether the attacks were related to the bus bombing in Rome and placed the death toll in the hundreds. Though many of the victims were tourists, locals had also been killed. It was being described as the French 9/11.

Harvath stood at the foot of his bed still holding his backpack. He had no doubt this attack was tied to the Rome bombing. He also felt responsible. He knew he shouldn't, but he did. The Old Man was going to be very angry. Harvath owed him a phone call, but before he spoke with his boss, he wanted to speak with Nicholas.

Setting his pack on the desk, he opened up the minibar. He grabbed a small bottle of whiskey, twisted off the metal cap, and poured it into a glass. Removing one of his clean cell phones, he powered it up and dialed the number for the Troll's satellite phone.

'You heard about Paris?' Nicholas asked. Ever fearful of the NSA's voice-printing capabilities, he was running the call through a special program on his laptop. The voice sounded robotic. There was a slight delay, along with an echo as it went up to the satellite and bounced back down.

'We were too late,' said Harvath.

'We couldn't have stopped it.'

'We could have and we should have.'

'There are going to be more,' replied Nicholas. 'Trust me. Let's focus on stopping those. We cannot bring these people back.'

Harvath took a sip of his drink. 'Tell me about Tony Tsui.'

'That's who hired Leveque?'

'Yes. Who is he?'

'He is a second-rate, digital pimp. That's who he is.'

'So you know him.'

'Unfortunately, I do,' answered the little man. 'But this is all starting to fit. When the assassin he hired failed to report back in, he proceeded right to the next step in his plan.'

'Which was implicating you in the Rome bombing.'

'Exactly.'

'Why would he want you killed?'

'I'm his leading source of competition.'

'Tsui is in the intelligence business?' asked Harvath.

'Tsui is barely a step above a peeping Tom, and not a very high step either. He's pure scum. He'd sell out his own mother if it meant a couple of bucks in his pocket. He has been trying to fish from my pond for years.'

'But why attempt to kill you now?'

The Troll was silent as he tried to fit the pieces

together. 'I sold him a piece of information recently.'

'How recently?'

'In the last year.'

'And that was the last time you communicated with him?'

'It's not like the man is on my Christmas card list.'

Harvath took another sip of his drink. 'What was the information you sold him?'

'Normally,' replied the Troll, 'I don't kiss and tell, but in this case I have no problem filling you in. It was the location of a secret military base in Mongolia run by the PLA.'

'What did he want with a secret base run by the Chinese military?'

'It was for a client.'

'Did he say who the client was?'

'As unprofessional as Tsui is, he knows how to keep his mouth shut.'

Harvath was having trouble connecting the dots. 'What's the base used for?'

Nicholas exhaled loudly. 'I've got no idea.'

'How about Tsui? Does he know?'

'Maybe. Maybe his client knows. All I brought to the party was the location.'

'And Tsui paid you for that information?' asked Harvath.

'Yes he did.'

'Any chance the information didn't pan out and so he wanted to whack you out of revenge?'

Nicholas laughed. 'That's not how our business works. If the information had been bad, he would have demanded his money back. And I would have paid him. But he never asked. Which tells me that the information was solid.'

'So he tried to kill you to get you out of his way.'

'Or to keep me quiet.'

Harvath needed to fill in the blanks. 'How many transactions have you done with Tsui over the years?'

'A lot.'

'And you never had any animosity? No problems at all?'

'There was plenty of animosity, but nothing that would rise to either one of us wanting the other killed. I told you, he's a despicable character. But from time to time he proved a useful and lucrative source. We flowed information both ways if the price was right. And we never let price prevent us from making money.'

It sounded to Harvath as if Tsui and Nicholas deserved each other. They were a couple of gossiping old ladies who talked trash behind each other's backs but would sit down and have coffee to trade gossip about everybody else if they got the chance. The only difference was that the 'gossip' they traded in was the stuff of state secrets and the kind of dirty laundry that brought politicians, business titans, and even countries to their knees.

Harvath swirled the liquid in his glass. All signs pointed to Tsui, but he wanted to be sure. 'Who else could have framed you with the Italians?'

'The pope himself could have done it.'

'I'm going to assume that you're exaggerating.

196

You haven't actually crossed the pope, have you?'

'I don't want to talk about it,' said Nicholas. 'Leveque gave you Tsui's name and I'm going to bet he didn't do so willingly.'

'No, it was under significant duress,' replied Harvath.

'Then you need to ask yourself how confident you are in what Leveque told you. Personally, Tsui makes perfect sense. He knows enough about me and what he doesn't know, he most likely has the means to find out.'

'What do you know about him?'

'Enough to make him very uncomfortable,' said Nicholas.

'I want to pay him a visit. How soon can you get me an address?'

'It'll probably take me a few hours.'

'Get started and call me back when you have something.'

After hanging up, Harvath downed the remainder of his drink and opened the minibar for a second. Though his ego was more bruised than his body, he was still sore from the beating he had taken from Dominique Fournier. But it was nothing compared to the beating he knew he was going to take from Reed Carlton.

After a couple of sips of his second whiskey, he picked up the phone and dialed.

27

Harvath had had only intermittent e-mail contact with his boss since leaving for Europe three days ago. It was time to provide Carlton with a full debriefing, which was exactly what he did. When it was complete, he sat back and readied himself for the recriminations he was sure would follow.

'So let me get this straight,' said the Old Man. 'You trunked two Basque separatists, Tasered a madam and her bodyguard — after she kicked your tail — then bagged and dragged her to some French farmhouse where you threatened to disfigure her, then iceboarded a concierge, shot three hotel security guards, kidnapped the wife of one of Russia's wealthiest mobsters, and are now sitting in a hotel in Marseille waiting for a callback from the man I sent you over there to apprehend. Is that about right?'

'Pretty much. All except the part of me she kicked. It definitely wasn't my tail.'

'Very funny, smartass. Have you seen what happened in Paris?'

Harvath changed his tone. 'Yes.'

'What am I supposed to tell DOD?'

'Tell them I haven't located the Troll yet.'

'You want me to lie to them?'

'Then don't tell them anything.'

'Which is it?' asked the Old Man.

'Are you pulling my chain? Because I can't tell.'

'I could say the same thing to you. I sent you over there to pick up your little buddy and bring him back, not to be his designated hitter.'

'He didn't have anything to do with Rome, Reed.'

'It doesn't matter. DOD wants him.'

Harvath tried to keep himself in check. His guilt over the second bombing had made him defensive. 'I thought DOD wanted whoever was behind the attack.'

'And the first rung on that ladder is your pal.'

'I agree. But the second rung is Fournier, the third Leveque, and the fourth is Tony Tsui. We're making progress.'

'Tell that to the people in Paris.'

Though Carlton probably didn't mean it that way, the rebuke stung. 'The Troll is a dead end. He had nothing to do with Rome. He was framed and the person who framed him is Tony Tsui. Tsui had prior knowledge of the attack.'

'Do you think Rome and Paris are connected?'

'I don't know yet,' said Harvath.

'I didn't ask you what you *know*, I asked you what you think.'

'I think they're connected.'

'Me too.'

There was silence between them. Harvath was the one to finally break it. 'Would you have connected these dots any differently than I have?'

'No.'

'Are you going to tell me my methods are too harsh?'

'No.'

'Do you think that I'm being too much of a cowboy?'

'You're doing exactly what I expected you'd do when I selected you.'

Harvath laughed. 'Are you telling me I'm predictable?'

'I'm telling you that you're a professional and you're reliable. I trust your judgment. You're the man in the field. If you have a choice between a flyswatter and a sledgehammer, would I rather you use the flyswatter? Of course. But that's for you to decide. That's your job. My job is to give you whatever you need to get things done.'

'Well, what I need right now is more time.'

'How much more?' asked the Old Man.

'I'll know better once I have a location for Tsui. In the meantime, tell DOD that we're making progress.'

'Body bags aren't progress, Scot.'

'I promise you,' said Harvath. 'I'm going to find who did this and I'm going to make sure they never do it again.'

'I agree with you. But first, give me something I can give DOD. If you can prove the Troll had nothing to do with this then bring me Tsui — alive. Do that and then we'll be able to take the next step.'

*　　*　　*

It was Sunday and the sun was just beginning to rise when Harvath's phone rang. 'I've got a location,' said the computer-modulated voice on the other end.

'Where?'

'Geneva.'

'That's terrific. How'd you find him?' asked Harvath.

'It's a long story. I'll tell you when I pick you up. Be at the General Aviation terminal at the Marseille airport in two hours.'

'What about customs in Switzerland?'

'Already taken care of,' replied Nicholas.

'Are you sure you're up for this?'

'I wouldn't miss it for the world.'

★ ★ ★

The white Learjet 45 touched down in Marseille and taxied to a revetment area near the General Aviation building. An attractive aviation services hostess walked Harvath to the plane. He was met at a set of air-stairs by the copilot, who offered to take his bag. Harvath politely declined and stepped aboard.

Argos and Draco were the first to say hello. The dogs weren't the only company Nicholas had brought with him. Surprisingly, Padre Peio had come along as well. He was dressed in a pair of tan trousers and a blue button-down shirt.

'Good morning,' he said.

'Good morning, Father,' replied Harvath, dropping his pack on one of the forward seats.

201

The Troll was lying on a leather couch toward the rear of the cabin. 'You should have stayed in Spain. You're not up for this.'

'That's exactly what I told him,' said Peio.

'And yet here I am,' replied Nicholas as he reached for the intercom. 'I want to get this over with.'

Harvath looked at Peio. 'You'll forgive me, Father, but I would think that this is something you wouldn't want to be mixed up in.'

The priest smiled wistfully. 'There is great evil in the world. I know that. Hundreds of people were killed yesterday. But I don't believe that the answer is more killing.'

'I wish it was that simple, Father.'

'For God's sake, Peio. Lighten up,' added the Troll. 'You of all people should know what's at stake here. When it comes to Muslim fundamentalists the only thing they respect is force. Imagine if Christian Europe had simply turned the other cheek at the Battle of Lepanto or the gates of Vienna. We'd be living in a much different world than we are now.'

'But we've come a long way since the Battle of Lepanto', said Peio, who then turned to Harvath. '*I'm* here because I was concerned about Nicholas making this journey alone.'

The Troll laughed as he activated the intercom and relayed instructions to the pilot. 'Don't believe him. He misses the intrigue. Don't you, Father?'

Harvath couldn't help wondering if maybe that was true.

28

Once the plane had reached its cruising altitude, Peio unbuckled his seatbelt and walked back to the galley. As he removed the trays of food that had been stocked for their flight, Nicholas explained to Harvath how he had tracked Tsui.

'So in other words, you planted a Trojan horse in his computer system.'

'A very expensive, extremely difficult to trace Trojan horse,' clarified the Troll. 'He's one of my key competitors, so I viewed it as an insurance policy. You can't trust anybody these days.'

'I'll keep that in mind,' replied Harvath. 'Have you put one of these on my computer?'

Nicholas looked sheepish. 'When this is over, I'll show you how to deactivate it.'

Peio emerged from the galley and could tell from looking at Harvath that he wasn't happy.

'Everything okay here?' he asked.

'Fine,' said Harvath as the priest set the food down. 'Nicholas is going to buy me a new computer when I get home. A very expensive and *extremely difficult to trace* computer.'

★ ★ ★

When the Learjet landed in Geneva, it taxied to a small hangar where it was met by two Swiss customs officers in suits.

Harvath watched through his window as the

copilot deplaned and handed over their passports. The officials stamped each one, handed them back, and then disappeared.

Once their passports had been returned, the three men deplaned and crossed the hangar to two waiting vehicles: a windowless panel van and a dark blue Range Rover. It had been decided that Peio would use the van to drive Nicholas and the dogs to the warehouse the Troll had rented, while Harvath would drive the Range Rover to the five-star Beau Rivage hotel they had traced Tsui to.

With the airport only six kilometers away from the city, Harvath arrived at the hotel within fifteen minutes of leaving the hangar.

It was an elegant, white stone structure in the tradition of the grand hotels of Europe. It sat on the Quai du Mont Blanc, facing the lake within sight of Geneva's famous Jet d'Eau; a magnificent fountain which shoots an enormous plume of water over 450 feet in the air.

Harvath valeted his car and checked into his room. He pulled out a Diet Coke and a jar of almonds from the minibar, then opened the laptop Nicholas had given him on the plane.

According to the Troll, Tsui had used the hotel's Wi-Fi service to plant viruses on the computers of multiple guests. Once the computers were infected, he could control them remotely, even after they had left the hotel. Without their owners being any the wiser, he used his network of zombie machines to covertly send and receive data without revealing his involvement.

Tsui, though, had made one mistake. All of his cleverly hidden, sophisticatedly encrypted data came and went via the hotel's Wi-Fi system. By accessing it and pushing small packets of data toward him, Nicholas believed his Trojan Horse would help them pinpoint the exact location Tsui was operating from. Or so he had hoped.

Harvath opened the French windows that looked out across the lake, settled in at the desk, and dialed his cell phone.

Nicholas answered on the second ring, his voice disguised as usual. 'I didn't get a chance to power the battery all the way up. This could take a while so make sure you plug the power cord in.'

Harvath fished the cord from his pack and plugged the computer into the outlet. 'Done,' he said as peered down at the Quai du Mont Blanc. 'I don't see the van. Where's Peio?'

'He'll be there shortly. Now, I want you to log on to the system, open a browser window, and surf over to any site you like. I'll take it from there.'

Harvath did as he was instructed. After entering his room number and agreeing to the charges, he plugged in the URL for the midget and dwarf wrestling federation.

'Very funny,' said the Troll, who was remotely monitoring the laptop.

Glancing back out the window, Harvath saw the van pull up. 'Peio's here.'

'Good,' replied Nicholas. 'Turn up the TV and leave the *Do Not Disturb* sign on the doorknob.'

'I'll talk to you from the van.'

Harvath stood up from the desk and closed the windows. Slinging his pack over his shoulder, he grabbed his Coke and his almonds and headed downstairs.

Peio was finishing up a conversation with Nicholas when he climbed into the van and shut the door.

'So where to?' asked Harvath as the priest ended the call and pulled away from the hotel.

'Nicholas wants us to stay in the area. Once he pinpoints Tsui's location, you're going to have to move fast.'

Harvath studied the man. 'You do miss the lifestyle, don't you?'

'Maybe a little,' he admitted.

'Are you hungry?' he asked, motioning to several small grocery bags on the floor behind them. 'I didn't know how long we'd be out.'

'I'm okay for now. Thank you.'

A couple of blocks from the hotel a parking space opened up and Peio pulled in. He put the van in park, but left the engine running.

Rolling down the window, he pulled out a pack of cigarettes and offered one to Harvath, who declined. The priest removed one from the pack, pulled out his lighter, and lit up.

He took a deep drag and out of respect for his nonsmoking passenger, blew the smoke out the window. 'I gave it up for Lent last year,' he said. 'Put on twenty pounds almost overnight.'

'Those things will kill you,' replied Harvath with a grin as he took a sip of his Coke.

Peio smiled back. 'My wife used to bother me

all the time about my smoking. I quit once, for her.'

'Didn't take?'

'I became so difficult to be around she begged me to take it back up again.'

Harvath laughed.

'Are you married?'

'No.'

The priest was silent for a moment. 'Assuming I am correct in what you do for a living, it must be difficult finding the right woman; someone who understands the demands of your job.'

'To be honest, Father, I found the right woman. She knows me better than anyone else in the world. She has no problem with what I do for a living. She not only supports me, she encourages me. She's an exceptional person in that regard.'

'Why do I detect a *but*?'

Peio didn't miss much. Harvath imagined he'd probably been a pretty good intelligence operative. 'My personal life isn't that interesting, Father.'

'Everyone's personal life is interesting, Scot. Yours I find particularly interesting. Tell me why you are hesitant. Were your parents divorced?'

Harvath laughed again. 'No. In fact, just the opposite. They were made for each other. After my father died, my mother never remarried.'

'I'm sorry,' said the priest. 'Is that your concern about marriage? Are you afraid something may happen to you and that you would leave this . . . I'm sorry, what is this woman's name?'

'Tracy.'

'Are you afraid that if something happened to you that you would leave Tracy alone?'

'I certainly wouldn't want to die, but if that happened, Tracy is an incredibly resilient woman.'

Peio looked at him. 'So this is about having children.'

Harvath couldn't believe it. The man had put his finger right on it. At least he had until he added, 'You're afraid that the same thing that happened to you could happen to your children. If you died, you'd be doing exactly the same thing to them that your father did to you.'

'Something like that.'

'It's nothing to be ashamed about. Obviously, your father's passing had a very profound impact on you. How old were you when he died?'

'I was already out of high school,' said Harvath, 'and if you don't mind, Father, I'd rather not talk about this anymore.'

'I understand,' said Peio as he took another drag on his cigarette and exhaled out the window.

Harvath doubted it, but he let it go and the two men sat in silence for several minutes.

'May I ask you how your father died?' said the priest.

'He was a SEAL. He died in a training accident.'

'Nicholas told me you had been a SEAL. Is that why?'

'I suppose that was part of it,' replied Harvath.

'I think your father would be proud of you.'

This was one of the biggest reasons Harvath hated conducting these types of ops with someone he didn't know. What they were doing was akin to surveillance. It was grindingly boring to sit around and wait to be set loose on a target. The boredom got to some people faster than others and when it did, they always wanted to 'chat.' And it was often about stuff that was entirely too personal.

'With all due respect, Padre,' he said, 'you don't really know that much about me.'

'Don't I? I know you care for Nicholas. I know you care for Argos and Draco. I know you care for your country and I know you care for this woman, Tracy. You are a good man. Nicholas told me so and I can see it for myself. And no matter what has happened to you up to this point in your life, I want you to know that God wants you to be happy.'

'Even if I want to kill all the Muslim fundamentalists in the world?'

It took Peio a moment to ascertain whether Harvath was pulling his leg. 'Let's leave the fundamentalists out of this.'

He was about to make a snappy remark that probably would have drawn the ire of the priest when his cell phone rang. It was Nicholas.

'I've got him.'

29

'My wife called,' said Paul Davidson as John Vaughan slid back into the Bronco and handed a Styrofoam cup of coffee over to him.

'Yeah?' replied the Organized Crime officer, pulling the passenger door shut. 'What'd she say?'

'She says she's naming you in the divorce decree as well.'

'Me? I only kept you out one night.'

'Yeah, but today is *punta* Sunday.'

'What the hell is *punta* Sunday?' asked Vaughan, vaguely recognizing the Spanish-sounding word.

'Today's the day, we, you know,' said Davidson awkwardly.

'Are you serious? You only have sex with your wife on Sundays?'

'*And* my birthday.'

Vaughan started laughing.

'Go ahead and laugh,' said Davidson, 'but this is going to affect you too.'

'*Me?*' he repeated. 'How the hell could this possibly affect me?'

'You'll see. Trust me.'

Vaughan rolled his eyes and peeled the lid off

210

his coffee. Examining the logs from the dispatch computer in Nasiri's cab, he had discovered a pattern. The Pakistani driver picked up fares in a certain part of the city at regular times of the day. As that area was nowhere near his apartment, there had to be another reason Nasiri favored it.

On a hunch, Vaughan cross-referenced the pickups with Muslim prayer times and his hunch paid off. Nasiri was picking up fares after he had gone to pray. The only problem was that there were no official mosques within the entire eight-block radius they were looking at. The keyword, though, was *official*.

With one phone call, Davidson was able to learn that there were unofficial, makeshift mosques and prayer rooms all across the city. Normally they were hiding right in plain sight. People just didn't know what to look for, such as an abundance of taxicabs in front, papered-over windows, Arabic writing, or the word *Masjid* written somewhere on the façade.

Once Vaughan and Davidson found out, it took them several hours, but they finally located what they believed to be Mohammed Nasiri's mosque.

Unlike American places of worship, Vaughan knew that it had been known for mosques, especially those frequented by fundamentalists, to be used to plot attacks, store weapons, and give sanctuary to terrorists.

'Anything else happen while I was gone?' he asked.

Davidson pretended to consult his notebook.

'Muammar Gaddafi dropped bin Laden and Zawahiri off for Sunday school, Jimmy Hoffa pulled up with a stack of union ballots in Arabic, and Amelia Earhart has been circling overhead with this really cool banner that says *Islam is the bomb*.'

Vaughan shook his head. 'Hey, don't take it out on me. My wife's not happy either and I'm sure it goes double for my kids. I normally cook pancakes on Sunday.'

'How old are they?'

'My wife would tell you her age is none of your business, but the kids are five and seven. How about you? Do you have children?'

'No. Just two extremely high-strung miniature Dobermans who piss the carpet if I shut the refrigerator too loud.'

'I hate tiny dogs.'

'Do you mind?' asked Davidson, his head pulled back. 'You're talking about my kids here.'

'Sorry.'

'Forget about it. I don't like tiny dogs either. Can you picture what I look like walking those little apartment rats when the wife is under the weather?'

Vaughan chuckled.

'How about you?' continued Davidson. 'Do you have any animals?'

'We've got a lab mix.'

'Mixed with what?'

'Pit bull.'

'Now that's a man's dog.'

'That's what Mrs. Vaughan tells me,' he said as he opened up a bag and offered Davidson a doughnut. 'Sorry. They didn't have any turkey or tofu sausage.'

'I'll let my wife know to add you to the wrongful death suit as well,' he said, reaching into the bag. 'Which one has the Crestor sprinkles?'

Vaughan was about to laud the health benefits of doughnuts when his eye caught movement across the street. 'I don't believe it.'

'Me neither. They're all glazed. There's not a single chocolate one in the whole bag. Who goes for doughnuts and doesn't bring back at least one chocolate?'

'I'm not talking doughnuts. Check out the guy who just got out of that car across the street.'

Davidson looked up as a fat man with a long gray beard and dark sunglasses was helped out of a car by two younger men. He looked to be in his late sixties and was dressed in traditional Muslim clothing with a length of fabric wrapped around his prayer cap.

'Look at his hands,' said Vaughan.

'Holy hand job, Batman. Where'd he get those back-scratchers?' exclaimed Davidson as he saw the man's two stainless steel hooks.

'Probably not from baking cupcakes.'

'You can say that again. Don't they cut off hands for stealing over there?'

'The Saudis do, and sometimes the Taliban. It's definitely an Islamic thing, but I've got a feeling this guy's a different story,' said Vaughan.

'Lose a hand and you end up becoming an instructor. Isn't that what you said?'

Vaughan nodded.

'Judging by this guy's qualifications, he must be teaching a Ph.D. course.'

'That's what I'm afraid of,' said the Organized Crime officer as he put the lid back on his coffee cup.

'Maybe we should hand this over to the Joint Terrorism Task Force now.'

'And tell them what? While looking for our hit-and-run cabbie we saw a man with hooks for hands? Everything from Nasiri's apartment is poisonous tree.'

Davidson knew he was right. 'But if what we think is going on, actually is going on, we can't just sit around and do nothing.'

'I agree. We need to do something, but the last thing we can afford to do is to be spotted. If that happens, everyone will scatter and this thing will go deeper underground. We've got one thread we're hanging on by and if we lose it, there's no telling how badly this will end.'

The Public Vehicles officer shook his head. 'I wonder if this was why 9/11 didn't get stopped.'

'We're not going to let another 9/11 happen. I don't care what we have to do. But the one thing we can't do is continue to sit here in your Bronco. We need a better surveillance vehicle.'

'The PI company I moonlight for has one,' said Davidson as he pulled out his cell phone.

'Why didn't you say anything before?'

'Because I don't like using it.'

'Why not?'

'It has a certain feature that's a real pain in the ass.'

'It gets hot and stuffy and begins to stink like

214

every other surveillance vehicle?' asked Vaughan.

'No, not at all. This thing is wall-to-wall luxury. It's like riding in a limo.'

'So then what's the problem?'

Davidson turned on the ignition and put the Bronco in gear. 'You'll see.'

30

Harvath didn't like flying blind. They should have had much more information before moving on Tsui. They didn't even have a description. All Nicholas could tell him was that Tsui was Asian, possibly Taiwanese. That was it. He didn't even have any idea how old he was, though based on their interactions, he believed he was young; mid to late twenties, tops.

He had tracked Tsui's signature to the servers at the University of Geneva. Once through the university's security protections, he narrowed the location down to a lab in the Computer Sciences department.

Tsui had been very careful in covering his tracks. If it wasn't for the Trojan horse Nicholas had planted in his system, they never would have even gotten this close. There remained, though, one problem. 'I can't find a student or a faculty member anywhere in Geneva with the name Tsui,' said the Troll.

'First things first,' replied Harvath as Peio drove the van across the river toward the university. 'Are you sure everything terminates in this lab? It doesn't get routed out again to Taipei, or Shanghai, or something like that, does it?'

'No. That's as far as it goes. Unless.'

The Troll's voice trailed off. 'Unless what?' asked Harvath.

'Unless it's a digital dead drop.'

'Meaning?'

'Meaning his traffic gets dumped onto a drive of some sort that gets physically collected and then rebroadcast from another location.'

Harvath thought about that. 'Either way there has to be a human being involved and that human being has to have access to this lab.'

'Yes, as far as I can tell.'

'Then that's where we'll start.'

Many of the university's buildings were southwest of Geneva's old town. Once they had located the building that housed the lab, Peio found a place to park. Harvath watched the foot traffic come and go and then exited the van and walked off campus. A couple of blocks away, he found what he was looking for.

The bar was noisy and crowded with students who were not paying attention to their belongings. He was in and out in less than five minutes.

He walked back with his backpack slung over his shoulder, and using the access card he had just liberated, entered the building Tsui's data was being fed in and out of. He found a directory and located the lab he was looking for. Students came and went. No one paid him much attention.

When he arrived at the lab, its door was locked. He tried his access card, but it didn't work. After checking the hallway to make sure no

217

one was coming, he removed a set of lockpick tools from his pack. Harvath preferred lockpick guns, but was able to get the door open in a respectable amount of time.

Slipping inside, he closed the door quietly behind him. The room was nothing special and exactly what he had expected. Rows of tables with computers faced a long wall at the other end of the room complete with blackboards, a retractable projection screen, a lectern, and a desk. Off to the right-hand side was a pod of offices.

Harvath made his way forward. There were at least fifty computers in the room, any of which could have been the one designated to send and receive Tsui's message traffic.

At the front of the room, Harvath saw that a message had been taped to each of the blackboards. It was written in French and English. It was dated one week ago and listed funeral arrangements for Professor Lars Jagland, as well as an announcement to his students that classes would resume with his teaching assistant on Monday. There was no explanation as to how the man had died, but Harvath had a pretty good feeling it wasn't an accident.

The door to the offices was unlocked and Harvath walked through. He studied the nameplates and decided to start with Jagland's.

His office was clean and sparsely decorated. Bookshelves and a small desk took up much of the room. There were no photos and no personal effects anywhere. On the wall near the window were two blank spots where artwork must have once hung.

Harvath took out his cell phone and stepped behind the desk. Dialing Nicholas, he fired up Jagland's computer.

'What have you got?' asked the Troll.

'There are about fifty desktop computers in the lab. There was also a notice about funeral services for a Professor Lars Jagland. Does that name ring a bell with you?'

'No, but I'm running it now. While I do that, I want you to ping the e-mail address I gave you.'

'It's asking me for a password before it will allow me on the system,' replied Harvath.

'Hold on. Let me see what I can do.'

'There's three other offices here. If you want me to check those computers, I'll probably also need passwords for them. But something tells me, Jagland is our guy.'

'Lars Jagland, Ph.D.,' replied the Troll, who had just pulled his obituary. 'Norwegian citizen age fifty-eight. Expert in the field of computational complexity theory and professor of same at the University of Geneva, at least until he was killed in a car accident just over a week ago.'

'Any family?'

'The obit I've got here doesn't recognize any.'

Harvath was about to ask Nicholas to see if he could uncover an address for Jagland's home when suddenly he heard a woman's voice.

'What are you doing in this office? Who are you?'

'Let me call you back,' said Harvath as he disconnected the call and stood up. Smiling he offered his hand. 'I'm sorry. The door was open.'

'I asked you who you are,' the woman repeated. She spoke English, but with a Germanic accent of some sort. She was in her early thirties, about five-foot-four with brown hair and trendy glasses. She was dressed in jeans and a T-shirt.

'My name's Jeff Hemmings. Who are you?'

'I'm Dr. Jagland's teaching assistant. What are you doing in his office?'

'We had a meeting scheduled,' said Harvath.

The woman looked at him and her posture softened a bit. 'You haven't heard?'

'Heard what?'

'Dr. Jagland was killed in a car accident.'

'When?'

'The week before last.'

'I had no idea.'

'The funeral was yesterday,' she said. 'I'm taking over until the university finds a replacement. Classes resume tomorrow.'

Harvath stepped out from behind the desk. 'And you came in to prepare and here I am.'

'Yes. Here you are. What is it you were supposed to meet with Dr. Jagland about?'

'I work for American Express. Dr. Jagland approached us about a project he thought our fraud-monitoring department would be interested in. We were supposed to meet here and go for dinner. He told me to dress casual.'

The teaching assistant smiled. 'You're a liar.'

'Excuse me?'

'You're after Michael, aren't you?'

'Who's Michael?' asked Harvath.

'Don't worry, I won't say anything. But I have to tell you that anyone who knows him won't be surprised.'

'Why is that?' he said, curious as to where this was leading.

'He's nothing more than an overeducated hacker.'

Bingo.

'He's incredibly rude as well,' the woman continued, 'and to tell you the truth, I don't know what Dr. Jagland saw in him. Love is blind, I guess.'

'So they were — '

The teaching assistant nodded. 'Disgusting, isn't it? Dr. Jagland was easily at least thirty years older than him. Why he couldn't find a boyfriend his own age is beyond me. So what did Michael do?'

'It's delicate,' replied Harvath. 'I'd rather not get into it.'

'He finally went too far. I'm not surprised. Are you going to arrest him?'

'Possibly. We have to find him first. Any idea where he might be?'

'He didn't even come to the funeral.'

'That sounds strange.'

'It's typical, selfish Michael. Afterward, we all went out for a couple of drinks and went by the house to give him a piece of our mind.'

'The house?' asked Harvath.

'Dr. Jagland's house. He and Michael lived together. But Michael wasn't there. It looked like he hadn't been there for a little bit.'

'Any idea where he might be now?'

The teaching assistant thought for a moment and then said, 'The chalet, I guess.'

'Do you have an address you can give me?'

The woman pulled out her iPhone and began going through her folders. 'We celebrated Dr. Jagland's birthday there over the winter. Here's a picture of the place,' she said, holding up her phone so Harvath could see it. 'Cute, isn't it?'

'It is,' he agreed.

'Here's a picture of Michael too.'

Harvath looked at him and he was exactly as Nicholas had so poorly described. 'If I give you my e-mail, can you send those pictures to me?'

'As long as you promise you won't tell Michael I gave them to you.'

'You don't need to worry. Michael and I have a lot of other things we need to discuss.'

'Good,' said the assistant with a laugh. 'I really hope he gets what's coming to him.'

31

Lars Jagland's chalet was located in a small village in the mountains two hours outside of Geneva.

Harvath and Peio had picked up Nicholas, who insisted on bringing Argos and Draco along. It was turning into a circus, but Harvath grudgingly agreed.

The fact that Tsui had set Nicholas up to take the fall for the attack in Rome had bothered him from the beginning. It didn't make sense. Why not let the terrorists take credit for the operation? It was obviously meant to be a distraction, but from what? Another attack? Was it meant to somehow help the terrorists pull off their Paris operation by siphoning away investigative resources? Or, was there another reason entirely?

Harvath suspected it might be a bit of both. The one thing he knew was that their best and only lead was Tony Tsui. He not only knew about the attack in Rome, he most likely knew about the attack in Paris and whatever else the terrorists had planned. As far as Harvath was concerned, he was the key to everything; most importantly, stopping any further attacks.

Based on satellite imagery Nicholas had downloaded, Harvath identified a secluded vantage point from which they could observe the chalet as they planned their next move.

While the teaching assistant blamed selfishness for the fact that Tsui, Michael, or whatever his name was, missed Jagland's funeral, Harvath had another theory. The man had gone to ground. The question, though, was *why*? Harvath thought he might have a good idea.

Somehow, somewhere, Tsui had screwed up and Jagland had found out about it. Maybe he had even threatened to expose Tsui. Whatever the case, Tsui was dangerous. He had already tried to have Nicholas killed, and now Jagland was dead. This was not someone that should be underestimated no matter how mild mannered he looked in the pictures the teaching assistant had forwarded. Tsui was a killer.

'There's no way you'll get close enough without him seeing you coming,' said Peio as he handed the binoculars back to Harvath. 'We'll have to wait until dark.'

'I don't want to wait,' said Nicholas. 'I want to go in now.'

'You don't get a vote,' replied Harvath.

'The hell I don't. Who's financing this operation? Who found Tsui?'

'Nicholas,' scolded Peio.

'Forgive me, Father, for I have sinned and am going to sin a lot more before the night is through, so get used to it.'

'I want you to promise me something,' began the priest.

Nicholas held up his hand. 'No. No promises.'

Peio looked at Harvath, but Harvath simply raised the binoculars to his eyes and went back to surveilling the chalet. The priest didn't belong here. He knew better than most what was going to happen once they got hold of Tsui. If he cooperated, things would be relatively easy for him. But if he refused to cooperate, it would get ugly fast. Peio wasn't toeing the edge of some imaginary line, he had crossed it. He had feet firmly planted in two different worlds and needed to decide which side he wanted to be on.

The men shared the food and water that the priest had purchased and waited for the sun to go down. They made very little small talk.

When it was dark, Harvath pulled the night vision monocular from his pack along with the other items he was going to need.

'Don't shoot him until I get there unless you absolutely have to. I want him to see my face,' said Nicholas. He turned to look at Peio, but the priest turned away.

Harvath stepped quietly out of the van. It was an overcast, moonless night and it was unseasonably cold, just like it had been back in Spain. *So much for global warming*, he thought as he turned up the collar of his coat.

Using his night vision device to help guide him, he carefully moved from one outcropping of rock to another.

When he got to the weather-beaten cowshed about one hundred meters from the chalet, he stopped and caught his breath. This was the last piece of concealment available until he hit the house. As he traversed the remaining distance, he would be completely in the open.

He would have given his eye teeth for a sniper providing overwatch for him. There was a chance that this quarry had night vision as well and had observed Harvath's entire approach. He could be inside at this very moment waiting for Harvath to step out into the open, waiting for him to get close enough to mow him down.

Harvath pushed the thought from his mind as he drew his Glock and prepared to run. Counting to three, he was about to charge the house when he heard the scatter of gravel behind him.

He spun just in time to see what looked like two enormous wolves barreling down on top of him. He leapt out of the way as Argos and Draco sped past. He recognized the lump clinging to the bizarre harness on Draco's back. It was Nicholas; he had jumped the gun and was going to screw everything up.

With nothing he could do to stop him, short of shouting, which would tip Tsui off, Harvath had no choice but to take off after them.

Owning a Caucasian Ovcharka of his own, he knew how fast the breed was, but Nicholas's dogs were amazing. He was still at least fifty yards behind them when the front door burst open and the shooting began.

32

Tsui was an idiot. He opened the door and silhouetted himself against the light from inside. As Nicholas and his two dogs barreled down upon him, he raised his shotgun and fired.

The odd thing was, the gunfire didn't come from Tsui. It came from somewhere to his right. There were sharp cracks as rounds splintered the doorframe around Tsui's head. He ducked just as Argos leapt into the air.

The enormous animal landed right on top of the man and knocked him backward into the chalet. Right behind came Draco and Nicholas.

Harvath hit the side of the structure and pulled up short. He pulled out his night vision device and was just able to catch a flash of a person taking cover nearby. Tsui must have had a sentry of some sort. Whoever it was, he had done a very good job of remaining hidden while Harvath had been doing his surveillance of the chalet. He had never seen the man.

Harvath snuck around the back of the chalet and over some rocks behind it. He tried to make as little noise as possible. He used his night vision device to guide him.

Finally, he located the outline of the shooter, taking cover behind a large store of firewood. Creeping up behind him, Harvath leveled his Glock and said, 'Don't move,' and then repeated himself in French just in case.

Turning his head, the figure replied, 'It's me.'

Harvath recognized the voice immediately. It was Peio.

There was no time to say anything as a scream was raised inside the chalet. It was Tsui, and Harvath knew what was happening. Nicholas was exacting his revenge.

'The balls! The balls!' the Troll was yelling at Argos in Russian. 'Bite his balls!'

Tsui was kicking wildly at the dog trying to get him off. His pants were shredded, and the man was bleeding badly.

'Nicholas,' Harvath yelled as he burst into the chalet. 'Enough!'

On top of the kitchen table was a terrified Yorkshire terrier with a rhinestone collar and a ridiculous blue bow atop its head yipping wildly. Draco circled the table growling, holding the smaller animal at bay.

The Troll ignored Harvath and taunted his victim as Argos tore into him. 'Look at my face, you motherfucker. Look! Look what you have done to me.'

Tsui was screaming for help, the tears streaming down his face as he continued kicking at the dog and thrashed to get away.

Harvath grabbed for Argos and the animal turned and tried to bite him, his snout covered in blood.

'Call him off or I'll kill him,' Harvath ordered.

The dwarf didn't comply, so Harvath lifted his pistol and put a round through the wall.

Reluctantly, Nicholas complied. He stepped away from Tsui and called his dogs to him. From the top of the table, the tiny Yorkie jumped down and ran to its injured master.

Peio stepped through the doorway. Harvath spun and leveled his pistol at the man's head before recognizing it was him again. 'Jesus, Padre.'

The priest let the remark slide. He tucked his pistol into his waistband and picked up Tsui's shotgun from the floor. He checked the breech and then turned it around for Harvath to see. 'Empty.'

In the corner, Tsui was crying and writhing in pain. Harvath grabbed a couple of dish towels sitting near the sink and threw them to Peio. 'Make sure he doesn't have any other weapons on him and then see if you can stop the bleeding.'

Harvath turned to Nicholas. 'You were going to kill him.'

'More like maim, actually.'

'You told Argos to bite his balls off. He could have bled to death.'

'If he lives long enough to tell us what we need to know, who cares?'

Harvath shook his head. He was going to have it out with both Nicholas and Peio, but now wasn't the time.

The Yorkie had started barking again and was trying to bite Peio as he attended to Tsui. Harvath was getting a headache. Walking over to Peio, Harvath reached down and grabbed the dog by the back of the neck. Gently, he picked it up along with its water bowl, moved it to the furthest room in the chalet, and locked it inside.

When he came back, the priest was helping Tsui into one of the chairs at the kitchen table. Nicholas stood off to the side with his two dogs, both of which were growling.

Harvath leaned up against the sink and set his pistol on the counter next to him. 'This is either going to be fast and easy or it's going to be long and very painful.'

'I'm going to wait outside,' said Peio as he wiped off his hands and stepped away.

'Why are you doing this to me?' Tsui sobbed, his crying beginning again in earnest. 'I didn't do anything to you. I don't even know who you are.'

'Look at my face!' the Troll yelled again. 'You did this to me.'

'No I didn't! I didn't!'

The man was hysterical. Harvath studied his face for any indication he was lying, but there was nothing. 'What's your name?'

'Please, I need a doctor.'

'What is your name?'

'Michael Lee. I need a doctor. Please get me to a doctor,' he begged.

'Tell me about Tony Tsui,' said Harvath.

'I don't know anyone named Tsui.'

'You're a liar,' spat Nicholas.

Harvath waved him off. 'We know you were washing your Internet traffic through Lars Jagland's computer lab at the University of Geneva. We know about everything.'

'Washing my traffic? What traffic?'

'Just kill him and let's get this over with,' said Nicholas.

'Shut up,' replied Harvath.

Lee looked at him and pleaded. 'I need to see a doctor. Please.'

'Not until you answer our questions.'

Lee was whimpering. 'You're not asking me anything I know the answers to.'

'Why wasn't your gun loaded?'

'I don't know,' he said emphatically. 'It belonged to Lars.'

'You were expecting us, weren't you?'

'I wasn't expecting anyone. When Sugar started barking, I looked outside and saw someone coming toward the house. I just wanted to scare you away.'

'How long have you known Gaston Leveque?'

'I don't know anyone named Gaston Leveque.'

'Why did you hire him to contact Dominique Fournier?'

'I don't know any of these people,' stated Lee. 'Please, you have to call an ambulance for me.'

Harvath had continued to watch for any sign that Lee was lying. There wasn't any; not one single tic, tell, or facial cue. He had a very bad feeling that they had the wrong person.

'How long have you known Lars Jagland?'

'I am in a lot of pain.'

'Answer the question.'

'Six years, okay? I was a graduate student of his before I became his TA.'

'When did you start hacking?' asked Harvath.

Lee didn't respond.

'Answer the question.'

'Screw the question,' interjected the Troll. 'Kill him.'

'If you don't zip it,' Harvath warned, 'I'm sending you outside.'

'I started when I was sixteen.'

'And what did Lars think of your hacking?'

'What do you think he thought? He was Mr. Straight Arrow. He hated it.'

'But you kept doing it.'

'Is that why you're here? Is this how companies get even now?' replied Lee. 'Like casinos? Is this payback time? Are you the leg breakers?'

'We're much worse than that,' said the Troll.

'Why didn't you go to Jagland's funeral?'

Lee looked at Harvath. 'None of your business.'

Pointing to the dogs he said, 'You can tell me, or I bring them over and put them back to work.'

'What about a doctor? I think I'm going to pass out.'

'As soon as you answer my questions, we'll get you a doctor.'

Lee readjusted himself in the chair and winced. 'His family hated me. It was bad enough for them that Lars was gay, but to have an Asian boyfriend was too much for them. They always made comments about searching for a cure for Lars's *yellow fever*. They were the most hateful people I'd ever met. I brought some of Lars's ashes up here so I could say good-bye to him alone.'

'What was his financial situation?'

'For a university professor I guess he was paid okay.'

'Did he have any enemies?'

232

'Lars? No. Not at all.'

Harvath watched his face very closely. 'Did you have access to his university computer network?'

'No,' he replied. 'I mean yes. Well, not anymore.'

'Which is it?'

'I told you he was lying,' said the Troll.

'I'm not. I just want to answer your questions so I can get a doctor.'

'So which is it?' asked Harvath. 'Either you did or didn't have access to his university network.'

'When I was his teaching assistant, I did.'

'What happened?'

'I did some things I shouldn't have done.'

'Finally, some truth,' snapped the Troll.

'What kind of things?' asked Harvath.

'I made a stupid mistake that got traced back.'

'A mistake on a hack?'

Lee nodded. 'It cost me my job at the university. Lars made me promise never to do it again.'

'But you kept on hacking, didn't you?'

'It was dishonest, but in my mind I was promising not to make the same stupid mistake again, not to stop hacking.'

'So you lied to Jagland.'

'Yes. Now, please can I see a doctor?'

'I don't believe that your access to Jagland's network was cut off.'

'It *was*. He started changing his password and didn't even access the university system from home.'

'So no one had access to it but Jagland?'

'And his TA. The one he hired when I left.'

'The woman with the glasses?' asked Harvath.

'That's her. Dripping with talent, but cold. Ice cold.'

At that moment, Harvath realized that they had made a very big mistake. Rechecking Michael Lee's wounds he said, 'We're going to get you to a doctor, but first I'm going to need you to do something for me.'

33

Adda Sterk awoke from a strange dream. In it, she had purchased a very expensive new car, but couldn't remember where she had parked it. There was something about the car that wouldn't allow her to go to the police or friends for help. As she continued to search her neighborhood, she became more and more distraught.

When she opened her eyes, the nightmare should have been over, but it was just beginning.

The man standing over her bed was rough and very strong. His face was covered by some sort of mask. He placed a piece of tape over her mouth and bound her hands painfully behind her back. She felt certain that he was going to rape her until he bound her feet and then placed a hood over her head. She struggled, but it made no difference to her situation.

As he lifted her from the bed, he pulled off the top sheet and covered her with it. She wanted to believe that this was an act of decency on his part, an attempt to conceal her nakedness because of the goodness, the humanity in his soul, but she knew that wasn't why he was doing it. He was doing it to conceal her altogether. And

235

with that realization, she knew in her core that whatever was in store for her was going to be worse than rape.

Adda Sterk fought to purge her mind of the fear and to focus. If she knew who was doing this to her perhaps she could negotiate her way out of it. After all, she had only been the messenger. One didn't kill the messenger.

The man carrying her paused near the glass doors to her balcony and her heart seized in her chest. *He was going to drop her to the pavement!*

The man then bent down and picked something up with his other hand. They were close to her desk. Was it her laptop? Was that what this was about? Did he want information? Maybe she would be able to bargain with him after all.

In the hallway, he moved quickly past the elevator and into the stairwell. He was very strong indeed to be able to carry her down so many flights of stairs. He was obviously being careful too. He hadn't risked the elevator. The chance he could have bumped into a neighbor, even at this early-morning hour, would have been too great. In addition to being strong, he was intelligent, or at least experienced.

If only she had been more attractive, she might have also been able to use her body to entice the man to spare her life, but she had been born with neither good looks nor an attractive physique. The only thing God seemed to have blessed the teaching assistant with was an incredible mind.

That said, how had this man found her? As an average citizen, she had no value as a kidnap victim. He, or the people he was working for, somehow knew what she really did for a living and therefore understood her true value. And for that to have happened, somewhere along the line, despite all of her safeguards to prevent this very thing, she had made a mistake.

* * *

In the parking structure, she was placed facedown inside a van with a sliding door. The man bent her legs upward and secured the restraints around her ankles to those around her wrists. The vehicle's metal floor was cold and the thin sheet did little to insulate her body.

There was a faint, lingering odor as well. Something she vaguely recognized. As her lungs constricted and she began having trouble breathing, she knew what it was — dog hair. Underneath the hood, her eyes wide with terror, Sterk's greatest fear rushed to the front of her mind. She was going to suffocate to death.

After leaving the garage, the van made so many turns she would have given up trying to follow its path had she been paying attention. Instead, she was trapped within a horrific nightmare. She felt a warm, wet sensation grow beneath her stomach and realized that she had wet herself.

Outside the van's thin metal sides, she could hear the din of morning traffic. She wanted to scream. She wanted to yell for someone to save her, but even without the hood and tape over her mouth she would have been unable. She was in the midst of a full-blown asthma attack.

★   ★   ★

When the van pulled into the empty warehouse on the outskirts of the city, Sterk was only semi-conscious. The pungent scent of urine and sweat greeted Harvath as he opened the vehicle's door. The fact that she wasn't moving told him something wasn't right.

Hopping inside, he pulled back the sheet and snatched off her hood. He tried to hold her head up, but it just lolled to the side.

'And you told me I went too far with Lee,' admonished Nicholas from just outside the van.

Harvath tore the tape from her mouth and checked her breathing and vital signs. She was on the verge of death.

'Her purse is on the front seat,' said Harvath. 'Get it.'

Nicholas climbed up into the van, retrieved the purse, and brought it back. Harvath unzipped the bag and dumped its contents on the floor. He found her inhaler, shook it, opened her airway, and injected the inhalant. Because he was administering it to her without her being able to actively breathe in the medication, he repeated the process two more times before pulling her from the van, cutting the restraint that bound her hands to her feet, and laying her on the cement floor.

When her breathing began to normalize, he

picked her up and moved her to the center of the facility where he secured her to a column and waited for her to fully regain consciousness.

The first person she saw was Michael Lee. He lay with his legs akimbo and his arms bound behind another support column. His trousers were tattered and he was covered in blood. To his left stood two enormous dogs, their faces also covered in blood. Sterk knew who the beasts belonged to. Had she any question, it was all but settled when the little man waddled into her field of vision and spoke.

'You are much more intelligent than I ever gave you credit for,' said the Troll as he came closer. 'Here I thought Tsui was some little hacker operating out of his parents' basement somewhere. I was obviously very wrong. I shouldn't have let my prejudice get the better of me.'

Sterk turned her eyes away.

'Why so shy, my dear? Don't you want to see what you have accomplished? Granted, as friends remind me, I wasn't very pretty to begin with, but I'm downright hideous now, wouldn't you agree?'

The woman who had built a burgeoning intelligence dynasty as Tony Tsui remained silent.

'Own it!' the Troll screamed. 'Look at me and own what you have done!'

Sterk looked up at him and as she did a tear rolled down her left cheek.

'Oh that's good,' said Nicholas. 'That's very, very good.'

With a calm and perfectly placid expression, he drew back his small arm and struck her across the side of the head with the wrench he had removed from the van's emergency toolkit. Harvath, who was standing behind Sterk, looked at Nicholas and drew a hash mark on the dusty support column she was tethered to.

'My, what a horrible gash,' said Nicholas as he studied the wound he had inflicted upon her.

Sterk had never had any of the bones in her face broken, but she was fairly certain that her cheekbone had just been shattered. 'You like to hit women. You're pathetic.'

The Troll wound up and hit her again, this time on the other side. Sterk cried out from the intensity of the pain.

Harvath ticked off another hash mark on the column.

'You've been a very, very bad girl, Adda,' said Nicholas as he hit her again.

Harvath put yet another hash mark on the board and was fairly certain the little man was going to start popping stitches.

Blood was rolling freely down both sides of her face. 'I hope the woman I sent was a good lay, because she was obviously a terrible assassin.'

Nicholas was about to hit Sterk again, but he stopped. Michael Lee had been right about her; about both her asthma and her pride.

He dropped the wrench, and without a hint of irony, smiled and said, 'Now we can speak freely.'

'If you're going to kill me,' she said, 'get it over with.'

Nicholas got a considerably good laugh out of that. 'Kill you? You're worth much more to me alive than dead.'

Sterk looked at him.

'I have big plans for you. First I'm going to cut out your tongue and seal your rather bland face inside an iron mask. Then I'm going to sell you to an unusually perverse Saudi prince who will chain you outside his tent in the middle of the desert, naked. Between the Arabs and the camels, you're going to be the belle of the Bedouin ball.'

'And the award for S&M fiction goes to the man with the world's smallest penis,' said Sterk.

Nicholas lunged for his wrench and struck the woman again. This time he tore open a wound along her forehead.

Harvath tallied his fourth hash mark. Nicholas would be allowed only one more swipe at her before he stepped in.

The Troll set the wrench down, quietly this time. 'Do you know that man across from you?'

The woman didn't reply.

'Of course you do. That's Michael Lee,' Nicholas continued. 'He's the man you set up to take the fall as Tony Tsui if the heat ever got too close to you.'

'I don't know what you are talking about.'

'Do I need to pick the wrench back up, Adda? Or perhaps you would like to meet my dogs?' Nicholas snapped his fingers and the dogs began growling. 'In fact, I'm going to even go so far as to suggest that the untimely demise of Lars Jagland wasn't an accident, but that he somehow

241

stumbled on to what you were up to and you killed him.'

To frighten the woman, Lee had been bound to the other column facing her. And in order to make him look like a real hostage, which in part he was, and also to make sure he didn't say anything he shouldn't, Harvath had placed a piece of duct tape across his mouth. The man now struggled against it. His eyes bulged as he cursed her and yelled from behind the tape.

'I agree with you. I think Lars was probably murdered, but I didn't have anything to do with it.'

'I don't believe you,' said the Troll. 'I think he discovered what you were up to and you killed him. Didn't you?'

'No, I didn't.'

'I have to hand it to you. The Tsui persona was exceptional. You not only had me fooled, but you covered your tracks quite well. And the icing on the cake was positioning Michael Lee to take the fall if things ever got bad. Brava.'

'I didn't kill Lars,' Sterk insisted.

'But you're not denying you set up Michael, are you?'

Sterk said nothing.

'I have no reason to believe anything you say. You tried to have me killed. What's one more?'

Sterk remained silent.

'You always have a fallback, don't you?' said Nicholas. 'When the assassin you sent after me failed, you implicated me in the bombings in Rome. What about Paris? Are my *fingerprints* going to surface there too?'

At that moment, something in the woman's face shifted.

Nicholas motioned his dogs over. 'You really have been a very, very bad girl.'

'What are you going to do to me?' Sterk demanded.

'That depends on how you answer my questions.'

34

'Is there another assassin looking for me?' asked Nicholas.

Sterk didn't respond, and Nicholas bent down and picked up the wrench again.

'No,' she responded.

'None at all?'

'I'm sure you have plenty of enemies, but when Leveque's woman in Spain failed to return, I assumed you had killed her and had gone deeper to ground.'

'So you moved to plan B: implicating me.'

The woman shook her head. 'Alive or dead, you were always going to be implicated.'

'Why? Why implicate me?'

'My employers wanted a diversion.'

'Who hired you?'

'Someone I fear much more than you.'

Nicholas tapped the head of the wrench in his tiny palm. 'I'll give you one more chance.'

Sterk shook her head.

Nicholas brought back his tiny arm and swung.

The wrench met its target and blood began to pour from a tear behind the woman's ear.

Harvath tallied his fifth and final hash mark on the column and stepped out from behind her. It was time for him to take over. Producing a roll of duct tape, he tore off a piece and placed it across her mouth. He then put the bag back over her head as Nicholas said to Sterk, 'Oh my. Things are about to get very bad for you indeed.'

Harvath cut the rope binding her wrists to the support column, stripped the sheet from her naked body, and carried her back to the van. He had no idea what had triggered the asthma attack the first time. He suspected it was stress, though it could have been something else. Either way, he was determined to re-create the circumstances as closely as possible to bring about another one.

He tied her back down in the vehicle exactly as he had before and closed the door. From the front seat, he grabbed two water bottles and then searched the warehouse until he found a suitable length of hose.

The good thing about gasoline was that it was so pungent Harvath wouldn't need much for what he had planned.

He made a big deal of banging around the rear of the van. He opened one of the water bottles and poured out some of the water. He then carefully siphoned a small amount of gasoline out of the van and into the bottle.

With Nicholas in tow, he stepped back around to the other side and opened the sliding door. He studied Sterk. Her breathing was rapid, as it should be for anyone in her situation. She was frightened. She wasn't yet, though, suffering from another attack.

'You can't do this,' said the Troll as Harvath stepped into the van. 'What if you don't just burn her, but you end up killing her?'

There was a long list of harsh interrogation

techniques he could have tried on Sterk — sleep deprivation, stress postures, sensory bombardment, or even extreme cold — but he didn't have the time. Frankly, after the beating the woman had taken from Nicholas, he was surprised she hadn't already broken. She was a much tougher character than he had expected. He had no idea if she had undergone training to resist hostile interrogation or if she was just one tough woman. It didn't matter. Everyone broke eventually, the key lay in discovering exactly how to break them and if time was of the essence, as it was here, how to do it as quickly as possible. Whether Adda Sterk was left physically or psychologically wounded by the ordeal was of no concern to Harvath. She held all the cards and could end the experience at any point she wanted.

The more one knew about one's subject, the better equipped one was to carry out a successful interrogation. Considering the fact that up until several hours ago they had believed Adda Sterk was a young male hacker of Asian descent by the name of Tony Tsui, it was plain they didn't have much to go on. But they did have one thing.

On the scale of harsh interrogation methods, one of the stronger tactics that can be employed is the exploitation of a prisoner's phobias. The fact that Sterk was asthmatic left no question in Harvath's mind that she harbored a fear that most asthmatics shared, *asphyxia*.

Opening the bottle filled with the gas-water mixture, he poured the contents over the woman's hood. Panic quickly overtook her as she began writhing and struggling against her restraints.

He followed by pouring the second bottle of water over the rest of her body. Her nostrils were so filled with the scent of gasoline, she would assume that she was now covered with it from head to toe. The gas seeping into her hood had probably found its way into the open wounds around her face and head.

Harvath didn't have to wait long. Whether there was some trigger like dog hair on the floor of the van, or if it was the stress of believing she was about to be set ablaze, Sterk was soon consumed by another intense asthma attack.

Lifting her from the van, he carried her several feet away and set her on the warehouse floor. He pulled the hood from her head and tore the tape from her mouth. He pulled out her inhaler and showed it to her. 'Are you going to answer my questions?'

Gasping for air, Sterk nodded feverishly.

Harvath shook the inhaler, placed it in her mouth, and administered the medication.

He waited until her breathing became less labored and then dragged her back to the support column. Now it was time to see if she would co-operate or not. He studied her face as he asked his first question. 'When I met you in Jagland's office, why did you give up Michael Lee?'

The woman coughed repeatedly before answering. 'Because I didn't need him anymore.'

'But he was your cover.'

'It didn't matter. That cover became useless

when Lars was killed.'

'You're not making any sense,' said Harvath.

'I knew that someday, someone might come looking for me. That was why I had created the whole Tsui persona. It was a layer of protection. I set it up so that everything traced back to Lars and from him to Michael. But when Lars was killed, my backstop was gone.'

'Who killed him?'

'I don't know. The police say he died in a car accident.'

'You don't believe that. I can tell by looking at your face.'

'I don't know what to believe,' she said. 'Could what happened to Lars have been an accident? Possibly. But I'm not certain. That's why I was waiting to see what happened to Michael.'

'You mean you were waiting to see if he would be killed as well?' asked Nicholas.

Lee shouted at the woman again from behind the duct tape covering his mouth. He pulled against his restraints and there was no doubt in anyone's mind, including Sterk's, that if he managed to break free, he would kill her.

'That's why you gave him up to me,' replied Harvath. 'You wanted to see if I had been sent to finish off Tony Tsui.'

'Obviously.'

'Then what?'

'Then, when I thought it was safe, I would have started over under a new persona.'

The woman was absolutely mercenary, but as far as Harvath could tell, she was telling the truth. 'So who killed Jagland?' he asked.

Sterk looked down at the floor and refused to answer.

'I want to make something perfectly clear,' said Harvath. 'Right now, the only person in this entire world you should fear is me. If I even suspect you're holding out on me, I'm going to light you on fire. I will let you burn and then I will put the fire out before it kills you. The pain will be worse than anything you have ever experienced. The heat will sear your lungs and you're going to suffer from smoke inhalation. It's going to be severe.

'I'll repeat this process until you're dead or you give me what I want. Which will it be?'

'My life's worth nothing if I survive. They'll find me and they'll kill me just like they did Lars, and I'm certain it'll be in a manner much worse than anything you can possibly devise.'

'Who are *they*?'

Sterk didn't respond.

Harvath turned to Nicholas, 'See if there are any matches in the van. If there aren't, heat the cigarette lighter.'

The Troll nodded and headed for the van.

Sterk looked at him. Both sides of her face were beginning to swell. 'Just kill me and get it over with.'

'You don't have to die.'

'I'm dead anyway.'

'We *can* protect you.'

'You don't even know what you'd be protecting me against. These people have resources beyond your imagination.'

'So do I,' he replied.

The woman laughed and shook her head.

'What if we gave them Tony Tsui?'

From the other support column, Lee's eyes bulged.

'How would you do that?'

'Never mind,' said Harvath. 'What if we can give them Tsui, or at least make it look like Tsui isn't someone for them to worry about anymore?'

'These are not stupid people. They can't be easily fooled.'

'I wouldn't expect them to be.'

Nicholas returned with the van's cigarette lighter and held it out to Harvath. 'Let's burn the witch.'

Harvath took it and looked at Sterk. 'It's your call, Adda.'

The woman studied the faces of her two captors and thought about her options. After several moments she said, 'I'll cooperate, but on one condition.'

'You're trying to negotiate? You've got to be kidding me,' stammered the Troll.

'What do you want?' Harvath demanded.

Sterk focused her gaze on him and replied, 'A little added insurance.'

35

John Vaughan sat in a plush leather captain's chair inside the most comfortable surveillance vehicle he had ever seen and wondered what Paul Davidson's problem was.

Josh Levy, the owner of Surety Private Investigations, Ltd., and Davidson's boss when he was moonlighting as a PI, couldn't have been more personable, polite, or professional if he had tried. He was a handsome, well-dressed man in his late fifties and very experienced in private investigative work. There was no question in Vaughan's mind that Levy had easily spent over a hundred thousand dollars on his surveillance van. It really was decked out like a limo inside and the electronic equipment rivaled anything the CPD or the FBI owned. Unless this guy had a DVD carousel loaded with animal porn, Vaughan couldn't find anything even remotely questionable about him. It was beyond him why Davidson so disliked doing surveillance with his boss.

'Is the temperature okay for you?' asked Levy. 'There's plenty of juice left in the batteries to run the air exchangers.'

As the man bent down to flip a switch,

Davidson looked at Vaughan and rolled his eyes.

'The air's real good, Josh. Thank you,' said Vaughan, ignoring Davidson.

Levy righted himself, leaned over, flipped open a mini-fridge and pulled out a cup of yogurt. Davidson tapped Vaughan on the shoulder with the back of his hand.

'Anybody want one?' asked Levy.

'No thanks, Josh,' responded Davidson. 'We're all good.'

Vaughan watched as Levy peeled back the lid and licked the yogurt from the top. When he was done, he placed the lid on the narrow counter beneath the surveillance equipment and went to work folding it into eighths, before dropping it into a Ziplocked garbage bag hanging from the wall.

While he was fishing a spoon from a drawer near the fridge, Davidson tapped Vaughan again and rolled his eyes. The Organized Crime cop looked back at him and shrugged. He had no idea what Davidson's problem was.

Levy took a bite of his yogurt and then picked up the copy of Mohammed Nasiri's picture. 'So this is our guy, but we don't know if he's inside the mosque. Correct?'

'That's right,' said Vaughan. 'Based on the calls we've made, he hasn't gotten on any airplanes out of town.'

'But he could have hopped on a bus, a train, or borrowed a car and left.'

'That's correct.'

Levy took another bite of yogurt. This time, he licked both sides of the spoon afterward. 'Why do you think he's inside?'

Vaughan could feel Davidson's glance, begging him to notice how Levy was licking the spoon, and he tried to ignore it. 'We saw a lot of this stuff in Iraq. The bad guys know we won't come into a mosque unless we've got a mountain of overwhelming evidence. Especially in the U.S., it's political suicide. The mosque is a sanctuary for these guys. We'd never in a million years think of doing in a church or a synagogue what they do in their mosques.'

'Nor would any priest or rabbi put up with it,' added Davidson. 'I can't imagine what my priest would say if I told him, 'Father, we're going to go shoot up a girls' school, plant a few roadside bombs, and be back for lunch. Don't let anyone into the room downstairs where we keep all of the rifles and grenade launchers, okay?''

Levy chuckled, though they all appreciated the fact that the reality of it wasn't that funny. 'I guess that's one of the many differences between Islam and the rest of the world.'

'You can say that again.'

Vaughan looked at the monitor feed for one of the infrared cameras mounted in the van's side-view mirrors. 'In Iraq, we'd know guys we wanted were inside a particular mosque, sometimes we'd chase them right up the front steps, but then we couldn't do anything. We'd have to wait until Iraqi soldiers got on site.'

Levy licked both sides of his spoon once more and said, 'That's the dumbest thing I have ever heard.'

Vaughan nodded. 'I agree.'

'So they think we'll treat their mosques here in the U.S. the same way we do in Iraq?'

'Up to now, that's exactly how we've treated them. It's not just hands off, it's hands *way* off.'

Levy shook his head. 'Political correctness is going to be the death of Western civilization.'

'I hope you're wrong, but there's no question that our enemies are using political correctness against us.'

'You can say that again,' replied Davidson. 'Muslim 'honor' killings are becoming an epidemic in the U.S., but do you think it gets reported by the media? No. Wife and child beatings are through the roof, but the media ignore those as well. Point out what's wrong with Muslim culture and you're automatically labeled a racist. It's like shunning the guy on the *Titanic* who says he sees water in the forward bulkhead.'

Levy finished his yogurt and placed the empty cup in the bag and zipped the top shut again.

Vaughan checked his watch. 'The evening Ishaa prayers will be over soon.'

'Think Nasiri will stick his head out?' asked Davidson.

'You never know. Terrorists make a lot of stupid mistakes.'

'Not this guy,' said Levy.

Vaughan and Davidson both looked at him. 'How would you know?' asked Davidson.

'If he's up to what you think he is, you have to assume he didn't get his job by being stupid. And if he felt the heat was so intense that he had to flee to the mosque, even a storefront mosque, then you have to give him enough credit that he won't pop his head out until he thinks he can get away with it.'

Vaughan nodded in agreement.

'Which means,' continued Levy, 'that eventually we're going to have to do more than just sit outside here watching the front door.'

He was right, and neither of the other two men in the surveillance van could argue with him.

'What are you thinking?' asked Vaughan.

Levy tapped two black Storm cases with the toe of his boot and said, 'I think we're going to have to get more aggressive with our surveillance.'

36

Levy opened the cases and showed his guests what he had brought. Vaughan reached down and plucked out a wireless camera embedded within a hard, black baseball-sized shell. 'What's this?'

'Brilliant Israeli military technology.'

Davidson looked at it. 'Then how come it says Remington on the side?'

'Because they licensed it for the U.S., but couldn't get it off the ground. I bought this sample kit from the rep.'

'How does it work?' asked Vaughan. 'You just drop these where you want them?'

'Better than that. You can actually throw them. When they stop rolling, they right themselves on those little stubby feet on the bottom. You can toss them on a roof, over a wall, anywhere.'

'And those are fiber-optic cameras in the other box?'

Levy nodded. 'If you've got balls big enough to get close to the door or drill down from the ceiling, then we'll really get a good view inside.'

'What are the baby wipes for?'

'You should see how dirty this stuff gets,' he said as he pulled another one of the camera balls out of its case.

As he did, Davidson jabbed Vaughan in the ribs and raised his eyebrows as if to say, *See?*

Vaughan waved him off. All he saw was a guy

256

who was particular about how he ate his yogurt and who liked to keep his gear clean. Big deal. In fact, he'd take Josh Levy over most of the sloppy cops he'd been forced to sit through stakeouts with.

'If we can drop a couple of those in the alley behind the building, will you be able to pick up the signal out here?'

'I should.'

'Will they work okay in low light?'

'They've got an IR illuminator, but it puts an extra drain on the batteries. We won't be able to run them all night.'

'Hopefully, we won't have to.'

Davidson used the cameras mounted outside the van to check for foot traffic along the street. They were in a small honor-system parking lot where you placed your money in a slot on a big board beneath the number that corresponded to what stall you were in. Levy had picked the lot himself, preferring it to being parked out on the street. The view wasn't as good, but it was acceptable. It was his opinion that a windowless van parked too near the mosque might draw undue attention to itself. Vaughan had agreed.

'How do you want to do this?' asked Davidson.

'We've got your Bronco parked around the corner,' replied Vaughan. 'From this distance, I don't think anyone is going to notice us getting out of the van.

'I'll stay here and monitor the feeds while you take Josh with you. He'll ride shotgun and can drop three balls. One at the beginning of the alley, one near the back door of the target building, and one before you turn back out onto the street.'

Levy shook his head. 'I don't leave the van.'

'Why not?'

'I just don't.'

Vaughan looked at Davidson for some sort of explanation but the Public Vehicles officer just looked back at him and smiled as if to say, *I told you so.*

He turned back to Levy. 'How are we going to know if we got the balls placed correctly?'

The PI pulled a radio from a charger rack and handed it to Vaughan. 'It's not rocket science. You roll down the window and drop them out. I'll radio you and let you know how the picture looks.'

'What if I screw it up and one of them rolls underneath a Dumpster?'

'Don't screw it up.'

Satisfied that the argument was settled, Levy unzipped the gym bag hanging from the arm of his chair and removed a small hand towel. Unrolling it across his lap, he fished his key ring from his pocket.

'That's good enough for me,' said Davidson, taking the radio from Vaughan, suddenly anxious to leave. 'Let's get going.'

Hanging from Levy's key ring was a gold nail clipper. The PI pivoted open the handle and studied his nails.

'The street's as quiet as it's going to get,' said Davidson as Vaughan watched Levy. 'Let's get this done before evening prayers are over with.'

He poked the Organized Crime cop with the radio's antenna, breaking the spell and getting his attention.

'Make sure to do a radio check when you get to your truck,' stated Levy as the two men parted the heavy blackout curtain and exited the van through its back door.

Cutting through the alley behind the parking lot, Vaughan said, 'I've never known anybody who carries a nail clipper on their key ring. Is it solid gold?'

'Probably,' said Davidson with a shudder. 'I can't watch him clip his nails. It creeps me out.'

'If that's the worst of his behavior, then you've got it pretty good.'

'That's the thing. It isn't just one quirky thing with him. It's a million. And they all add up.'

'And that's why you don't like doing surveillance with him?'

'Damn straight,' replied Davidson. 'The guy's an investigative genius, but there's something just not right about him. It's like if Magnum PI and Rain Man had a baby. You saw how he wouldn't leave the van.'

'So?'

'So Judge Wapner probably comes on in ten minutes.'

Vaughan shook his head. 'The guy's a little eccentric. So what? You need to lighten up.'

Davidson smiled. 'Give it another hour. You'll want to beat the guy to death with the heel of your shoe.'

He doubted it and they walked in silence the rest of the way to the Bronco and climbed in.

While Davidson did a radio check, Vaughan received an e-mail from one of the forensics specialists going over Nasiri's taxi. The piece of plastic that had been recovered at the scene of the hit-and-run was indeed from a radiator header, and the radiator header in Nasiri's cab was new. Everything they were telling him jibed with what the Pakistani mechanic from the Crescent Garage had told them.

The bad news was that there was no blood, hair, or tissue anywhere on the outside of the vehicle. Worse still was what the tech told him next.

Skirting the poisonous tree issue had not been easy. The only thing Vaughan could do was to ask his forensic pal to search the interior of the cab, as well as the trunk, for traces of any chemicals. He said he was looking for any sign that Nasiri had washed down his cab with solvents in an attempt to hide evidence of the hit-and-run. His real hope was that they would come back with hits for TATP or the precursors for the compound. The bad news from forensics was that the cab contained no traces of chemicals whatsoever.

Vaughan shared the bad news with Davidson as they pulled away from the curb and headed toward the alley.

'I'm not surprised,' replied Davidson. 'If that stuff is as volatile as you say it is, they're not going to want to move it until they absolutely have to. If Nasiri was transporting anything, it was bottles of peroxide and cans of drain cleaner; all nice and sealed.'

Vaughan didn't like it, but he had to agree. 'So we've still got nothing.'

'What do you mean nothing? You've got Josh Levy's balls in the palm of your hand.'

He held up one of the cameras and looked at it.

'Now, Josh may think his balls are made of brass,' said Davidson, 'but I still think you should drop them out the window delicately. Nobody likes to have their balls busted.'

'Are you done?' asked Vaughan as he rolled down his window.

'Since you asked, you have to admit that even though he wanted to stay in the van, Josh really does have big balls.'

'Is that all of them?'

'All of my ball jokes?'

'Yeah.'

'For the moment.'

'Good,' said Vaughan. 'I'd like to concentrate on what's happening at the mosque.'

'Like Captain Hook.'

Vaughan nodded.

As they rolled up to the stop sign half a block from the alley, Davidson snapped the clip on the metal clipboard wedged between his seat and armrest. 'You know what that is?'

'No. What is it?'

'The sound of *no* hands clapping.'

Vaughan shook his head. 'Can we please concentrate on what we're about to do?'

'So you're asking me to give you a *hand* with this part?'

'You know, Levy probably isn't the one I'm

going to beat to death with my shoe tonight.'

'All right. I get it,' said Davidson. 'You lawyers have no sense of humor. How fast do you want me to drive down the alley?'

'Fast enough to look like you know what you're doing and are just cutting through.'

Davidson put his left hand over his eyes and waved his right index finger over the speedometer before landing on a speed. 'Okay, got it. Anything else?'

'Yeah. You'd better put your thinking cap on. If this surveillance doesn't pan out, we're going to need a really good plan B.'

37

Vaughan lowered the radio and looked at Davidson. They had just driven out of the alley after dropping all three covert surveillance balls. 'Is the placement of the second camera 'not right' because it's not right, or because Levy's *not right?*'

'Despite what I told you, he knows what he's doing. He wouldn't ask you to tweak it if he didn't have a good reason.'

Levy's voice came over the radio again. 'Did you guys copy that?'

'Ten-four,' said Vaughan. 'We heard you loud and clear.'

'You didn't pitch it under a Dumpster, but you did manage to get it wedged behind a garbage can,' added Levy. 'I wouldn't be expecting a call from the White Sox this year.'

Davidson looked at him. 'Is he pissing you off yet?'

'He's getting there.'

'So what are we going to do?'

Vaughan really wanted a view of the back door of that building. 'I'll fix it.'

He climbed out of the Bronco and made his way into the alley. It was cluttered with empty boxes, splintered pallets, Dumpsters, and garbage cans. Though he didn't have a terrific view, he did have lots of good concealment and he carefully picked his way forward.

Just before the building that held the mosque, he stopped and took a slow look around. If he was going to move the camera, he might as well put it in the best spot possible. Now that he was here, he wished he'd brought along a couple of the fiber-optic cameras as well. Having come this far, it would have made sense to go the rest of the way and get the best look at what was going on inside as they could.

The back of the building was covered in gray brick. The basement windows had been painted black and were covered with iron bars. The first-floor windows were covered with newspaper and also covered with bars. A broken lightbulb hung over the back door. The ground was littered with cigarette butts, despite a coffee can filled with sand, which the building's smokers must have figured was a doorstop.

Vaughan identified a spot for his camera and stacked a few empty boxes around it so it would run less of a chance of being noticed. With a new hiding place ready, he went looking for the hard, black sphere.

There was a row of about five trashcans. The ball was fairly heavy for its size, and when he dropped it out the window he hadn't expected it to roll very far. They must have been driving down the alley at a higher rate of speed than he had thought.

Pulling a flashlight from his pocket, he leaned over, tilted back the first can, and looked. There was nothing there. He slid out the second can and came up empty as well. It was the same story with the remaining three cans. *Where the hell had that thing gone to?*

Vaughan studied the alley. There were buildings, cans, Dumpsters, and trash on both sides. The camera could have rolled to the other side, but he doubted it. He had dropped it on the east side of the alley. That was where it had to be.

He came back down the row of cans, tilting each one out, and this time he saw it. Even if his life had depended on it, he couldn't have made such a one-in-a-million shot. Sitting wedged inside a laundry vent or a drain opening of some sort was his missing surveillance camera. He pulled back the can and bent over near the wall to free the ball.

He was just beginning to stand when he heard something behind him. Vaughan had no idea who it was and had learned a long time ago that discretion wasn't always the better part of valor. He was in a dark alley in a bad neighborhood on the trail of even worse people. He went for his Glock.

The move was met with a searing pain in his right hand as he was struck with a piece of rebar and his wrist was broken.

Vaughan spun and came up with his left hand in a fist. He connected with his attacker's jaw and sent him stumbling backward. At that moment, the barrel of a gun was shoved into his face and a flashlight was shined in his eyes.

Though it hurt like hell on his right side, Vaughan raised his hands. 'I don't know who you are, but I'm a police officer.'

The light was taken out of his eyes and, for a

moment, he thought he was going to be let go, until he felt his Glock being removed from his holster and saw the man he had punched out gather himself off the pavement and come forward. The man was Middle Eastern. This wasn't good.

Walking over to him, the man drew his fist back and struck him right in the gut. Vaughan doubled over.

The man grabbed him by the hair and jerked his head up. Vaughan had been in plenty of fistfights in his time and he readied himself either for a knee to the face or for the man to punch down at his head. Either way, he knew it was going to hurt.

Suddenly, he heard a voice from behind his attackers. 'This isn't even a fair fight. You assholes didn't bring enough guys.'

Vaughan looked past the man with the gun to see Davidson right behind him with his own gun pressed up against the back of the man's head.

The man holding him by his hair let go and Vaughan straightened himself up. His relief at seeing Davidson was short-lived. Four other men were now standing behind him with weapons pointed right at him.

'Well, it looks like maybe you did bring enough guys,' said Davidson. 'Why don't we put our guns down and settle this like men?'

One of the men stepped forward and struck him in the kidneys with the butt of a rifle. Davidson's knees buckled from the pain and he collapsed to the ground.

As his gun was taken away from him,

Davidson looked up and said, 'That's it. You're all under arrest.'

The man who had broken Vaughan's wrist smiled and punched Davidson in the mouth.

Someone gave a series of orders in rapid Arabic and the two police officers were dragged from the alley and into the building.

As the heavy metal door clanged shut, Vaughan wondered what was going to happen, but part of him already knew. All of the bad feelings he'd had since going after Nasiri came flooding back. This was no longer Chicago, and he was no longer a cop or a lawyer working for the family of a young woman who'd been struck by a fleeing taxi. He was a Marine and he was being dragged into a terrorist hellhole worse than anything he had ever seen.

38

The speed with which Reed Carlton worked was a testament to the efficiency of the private sector. Within hours, he had not only helped plug the holes in Harvath's plan, he had gotten the train on the tracks and out of the station.

It was agreed that Michael Lee had seen and heard too much to be let go. For the time being, he was going to have to be held on to. And while Peio was a decent field medic, he wasn't a trauma doc. Lee was stable, but he needed a professional to look at his wounds. There was an American surgeon based in Paris who was being flown in. She had some sort of relationship with the Department of Defense, but other than that, Carlton didn't elaborate. All he added was that she was equipped to keep an eye on Lee until they decided what to do with him. Harvath had trouble imagining what a surgeon could do, short of keeping Lee drugged up, but he figured Carlton knew best and let it go. There were several more pressing items that needed to be worked out anyway.

As the attempted murder of the Troll had been orchestrated from within Switzerland, the United States didn't have any jurisdiction. They also

268

didn't have any jurisdiction over the alleged murder of Lars Jagland. Not that anyone in the United States cared very much about either. All they cared about were the Rome and Paris attacks. That and Sterk's material support of terrorism and how it had resulted in the deaths of hundreds of American citizens.

Harvath was a big believer in the merits of enhanced interrogation. He also had no problem with torture when the situation called for it, which this one definitely did. There were very likely more attacks on the horizon, and Sterk possessed information that could help stop them. The key lay in applying as much pressure as was necessary to get her to play ball. Once she began cooperating, the pressure could be dialed back, but the threat of it ramping back up needed to hover over everything they did in order to ensure her continued collaboration.

If they'd had more time to interrogate her, Carlton and the higher-ups at the DOD might not have been so willing to cut a deal. But as it was, everyone, including Harvath, agreed that preventing further attacks was more important than prosecuting her.

Painting Sterk as a covert intelligence source for another agency, an immunity agreement was drafted. So long as she cooperated, Sterk would not be prosecuted.

With that demand met, they set to work on 'closing out' Tony Tsui.

Sterk had been dead set against having it happen in the United States. 'Too suspicious,' she had argued, believing that it would raise too many questions and sow too many seeds of doubt.

The woman preferred that it take place in an Asian or Latin American country.

That made things difficult for the Old Man. It had to be done correctly and with people he knew he could trust. The best was if it could be done through someone who owed him a favor. There were several of those scattered around the globe, but not all of them could lay their hands on a fresh 'John Doe' Asian corpse.

The woman finally agreed to the closeout taking place outside Frankfurt, Germany. The gun battle between Tony Tsui and an elite GSG9 team began shortly before eleven o'clock local time and raged for over forty-five minutes. When the unit finally stormed the small house, news vehicles from every media outlet in Frankfurt were already stacked three deep behind the police cordons. None of them had any clue that the man returning fire from inside the house was not Tony Tsui, but was one of the GSG9 counterterrorism operatives from the German Federal Police force.

As dead bodies do not bleed, the operative inside the house had pumped plenty of fresh blood through the corpse as he simultaneously pumped it full of rounds from his MP5. A forensics team was brought in, and a big show was made of a single laptop being removed from the house. It was placed into an official police vehicle along with the GSG9 team and driven away in one of the longest and most secure convoys any of the media had ever seen. One reporter remarked that not even foreign heads of state traveled with that much security; not even the American president.

The first piece of disinformation was leaked to the popular German weekly *Der Spiegel* and appeared on their Web site within the hour. German counterterrorism forces had decided to move on a known espionage figure who dealt in the sale and trade of highly classified state secrets. This figure was reported to have had wide-ranging ties, including several high-level terrorist contacts. The suspect had been shot and killed by German counterterrorism forces.

The next leak went to the *Frankfurter Allgemeine Zeitung,* which reported that the house, located in a largely rural area, contained a significant stash of weapons and cash. It went on to say that while the victim's identity had yet to be established, it was believed to be an Asian male in his late twenties or early thirties.

By the time *Hessischer Rundfunk Television* updated its viewers, the narrative was almost perfectly formed. Along with the weapons and money found at the house of the suspected black market information broker were several passports which the suspect had attempted to destroy. The name of the suspect and any names at all gleaned from the passports were being withheld by German authorities pending investigation.

While the names were being withheld from the German citizenry and its press, they were already

271

being circulated through international intelligence channels. Mixed in among them was the name Tony Tsui.

Finally, *Der Spiegel* did a follow-up piece identifying the laptop removed from the scene as being suspected of containing sensitive German military secrets. Because the laptop was protected by an extremely sophisticated encryption system, it was very likely the government would seek outside specialists to help crack it.

Other international media outlets were already picking up on the story and running with it. Tony Tsui was as good as dead. That was the easy part.

Reed Carlton was a master spy who had spent a lifetime in the espionage and counter-terrorism arenas building a network of friends, contacts, and people who owed him favors, but there wasn't anything he could do to satisfy Adda Sterk's second and final request before she would cooperate.

Looking at Nicholas, she said, 'I want his dogs.'

Before Harvath could even respond, Nicholas had told the woman to go perform an impossible sex act upon herself and had lunged once more for the wrench.

'Why do you need the dogs?' Harvath had demanded.

'Collateral. As long as I have them somewhere where he can't get to them, I know he won't allow anything to happen to me.'

'At this point,' cautioned Harvath, 'you've got

a lot more to worry about from me than you do from him.'

The woman looked at him. 'If I have the dogs, it's in his best interest to make sure I'm safe from everyone, including you. When I'm someplace safe, I'll make sure the dogs are returned. Take it or leave it.'

It was a discussion Harvath hadn't wanted to have in front of Sterk so he had called Peio in to keep an eye on her while he walked Nicholas outside to talk to him.

It wasn't surprising that a dwarf would hit below the belt and Nicholas took the low road right from the minute they exited the warehouse. He said that because Harvath didn't have children, he would never understand what it was that Sterk was asking. Nicholas not only ranted at him, he threatened to have Harvath killed if he caved to her demands. As far as he was concerned, they were going to have to go back inside and start torturing her again because there was no way he was going to hand over his dogs to her. They would not be used as an insurance policy. End of discussion.

The man's love for his dogs was one of the things Harvath had long respected about him. He could have berated him for beating Sterk so badly with the wrench. He could have blamed him and told him that's what he got for taking out his anger on her in such a way, but he didn't. He had done the same and worse in his life. Sterk had tried to have Nicholas killed and Harvath would have expected anyone in that situation to want revenge.

'We're not going to give her your dogs,' he said.

'Then what are we out here discussing?'

As Harvath explained his plan, a smile crept across the little man's face. When they stepped back inside, Harvath watched as Nicholas said a convincing good-bye to his dogs and then turned to face Sterk.

'If anything happens to my animals,' he said, 'I will make sure you die a death even you couldn't imagine. Am I clear?'

Sterk grinned and Nicholas raised his hand to strike her, but Harvath stopped him. 'Enough.'

* * *

The doctor arrived an hour later. She rang Harvath's cell phone to tell him she was there.

He stepped outside the warehouse to find a very fit, very attractive woman in her early thirties. She was leaning against a van identical to the one that was parked inside. Her reddish-brown hair was pulled back in a ponytail. She had blue eyes, full lips, and a wide mouth.

'I'm Scot,' he said offering her his hand. When she took it, he felt a bolt of lightning pass between them.

'Riley,' she replied, breaking off the handshake when she realized it had gone on a few seconds too long. 'I'm sorry it took me so long. That was quite a to-do list I was handed.'

'How'd it go?'

'You can see for yourself,' she replied, stepping

away from the door.

Harvath slid it open and looked inside. There were two large crates with two large, white dogs inside. Stacked next to them were boxes filled with Adda Sterk's personal belongings from her home and office as well as two laptops, three desktop computers, and stacks of portable drives. 'That's what I call a house call. You work fast. I'm impressed.'

'That's why they pay me the big bucks.'

He stepped back and closed the door. 'The Old Man said you do security too?'

'That's also why they pay me the big bucks.'

Harvath was definitely intrigued, but he didn't have time to ask the questions that were going through his mind. 'We'll bring your patients out shortly.'

'I'll be standing by.'

Harvath fought the urge to look back over his shoulder at her as he walked back into the warehouse. Though he couldn't be completely sure, he was fairly confident that she was watching him.

Back inside the warehouse, he made a beeline for Adda Sterk.

'I'm thirsty,' she said.

'Too bad. I'll give you one more chance to leave the dogs out of this.'

'No. No dogs, no deal.'

'Fine,' he said as Nicholas handed him his laptop.

Based on Sterk's instructions, they logged on to a Swiss discussion forum under her account. Harvath looked up the user name she had given him and typed a quick message. Five minutes later he received a response.

When the instructions were complete, Nicholas loaded the dogs into the back of his van and watched as Peio drove them out of the building.

He returned twenty minutes later. Harvath had him help Riley load Michael Lee into her van and then he stood guard outside.

When Harvath checked the forum, there was a message waiting. The handoff had taken place and the dogs were being taken to 'the country.'

He had no idea who the person in the discussion forum was. It could have been Sterk's boyfriend, a student who owed her a favor, or a neighbor. He didn't care. All he wanted was the information he needed to stop any more bombings and nail the people responsible.

Though the handoff had moved faster than he had anticipated, they had wasted a lot of valuable time.

He showed Sterk the confirmation message and said, 'I've done everything you asked; now it's time to live up to your end. I want to know who is behind the bombings and how I stop them.'

'I'm still thirsty,' she replied.

'As far as anyone is concerned, Tsui's dead. You've also got the dogs. I'm not giving you anything else until you begin cooperating with me.'

'Fine. Although without water, I'm probably going to have some trouble speaking.'

Harvath was done getting jerked around.

Turning to Nicholas, he said, 'Go heat the cigarette lighter back up.'

As the Troll walked toward the van, Sterk looked up at Harvath. 'That won't be necessary. I'll give you what you want.'

39

'I never met the people who hired me,' Sterk said as the Troll returned with the cigarette lighter.

'But you know who they are,' replied Harvath.

'That's just it. I don't know. All of our transactions were via digital dead drops and wire transfers.'

'So why are you so afraid of them?'

'Because I have seen what they can do.'

'What? The Rome attacks? The Paris attacks?' Sterk shook her head.

'The hell with this,' interjected the Troll. 'I want to know why you were trying to have me killed.'

Harvath motioned for him to be quiet.

'This bitch tried to murder me. I'm not going to be quiet. I want answers.'

'We all want answers,' he said firmly as he turned his attention back to her.

'It's all connected,' she replied.

'Why was I targeted?' Nicholas demanded.

Sterk looked at him. 'There was a certain piece of business we did together. The people who hired me wanted any and all traces of it to be wiped away.'

'And that meant wiping me away as well.'

'Yes.'

'I imagine that it also helped to provide the authorities with a false trail to follow.'

Sterk nodded. 'That's why I had the dogs and

the dwarf flown to Sicily.'

'So you knew about the bombings in advance,' said Harvath.

It took her a moment to respond. Finally, she said, 'Yes, I did.'

He shook his head. 'How do you charge for something like that? Is it a flat fee? Or is it on a sliding scale based on how many are killed versus maimed and wounded?'

It was a rhetorical question. She didn't bother answering.

'This is about the last piece of business we did together, isn't it?' said Nicholas. 'I sold you the location of site 243.'

The woman nodded. 'I was hired to help steal what they were working on.'

'I was actually surprised when you contacted me about buying the coordinates. The level of secrecy surrounding it was amazing. I was only able to get its location; and even that took some doing.'

'What is it?' asked Harvath.

'The more appropriate question would be, what *was* it,' stated Sterk. 'Two weeks ago, site 243 was destroyed.'

'By whom?'

'By my clients. They were able to launch an attack inside China on a Chinese military base and not only kill everyone on the base, but they then tracked down the remaining Chinese intelligence officers who had any knowledge of what was being worked on at site 243 and they killed them as well.'

'This was a Chinese operation?'

The woman nodded. 'You wanted to know why I fear my clients. That's why. Who mounts an attack on a Chinese military base, slaughters everyone on it, and then hunts down high-ranking Chinese intelligence agents inside and outside of China? Who has the skills and the resources to do something like that?'

'I still don't understand what this has to do with the attacks in Rome and Paris.'

Sterk took a deep breath. 'The Chinese know that they can't defeat America on a conventional battlefield. They've known that for a long time. To win a war against America, the Chinese would have to engage in unconventional warfare.

'They created a military base in the middle of nowhere in Mongolia with the sole purpose of studying America. Its operatives spoke only English, ate only American foods, read American books, watched American television programs, played American video games, and surfed nothing but American and Western Web sites. It was as close as you could be to the United States while still remaining under China's umbrella.

'They were steeped in American culture and the American way of thinking. Their job was to study America, find its weaknesses, and develop the most devastating attack they could conceive of. They were encouraged to think outside of the normal military mind-set.'

'And suicide bombers were the best they could come up with?' asked Harvath.

'Look at the impact of 9/11,' replied Sterk. 'Look at what it did to America's psyche and its economy. How many billions were lost? How many billions more were spent preventing another similar attack? Massive governmental agencies like your Department of Homeland Security and the TSA were created as a response. Now multiply that impact across the United States in all new waves of attacks. Pick whatever targets you want: movie theaters, shopping malls, churches, hotels, schools. Your country would grind to a halt, its people paralyzed with fear.'

'But the attacks aren't happening in America, they are happening in Europe.'

'Not yet.'

'What do you mean, *not yet?*' replied Harvath.

'Through site 243 the Chinese had created an entire terrorist network. My clients have not only hijacked it, they have activated it.'

'And they are planning on targeting American cities?'

'Yes.'

'How do you know so much?'

'It's my job. I deal in information. Information is power.'

'And she probably spies on and steals from her own clients,' added Nicholas.

'The bigger the picture I have,' she replied, 'the better I am able to connect the dots. When I know what pieces I'm missing, I go after them and secure them. My customers don't come to me to purchase incomplete intelligence.'

'So in other words, you snuck a peek at what your clients were paying you for.'

'I didn't get to see all of it.'

'But you got to see some of it.'

Sterk nodded.

Harvath was trying to make sense of it all. 'Why would they bother targeting Americans in Europe? Why not move right to attacks on American soil?'

'I don't profess to understand the mind of the Chinese,' Sterk said with a shrug.

'Try.'

She thought about it for a moment. 'The easiest answer is that Muslim attacks in Western Europe erode support for the wars in Iraq and Afghanistan. The less support America has from its allies, the deeper it will get drawn into those conflicts. Its military is stretched too thin. Stretch it even further, maybe open up another war somewhere, and all that stretching could lead to a snap.'

It was a good point and one that Harvath and others had grown increasingly concerned about. With the Madrid train bombings, Islamic terrorists had proven that they could influence Western elections and help catapult politicians to power who would withdraw support for American military actions. Why wouldn't the Chinese have picked up and expanded upon this as well? It was an exceptional tactic.

The other thing that troubled Harvath was the knowledge that with each attack in Europe, the United States would be focusing more and more of its limited resources abroad. That invariably meant less attention to what was going on at home. Sooner or later, America wouldn't have enough eyes on the ball in its own backyard, and that's when its enemies would strike.

'What U.S. cities have been targeted?'

'I don't know.'

'Bullshit,' spat the Troll.

'I'm telling you the truth,' Sterk insisted. 'They're playing the American attacks close to the vest.'

'How about *when?*' asked Harvath.

'After the bombings in Europe have all been carried out.'

'How many are left?'

Sterk was silent.

Harvath grabbed her throat and clamped down. 'How many?'

'Two,' she finally coughed. 'Please. I can't breathe.'

'Where?'

'Please, I can't — '

Harvath squeezed harder. 'Where?'

'London and Amsterdam.'

'Where in London and Amsterdam?'

'Piccadilly and the Dam Square.'

'When?'

'Tomorrow night. Now, please. My throat — '

Harvath dug his fingers in. 'How do we stop them?'

'You can't. They're fully operational. The cells have gone dark.'

'The Brits need to shut down Piccadilly and the Dutch need to shut down Dam Square,' said the Troll.

Sterk could no longer speak. She shook her head.

Harvath relaxed his grasp.

'It won't work,' the woman said as she gasped for air.

'Why not?'

'Both cells have alternate targets. No one but them knows what they are. If you shut down Piccadilly and the Dam Square, they'll just move to the second location on their list.'

There was more that Harvath wanted to know, but Carlton needed this information right away. He stepped to the other side of the warehouse and pulled out his phone.

40

Vaughan and Davidson both had their hands tied behind their backs and their ankles bound to the legs of the chairs they were sitting on.

They were in a dank room somewhere in the basement. Their pockets had been turned inside out and all of their belongings were now laid out on a table.

One of the men from the alley did all of the talking. 'You are police?' he said.

'You're damn right we are,' stated Davidson, 'and you're in a lot of fucking trouble, my friend.'

The man walked over to Davidson and punched him so hard in the face, his chair rocked onto its rear legs and almost fell over.

He then looked at Vaughan. 'Tell me what you are doing here.'

The pain of having his wrist broken was nothing compared to his conviction that these men were up to something very bad and had nothing to lose. He felt certain they wouldn't think twice about killing them. 'You have taken two Chicago police officers hostage,' he said. 'This entire building is going to be crawling with police very soon.'

The man drew back his fist and hit Vaughan even harder than he had hit Davidson. The Marine was knocked so far backward that his chair fell over and even having his arms tied behind his back couldn't stop his head from cracking against the cement floor.

Immediately, two of the other men stepped forward, picked his chair back up, and returned to where they had been standing.

The man bent down and looked into Vaughan's eyes. He was so close the Marine could smell his foul breath. 'Back in my country, I spent ten years as an interrogator in one of the worst prisons you could ever imagine. My colleagues and I laughed at your Abu Ghraib scandal. I know what real torture is and I will show you unless you answer my questions.'

'We're the Chicago police, asshole. We're not answering shit,' stated Davidson.

The man turned his attention to the Public Vehicles officer and smiled. He then gave a command to one of the other men, who opened the door and exited the room. Vaughan's Arabic was not the best. It sounded like he had sent the man for water.

The interrogator then focused on Vaughan. 'I will ask you again. What are you doing here?'

Davidson, his face swelling, said, 'We were looking for your sister.'

The man was about to strike the cop again, but caught himself when Vaughan admonished Davidson. 'Cut it out. That's not going to help.'

'It won't. You are right,' said the interrogator.

'What will help you is if you tell me why you are here.'

'We have your mosque under surveillance,' replied the Marine. His jaw, his head, and his wrist were all throbbing.

'Who is *we?*'

'The Chicago Police Department.'

The man lined up his captives' credentials and studied them. 'And while you are on police business, you carry other business cards and badges as well?'

Davidson didn't know when to shut up. 'Tell him to fuck off.'

'Listen,' Vaughan continued, blood running from his mouth. 'You may think you know how this works, but you don't. The police will not negotiate for our release.'

'I don't expect them to.'

'What do you want then? I already told you that your mosque is under surveillance.'

'But you haven't told me who is monitoring it.'

'I have. The Chicago Police Department.'

The interrogator smiled. 'You're lying.'

Vaughan knew that if he told the man the truth, if he told him nobody else except for Josh Levy even knew they were here, they were as good as dead. Their only hope was that Levy would realize something had gone wrong and that he would bring reinforcements.

Vaughan was trying to come up with a response when the door opened and the man who had left a few moments ago returned. He was carrying a case of large water bottles with two towels laid across the top.

'I'll pass on the sponge bath,' shot Davidson, 'but there's a couple of you who should definitely consider it. Maybe some back waxes too.'

The interrogator picked his foot up and kicked Davidson over backward. The sound of his head cracking against the floor could be heard across the room.

Calling two of the men over, the interrogator had them tilt Vaughan back. Another man grabbed a towel, and though the police officer resisted, managed to wrap it around his face and pull it tight at the back of his head.

The interrogator opened half of the bottles and sent the man to go get more. Picking up two of them, he walked over and stood looking down at the Marine. 'We have much more water and I have all night. Let's see if we can decide once and for all whether or not this is torture.'

41

Rashid had seen enough. He opened the door and stepped back out into the hallway.

Marwan Jarrah was waiting for him and could read the younger man's face. He signaled for him to hold his tongue until they got upstairs.

The two men proceeded in silence to the mosque's office, the faithful having long dispersed since the end of evening prayers. Once they were inside and the door was closed, Rashid wasted no time getting to the point. 'We're in big trouble.'

'Everything will be fine, Shahab,' replied Jarrah.

'No, it won't. Do you have any idea how serious this is? You have two Chicago policemen as prisoners in your mosque.'

'A police officer does not carry a private investigator's badge when he is on duty as a policeman. Nor does another carry business cards identifying him as an attorney and a little notebook with the information about his case.'

'It doesn't matter what they were carrying, Marwan, they're still *cops*.'

'I understand the situation,' said Jarrah. 'I also understand that they were carrying a picture of Mohammed Nasiri and that it wasn't my idea to bring Nasiri here. It was yours.'

'We had no choice.'

'We should have killed him.'

'Please, Marwan. We've been through this. We need Nasiri.'

'So what do we do now?'

'You mean now that your thugs have tortured those two cops?'

'It's not the time for recriminations,' replied Jarrah.

'I told you that those guns were supposed to stay in the mosque until we were ready to use them.'

'Shahab, what is done is done. We need to plan.'

'You want to make a plan?' said Rashid. 'Here's *my* plan. We pack everything up, send everyone home, and put this entire operation in a box and bury it for at least two years; maybe longer.'

The man shook his head. 'We can't do that.'

'You don't have a choice.'

'There are always choices.'

'Marwan, your thugs *tortured* two cops. Do you understand that? Maybe we could have made up a mistaken-identity story about how we thought they were breaking into the mosque when we found them, but not now.'

'Then we need to kill them.'

Rashid shook his head. 'We could, but that might not be the right move; not yet.'

Jarrah looked at him. 'Then what would you like to do?'

The younger man thought about it for a moment and then said, 'Obviously, the mosque is no longer safe. We'll need to move everything and we need to do it right away.'

'Move it where?'

'You know where.'

Jarrah now shook his head. 'No. Absolutely not. It is too dangerous.'

'You wanted choices. You can stay here, compromised, or you can move the operation. Just know that if you decide to stay, you'll be staying without me.'

'You would leave?'

'If you force me to, yes.'

'For the sake of argument,' Jarrah replied, 'let's say we move. What will we do with the policemen?'

'We'll move them too.'

'Why do you want to take that risk? It seems easier to just be done with them.'

'I know it seems that way,' said Rashid, 'but they could end up being worth more to us alive than dead.'

'No. They're a complication. We need to be rid of them.'

'Marwan, you agreed to let me run this cell and this part of the operation. I've done everything you've asked. Do you not trust my judgment?'

'Of course I trust your judgment. You are like a son to me.'

'How many times have I risked my life for you?'

'More than once, Shahab. More than once.'

'So?'

After a short period of reflection, the man finally relented. 'Okay, we'll move. I'm not happy about it, but I agree with you. We cannot stay here.'

Rashid remained quiet.

'And we will bring the police officers,' he added.

'It's the right choice.'

Jarrah shrugged.

Rashid removed his cell phone as he opened the office door. 'We'll need to start as soon as possible and do it in two trucks.'

They continued discussing their plans as they walked downstairs to the basement. The men who had captured the police officers were standing in the narrow hallway talking. One of them was smoking.

Seeing the men standing there, Rashid's anger resurfaced. In rapid-fire Arabic, he berated them for their mistakes. There was no excuse for it.

He was lecturing them on how stupid they had been to carry their weapons outside the mosque when the door to the alley burst open.

The men were caught completely off guard. A bright flashlight clamped to the barrel of the intruder's weapon blinded the men as they pulled out their guns and attempted to shoot.

'Drop your weapons!' the intruder yelled.

None of the men complied.

As the first pistol was pointed in his direction, Levy pulled the trigger of his Remington 870 shotgun and hit the two men closest to him.

Racking the slide, he prepared to fire again, but before he could pull the trigger, two shots rang out and he was knocked backward into the alley.

Smoke was still rising from the barrel of his pistol as Abdul Rashid pushed past the men and rushed to the door.

He kicked the intruder's shotgun away. Pointing his weapon at the man's head, he said, 'Don't even think of moving.'

With pain spreading through his body and blood soaking through his clothes, Josh Levy did exactly as he was told.

42

Harvath flew out on the private jet Carlton had arranged for him, leaving things back in Geneva in the best state he could.

Nicholas remained in the warehouse while Peio helped Harvath transport Adda Sterk to the Carlton Group safe house. Riley was already there tending to Michael Lee, and she secured the woman in one of the bedrooms. The priest agreed to stay until the interrogation team Carlton had en route arrived. He had no desire to watch them wring whatever else could be wrung from the woman.

Harvath still wanted to have a discussion with the priest about what had happened at the chalet, but the opportunity never really presented itself. It was none of his business, and he figured he should probably drop it and leave the man to his own conscience.

He had fed everything he was able to download from Sterk, including her medical condition, back to Carlton in Virginia. Outside of the dates and locations, she seemed to know very little about the attacks themselves.

She believed the cells were composed of Muslim males, but was uncertain of their ethnicity. They would be using homemade bombs packed with marbles, ball bearings, nails, or screws to act as shrapnel to maximize their killing power.

Sterk also couldn't tell him if the men would be wearing suicide vests, if the bombs would be carried in backpacks, or if they would be packed in a car. She didn't know how many bombs there would be or how they were designed to go off. She couldn't say if the men would be hiding their explosives and leaving as had been done in Rome, or blowing themselves up as had been done in Paris. She also had no idea if there was one bomb intended for Piccadilly and one for Amsterdam's Dam Square, multiple bombs at both, or one bomb at the former and multiple bombs at the latter.

As much as he wanted to, Harvath couldn't be two places at once. With such sketchy information, the choice of which city to try to head off an attack in was a toss-up. It all came down to the numbers. He would go where the most American lives were at risk and it was the Old Man who made the call — London.

Carlton had excellent contacts in Great Britain; experienced people he could trust. He also had something else — a Delta unit training with the British SAS at a classified site in Wales. With one call from the Old Man to the DOD, the unit was packing its bags and heading for London.

When Harvath arrived, he was met by one of the deans of MI5, Robert Ashford. He was a barrel-chested man of medium height with steel-gray hair and a broad, flat nose. He looked very capable of handling trouble and also looked like he had probably dealt plenty of it out over the course of his career.

Ashford introduced himself and handed over his card. 'Bob Ashford. Welcome to England.' Looking at Harvath's bag, he added, 'I understand there's nothing special you need to declare, correct?'

As the capability kit at the safe house in Geneva wouldn't cover Riley and the interrogation team, the Old Man had instructed Harvath to leave his gear behind. 'Correct,' Harvath said, tapping his bag. 'I only brought my toothbrush and a change of underwear. I was told you know all the best places to shop.'

Ashford smiled, removed his credentials, and navigated Harvath through the passport control and customs checkpoints. Parked in a fire lane just outside was a black BMW. The MI5 man directed Harvath to the passenger seat and then walked around and got behind the wheel.

'Seatbelts, please,' he said as he shut the door and started the vehicle. 'Peaches would never forgive me if something happened to you.'

'*Peaches?*' repeated Harvath.

'A little joke amongst his friends. I assume you refer to him as Mr. Carlton or some such back in the States.'

'Either that or boss. Sometimes known simply as the Old Man.'

Ashford chuckled softly, applied his turn signal, and pulled away from the curb. 'We weren't always old, you know. We were once quite young. Younger than you even.'

Harvath didn't need a reminder of his age. He still had a swollen testicle and a couple of bruises that five years ago would have been gone by now.

'Reed's a good man and an even better operative,' Ashford added.

'Is that where the nickname Peaches comes from, or should I ask Mrs. Carlton about it?'

The MI5 agent smiled. 'Suffice it to say, the nickname was meant as an antithesis. Your boss was anything *but* sweet. No matter how unsavory a tactic the enemy employed, he could always one-up them. He never hesitated doing what needed to be done. And you should have seen him interrogate. My goodness, within minutes, even I was ready to tell him everything I knew, and *I* was on his side. In a word, he could be bloody ruthless, ergo the name — '

'Peaches.'

'Exactly,' replied Ashford as he changed lanes, cutting off a cab driver who honked in protest. 'He has always been a gentleman, though. Exceedingly polite, your boss.'

'He speaks very highly of you too,' said Harvath.

'He damn well should. Without me, he never would have been allowed back into the U.K. again.'

Harvath had heard rumors around the Carlton Group offices about the Old Man's past. 'He didn't really strike a member of Prince Charles' staff, did he?'

'He didn't *strike* him. He knocked him out bloody cold, mate.'

'All because the man had said something about Diana?'

'Reed was very fond of the princess. He had gotten to know the royal family quite well while working over here. They always insisted he be involved with their security when they came to the U.S. Whether that rankled the Secret Service or not, I don't know, but Reed always made sure the royal family had the very best agents. Some even said their security plans rivaled the president's.'

'He got called in for help after Diana's death, right? He was part of the secret team looking into whether the car crash was an accident or a homicide.'

Ashford nodded. 'When Reed arrived, everyone was very emotional. That's when a member of the prince's staff made a crude remark about Diana and Reed punched him out. I stuck up for Peaches, of course.'

'Which means you pulled your gun when Charles's security detail rushed him?'

'There are many conflicting stories as to what happened that night,' said Ashford as he switched lanes and cut off another vehicle. 'Let's put it this way, I understand why all my peers have been knighted and I haven't. But in the end, as long as I'm still recognized in the pub when I go back to Yorkshire, that's all that matters to me.'

Harvath smiled. 'Bullshit. I haven't met a Brit yet who doesn't dream of being knighted.'

The MI5 man smiled back and changed the subject. 'Reed's phone call has caused quite a bit of a stir.'

'I can imagine,' said Harvath.

'Obviously, we want to extend to you every professional courtesy, but we are taking the lead on this.'

'Based upon the intelligence we gathered for you and which specifically states that Americans are the target?'

Ashford downshifted and switched lanes. 'The targets may be American, but the attack is planned for Britain and British lives, as well as other nationalities, are also at risk. Besides, if the shoe was on the other foot, would you be giving us control over Times Square?'

The man had a point. 'No, we wouldn't.'

'Of course you wouldn't. Nobody wants an attack to take place in their own country.'

'As long as we work together.'

'We already are. Against our better judgment, we are not raising the terror-alert level and we are not going to close down Piccadilly Circus. You and your team will be able to work the area, but our teams will be there too.'

Harvath was about to reply, when he added, 'And before you say anything, I want you to know that you have nothing to worry about. You won't see my people.'

'Yes, I will.'

Ashford laughed. 'Okay, maybe *you* will see them, but I guarantee you the bad guys won't.'

Harvath loved the Brits. They were some of the most squared-away operators he had ever met, but he wasn't comforted by Ashford's assurance.

'And there's one final item which is not open for negotiation,' the man added. 'Any suspects taken into custody here shall belong to us and will be interrogated by us. It's the only way I could get this signed off. Is that clear?'

'Crystal,' Harvath replied. 'Interrogations make me squeamish anyway.'

Ashford looked at him. 'Somehow I doubt that.'

For the balance of the drive, the men made small talk and discussed politics.

Ashford soon brought his BMW to a stop in front of an immaculate Georgian town house in Belgravia, just southwest of Buckingham Palace.

'There's a package for you in the boot,' he said, activating the trunk-release as Harvath climbed out.

Harvath walked to the rear of the BMW, and inside was a large, hard-sided suitcase. Lifting it out, he walked back around to the front of the vehicle.

Ashford rolled down his window. 'Peaches has pinned a lot of his hopes on you. He says you have good judgment and that we can trust you.'

'You can,' replied Harvath.

'Good, because we've put a lot at risk. There are many people we've kept out of the loop for security reasons. When this goes down, they're not going to be happy that they weren't included.'

'They'll get over it.'

'Provided everything goes to plan. But, if a

bomb or bombs are detonated tomorrow and there are casualties, there will be hell to pay.'

Harvath had no trouble grasping who Ashford and the Brits intended to stick with the bill if something went wrong. 'We want to take as many of them alive as possible.'

'Let's hope we get them all,' said Ashford, putting his car in gear. He looked at his watch. 'We'll meet tomorrow morning at six. I'll pick you up here. If I hear of anything before then, I'll call you.'

Harvath thanked him and stepped back from the curb as the MI5 man pulled away. Opening the townhome's wrought-iron gate, he walked up the stairs to the front door. He punched the code Reed had given him into the keypad and stepped inside.

There was a cavernous silence. It was immediate, as if a television had just been shut off, but the echoes of a program still lingered in the air.

Harvath was suddenly aware that he wasn't alone. He set the case down and stepped into the living room.

For a moment, he thought that he had entered the wrong house. Then he saw the weapons, one of which had been picked up and was now pointing right at his chest.

43

The woman pointing the MP5 at Harvath turned to one of her colleagues and commented, 'I thought somebody said this guy was hot.'

The other five women in the room laughed.

'He's a lot better than that guy we had to work with in Dubai,' replied another. 'Remember him? What was his name?'

'Aswad.'

Most of the women groaned.

The woman holding the MP5 looked Harvath up and down. 'He's definitely better looking than *ass wad,* but is he into goats? That's the question.'

The women laughed again.

'There are a lot of things I'm okay walking in on a man doing,' the woman continued, 'but the goat thing isn't one of them.'

'I'm sorry,' said Harvath through the laughter. 'I must be in the wrong place. I'm looking for the Emily Dickinson reading?'

'He's also a smartass,' said the woman as she lowered her MP5. 'Just my type.'

So this was what an Athena Team looked like, Harvath thought to himself. He had heard the stories about Delta haunting high-end women's sporting events, recruiting the best female athletes to turn into operators, but he had never worked with any of them.

They were considered just as lethal as their

male counterparts and often posed as wives in husband/wife teams with male Delta operators, especially in countries or situations where sending in two or more men would raise too much suspicion. The ruse worked particularly well when posing as missionaries or NGO workers.

The women were also deployed as they were now, in all-female teams, normally composed of four to six members.

Harvath had every confidence in their abilities. He also liked the fact that they'd be harder for the bad guys to key in on.

In their mid twenties to early thirties, the women were all extremely fit. They were also very attractive and represented a cross section of backgrounds.

Harvath was trying to figure out who was in charge when one of the women stepped forward and introduced herself, 'I'm Gretchen Casey.'

She had brown hair pulled back and a slight southern drawl. It sounded as if she might have been from Texas.

'Nice to meet you,' Harvath said as he walked over and shook her hand.

After explaining that their sixth teammate had been injured in training in Wales and had been forced to remain behind, Casey went around the room and introduced the rest of the team. 'So from left to right, we have Julie Ericsson, Megan Rhodes, Alex Cooper, and on MP5, Nikki Rodriguez.'

Ericsson had jet black hair and looked like a Brazilian volleyball player. Rhodes was the tallest of the bunch, had blue eyes, and was the only blonde. Cooper had fine Ethiopian features with a light-brown complexion and brown eyes. Rodriguez was the shortest of the group, but despite her tough exterior was easily the best-looking, with dark hair and even darker eyes.

'Nice to meet you all.'

'We're not going to have any goat trouble with you, are we?' asked Rodriguez with a smile.

'Give the guy a break, Nik,' said Rhodes as she stood up and offered her hand to Harvath. 'It's bad enough he has to be surrounded by women who can shoot better than he can.'

'All right already,' said Casey. 'He may just be a Navy man, but I think he gets it.' She gestured to the women and then looked at Harvath. 'Tough ladies, get it?'

'Got it.'

'Good.'

'Are you hungry?' she asked.

'What do you have in mind?'

'We need to recon Piccadilly, but we can't all walk through en masse.'

'True.'

'I want to do it in teams; separated out over the next few hours. You and I will get a bite to eat and then when it's our turn we'll go in. When everyone's done, we'll meet back here to debrief. Sound good?'

'Sounds good,' Harvath replied. Smiling at the Athena Team as he headed for the hallway, he added, 'There's one more thing.'

'What is it?' asked Casey.

'Make sure I get the bedroom with the lock on it.'

The women snorted and rolled their eyes.

'Got your lock right here,' said Cooper, as she flipped Harvath the finger.

Ericsson made a lewd gesture while Rhodes blew him a kiss, and Rodriguez started stripping the MP5.

★ ★ ★

Harvath and Casey went over details as they ate at a small Thai restaurant off Regent Street. When they were finished, they walked to Piccadilly Circus to begin gathering intelligence. The area was packed with Britons and tourists alike. People took pictures of the blazing neon signs and of each other standing in front of the Shaftesbury memorial fountain.

Most of them appeared not to have a care in the world. Undoubtedly they were aware of the attacks in Paris and Rome, but if they were concerned, they didn't show it. Those who were out and about were all smiles and laughter.

Harvath reflected on what his friend Colonel Dave Grossman liked to say, 'Sheep only have two speeds — graze and stampede.' As a sheepdog, Harvath wanted to guarantee that nothing would happen to them. The sheer size of the traffic circle, or *circus* as it was known in Roman times, made him question whether they were doing the right thing. Even if they flooded the area with operatives, there was no way they could check every face; follow every suspicious person. It was an overwhelming task.

Casey had brought along a digital video camera. She used it to blend in with the other tourists and film as much of the area as possible. As she did, Harvath tried to put himself in the mind-set of the bombers.

Rome had been a single bombing, but Paris had been a quantum leap forward with multiple bombings in multiple locations. Each event was created to have maximum impact, but also to be different from the last. From a tour bus bombing to multiple bombings in one city, to simultaneous bombings in two cities, the terrorists wanted to keep shaking people up. They wanted to keep citizens and law enforcement off balance while continuing to create spectacular attacks.

Taking in everything as they walked, he asked himself how he would pull this off if he was them. Would he detonate in the Tube station and then have a secondary device waiting for all of the survivors who then flooded out on the street? How about placing a lone device or suicide bomber near the fountain with secondary bombers on every street leading away from the circus?

He tried to think of everything. He studied the fixed railings all along the sidewalks that funneled pedestrian traffic and only allowed crossing at recognized crosswalks. He studied what buildings people might run into for safety. He watched how traffic moved into, around, and out of the circle. He forced himself to examine every detail and by the time they left, he was exhausted.

Back at the Belgravia house, he and Casey compared notes. They discussed where the most efficient kill zones would be. They explored what a single bomb would do versus multiple bombs. Based on the devices used in Paris, they queried each other on where similar devices in London might be placed. Then they discussed the topic Harvath was most concerned with. What if it wasn't bombs in backpacks or suicide vests they were planning to detonate?

What if they were going back to a vehicle-bomb model as had been used in Rome? What if there was more than one? What if they all converged in Piccadilly at the same moment and detonated en masse? Buildings would be leveled, and the carnage would be off the charts. The only scenario Harvath feared more than that was actually being there when it happened.

Bob Ashford had been right to bring his people on board. There were too many what-ifs here and it was far too large an operation for Harvath and Casey to get their arms around by themselves.

When the rest of the Athena operatives had gathered at the house, they designated the dining room as a makeshift ops center. Sitting around the table, each team reported their findings and delivered an assessment.

Everyone was in agreement that screening and managing traffic in and out of Piccadilly Circus was far outside their ability. That task was going to have to fall to the Brits. But if the bombers came in on foot, as they had in Paris, then that would be a different story.

The largest gathering place for tourists was around the Shaftesbury fountain. That's where most people stood to take in the neon signs and it was also where the Tube stop was. This was where bombers leaving backpack bombs or detonating suicide vests would get the biggest bang for their buck.

It was also the most obvious, and that's what bothered Harvath. While it made the most sense to strike near the fountain, the terrorists weren't stupid. With the Paris bombing, security had already been stepped up at tourist sites across Europe, and London was no different. He and Casey had seen plenty of uniformed officers as they did their reconnaissance of Piccadilly and they had noted several plainclothes officers as well.

And they weren't limited solely to Piccadilly Circus either. They had picked up concentric rings of security the moment they had left the restaurant and had begun walking down Regent Street. The closer they got to Piccadilly, the more intense the police presence became. The terrorists would be doing dry runs as well and would have to know this.

So what were they planning? How did they intend to subvert the police and get close enough to strike? Harvath had reached out to Reed Carlton twice, hoping for news that Adda Sterk had revealed more information about the bombings to the interrogation team, without any luck. He'd inquired as to whether or not the Dutch authorities had had any success on the Amsterdam attack and whether or not the interrogators had come up with more information on who had hired Sterk, but so far everything seemed to be a bust.

With cameras everywhere, they knew the Brits would be scanning every face coming and going from Piccadilly. They also knew, though, that the cameras wouldn't prevent a determined terrorist attack. Whereas pickpockets and purse snatchers might be concerned with the police hunting them down after they had committed their crime, martyrs didn't really have that problem.

If the bomb or bombs were going to be vehicle-borne, Rhodes brought up a very good point. According to Sterk, the London and Amsterdam attacks were supposed to be simultaneous. That meant that a vehicle, or vehicles, would have to arrive at Piccadilly at a precise time. This would mean that the terrorists would have to commit drivers. They couldn't simply plant a bomb as they had done in Rome and hope that the vehicle they had planted it in arrived at Piccadilly on time and didn't get held up or change course.

It was an excellent point. Harvath made a note to bring it up with Ashford. They needed to make sure that any regularly scheduled traffic that passed through Piccadilly, such as public buses or guided tours with set routes and pickup/drop-off times, were monitored.

If the terrorists did try to drive in, then hopefully, London police would be able to identify and neutralize them before they reached

Piccadilly, and before they could detonate their explosives.

Harvath didn't like having to hope for successful outcomes. He liked to tilt the playing field so far to his advantage that his opponent didn't have a chance. This was a different game entirely.

He was still very concerned with how little they had to go on. The odds were much more in favor of the terrorists. Maybe keeping the alert level low was a mistake. Maybe people did have a right to know.

With his cognitive abilities nearing zero and his head still filled with doubts, Harvath walked upstairs to grab a few hours of sleep before Ashford came to pick him up.

He thought about calling Reed again but realized the Old Man would call him when he had something to report.

Climbing into bed, Harvath forced his mind to relax and he fell into a deep, dreamless, black sleep.

Three hours later, a buzzing near his ear dragged him back. He was more tired than when he had first turned in and it felt like he had been asleep for only a few minutes. He brushed at his ear and reached for his watch to see what time it was. That's when he saw the light on his phone blinking as it vibrated on the nightstand.

Picking it up, he flipped it open. 'Yeah?'

'It's Ashford. Scotland Yard just got a tip. They're moving on the target within the hour.'

Harvath swung his feet out of bed and sat up. 'What target? What tip?'

'A car will be there in ten minutes. I'll explain when you get here.'

With that, the MI5 man disconnected the call and the line went dead.

44

TUESDAY

By the time Harvath stepped outside, his ride was already waiting for him. It was an older, navy blue van with the words *David's 24 Hour Plumbers, Home of the Royal Flush* painted along the side. The driver looked like a heavily tattooed thug, barely into his twenties.

When he spotted Harvath, he stepped out of the vehicle and opened the sliding door. 'You'll have to ride back here.'

Harvath climbed inside and tried to get comfortable. It was still dark outside and the morning rush was several hours off.

The van headed east. The driver didn't speak. A half hour later, it pulled into the garage of a plumbing supply warehouse in East London.

When Harvath's door was opened, Bob Ashford was waiting for him.

'Sorry for the subterfuge,' he said. 'Unfortunately, in this neighborhood Anglo-Saxons stick out like sore thumbs.'

'I've ridden in worse conditions. Don't worry about it. What have you got?'

Ashford led Harvath to a small office with a coffeemaker and a scarred conference table. The walls were lined with shelves stocked with plumbing parts. In the corner was a television set. The MI5 man switched it on while Harvath helped himself to some coffee.

A thin Pakistani man sat at a small desk. There were what appeared to be two plainclothes detectives in the room with him. One was sitting while the other stood leaning against the wall.

'That's a feed from the room down the hall,' said Ashford as he followed Harvath and poured a cup of coffee for himself. 'The man you see there is named Saud Wadi. The men with him are Metropolitan anti-terror police.

'Mr. Wadi is one of their informants. Last night, he learned of a terror cell planning to carry out an attack in the very near future.'

'How do you know it's the cell we're looking for?'

'Because his youngest brother, Rafiq, is a member.'

Harvath turned and looked back at the image on the TV as Ashford continued. 'Apparently, Rafiq has already made his martyrdom video, but he got cold feet. He reached out to his big brother to help him figure a way out. But before Saud could do anything, Rafiq disappeared.'

'And Rafiq told him everything?'

'Unfortunately, no. All he said was that it was a martyrdom operation geared for central London.'

'Did he mention Piccadilly?'

'Yes.'

Harvath couldn't believe it. 'Do we have any idea where Rafiq may be?'

'We think the cell is operating out of a mosque

313

four blocks from here. The police are assembling their tactical teams now.'

'Did he mention what kind of attack they had planned or what their secondary target was?'

Ashford shook his head. 'No.'

'How well do you trust this source?'

'I don't know him. He's run by the Yard. They say he has always produced good intelligence for them in the past. But it's never been on this kind of scale before.'

'How long have you been watching the interrogation?'

'Since they brought him in. I think he's genuinely worried about his brother.'

Harvath was running the options through his mind. 'If Rafiq got cold feet, they may have killed him already.'

'Or they may have wooed him back. An already-recorded martyrdom video can be a very successful tool for cultural blackmail. They also may have threatened his family. We don't know and frankly, I don't care. I just want to stop this attack.'

'So do I.'

'Good, because as soon as we have our ducks in a row, we'll launch the teams.'

Harvath pulled out a chair and sat down at the table. He watched the two cops continue their interrogation. 'Do we know if their attacks were going to use explosives?'

'That's been confirmed, but it appears to be the limit of what Saud was able to glean from his brother.'

'When you say operating out of the mosque,

what do you mean?'

'We think they're headquartered there,' said Ashford.

'Do you think they're building the bombs there too?'

'It's possible. These people are smart. They know we'll raid a mosque, but only as a last resort and only if we really have to. The PR fallout in their community is terrible. The PC moonbats everywhere else also go crazy.'

'Makes you wonder whose side they are all really on.'

'I know,' said Ashford. 'What's more, from a strategic standpoint, if the bombers have a willing imam, they're probably better protected in a mosque than in a house or an apartment.'

'And if that is what's happening, you know the imam will claim he knew nothing about it.'

'Exactly.'

Harvath took a sip of his coffee. 'If today's the day the attack happens, they're going to be on edge.'

'They probably have been up all night praying and getting ready. Hopefully, they'll be sluggish when the entry teams hit the mosque.'

'What if they're not? What if they're prepared for the teams?'

'We have the element of surprise on our side,' the MI5 man replied. 'What's the motto Peaches was always so fond of? Speed, surprise, and violence of action?'

Harvath nodded. 'But what if they're buttoned down?'

'Meaning they have their fingers on the proverbial switch?'

'Exactly. What happens if your teams kick the doors in and they detonate their packages?'

'That's one of the reasons they call it a high-risk entry. These teams have gone after bombers before. They know what's at stake.'

'With all due respect, they don't know what's at stake,' said Harvath. 'This isn't just about Piccadilly; one cell and one attack. This is about an entire terrorist network. We need these guys alive.'

'What do you suggest then? Should we knock on the door and ask *Mother, may we come in?*'

Harvath brushed aside the man's sarcasm. 'What information do you have about the mosque?'

Ashford rolled his chair back and withdrew a file folder from his briefcase and slid it across.

It was a general briefing and contained only a couple of pages. Harvath skimmed it until he found what he was looking for. 'What if we could get operators inside?'

'That sort of thing takes time; a commodity we have precious little of right now.'

'It says in here that Scotland Yard has a confidential source unaffiliated with the Wadi family who attends this mosque.'

Ashford nodded. 'They've already dispatched a team to collect him. He's going to provide us with detail as to the layout.'

'What if he can also walk a small team of operators inside?'

'Even if I could get all my guys together who

316

fit the bill culturally, if Saud is correct about what is going on in that mosque, there's no way they would allow a bunch of strange men in. Not today.'

Harvath looked at him and replied, 'Who said anything about men?'

45

By the time Casey, Rhodes, Cooper, Ericsson, and Rodriguez arrived at the plumbing supply warehouse, two of the British tactical teams were already on site.

Harvath had informed them that the Athena Team would be coming in with most of their own gear, but as a courtesy, they had set up a table with an assortment of items they thought the women might need. Once again, Harvath was reminded of how professional the Brits were and how much he enjoyed working with them. They were truly one of America's best partners in the war on terror.

The ladies stepped out of another nondescript van, each carrying a duffel bag and a large black Storm case. The only explanation Ashford and the tac team leaders had been given was that the women were part of a highly trained, U.S. covert operations team. Neither Delta nor the Department of Defense was mentioned. Harvath introduced them to the women and after checking out the equipment table the group walked back to the small conference room.

In addition to coffee, bottled water and food had been brought in. The women helped themselves and then sat down and waited for the briefing to begin.

Moments later, a gray-haired woman in her early sixties strode in and took over the meeting.

'Good morning, ladies and gentlemen,' she said. 'My name is Rita Marx. I'm a detective with Scotland Yard's SO15, or for the benefit of our American friends in the room, the Counter-Terrorism Command.

'The mosques of East London in general and the Darul Uloom Mosque in particular fall under my jurisdiction. The man you will soon meet, Yusuf al-Fihri, has been a Scotland Yard asset for the last two years and has been attending the Darul Uloom for the last four.

'Mr. al-Fihri hasn't been told what will be taking place this morning, though I suspect he has a fairly good idea. Nevertheless, he has agreed to help get the team into the mosque. For that we owe him our thanks and the commitment to do everything we can to keep him safe. Is that clear?'

Casey and company nodded.

'Good,' said Marx, who nodded to a detective standing next to her. 'As we've never conducted formal surveillance on the Darul Uloom and as we don't have female tactical operatives, our information on it is rather incomplete. Jackets are being handed to you now with the pertinent information.

'Mr. al-Fihri will be accompanying you to morning prayers and presenting you as female relatives. Once you have secured entry to the mosque, you will go to the section reserved for women and children. This next point is very important, so please listen closely. Neither the Metropolitan Police, MI5, nor the British government will tolerate any casualties.'

Ashford cleared his throat to get the woman's attention. 'I believe we're willing to tolerate *certain* casualties.'

Marx grasped what he was implying. 'These bastards like to hide behind women and children,' she said with a smile. 'Let's make sure they don't get that chance.

'Now, before I bring in Mr. al-Fihri, I want to introduce you to Mr. Saud Wadi. He is also familiar with this mosque and will help give you a feel for its general layout. Mr. Wadi is our source that provided the mosque intelligence and he is also the gentleman whose brother was a member of this cell before he went missing. If Rafiq Wadi is inside the mosque and you are able to facilitate his release, we'd like you to help extricate him.'

Saud Wadi made his presentation, and pictures of his brother were handed out. He discussed what he knew of the plot and answered questions from the team. The ladies were then introduced to Yusuf al-Fihri, who would be taking them inside. He made sure the women were familiar with how to perform *Salaat*, the Islamic ritual prayer, and gave them tips on how to behave and where to go once they were inside the mosque.

The female operators then asked al-Fihri questions about the layout of the mosque, where certain rooms could be found, how many people would be there, and so forth. Once they were satisfied that they had obtained all of the information they could from him, Rita Marx thanked al-Fihri and had him taken to another

320

room to wait. It was time to talk about the assault itself.

Al-Fihri had insisted that he could take in only three of the women. Casey didn't like odd numbers and under pressure, al-Fihri had agreed to four. This way the women could break off into two, two-member fire teams. Deciding which of the women would go was another matter.

All of them wanted in and all of them were qualified for the assignment. They each understood Muslim culture, could converse in a handful of languages spoken throughout the Islamic world, and were incredibly well trained in close-quarters battle. In the end, the decision came down to appearance. Megan Rhodes was too tall and too fair. She would be the odd woman out.

That meant that Gretchen Casey, Julie Ericsson, Nikki Rodriguez, and Alex Cooper would be the ones to go in.

The tac team commanders discussed strategy with their American counterparts and a plan was settled upon. It was simple, but simple plans were often the best, especially when violently executed. The only way success could be better assured was to have the plan well rehearsed. With the clock ticking down to morning prayers, rehearsals were not something they had time to carry out.

Detective Marx left the conference room and came back with four shopping bags containing the Islamic garb the women would be wearing.

From an ops standpoint, Casey and her team loved burqas. They allowed them to mix in the

321

Muslim community without drawing undue attention to themselves and a lot of gear could be secreted beneath. The fact that they were employing one of the most preeminent symbols of Islamic oppression against women to get up close and stick it to the bad guys was an added piece of sweet irony.

Opening their Storm cases, the team selected the weapons and equipment they were going to use. One of the items was a device Harvath had heard about, but had yet to deploy with — the new semiautomatic, multishot Taser X3. The new ECD, or Electronic Control Device, provided the opportunity to deploy a second and third cartridge immediately and could even incapacitate three subjects simultaneously.

It was a sexy-looking piece of gear with a cool space-age design. It had dual laser sights, a thirty-five-foot range, and unlike the bright yellow device Taser was so well known for, this was as black as night. It also matched their burqas, an observation Harvath decided to keep to himself.

Casey and Rodriguez walked back into the garage and selected several pieces of equipment from the tac team table and then Marx got them outfitted with radios. Before anyone knew it, it was time to launch.

They gave their weapons and radios one last check before climbing into Yusuf al-Fihri's car.

As they pulled out of the garage and the vehicle disappeared down the street, Harvath had a bad feeling. But like his burqa observation, he kept it to himself.

When he climbed into one of the backup vans and took his place alongside Rhodes, he could tell by the look on her face that she was feeling exactly the same thing.

46

Gretchen Casey sat in front and studied Yusuf al-Fihri as they drove toward the mosque. She could tell he was nervous. 'Are you a smoker, Mr. al-Fihri?' she asked from beneath her burqa.

'Yes, miss,' he replied.

'Why don't you have a cigarette? It won't bother us.'

'I don't like to smoke before prayers.'

'It will help calm your nerves. I think it's a good idea.'

'Yes, miss,' said al-Fihri, who then fished out his cigarettes and lit one. He took a deep pull of smoke into his lungs and the soothing effect the nicotine had on him was instantly apparent.

'You're doing the right thing, Mr. al-Fihri. Remember that.'

'I know, miss.'

★ ★ ★

They found a parking space and then, as instructed, walked behind al-Fihri the rest of the way to the mosque. Casey reminded him to take his time. They wanted to get there as late as possible. They had no desire to stand around socializing before prayers.

Approaching the front doors, al-Fihri nodded and said hello to several men he knew, but kept moving. He accompanied the women to a side entrance where he spoke a few words to a burqa-clad woman who appeared to be a greeter of some sort. Per the plan, he then berated Casey for making him late, shoved her inside along with the other women, and hurried back to the main entrance, which was for men only.

The greeter further chastised the women, and after they had removed their shoes, rushed them up a narrow set of stairs.

On the second floor, she shooed them into a small bathroom and waited outside while they performed their ritual purification. As they conducted their faux ablutions, Casey radioed a quick update over the bone mic in her left ear.

When they reemerged, the doorkeeper hurried them into the packed women's prayer room and pointed to where she wanted them to stand in the back row. She then took up a spot right between them and the door.

The team was professional and maintained radio silence. Casey didn't need to hear anything; she knew exactly what they all were thinking. The doorkeeper had just gone from being a pain in the ass to an actual impediment that would have to be dealt with.

With their heads down, feet shoulder-width apart and their hands at their sides as they faced in the direction of Mecca, the ladies pretended to quietly utter their intentions to perform Salaat, the Islamic ritual prayer.

A voice crackled over the loudspeakers at the front of the room in Arabic and the Salaat began.

The Athena Team followed along, voicing the appropriate phrases and adopting the proper postures, until Casey signaled over the radio that she was going to take out the doorkeeper.

Rising from the floor, Casey wrapped her midsection and bent over as if she was in pain. She sat in that position until she could tell that she had gotten the doorkeeper's attention. Standing up slowly, she then moved toward the exit.

The doorkeeper met her halfway and tried to stop her from leaving.

'I'm going to be sick,' she mumbled in Arabic and then added in heavily accented English, 'Need toilet. Sick. Sick.'

The woman stepped out of her way, but followed Casey toward the women's bathroom.

Approaching the door, she pretended to falter and the woman rushed forward to grab her arm.

She helped steady Casey and steer her into the ladies' room. As she did, she took the opportunity once more to chastise her. 'Shame on you,' she hissed. 'You should know better than to come to mosque when you are sick.'

'I'm not sick, darling,' said Casey in her best Texas drawl as the door shut behind them and she reached over to lock it. 'But I am getting pretty tired of what a bitch you're being.'

'I, I, I,' the woman stammered, suddenly aware that something very bad was happening.

'Yup. You, you, you,' replied the Athena Team leader as she pulled her Taser from beneath her burqa and stun-drove it into the woman's chest.

The doorkeeper's muscles seized up and Casey caught her as she fell forward. She was in the process of removing the woman's burqa to bind and gag her when she heard Ericsson's voice over her earpiece, 'We're in the hallway. All clear.'

Casey reached up and unlocked the door. Rodriguez and Cooper helped her secure the doorkeeper in one of the stalls as Ericsson continued to keep watch. Once they had her out of the way, Casey radioed Harvath that they were heading to the basement. Morning prayers would not last long, so they needed to move quickly.

With suppressed weapons at the ready beneath their burqas, they descended the narrow staircase. Casey took the lead, followed by Cooper, Rodriguez, and Ericsson.

On the ground floor they retrieved their shoes and proceeded to the end of the hallway where they found the door al-Fihri claimed led to the basement. Casey reached out and tried to open it, but it was locked.

She stood back and signaled Cooper, who stepped forward, checked the door for any sort of alarm, and then pulled out a lockpick gun. Within seconds, she had the dead bolt taken care of. Nodding at Casey, she stepped away from the door, replaced the lockpick tool beneath her burqa and readied her weapon.

Casey grabbed hold of the door handle and counted down quietly from three. When she said 'Go' and opened the door, they followed her into the stairwell and down the stairs.

Their presence on the stairs was greeted with a string of sharp words spoken in Arabic. A young man, no more than twenty-two years old, with a Glock placed on the prayer mat in front of him, demanded to know what they were doing.

'*Salam, salam,*' *peace*, repeated Casey in the traditional Muslim greeting as she continued down the stairs toward him.

The man was nervous. The women didn't belong there.

Had he not had a weapon sitting right in front of him, Casey would have transitioned to her Taser, but her primary duty was to protect her life and those of her teammates.

Don't go for the gun, she begged him under her breath, but he did. It was a bad decision and the last one the young man would ever make.

Casey fired two suppressed rounds from beneath her burqa, both striking him in the face. It was a very difficult shot, especially having to aim down a set of stairs and firing from behind clothing.

The young man was still alive as they reached the last step, but barely. Pulling out her MP5, she popped him twice, just above the bridge of his nose, finishing the job.

'Contact,' she said over the radio. 'Tango down.'

The man had collapsed on his prayer mat and Cooper and Ericsson used it to drag him underneath the stairs before the blood soaked through and stained the floor. Once they had him stashed they all removed their burqas. There was a distinct chemical odor in the air.

With Rodriguez covering the door at the top of the stairs, they got ready to clear the rest of the basement.

The fact that they had encountered an armed man told them two things. Not everyone had gone upstairs for morning prayers, *and* there *was* something down here someone felt very serious about protecting. Judging by the odor, whoever was down here wasn't preparing cookies for the mosque bake sale.

The hallway ran the length of the building above with four doors along each side. The amplified voice of the imam radiated down through the ceiling and vibrated the dusty light fixtures above them.

Casey withdrew a special device with a long piece of fiber-optic cable from her pocket. She hit pay dirt with the very first door. Slipping the cable beneath it and raising the unit to her eye, she saw a makeshift lab, complete with long tables, jammed with glass jars, soldering guns, nylon bags of some sort, and stacks of discarded electronic equipment. She signaled for the team not to move. Beyond the tables, she could see at least six men, prostrated on prayer rugs.

Pulling the cable back out from under the door, she turned to her teammates and drew a quick diagram on the floor.

The room appeared to run the entire length of the building on its south side. It must have been subdivided into offices or separate storerooms at some point as it had four doors leading into it. Casey planned to use this feature to their advantage.

Moving down the hallway, so she could get a good look at the men from the front, she positioned herself near the last door and fed the cable only partway beneath it.

She noticed that the voice of the imam above was even louder here and figured there must be speakers in this basement room, just as there had been in the women's prayer hall.

Once again, she counted six men, all of whom had weapons with them on their prayer mats. At the very end, furthest from the door, was Rafiq Wadi. Gone was the beard he'd been wearing in the photo his brother Saud had showed them back at the plumbing warehouse. Like the five other men he was praying with, all were clean-shaven. That was a bad sign that this group had performed the Islamic ritual cleansing rites intended to speed their way into paradise. They appeared ready indeed to go operational.

Casey studied the men, trying to discern who was in charge, but it was impossible to figure out. Carefully, she withdrew the cable and backed away from the door.

The prayer service was almost over. She checked to make sure none of the doors were wired and then quickly cleared the other rooms. They were all being used for storage of one sort or another and one even appeared to be a bike room.

She searched for a fuse box or a circuit breaker, but couldn't find one. They would have to come up with some other kind of distraction.

Based on the smell and the compounds known to have been used in the other attacks, Casey had no doubt these men were constructing organic peroxide explosives. This was going to be one of the trickiest assaults they had ever conducted.

One wrong move and the entire building could be leveled; maybe even the entire block. Their job was made even more complicated by the fact that they needed to take as many of the men inside alive as possible.

Casey didn't have time to formulate an elaborate plan. They also couldn't risk using flash bangs for fear of setting off the bombs inside. They were going to have to go in hard and fast and hope that the element of surprise would give them enough of an edge.

She decided to pull Nikki off of covering the door at the top of the stairwell. Though this would leave their rear vulnerable, right now the men in that room posed a greater threat than anyone who might come down the stairs.

The room's occupants were praying between the third and fourth doors and that's where Casey decided to hit them. She would take door number four with Cooper, while Rodriguez and Ericsson took door number three. Cooper and Ericsson would be armed with their MP5s while she and Rodriguez, the fastest and most accurate shooters on the team, would be armed with their Tasers. The idea was to incapacitate all of the men if possible. If any of them were able to pick up their weapons, it was up to Cooper and Ericsson to take them out.

When both fire teams were positioned at their respective doors, Casey tightened her grip around the X3, took a breath, and then once again counted down from three.

47

Though the sight of four heavily armed women kicking in the doors of their bomb factory scared the hell out of them, the six Islamist terrorists had been trained well and didn't allow their fear to paralyze them.

They were in the process of rising from their prayer mats when the two doors exploded inward. In various stages of standing, they reacted quickly, scrambling for their weapons almost in unison; all except for Rafiq Wadi.

There was a series of pops as Casey and Rodriguez deployed their Taser cartridges. Cooper fired two rounds from her MP5, hitting one of the terrorists in the arm and upper chest. Ericsson fired her MP5 as well, hitting one of the men in the hand and the neck as he lunged for his weapon.

It was chaos as the men fell to the ground. The terrorists with the neck and chest wounds were already bleeding out.

Rafiq Wadi lay down on his prayer mat with his hands over the back of his head. He was yelling, 'Don't shoot. Don't shoot.' As a precaution and just to get him to shut up, Casey Tasered him anyway.

Cooper covered the men, while Ericsson entered the room and secured their weapons. As she did, Casey activated her radio. 'Six tangos in custody, two with multiple GSWs.'

'What about explosives?' replied Harvath.

'Stand by.'

The team secured the prisoners while Casey began searching the room for bombs. She went directly to the bike messenger bags and sure enough, they were loaded with explosives. There was a row of panniers and they had been loaded with explosives as well.

'I've got multiple explosive devices here. At least fifteen, maybe more. The compound appears to be TATP and it has been packaged in bicycle messenger bags and large panniers. It looks like they have been packed with ball bearings.'

'Roger that,' replied Harvath, who now realized how they were going to navigate traffic and all enter Piccadilly at the same time. It was not only extremely low-tech, it was incredibly creative. This method had been used in both Pakistan and Afghanistan. People rarely gave bike messengers or bike riders a second glance. While police would be keeping their eyes out for backpacks, bicycle-borne bombs could very well escape their scrutiny. They could weave in and out of traffic and park just about anywhere. Not only would it work well in London, where riders with their heads down could obscure their faces from surveillance cameras, the tactic would be brilliant in bicycle-choked Amsterdam. 'Do you see any bikes?'

'Affirmative. There's a roomful across the hall.'

'Don't move any of them. They could be packed with explosives too,' cautioned Harvath, who pictured bike shrapnel in addition to the ball bearings in the bags tearing people apart.

'Roger that.'

'Are the bags armed?'

'Checking,' said Casey as she examined one of the bags more closely. 'There are wires leading to some sort of reflection beacon. I'm assuming that when the beacon gets turned on, that's when the bags blow.'

'We'll leave that for the bomb technicians.'

'Affirm — ' began Casey but then her voice broke off.

'You're breaking up. Repeat, please.'

'The bags are hot,' she said. 'All of them.'

'Are you talking about the beacons?' replied Harvath.

'Negative. Each bag has a chicken switch. They're wired to cell phones and the cell phones are powered up.'

Harvath looked at Ashford and Marx sitting in the van next to him listening in. 'Any way we can jam cell phone signals from entering that mosque?'

'We don't have any jamming equipment with us,' replied the MI5 agent.

'How quickly could we get it?'

Marx looked at her watch. 'Ours would probably take at least an hour.'

'How about MI5?' Harvath asked Ashford.

'Probably the same amount of time depending on where the nearest gear is.'

Casey's voice came back over the radio. 'What do you want us to do?'

It was clear the jammer route was closed. They'd have to do something else. 'Can you describe the setup to me?' Harvath replied.

'It looks like the phone from the undetonated device in the 2004 Madrid bombings. Same stuff they have been using in Iraq. There are two wires protruding from the interior of the phone to a small circuit board taped to the front of the phone with clear plastic tape.'

'How's the signal strength?'

'Three bars.'

That was not good news.

'The circuit board appears to be wired to two detonating caps,' she continued. 'I'm assuming the entire set-up leads back to the phone's ringer. As long as that's not a booby trap, we should be able to snip the wires and deactivate that secondary trigger.'

'Was Rafiq Wadi injured in the assault?'

'No, he just rode the bull.'

Turning his attention back to Casey, Harvath said, 'Get him away from the others and ask him what he knows about the bombs. After that, I want you to verify the primary and secondary targets.'

'Roger that.'

The terrorists had been bound hands and feet with EZ Cuffs, gagged with duct tape, and made to lie facedown on the floor. The barbed Taser probes were then pulled from them as they each had their pockets emptied and the contents placed in piles so that the Athena members could ID what belonged to whom.

Next to the bombs' being detonated, Casey's biggest concern was that there could be more terrorists upstairs who might be on their way down now that the service was over. She dispatched Rodriguez and Cooper to make sure the upper door was locked and to cover the stairs. Ericsson was left to watch the prisoners. The two men who were bleeding out would not be given medical attention until the situation was completely under control.

Casey walked over to the terrorists. They looked up at her as she pretended to decide which one of them to select. Finally, she grabbed Rafiq Wadi and yanked him to his feet. The man next to him began mumbling something from behind the duct tape across his mouth and Casey kicked him in the ribs, hard.

She shoved Wadi out the door and closed it behind them. In the hall, she pushed him up against the wall, drew her knife, and placed it against his throat. She held her fingers to her lips and motioned for him to be quiet. His eyes reflected how frightened he was. He nodded once, very slowly, and Casey peeled the duct tape back from his mouth.

'We have Saud,' she said before Rafiq could speak. 'He will remain safe, only as long as you cooperate. If you understand, nod your head once.'

Rafiq nodded.

'Good. I know everything about what is going on here. If you lie to me, I will gut you like a pig and let you watch your insides spill out. Do you understand me?'

Again, Rafiq nodded.

'Are there any more bombs?'

The man nodded and flicked his eyes across the hallway.

'The bicycles?'

Rafiq nodded.

'Are the bombs armed?'

The man nodded, but then shook his head.

'Which is it?' demanded Casey.

'The bags, yes. The bicycles, no.'

'How are the bags armed?'

'Each one has an electronic light.'

The woman studied his face and then said, 'I'm sorry Saud will have to die because his brother lied.'

Rafiq became even more panicked. 'I am not lying. They're beacons that flash. Twenty seconds after they are activated the bombs detonate.'

'Tell me about the cell phone triggers. How do you defuse them?'

'I don't know.'

'You're still lying to me.'

'I'm not lying. Why would they want us to know? The cell phone is their guarantee. If we don't go through with it or our primary detonator doesn't work, this is how they make sure the mission goes forward.'

The cell phone detonators were a fail-safe. These Rafiq would not have been taught how to deactivate. Casey moved on to her next question.

'What's your target?'

'Piccadilly Circus.'

'When?'

'Tonight, during the evening rush hour.'

'What is your secondary target?'

'I don't know. We surveyed many targets. It

could be any of them. The London Eye, Covent Garden, several of the theaters.'

'Who's in charge of your cell?'

Rafiq Wadi seemed reluctant to answer and Casey applied pressure to her knife.

'The man who was shot in the neck,' he said finally.

'And who does he report to?'

'I don't know.'

'How do they contact each other?'

'I don't know. Please.'

Casey placed the tape back across his mouth. They'd have to interrogate all of them.

Her thoughts were interrupted when Julie Ericsson's voice came over her earpiece. 'You need to get back in here.'

'Why? What's up?'

'One of the cell phones just began vibrating.'

48

Gretchen Casey quickly steered Rafiq Wadi back into the room and had him lie facedown with the other prisoners.

'Which one?'

Ericsson pointed to the cell phone in question. It was in a pile of pocket litter belonging to the terrorist who had been shot in the neck; the man Rafiq Wadi had identified as the cell leader. She could tell by looking at him that he wasn't going to make it. He'd already lost too much blood. There wasn't anything they could do for him. Casey picked up his phone and stepped to the back of the room where she radioed Harvath.

'One of these guys just received a text message.'

'What did it say?' Harvath replied.

'Someone wants an update.'

'What did Rafiq say about the bombs?'

'He said the cell phone triggers are a fail-safe in case one of the devices fails to detonate.'

'Do you believe him?'

'I do.'

'What about the secondary target?'

'He doesn't know. They surveilled several potentials.'

'Do we know who the cell leader is?' asked Harvath.

'The guy with the neck wound. He's not going to make it. Right now, though, we need to focus on these bombs. What do you want to do?'

Harvath knew what he wanted done, but it was up to Casey whether she wanted to do it. 'How do you feel about deactivating the cell phones?'

'As long as they're not booby traps, we've done these before, so I've got no problem with it.'

She was a brave woman. 'Good. Grab one of the prisoners and make him stand with you when you do it. They may know more than they are letting on.'

'They might still also want to go to Paradise, in which case — '

'In which case,' Harvath interjected, 'it should be written all over each of their faces. Watch for them to start sweating or rocking back and forth, mumbling their prayers. Now, do you see any wire clippers there?'

'I'm already ahead of you,' replied Casey as she picked up a pair off the table. She walked back to the prisoners and pulled one of the men to his feet. She jerked him over to the table with all the messenger bags and panniers assembled on it. She could feel his body tense beneath her grasp.

Opening the first bag, she pointed at the cell phone and the wires leading from it. The man stared at it and then back at her. Casey made a clipping motion with the cutters. The man didn't respond.

'This guy doesn't like that we're standing near the bombs,' she said to Harvath, 'but other than that, he's not giving me any other signals. I'm going to cut the wires coming out of the phone to the circuit board. Everybody get ready.'

Casey paused, took a deep breath, and then let it out. As she did, she gritted her teeth, placed the wires in the mouth of the cutter, and clipped them both at the same time.

Harvath was anxious to know what happened, but he remained quiet, ready for whatever the outcome might be, but hoping for the absolute best. He hadn't realized he was holding his breath until Gretchen Casey's voice came back over the radio.

'Chicken switch number one deactivated,' she said. 'Moving to number two.'

'Roger that,' replied Harvath. 'Good job.'

When all of the cell phone detonators had been deactivated, Harvath had Casey remove them from the bags and place them in the order she had retrieved them. She then took care of the beacons.

With the bombs deactivated, Ashford and Marx were eager to send the tactical teams into the mosque. Harvath wasn't so sure that was a good idea.

'Why not?' said Ashford.

'There are two men dying in there,' added Marx.

'With all due respect,' Harvath replied. 'I don't care about two dying terrorists.'

'What if they have intelligence we can use?'

'The cell leader isn't going to make it. And if the second one dies, that's two trials the British taxpayers have been spared. I'm more concerned with finding out who's behind this attack.'

Ashford looked at him. 'So then why not secure the mosque and begin interrogating these men?'

'Because we'd lose our advantage,' explained Harvath.

'Which is what?'

'That nobody knows we're in there.'

'Except the terrorists,' clarified Marx.

'Correct. And we've cut them off from whoever their controller is. That's the person we need to get to.'

'Let's try to trace the number that text message came through on.'

'I guarantee you it'll be a throw-away phone. If the right text response doesn't come back soon, whoever originated that message is going to abandon that phone.'

'Then we check the cell phone detonators. Whoever selected them would have tested them to make sure they received incoming traffic without any problems.'

'I can have Casey pull off the tape and circuit boards to see if there's a list of previous activity,' said Harvath, 'but if it was me, I'd have deleted all the logs.'

Ashford thought about it for a moment and then nodded. 'You're probably right.'

'How about the six men we have in the mosque?' asked Marx. 'In addition to interrogating them, shouldn't we check their phones for any common numbers?'

'I can ask Casey to do that, but I don't think that'll provide much either.'

'Then what *do* you want to do?'

'I want to force their hand.'

'How?'

'I want whoever is running this cell to think the operation is in jeopardy and I want them to expose themselves. If we do this right, when they do, we'll be able to nail them.'

49

Word of a major gas leak in East London was in reality a heavy release of mercaptan, the substance added to natural gas to make it smell like rotten eggs. Residents in a four-block radius surrounding the Darul Uloom Mosque were evacuated. Shortly after the evacuations began, the reporters showed up.

A cordon had been established and the news crews, as well as onlookers, were kept a safe distance away.

With Ashford's approval, Harvath had decided that the BBC should be allowed the 'scoop.'

When the time was right, the BBC news team on site was tipped off about some strange activity only a block from their location. Hot for a story, the reporter ran for it with her cameraman in tow. They arrived just in time to see teams of heavily equipped, black-clad, balaclava-wearing anti-terrorism police piling into four gas company vans. The cameraman was able to capture all of it.

Rushing back to their own van, they uploaded the footage to the BBC, who broke into their morning news programming for a 'strange development' in the East London gas leak story. Within seconds of the footage being received, the BBC's helicopter was diverted to East London and the completely predictable speculation began. *Was the gas leak terrorism? Was it a cover for an anti-terrorism raid? Why was the British government keeping its people in the dark? Don't the people have a right to know? Should the prime minister resign?* They played right into Harvath's plan. Moments later, the other networks had picked up on the story.

Anyone watching TV now knew that there was a lot more happening in East London than a gas leak. Anti-terrorism units were not normally sent in to handle utility problems. Harvath was hoping that whoever controlled the cell at the Darul Uloom Mosque was watching TV as well.

The architecture of any human network, whether it was created for gathering intelligence or committing acts of terror, was pretty easy to understand. As you climbed the food chain, each layer was designed to protect the operative positioned above it. Those layers were people, and they were known as 'cutouts.'

At the ground level was the cell itself. The number of people in that cell was dependent upon their specific assignment and the overall goal of the network.

The cell had a leader whose job it was to make sure that the cell operated efficiently and to communicate up the food chain. The next rung on the ladder was the controller. He or she might control only that one cell or he or she might control many cells, but that person's primary job was to act as a go-between and protect the identity of the regional controller.

The regional controller could be limited to controlling all of the network's activity in a particular region, in a particular country, or even

345

a group of countries. The regional controller then reported to a figure known as 'tight control.'

'Tight control' was in charge of the entire network worldwide. Despite site 243 being a Chinese project, Harvath doubted that any of the controllers were Chinese. Most likely, they were all Muslim men who totally believed they were operating within a true Islamic terror network. That was the brilliance of the operation.

Whoever 'tight control' was, Harvath was confident he didn't live anywhere near China. He very likely operated similarly to bin Laden prior to 9/11, as the guest of a country sympathetic to the Islamist agenda. Pulling his strings would have been achieved through coded communications. For all intents and purposes, the man could very well have believed he was working directly for the al-Qaeda hierarchy, even though he'd probably never met any of its members face-to-face.

It was the perfect turnkey operation. Why go through the trouble of building your own Muslim network when you could hijack one from the Chinese? What Harvath couldn't figure out, though, was *why* they had done it. Why unleash the carnage? What was the point?

To figure that out, they were going to need to get to 'tight control'; and to get to him, they were going to need to work their way up the food chain one bite at a time.

They all agreed that the terrorist who had received the text was most likely the cell leader and the sender of the message had been the cell controller. While Harvath would have liked to have applied 'pressure' to the terrorist, he was barely clinging to life as it was and would not have withstood interrogation.

What's more, reverse engineering a network was very delicate work. Members were taught distress codes and could easily relay to their controllers that the cell had been compromised. They didn't even need to send the message themselves. Often they could trick their captors into doing it for them. It could be as simple as a chalk mark in the wrong place, a window shade at the wrong height, or the wrong color or style of font in a chat room.

Knowing full well the pitfalls, Harvath decided it best to force the controller out into the open. But to do it, Robert Ashford and Rita Marx had to call in nearly every favor they had ever accrued. For the first time in Britain's modern history, its entire electronic surveillance apparatus was focused on one objective and one objective only — locating a single phone somewhere within the United Kingdom.

When everyone was in place, Ashford radioed for the tactical teams to move in on the mosque, whose morning worshippers had already departed.

High above, television helicopters were broadcasting the entire thing. All the rest of the team could do was wait and hope that the cell's controller would expose himself.

The gas company trucks converged on the mosque from opposite ends of the street. When the officers poured out, they were all heavily armed, armored, and wearing gas masks.

Rounds and rounds of tear gas were fired through windows as the officers rapidly advanced on the mosque. Across the country, viewers were undoubtedly glued to their sets. If the cell's controller was watching, which Harvath prayed he was, all he would be able to surmise was that the mosque his men had been using for their headquarters was compromised and was now under a full-scale assault.

The fact that he hadn't been able to reach any of his cell members would only heighten his anxiety. Very likely, the only question greater in his mind than how the cell had been discovered, was why his men hadn't yet detonated their explosives. That was what their training would have dictated.

The only thing the controller would have been able to attribute the delay to was that the cell members were trying to draw more police officers into the mosque before blowing it up.

That sort of deviation definitely would have been against protocol. Their job would have been to detonate, not fight it out or try to take as many officers with them as possible.

There was one other option that the controller would have had to consider. He would have to entertain the possibility that the men had lost their nerve.

Either scenario was unacceptable. The controller would have been left with no other option than to engage the fail-safe.

When the tactical team hit the mosque's front doors, Marx's voice came over Harvath's headset. 'The cell phone detonators have begun lighting up.'

'Give me a location.'

'We're working on it,' she replied. 'Stand by.'

Precious seconds ticked down as the tac team flooded into the mosque. Harvath studied the faces of the Athena Team members sitting next to him. To the untrained eye, they would have appeared cold and even expressionless, but Harvath knew the look of operators about to go into battle. The women were the picture of professionalism.

He could also sense their impatience. He was feeling it too. This was their one shot and the window was narrower than almost any other he had ever dealt with. If the Brits couldn't get a lock on the controller, they were going to be dead in the water.

'We need that location,' Harvath repeated.

'Stand by.'

'Come on. Come on.'

Finally, Marx's voice came back over his headset, 'Got it.'

The woman from Scotland Yard rattled off a set of coordinates.

'Roger,' replied the helicopter pilot, who then announced to Harvath and his passengers, 'Hold on.'

The pilot banked the Agusta Westland Lynx and sped toward the center of London. It was the fastest helicopter in the world and speed was exactly what they needed right now. As Marx worked on pinpointing the exact building the controller was in, she had already begun sending undercover tactical teams in the general direction. But unless the teams were in the immediate vicinity when the address was revealed, Harvath had a strong feeling he and his team were going to be the first boots on the ground.

Buildings whipped beneath the belly of the helo as it rapidly closed the distance with their destination. Harvath had been surprised by the central London location. It wasn't that the cell's controller couldn't be fully integrated into British culture — the wave of British doctor attacks had proven that — it was just incongruous with what Harvath's experience had been. Normally, these guys used ethnic neighborhoods as cover. There, they could blend in and disappear. The neighborhoods were difficult for non-Muslims to penetrate and the close-knit, often ethnic makeup of their inhabitants provided an unending supply of lookouts and human trip wires.

That said, only hours earlier, Harvath had cautioned Bob Ashford not to underestimate their enemy, and now he reminded himself to heed his own advice. Expecting the controller to be holed up in some blighted Muslim neighborhood sitting on a carpet drinking tea while he coordinated bombings was sloppy thinking on his part. He was trained better than that. This guy could be a banker or a professor at the London School of Economics for all he knew.

As the Lynx banked again and raced up the Thames, Robert Ashford's voice came over Harvath's headset. 'We've lost the signal.'

50

'Just try to breathe,' said John Vaughan. 'In and out. Nice and easy. You're going to be okay. Just relax and breathe.'

'Jesus, it hurts,' said Levy. 'I think I'm having a heart attack.'

'Focus on the sound of my voice, Josh. Listen to me. You're going to be okay. We're going to figure out a way to get out of here.'

'They're going to kill us, aren't they?'

'If they were going to kill us, they'd have done it already.'

'Either way,' added Davidson, 'I'm a dead man. If they don't kill me, my wife will. How many days have we been here?'

All three were bound and hoods had been placed over their heads. As a Marine, Vaughan was the only one who had been trained to withstand captivity and interrogation. He knew that most of it was a mental game, and that meant that he had to help Davidson and Levy get through this.

'We've only been here about twenty-four hours, give or take an hour or two.'

'That's it,' said Davidson. 'My marriage is definitely over. My wife is never going to believe

351

I was taken hostage.'

Vaughan kept his attention on Levy. 'Josh, I want you to describe to me how you're feeling.'

Levy took a moment to form his assessment. 'My shoulder hurts like hell, and I have a lot of pain in my chest. My back hurts and so does my neck.'

'Welcome to what it feels like to have been shot.'

'But I was shot in the shoulder, not in the chest.'

'Your torso absorbed a lot of blunt force trauma. You're going to feel it everywhere.'

'I have tightness and trouble breathing.'

'That probably has more to do with anxiety than anything else.'

'He's right, Josh,' said Davidson. 'Try not to think about how long it has been since you last clipped your nails.'

'Up yours.'

As Levy and Davidson started laughing, Vaughan felt relieved. They needed to keep their spirits up.

Ever the wiseacre, Davidson said, 'Hey, do you guys know what the only thing in the world shorter than a Muslim terrorist's dick is? His *to do* list.'

There was another roll of quiet laughter, but the elevated mood didn't last.

'What do you think they're going to do with us?' Levy asked.

'We gave them everything,' replied Vaughan, 'so I don't know that there's any other information they could squeeze out of us.'

'Which reminds me,' said Davidson. 'I thought you big, tough Marines were supposed to be able to hold out indefinitely under interrogation.'

'No one can hold out indefinitely, Paul. That's just in the movies.'

'But we told them everything,' said Levy. 'What possible value could we still have for them? They know we came looking for Nasiri and that this wasn't official police business.'

Vaughan had been thinking about that too. 'We should take it as a good sign that we're still here. As long as we're alive, there's a chance we're going to get out of this. We're all married, so let's focus on our wives and children.'

'Way to ruin it for me,' said Davidson.

'Come on. Your wife can't be that bad.'

'When we get out of here, you can stay at my house for a week with her and her two dogs, okay?'

Vaughan smiled beneath his hood. 'Think about fishing then.'

'I have been. And I've been thinking about how I'm never going to take my cell phone on vacation again.'

'If it makes you feel better to blame me for all of this, go ahead.'

'When the turban fits.'

'By the way, who were you really fishing with when I called? I know you didn't threaten to kill your priest.'

'You should hear the kind of stuff he threatens me with.'

Vaughan still didn't believe him, but he laughed anyway.

'I've been thinking about my wife,' Levy interjected, his tone morose. 'We had an argument yesterday. A bad one.'

'You've got to stay strong, Josh,' said Vaughan. 'We're going to make it.'

'What if we don't?'

'We will.'

'How? Nobody knows where the hell we are. We don't even know where we are.'

'I guarantee you that our wives are raising holy hell right now,' replied Vaughan. 'The fact that Paul and I are cops means that CPD will be working extra hard to find us.'

'I didn't tell my wife where we were going or who we were surveilling,' said Levy.

There was silence. Finally, Davidson admitted, 'I didn't give my wife specifics either.'

Beneath the darkness of his hood, Vaughan could feel the other men's eyes shift toward him. He knew what they wanted to hear. He knew what they needed to hear and so he said, 'Then I guess it's a good thing I told my wife everything.'

The other two didn't respond. They knew he was lying.

51

'Talk to me, Bob,' said Harvath as the Lynx flew over Westminster Bridge and decreased its speed as the pilot awaited further instructions.

'We had a flurry of activity and then everything stopped,' Ashford replied. 'Somebody pinged the cell members' phones from different numbers and when they didn't respond, whoever it was began trying to activate the detonators on the explosives. We had the caller traced to a one-block area.'

'How many buildings are we talking about?'

'The caller wasn't in a building. He was outside, moving.'

'Was he in a vehicle or on foot?'

'We don't know,' said the MI5 man.

'How about CCTV cameras? Were there any in the area?'

'Yes. Rita has already pulled the footage and we're rolling it back to the time the calls were placed. The first filter is people visibly using phones. The next is headsets or earbuds. If someone is seen using more than one phone or changing SIM cards then obviously we . . . ' the MI5 man's voice trailed off.

355

'Can you repeat?' said Harvath. 'I didn't get that last part.'

Marx's voice came back over the radio. 'I think we have our man. Arab male, early forties. Approximately two meters tall and eighty kilos.'

Harvath did the conversion in his head — six feet and around 175 pounds.

'He has short black hair and a goatee,' Marx continued. 'He is wearing a brown sport coat, a blue jumper, khaki trousers, and dark shoes.'

'What happened to Bob?'

'He seems to be having trouble with his radio,' said Marx.

'You're sure this is our guy?'

'Positive. We have footage of him operating three different devices.'

'Where is he and which direction is he headed?'

'We ID'd him off of footage from several minutes ago,' said the woman from Scotland Yard. 'We need to reacquire him. We're sorting the live feeds now. Stand by.'

Harvath turned to the pilot. 'Where can you set us down?'

'There's a helipad at the London Hospital in Whitechapel,' he replied, pointing down at his map.

'Too far,' replied Harvath, who then hailed Ashford again. 'Bob, I need to know which direction the subject was heading.'

'North, but as best we can tell, he doubled back,' replied Ashford, his radio working again. 'We're still trying to find him.'

'He's running SDRs.'

'Let him. We don't have anyone on him yet, so there's nothing for him to pick up.'

'What if he gets on the Tube?' asked Harvath.

'We've got cameras in all the stations. Hold on a second.'

'Do you have him?'

'I think so. Stand by. Is it confirmed?' Harvath heard him say over his open mic. Moments later he came back and replied, 'Yes, we've re-acquired him. The sport coat is gone. He's got the blue jumper on now along with a pair of wire-rim glasses. The khakis and shoes are the same.'

'He's definitely running SDRs,' said Harvath.

'Agreed. Right now he is on Waterloo Place, near the Sofitel headed toward Trafalgar. We're going to mobilize all the teams we have and flood the area. We're getting his picture out to police as well.'

'Don't do that,' Harvath cautioned.

'Why the devil shouldn't we?'

'If he's the controller of the East London cell, he's going to need to get in touch with his superior to sort out what just happened. They have no idea how deeply they've been penetrated and if other cells are at risk.'

'What if we lose him?' asked Marx now.

'The only way that will happen is if we spook him. So we won't spook him. The last thing we want to do is put the kind of surveillance on him that he'd be expecting.'

'And you think he won't spot your team of women.'

Harvath looked at Casey and the rest of the

Athena Team, who all flashed him thumbs-up. 'If your people can establish a loose cordon,' Harvath said, 'my team can work inside the bubble.'

'You realize that just because they're women, that doesn't mean he won't take notice of them. If he sees any of them a second time, we're going to have a problem.'

'So let's make sure we don't have any problems. Put your teams into the area, but hold them as far back as possible. We'll stay on the radios and you can give us CCTV updates as to what our man is doing. Meanwhile, try to find out who the hell he is and get me everything you can on him.'

'We will,' said Marx. 'Anything else?'

'Yes,' replied Harvath glancing back down at the map. 'I'm going to need you to make an important phone call for me.'

52

The Lynx helicopter flared as it came in and landed on the Horse Guards Parade exercise ground in Whitehall. Crowds of tourists, gathered for the famous changing of the guard, were kept a safe distance away by formally garbed Household Cavalry troopers.

Both Harvath and the Athena Team members were familiar with the Household Cavalry, as it was a highly respected operational regiment whose personnel, which included Prince Harry, had served courageously in both Iraq and Afghanistan.

A special contingent of troopers spirited the helicopter's passengers to the archway that led to the street. There were shouts of 'Coming through. They have an ivory!' as the team passed beneath the ceremonial arch reserved solely for the queen and those who had been given the queen's permission to pass in the form of a formal ivory invitation. Harvath had no idea if Marx had contacted the queen, but the speed and professionalism with which they were ushered through was remarkable.

Out on the street, they divided up into teams and Harvath watched as the women transformed right before his eyes. They made subtle adjustments to their clothes and hairstyles that could later be changed at a moment's notice and would result in their appearance's being significantly altered. Like their male colleagues, this Delta Force detachment was exceedingly well trained.

Once again, Harvath was teamed with Gretchen Casey. Cooper went with Ericsson and Rodriguez went with Rhodes. Halfway up the street, he watched Cooper and Ericsson duck inside a T-shirt shop. He could see the scene playing out in his mind without even being there. In a hurry, their tour bus leaving momentarily, two tourists wanted to stock up on a bunch of souvenirs.

If they were smart, which Harvath already knew they were, they'd be buying a bunch of clothing to help further alter their appearance. The bonus was that the bags they'd be carrying would make them look even more like tourists.

As they approached the statue of Sir Henry Havelock with Lord Nelson's column and Trafalgar looming behind, Harvath was amazed at the number of people that were out. Black cabs, double-decker and tour buses disgorged people on every corner, and somewhere in that mass of humanity was the man they were looking for.

Because of the number of operatives now involved, Ashford wanted firm call signs and Harvath's team had been designated *Corona*. He was Corona One; Casey, Corona Two; Cooper, Corona Three; Ericsson, Four; Rodriguez Five; and Rhodes Six. Ashford took the call sign *Viceroy*.

Harvath and Casey had picked up a tourist map, while the other women used maps that they had found on the Web via their iPhones.

They gave Trafalgar a wide berth and stayed well across the street. Via the bone mic he was wearing, Harvath pretended to consult his map with Casey and said, 'Okay, Viceroy. Where's the subject?'

'He's heading into the National Gallery.'

Before Harvath could respond, Cooper said, 'This is Corona Three. We've got him.'

The dance went on for over an hour. The man they were following used channels, stair-stepping, intrusion points, and timing stops. He also changed his appearance several more times, but it made no difference. He never spotted Harvath's team and was therefore unable to shake them.

He walked into an Internet café on Charing Cross Road with Megan Rhodes right on his heels. It was a small, storefront operation that sold newspapers, cigarettes, and Western Union services in addition to Internet access. The space looked like it had once belonged to a grocer and they also offered Skype, IT maintenance, Web design, computer networking, and Web and data security. It was an odd hodgepodge to say the least.

Chewing gum and clicking away at her iPhone, Rhodes was directed by an overly pierced clerk to the only remaining terminal, the one right next to the man she was following.

Having pulled out her earpiece before walking into the café, Rhodes was now communicating via text messages with Gretchen Casey, who, along with Harvath, was two blocks away and closing.

Nikki Rodriguez took up a position outside, while Cooper and Ericsson split up to cover any rear exits. Ashford's men maintained their perimeter, ready to move in as soon as Harvath gave the command.

'Shut up,' Rhodes snorted as she popped her gum, rolled her eyes, and thumbed out another text message.

The controller cursed the 'ugly American' under his breath and tried to tune her out as he opened up his Web browser.

Rhodes set her phone down next to her computer and opened her Web browser as well and began slowly surfing through a series of tourism links for the Cotswolds.

The man next to her logged on to his Skype account, picked up the headset next to his computer, and initiated a VOIP call.

'The oranges were no good,' he said in Arabic. 'I have no idea why,' he added after a pause to listen to something said by whoever was on the other end. 'It might have been just this batch or it could have been throughout the entire crop.'

The cryptic call went on for several minutes as the men spoke in code. Rhodes's iPhone was recording the entire thing and broadcasting it to Casey.

'I understand,' the controller finally said. 'It is the right thing to do.' He then disconnected the call and removed his headset.

Rhodes paid no attention to the man as he stood up to leave. Once he was at the door, she picked up her phone and said, 'He's coming out. Take him down.'

In case the man had some sort of a relationship with the café, they waited until he was half a block away and then Harvath and Rodriguez did the honors with a blast from one of the Taser X3s.

By the time Harvath had the man's wrists bound with a pair of EZ Cuffs, an MI5 van was in the street, its sliding door wide open.

He and Rodriguez chucked the man inside and then watched as it raced away. Turning to her, he asked, 'Did that guy smell like goat to you?'

Rodriguez shook her head and went back to join the rest of the team at the café.

A small, nondescript car pulled up to the curb, dropped off Bob Ashford, and then took off in the same direction as the van.

'Do we have any idea who he is yet?' asked Harvath as Ashford approached.

'We think he may be a former Yemeni Intelligence Service operative, but we're not sure.'

'Based on the way he conducted his surveillance detection routes, he's had formal training. And if that's true, he won't be an easy interrogation subject.'

'Suffice it to say that the people he's just been handed over to will get to the bottom of who he is, sooner rather than later,' said the MI5 man. 'Trust me.'

Harvath didn't doubt it. There were certain things the Brits did very well and were able to keep away from the press. One of those things was the interrogation techniques they used to drain intelligence from suspected terrorists.

He was about to ask if the techniques involved things the American press found so hateful like calling terrorists names and hurting their feelings when Casey emerged from the Internet café and hurriedly walked over to them.

'I think we may have caught a break, but we're going to need some real muscle in there.'

'Let's get to it then,' said Harvath.

He took a step forward but Gretchen put her hand against his chest and stopped him. 'Not your kind of muscle, Prince Charming,' she said, turning to look at Ashford. 'His.'

53

Once Casey explained what she wanted and why she believed the café manager not only had it, but was lying to her about it, Bob Ashford went straight inside and turned the woman's world upside down.

Law enforcement in the U.K. had exceptional powers to deal with terrorism. Ashford also had an incredibly powerful personality. He had a way of being polite, yet terrifying all at the same time. He left no room for argument and was very clear about what would happen to the manager if she didn't cooperate, immediately.

When he asked her for identification and began to question her about any past difficulties she might have caused for police, her tough façade crumbled.

Within minutes, she had not only confessed to the café's keystroke-logging program, but had explained how it worked and had blamed it all on the café's owner. Casey had been right. The café not only spied on its customers, it probably trafficked in their personal data as well. Without an Iron Key, very few people were safe anywhere.

Ashford didn't much care about what the café did with its other customers' data. What he wanted was what the man they had apprehended outside had typed into his computer.

The manager pulled up the information for

the terminal and printed out all of the man's keystrokes. Unfortunately, there weren't very many. He had logged on to his Skype account, searched for another Skype user named Jamal, and made one call before leaving the café and being taken down.

Casey sat down and pulled the man's Skype account back up, but he had deleted everything.

'I just did a search for any accounts with the name Jamal,' she said.

'And?' asked Harvath

'And there's so many, Skype doesn't even list them all. Without knowing which drop-down menus he clicked to focus his search, we won't be able to zero in on him.'

'What about going to Skype directly?' said Ashford. 'They have London offices.'

'You can try, but they're not going to do anything other than talk to you without a judge's order.'

Harvath removed one of his cell phones and sent a text message to Nicholas. Moments later, a response came back. *Yes. The Israelis are rumored to have already cracked it.*

Excusing himself, Harvath stepped outside and called the Old Man.

'Did you get him?' Carlton asked when he picked up his phone.

'We did. He ran SDRs for about an hour and then slipped into an Internet café where he made a Skype call.'

'Do we know who he called?'

'No. All we know is that it was another Skype user named Jamal. The Brits can lean on Skype via their offices here, but that could take a while. Word on the street is that the Israelis have cracked Skype.'

'A few months ago, I'm told,' said the Old Man. 'But you have to give me more than somebody named Jamal who received a Skype call within the last hour.'

'How about our guy's username and password?'

'That's better.'

Harvath rattled off the information and Carlton told him he'd reach out to some friends he had in Tel Aviv and get back to him as soon as possible.

When he stepped back inside, Ashford was bagging the keyboard and headset as evidence. He then asked Rhodes to e-mail the recording she had made so he could see if there was a voiceprint of the man on file somewhere.

Those tasks complete, he looked at Harvath. 'It's your call. What do you want to do now?'

'Where are you doing the interrogations?'

'At a lovely country estate outside the city,' said the MI5 man. 'Why? You want to watch them? I thought interrogations made you squeamish.'

'Only if I don't wait at least a half hour after eating before jumping into one.'

Ashford smiled as his phone vibrated. He removed it from his pocket, unwrapped the earbuds, and read the text message that had just come in. 'If we're done here, I've got transport for us outside.'

Harvath looked at Casey. 'Are we done?'

The Athena Team leader nodded. 'We're all good.'

Outside there were two passenger vans waiting. Ashford turned to Harvath with a suggestion. 'Why don't you and your team get something to eat? I've assigned two of my best men to you. They were both Royal Marines. Whatever you want, they'll see to it.'

'Where are you going?'

'I'm going to drop the evidence at my office and then pay an unannounced visit to the Skype people over on Lexington Street.'

'I want to come with you to Skype.'

The MI5 man pointed over his shoulder. 'This was just a warm-up. If I encounter resistance from Skype, that visit is going to be considerably more unpleasant.'

'I can probably help bring some pressure to bear.'

'I don't doubt it,' he said, putting his hand on the younger man's shoulder. 'You and Peaches do seem to have a very similar approach. Neither of you ever take no for an answer.'

Harvath was flattered to be compared to the Old Man.

Ashford looked at him. 'In my country, the fact that I have to order you to take five very attractive ladies to lunch would be grounds for immediate dismissal.'

'What about Amsterdam?'

'Let's worry about Skype first. Without that, there is no Amsterdam,' he said as he removed his hand from Harvath's shoulder. 'Relax and eat with your team. I'll let you know what happens at Skype, and if we somehow get a break in the interrogations, I'll call you immediately.'

'You've got all my numbers, right?'

'Yes,' said Ashford as he walked toward his vehicle. 'Don't worry.'

Harvath watched as Ashford climbed into the number-one van and it pulled away. A tall, well-built man in his early thirties, dressed in a sharp blue suit and perfectly polished shoes, stepped out of the remaining vehicle and walked over to Harvath.

He stuck out his hand and said, 'My name is Bloom. Commander Ashford has instructed us to take care of you.'

They had gone from one hundred miles per hour to five, and Harvath hated it. All-ahead-stop was not a maneuver he was fond of. He didn't know how to channel his energy. If he wasn't careful, it could wind up as anger.

He shook the man's hand and tried to be nice. 'You're aware that the situation we're in is still active, correct?'

'Yes, sir. The commander briefed us.'

The Brits were so damn professional, and polite. 'I guess we need to eat,' he said and then added, 'Someplace where we can keep the vehicle close in case we have to move quickly.'

'Understood, sir.'

'It would also be nice if we could eat someplace where we're not going to stick out and the ladies won't be bothered.'

'Absolutely, sir.'

Once the team was in the van, Bloom and his colleague, Michaels, took the team to Number 8

Herbert Crescent. It was an unremarkable Victorian building behind Harrods department store in Knightsbridge. It was perfect and Harvath had no doubt that Ashford had made the reservations himself.

There was no name plaque on the shiny, black door; only a brass lion knocker with a buzzer recessed into the frame. Up above, a camera recorded the comings and goings of guests.

Bloom pressed the doorbell and when the door clicked open, ushered his charges inside. Standing in the small, carpeted foyer was a well-dressed man cradling an MP5. They had just entered London's Special Forces Club.

Harvath's suspicion that the lunch had been put together by Ashford was confirmed by the fact that there was already a table waiting for them under Bob's name.

The club's membership was open to anyone who had a clandestine role in or out of uniform. Its motto was: Spirit of Resistance. Simply put, it was *the* private club for current and former secret agents, Special Forces operatives, MI5, MI6, and CIA officers in London.

They were led to a large table in the dining room. After they were seated, menus were passed around and the day's specials were explained. Bloom and Michaels sat at a table nearby.

None of the team felt they were dressed appropriately for a private club, but none of the other members seemed to mind. Perhaps some of the more wily intelligence operatives suspected what kind of work their American guests were up to, but if they did, they didn't let on.

They were halfway through lunch when Harvath's cell phone rang. Standing up, he walked back down to the entry hall to take the call. It was Reed Carlton.

'The Israelis broke the Skype transaction for us.'

'You've got the regional controller's location? Where is he?' asked Harvath. 'London?'

'No,' replied Carlton. 'Amsterdam.'

54

Abdul Rashid rubbed the stubble on his cheeks and massaged his eyes with the heels of his hands as he poured more tea. It had been a long night.

It was bad enough the two police officers had happened upon them, but then the third man had come in through the alley door with his shotgun and the shooting had happened. Rashid had been forced to act quickly.

The first thing he had done was to call the police from one of his prepaid cell phones, which he promptly disposed of afterward. He reported shots fired, but gave the location as four blocks away. He also made up descriptions of the shooters, the vehicles they were driving, and the direction they were headed in.

Though the building they used as a mosque was in a largely commercial area and the shots had been fired late at night, there was still a chance that someone might have heard the exchange and reported it. Unless they were looking out a window onto the alley where it happened, they wouldn't be able to give the police much more to go on than that they heard gunshots nearby. By phoning in a believable account of a gangbanger shoot-out four blocks away, Rashid all but guaranteed where the police would focus their efforts. That, though, would buy them only so much time.

The explosive compounds and all other incriminating materials had to be moved right away, as well as the hostages. Without time to go fetch two of Marwan's trucks, they had to use the vehicles of the cell members at the mosque.

Pulling the vehicles into the alley, they loaded them as quickly as possible. Rashid personally kept watch for any other surprise visitors.

Once the vehicles had departed, he had one of his men follow him in the police officers' Bronco, which he abandoned in a rough neighborhood several miles away. With any luck, it had been stolen within minutes.

It looked as if they had dodged a bullet. The only remaining loose end to be tied up was the mosque's imam, whom Marwan handled with a phone call. Should the police come to question him about anything, he would simply tell the truth; after the faithful had departed following the final prayers of the evening, he had locked up the mosque and had gone home. He knew better than to reveal that things were happening in the basement. If the police wanted to look around, he was instructed to accommodate them. There was no incriminating evidence anywhere in the building.

So far, the police hadn't showed up. Rashid doubted they would. For the time being, they were still safe. Or so he had thought.

'The timetable must be changed,' Marwan

said as Rashid brought over tea for their guest.

'We should not speak in front of him,' the guest responded in Arabic, slicing one of his hooks through the air as if physically cutting off the conversation.

His name was Aazim Aleem. He was British by birth and had fought against the Soviets in Afghanistan. It was there that he had both hands blown off allegedly trying to deactivate a landmine close to a school. Only the truly naive believed the story. In truth, he had lost both of his hands when a bomb he was building prematurely detonated.

Rashid had met him once before, in Pakistan while he was travelling with Marwan. Aleem was a respected Islamic scholar who had studied at Egypt's prestigious Al-Azhar University in Cairo. He was famous for his writings about jihad, as well as his sermons, the audio recordings of which were disseminated throughout the Islamic world and across the Internet. He was known as the 'Mufti of Jihad,' but he never made any public appearances. Very few knew his true identity. Not even British or American intelligence agencies knew who he was. Back in the U.K., the man lived on a full disability pension paid for by the same government he plotted against and deeply desired to overthrow.

Rashid had been surprised to see Aleem at the mosque. It was completely unexpected and, happening so close to his cell going operational, he was quite sure that it wasn't a coincidence.

He set down the tea and said, 'I understand Arabic.'

Like an angry sea crab, Aleem leaned forward and snapped his hooks at him. 'You are not one of us,' he hissed in English.

Rashid looked at Marwan. 'I'm confused. Sheik Aleem grew up in the U.K. He speaks better English than I do and yet he's got trust issues with me?'

'You were not a mujihadeen who fought against the Soviets.'

'With all due respect,' replied Rashid as he looked at Aleem, 'the jihad against the Soviets is over.' He pointed at his chest for emphasis. 'I represent the *current* jihad; the one that is actually being waged right now.'

Aleem smiled and addressed Marwan. 'He doesn't know his place very well, but he is passionate.'

Marwan Jarrah held his hand out to calm his protégé. 'You will show our guest the respect he deserves, Shahab.'

Rashid did as he was told. 'I apologize.'

'You are able to temper your passion,' noted Aleem. 'That is important.'

'Important for what?'

'We've had a change of plans,' said Marwan.

Rashid looked at their guest and then back to his boss. 'So Sheik Aleem is involved in our struggle?'

Aleem laughed. 'I have been involved in this struggle since before you were born, boy.'

'Yes,' said Marwan. 'He's involved. There has been a problem in Europe.'

'What does Europe have to do with us?'

'He has much to learn,' replied Aleem.

375

Rashid was tempted to give the hook-handed old man a piece of his mind, but held his tongue. 'So we are working in concert with the brothers in Europe.'

Marwan nodded.

'You could have told me.'

'The need for compartmentalization has always been greater than your need to know.'

'So why are you telling me now?'

'Because you are being promoted,' said Aleem as he raised one of his hooks and mimicking Rashid, jabbed himself in the chest for emphasis. 'Because while you may represent the current jihad, I am the one who orchestrates it.'

Rashid didn't respond.

'Smile,' continued Aleem. 'Allah has just called you for something very special.'

55

'My name is Anneke van den Heuvel,' said a tall, uniformed woman with curly hair who met the team when they stepped off the plane. 'Are you transporting any weapons?'

There was no 'Hello' or 'Welcome to the Netherlands,' not even a 'Thank you for trying to help us head off a major terrorist attack.' Instead, the woman's only concern was if they were bringing weapons into her country.

'We're not carrying any weapons,' replied Harvath.

'Not yet at least,' Nikki Rodriguez added quietly from behind him.

Harvath had been informed that bringing in weapons would only slow the team down.

'Good,' the woman said as she motioned the team to follow her into the terminal. 'First we will proceed through passport control, and then customs. There are two flights that have just landed, so I suggest we move quickly in order to gain the advantage of the queue.'

'Gain the advantage of the queue?' commented Cooper. 'How about some professional courtesy and we skip the queue altogether?'

'Is there a problem?' the woman asked.

Casey held up her hand to silence her team.

'We require all police officers to file certain paperwork upon arrival to the Netherlands.'

'Well, we're not police,' said Harvath.

'That's not what I was told.'

'Our trip has been cleared by the — ' he continued, but he was cut off.

'If you are not police officers, then we have a problem.'

'We are working for the American government.'

'Do you have any government identification?'

'No,' replied Harvath, trying to melt the ice around her a bit with his tone. 'Our group is not issued ID cards.'

'If you are not police and you do not have proper identification from your government, we will need to get this straightened out. Have a seat, please,' she said, pointing to a row of orange plastic chairs bolted to the gray tile floor.

Harvath tried to explain but she turned her back on him, raised her radio to her mouth, and began speaking to someone in Dutch.

Casey stepped over to Harvath and said, 'The religion of peace is going to blow up their city in a matter of hours and she's jerking us around on entry requirements? I thought you had this handled.'

Harvath was just as angry as she was. 'Don't worry about it,' he said, removing his cell phone.

He scrolled to a number in his address book and sent a quick text. *An immigration officer is holding us up. Where r u?*

A couple of seconds later, his phone vibrated

with a response. *Look up.*

Coming down the hallway were three men, all well over six feet tall. The men on the left and right were blond-haired and blue-eyed while the man in the middle, who was sliding his cell phone back into his pocket, had a shaved head and narrow, dark eyes like a hawk.

They looked like three Rugby captains walking out onto the field — if Rugby captains wore Italian suits, polished shoes, and Secret Service earpieces.

The man on the left ID'd van den Heuvel as the reason for the holdup and went straight for her. Though neither Harvath nor the Athena Team spoke Dutch, they got the gist of the serious dressing down he gave her.

With van den Heuvel incapacitated, the bald man came over and shook Harvath's hand. 'I'm sorry we're late. There have been a few developments since we last talked. We have cars waiting outside.'

As they were whisked through immigration and customs, Harvath introduced Martin de Roon of the AIVD to Casey and the rest of the team.

AIVD was the acronym for the Netherlands' General Intelligence and Security Service, the Algemene Inlichtingen- en Veiligheidsdienst, which was charged with combating both domestic and international threats to national security. After the murder of Theo van Gogh and the discovery of the Muslim Hofstad Network, AIVD had become particularly focused on the Islamic fundamentalist threat to Dutch society.

The two blond men fell to either side of the group, their heads on swivels, as Harvath and de Roon took the lead. Martin swept an ID through a card reader, pushed open a fire door, and led them all up a short flight of stairs. Opening another door, they found themselves outside. Parked in front of them were three armored BRABUS SV12 R Mercedes-Benz S600s. Recognized as the fastest sedans in the world, they were all black with deeply tinted windows.

Harvath and Casey climbed into the back of the first Mercedes. Cooper and Ericsson got into the second, and Rhodes and Rodriguez the third.

De Roon was sitting in the front passenger seat. The car was so quiet, it was like being in a bank vault.

Once the convoy was ready to roll, de Roon raised his sleeve mic to his mouth and gave the command to his drivers to move out.

As the convoy sped out of the airport, Harvath asked, 'What have you learned about the target?'

The Dutch intelligence officer prepared his driver and then told the rest of the team over the radio to move two lanes. He then turned around in his seat to address Harvath. 'The target is an accountant named Khalil al-Yaqoubi, with no record of any sort. The only thing we could find out about him is that he does the books for one of the most radical mosques in Holland. He answered the Skype call from London in his office.'

'Is he still there?'

De Roon nodded. 'He is. We have a surveillance team on him. We also have active surveillance on his apartment, as well as the mosque.'

'How close together are the locations?'

'It's all the same neighborhood, but it's an S-U-A.'

'*S-U-A?*' said Casey.

'It's Dhimmi-speak, for *Sensitive Urban Area*,' replied Harvath.

De Roon looked at her. 'It's actually EU-speak, but Scot's essentially right. The subject operates in an all-Muslim neighborhood.'

'So what? It's still part of the city of Amsterdam, isn't it?'

'Technically, yes. But the police won't go there.'

'Well, as we stated upon arrival, we're *not* the police and just so you know, there's no place my team is afraid to go into.'

Harvath met de Roon's eyes, 'They're the ones who took down the mosque in London.'

'Then maybe she should be in charge.'

Casey held up her hand. 'This is Scot's operation.'

'Do you know what a *klootzak* is?' he asked her.

'No, I don't.'

'That's what we call men like him here in Holland.'

Harvath gave de Roon the finger.

'See?' said the Dutchman. 'That's the behavior of a *klootzak*. They always want the most dangerous assignments and if you're not ready to move when they are, they leave without you.'

381

'I think you're referring to what we call a *cowboy*.'

'I suppose you could call him a cowboy, but *klootzak* is more offensive, and more accurate. Therefore, he is a *klootzak*.'

Casey looked at de Roon. 'Do you two have some sort of history I need to know about?'

'It all started when Marty placed an ad in the *Village Voice* — ' began Harvath.

'I'm not talking to you,' she said, cutting him off.

'A Dutch journalist was speaking at an event in New York City to raise awareness about Islamic fundamentalism,' said Harvath. 'There were several other big-name speakers at the event like Robert Spencer and former Dutch Member of Parliament Ayaan Hirsi Ali.

'A group of bloggers at a site called the Jawa Report, which specializes in taking down Islamist Web sites, uncovered a terror plot against the event. I knew several of the security people involved and when they learned of the threat, they asked me to come in and consult.'

'And was there actually an attempt on the event?'

'Yes, but we stopped it.'

'He means that *he* stopped it,' said de Roon.

Casey looked at Harvath. 'Is that true?'

'Some radical American Muslim wounded two police officers and three hotel security guards trying to get into the ballroom. The man was not only heavily armed, he was also wearing a bomb vest. He would have killed all of the presenters and many of the attendees if

Scot hadn't killed him first.'

'I got lucky,' replied Harvath.

'You can say that again,' replied de Roon. 'If I had snuck out of the ballroom looking for a Red Bull, maybe I would have been in the right place at the right time too.'

'So that's how you two know each other?'

Harvath nodded. 'Marty invited me to come over and do some training with his unit.'

'Dumbest thing I ever did,' said de Roon.

'Why?' asked Casey.

'Because,' said Harvath, 'when the powers that be saw how good he was, he got promoted. He went from being a special police officer protecting Dutch dignitaries to AIVD where he now gets to deal with whack jobs on a daily basis.'

'And unfortunately today is no different,' added de Roon. 'We need to decide what we're going to do.'

Scot glanced at his watch. 'The attack is supposed to happen during the evening rush, so we'll have to take him at his office. Describe it to me.'

De Roon pulled up the file on his BlackBerry and rattled off the salient details. 'The office is on the ground floor of a three-story building. Plate glass windows. No rear exit.'

'How many people working there?'

'Besides al-Yaqoubi? Three men.'

'Do we have histories on them?'

'No, they're all clean.'

'Ages?' asked Harvath.

'Al-Yaqoubi is forty-five and the three other

men are forty, forty-three, and fifty-five.'

'And we have no idea if they have any role in this or not?'

'No, we don't. They could be cell members or function in some other capacity within the network.'

'Which means that if we grab him, we're probably going to have to grab them too,' said Harvath.

'Unless being an accountant is al-Yaqoubi's legitimate cover and these men know nothing about his terrorist activities.'

'But with no way of knowing, we have to assume that they're involved. If their firm does the books for the most radical mosque in Amsterdam, we can guess where their sympathies probably lie.'

'That's true,' replied de Roon.

'Is there anything covering the windows?' asked Harvath. 'Shutters? Blinds?'

'No.'

'Any other rooms?'

'From what we can tell, there's a storeroom of some sort and a toilet. That's all. The entire office is in full view of the street.'

'Which is a big problem.'

The Dutch intelligence officer nodded. 'Keep in mind that if we're going to grab all the men in the office, we have to be in and out in less than a minute. Any longer than that and it won't happen.'

'Why? Can the locals organize a riot that fast?'

'They can. They're experts at it. Believe me.'

'How do we transport them?' asked Harvath.

'We can use the van and my agents who are surveilling the office now.'

'Since we can't conduct the interrogation at the accounting office, what's our alternative?'

De Roon pulled up a picture on his BlackBerry and turned it around to show Harvath. 'There's a Liberian freighter in the port. We arrested the crew two days ago for smuggling. I have two men there now. You'll have the whole ship to yourself.'

'How long will it take to get there?'

'Ten or fifteen minutes depending on traffic.'

'That's too long. What do you have closer?'

'For the kind of interrogating you're going to want to do, that's it.'

Harvath let that sink in. 'Our larger problem is that with no back door, we're not going to be able to get them out of the office and into the van without people seeing it happen.'

'Exactly. And word travels fast in the Muslim neighborhoods.'

Harvath was frustrated. No matter how he spun it in his head, he couldn't come up with the right way to conduct the snatch.

Casey had already given up on forcefully taking al-Yaqoubi from his office. 'Can we draw him out?' she asked. 'What are his pressure points? Is he married? Does he have kids?'

De Roon scrolled through the file and read. 'He is a Dutch citizen of Moroccan extraction, Rabat to be exact. According to our records, he has three wives and eleven children, but despite the fact that they receive Dutch social assistance — '

'Wait a second,' said Harvath. 'This guy is an accountant and his family receives welfare?'

The intelligence man shook his head. 'The system has a lot of problems, including the fact that we cannot find any proof of current residency for the family.'

'None?'

'No. We have no Dutch medical, Dutch school, or Dutch employment records for any of them.'

'Which means they're probably back in Morocco.'

That gave Casey an idea. 'Do we have full names and dates of birth for the family?' she asked as she removed her cell phone.

De Roon pulled it up and handed his BlackBerry to her.

'What are you doing?' asked Harvath.

Casey highlighted a number in her address book and activated the call button. 'I know a few people in the Moroccan secret police,' she replied. 'If that's where this guy's family is, we might not have to walk into his office at all.'

56

Martin de Roon ordered the other two vehicles to hang back. The less attention they drew to themselves, the better. One blacked-out Mercedes cruising through one of Amsterdam's worst Muslim ghettos was more than enough.

'There are two pistols in the armrest between you,' he said.

Casey opened it and Harvath fished out a pair of SIG-Sauer P226s and an extra magazine for each.

'It goes without saying that you didn't get those weapons from us.'

'Understood,' replied Harvath as he handed Casey a pistol and a spare magazine. 'Have you heard anything back from Morocco?'

She checked her phone again. 'They're approaching the house. That's all I know.'

Harvath glanced at his watch. They were running out of time. 'What's plan B if the house is empty?'

'We create a distraction on the next block,' said de Roon. 'Something big. Something that will draw people out of houses and shops. We pick a building and send in fire trucks and ambulances. We send them in fast and loud. We make police go in and set up barricades to hold people back.

'As soon as the crowds begin to gather and enough people have gone to see what is happening, we pull up in the van and grab al-Yaqoubi and the other men in the office.'

'How quickly could you get all of those emergency responders there?' asked Harvath.

'It would only take a matter of minutes.'

'I don't think that's going to be necessary,' said Casey as she read the message that had just come across her phone. 'Two of al-Yaqoubi's wives and several of the children are apparently at the Rabat house. My DST contact wants to know how he should proceed.'

'Tell him to take the house.'

'Roger that,' replied Casey, who called her contact in Morocco's secret police, formally known as the Direction de la Securité du Territoire, or DST.

Above a wooded gorge, south of Rabat's diplomatic district at Ain Aouda, the United States had helped Morocco build an interrogation and detention facility for its al-Qaeda suspects. It was run by the Moroccan DST, and Gretchen Casey had participated in several interrogations there over the last two years.

She put the call on speaker phone so Harvath and de Roon could listen in to the takedown. Commands were issued in Arabic as men could be heard jumping out of cars and pounding on a door.

In typical Arab fashion a woman could be heard arguing with the men, and when that didn't work, she slipped into sobbing hysterics, claiming she didn't know anyone named Khalil al-Yaqoubi.

Finally, the DST man in Rabat told Casey

they were ready to make the call. 'How close are we?' she asked de Roon.

'Four blocks. Less than two minutes out,' he replied.

'Proceed to the target.'

The intelligence officer nodded and instructed his operative to take the next left. They stopped there and waited for the second Mercedes. When de Roon's operative had gotten out, he retrieved several items from the trunk and then slid behind the wheel. Casey joined him up front while Harvath remained in the backseat.

When they were half a block away from the target, Casey told her contact in Rabat to make the call.

They pulled up in front of the accounting office just as the phone began to ring. The DST operative had called from inside the house in Rabat. Casey could hear everything from his end, including when he put al-Yaqoubi's wife and then one of his children on the phone.

The instructions were very clear. The DST operative told al-Yaqoubi to look out the window. When the accountant confirmed that the black Mercedes had just pulled up, the DST man told him to stand and without saying a word, hang up the phone and exit the office. If he was seen to utter even a single syllable, his family would be killed.

It was a despicable tactic, but one Harvath had learned long ago to accept. In the war against Islamic fundamentalists, often the only tie greater than the tie to their god was their tie to their families, especially when children were involved. It made Harvath wonder if maybe he was actually better off without children himself. Maybe Tracy had been doing him a favor. He could only imagine how horrifically gut-wrenching it would be to be on al-Yaqoubi's end of the phone right now.

They watched as al-Yaqoubi hung up the receiver, stood up from his desk, and exited the office. The team in the surveillance van watched and confirmed that he had not spoken a word to his confused colleagues.

Walking up to the Mercedes, he opened the door and got in. Harvath pointed the SIG-Sauer at his chest and told him in Arabic to sit down. The man did so.

'Close the door.'

Al-Yaqoubi complied. Harvath looked at de Roon and said, 'Drive.'

'Who are you? What have you done to my family?' the man demanded in English. He was far from being frightened. In fact, he was indignant.

'How do we stop the attack?'

'I don't know what you are talking about.'

De Roon said, 'The surveillance team says the men in the office seem confused. They are all standing at the window trying to figure out what just happened. Should the men go in and get them, or do you want our guest to make the call?'

This was where Harvath was going to have to take a gamble. If the men in the office were in on the plot, al-Yaqoubi's sudden departure might seem odd, but they would likely rationalize that something had come up that he needed to take care of right away. As far as they would have been able to tell, he had left of his own free will. Besides, he had climbed into a Mercedes, not a police car. While indeed unusual, and while it may have put them in a state of unease, it wouldn't have been enough to cause them to ring any alarm bells. Not yet.

Harvath decided to leave them in the office. 'Tell your team to keep watching and to let us know if any of them pick up a landline or cell phone.'

'Understood,' said de Roon as he radioed the orders to his team.

'How do we stop the attack?' Harvath repeated to their passenger.

'I want to know what you have done to my family!' the man demanded once more.

Harvath nodded at Casey who brought de Roon's Taser up over her seat, aimed it at al-Yaqoubi's torso, and pulled the trigger.

Instantly, he cried out and his body seized as if he'd been overcome by rigor mortis. Harvath waited until it was safe and after tucking his weapon into his waistband, zipped the man's wrists together behind his back with a pair of Flex Cuffs. Pushing him back in his seat, he patted him down and removed the man's cell phone, keys, and pocket litter, which he set in a pile on the floor.

'How long until we're there?' he asked.

'Fifteen minutes,' replied de Roon.

Harvath looked at his watch. 'We don't have that kind of time. We're going to have to interrogate him here.'

He wrapped al-Yaqoubi's ankles with duct tape and then took the Taser from Casey.

Catching de Roon's eyes in the rearview mirror he said, 'No matter what happens do what I say and don't stop driving.'

57

'You tell me how I stop this attack,' said Harvath, who knew the fear that Moroccans had of their country's secret police, 'or I will tell the DST to begin torturing your family in Rabat.'

There was a flash of anger across al-Yaqoubi's face. He looked like he was about to spit at him, so Harvath pulled his fist back and broke the man's nose.

There was a crack of cartilage followed by a gush of blood that poured down the front of his shirt.

'We'll start with your children,' said Harvath.

'I don't believe you,' spat al-Yaqoubi. 'Your country and your president forbid you from torture.'

Harvath smiled. 'That's what you think?'

'That's what I *know*.'

'Let me disabuse you of that notion right now,' said Harvath, as he told de Roon, 'Speed up and do not slow down.'

He then slammed his fist into the accountant's stomach and shoved the man, doubled over, onto the floor of the backseat.

Reaching for the heavy, armored door, he opened it and forced al-Yaqoubi's legs outside.

'Faster,' he ordered de Roon.

The intelligence operative complied as Harvath bent down and yelled into the accountant's ear so he could hear over the rush of the wind

393

whipping past them. 'When I let go of this door, it'll pin your legs against the sill. When that happens, your knees will be forced to bend and your feet will begin dragging along the pavement.

'At this speed, your shoes will be burned through in a matter of seconds. Your socks will go even faster. Then the flesh from your feet will be ground away. The road underneath this car will eat through sinew and grind down your bones. The pain will be like nothing you have ever known.

'When I pull you back in, both of your feet will have been eaten away. You will beg me to kill you.'

'You cannot torture me. The Geneva and Hague conventions forbid it.'

'Those treaties prevent me from torturing lawful combatants. You're a terrorist. This is your last chance, Khalil.'

This time, the man was able to spit before Harvath could stop him. He caught it in the face and it was full of blood. He let the door go.

They all knew when al-Yaqoubi's shoes and socks had been burned away because the man began screaming.

Harvath pushed the door open just enough to pull him back inside. His feet looked like hamburger. 'How do we stop the attack? Tell me.'

Al-Yaqoubi's head lolled to one side and his eyes rolled up in their sockets.

'Oh no you don't, motherfucker,' said Harvath as he juiced him with the Taser again.

The accountant's body went rigid, and he screamed even louder this time.

Once Harvath could get him to focus, he said to Casey, 'Tell the team in Rabat to start with his youngest child. Make sure the family, and in particular the children, know that this is happening because their father doesn't care about them.'

Casey relayed the orders over her cell phone and then placed it on speaker phone and pointed it toward the backseat so al-Yaqoubi could hear the DST operator addressing his family in Rabat. The children immediately began sobbing and their mothers screamed at the news that they were to be held responsible for al-Yaqoubi's crimes.

Harvath watched as the man began to sob. He was breaking. Harvath leaned in to rub salt in the gaping wound that had been torn inside him. 'After the DST is done with them, your family's nightmare will only get worse.'

The accountant looked at him as if to say *How could it get worse?*

'We will make it known to al-Qaeda that you are a traitor and that you gave up the London cell. We'll then let them know where to find your family.'

Harvath let that sink in before adding, 'The DST is very creative, but al-Qaeda is going to come up with things for your family that no one has ever heard of before. They will make an example out of them that no one will forget.'

The tears were openly running down al-Yaqoubi's bloody face.

'You can stop all of this right now,' said Harvath. 'Your family will be spared.'

The man didn't reply.

Harvath looked back at Casey, who had withdrawn her BlackBerry. 'Khalil would like the DST to start torturing his family. But make sure to let them know that they are to leave them as close to alive as possible so that al-Qaeda gets their turn.'

As Casey took her phone off speaker and lifted it to her ear, al-Yaqoubi yelled from the backseat. 'No!'

'No, what?' replied Harvath.

'I will tell you what you want to know.'

'How do we stop the attack?'

Al-Yaqoubi started shaking. He was slipping into shock. Harvath slapped him to get his attention. 'Where is the attack going to take place?'

'The Red Light District.'

'You're lying.'

'I'm not,' pleaded al-Yaqoubi.

'We know the target is Dam Square,' said Harvath.

'That was before London was interrupted.'

'What time?'

'Sometime before midnight. I don't know exactly when.'

'How do we stop it?'

The accountant's shivering increased.

'How do we stop it?' Harvath repeated.

'You can't.'

'Bullshit. How are they planning to attack?'

Al-Yaqoubi's eyes were unfocused and when

396

he failed to respond, Harvath slapped him again and repeated his question.

'Explosive vests,' the accountant stammered.

'Not bicycles?'

'After London, everything was changed.'

'Do the men have cell phones? Can they be recalled?'

'The only phones are on the explosives they are carrying. They are in their final stage and are not supposed to have contact with each other or anyone else.'

Chicken switches, thought Harvath. *Just like London*. He believed al-Yaqoubi was telling him the truth. It also made sense. You wouldn't want your martyrs reaching out to a girlfriend or family member at the last minute only to have that bring about a change of heart.

'Someone will be watching them to make sure they carry out the operation, correct?'

The accountant nodded, his pupils beginning to dilate.

'Where will he be positioned?'

'I don't know.'

'What about the bombers? Where will they be?'

'De Wallen,' he mumbled.

Harvath looked up at de Roon.

'I know it,' said the intelligence operative, 'but it's only a general district. He needs to be more specific.'

Harvath shifted his attention back to al-Yaqoubi, who was decompensating. His pulse was rapid and thready, his skin cool and clammy to the touch. They were going to lose him.

Harvath tried slapping him again, but it had no effect. He yelled into the man's ear and knuckled his sternum without any success. 'He's crashing. He needs medical attention.'

'If we take him to a hospital, your interrogation is over,' said de Roon.

'If we don't, he's going to die.'

'You're a SEAL. You have experience with battlefield medicine. Can't you stabilize him?'

'With what?' asked Harvath, looking around. 'Duct tape?'

De Roon slammed on his brakes and pulled to the shoulder. As he leapt from the car, he yelled for Casey to climb into the backseat to assist.

He removed a trauma bag from the trunk and tossed it to Harvath as he got back in the car, put it in gear, and peeled back out.

Harvath quickly unzipped the bag and emptied out its contents. It was full of QuikClots, Israeli bandages, and other odds and ends. 'This isn't enough. This will only help me stop the bleeding. At the very least, he's going to need an IV and painkillers.'

Al-Yaqoubi had been laid across the backseat. Casey found a reflective space blanket in the supplies and opened it up and laid it across him, while Harvath began to tend to his wounds.

'If you had those supplies, could you stabilize him?'

'I'm not a doctor.'

'But could you do it?'

'Probably.'

The answer seemed to satisfy de Roon, who began issuing orders over his radio as he put his foot down even harder on the accelerator.

58

The rusting Liberian-registered freighter was called the *Sacleipea* and had the filthiest infirmary Harvath had ever seen. Nevertheless, it was well stocked and de Roon's men had everything Harvath had asked for ready and waiting when they carried Khalil al-Yaqoubi in.

Casey helped get an IV going and began administering pain meds while Harvath plucked as much road debris from the accountant's shredded feet as possible. Once he had cleaned and rebandaged the man's wounds, he taped up his nose and gave him a dose of antibiotics to begin fighting any potential infection.

Harvath opened a package of smelling salts and waved it under al-Yaqoubi's nose until he came to. The man shook his head violently to get away from the odor, but soon opened his eyes. He tried to move his arms, but they were Flex-Cuffed to the infirmary gurney.

'Where am I?'

'Not nearly close enough to save your family,' said Harvath as he tossed away the salts.

'I told you everything.'

Harvath was in no mood to argue. 'How many bombers are there?'

'Six.'

'Plus one making sure they detonate, correct?'

'Yes.'

'I want physical descriptions of all of them. I

also want to know where the bombs were assembled and how.'

The accountant nodded his assent.

'And, Khalil,' said Harvath, locking eyes with the man. 'The descriptions you give me had better be perfect. If we are unable to stop them, if even one bomb goes off, your family is as good as dead.'

★　★　★

Al-Yaqoubi's bombers had picked one of the most densely packed tourist areas in Amsterdam. De Wallen was the most popular red-light district and was located in the heart of the oldest part of the city. It was a network of alleys and small streets crisscrossing several blocks and canals south of the *Oude Kerk*.

Scantily clad women, midgets, hermaphrodites, and transvestites offered themselves from behind large windows or glass doors often accompanied by a red light. The prostitutes' places of business were often interspersed with sex shops, peep shows, hash bars, and live-sex theaters.

Tourists gawked at the women, but for the most part kept moving. The challenge for Harvath and Martin de Roon was how to field their teams. Dutch law enforcement officials were similar to their American counterparts and were easy to spot by their physiques and demeanor.

Regardless, no one spent hours upon hours wending their way through De Wallen. It wasn't that big. Anyone who did so would be pegged as unusual and therefore suspect. The last thing they wanted to do was tip their hand.

Harvath came up with an idea to put four of Martin's youngest operatives in soccer jerseys. They looked like athletes anyway and could convincingly pass themselves off as teammates out celebrating a win. De Roon thought it was a good idea and decided to okay it, suggesting the men park themselves at one of the hash bars in the center of the red-light district.

He also agreed that since most people never looked up, placing snipers out of sight along as many of the rooftops as possible was a good idea. Using small cameras to observe the streets below them, they acted as extra eyes in the skies and wouldn't need to expose themselves unless they were ready to take a shot.

The positions for the last assets to be placed in were the hardest to decide upon. While couples and bachelorette parties strolled through De Wallen, they kept moving and rarely passed the same location twice unless it was on their way home after a night out on the town.

Casey didn't need to be asked. She knew placing the Athena Team in the windows was the best way to watch the flow of people and they all volunteered. All that needed to be decided was which windows they would take. Once Harvath and Martin had identified the best possible locations, de Roon contacted a cop he knew and trusted who dealt with the red-light district and explained that he was running a very quiet sting. The occupants of the windows in question were paid a hefty sum of cash from Harvath's funds and given the night off.

Everything was ready to go except for one thing. The Athena Team members were probably some of the most attractive 'prostitutes' the red-light district had ever seen. Before the operation could begin, they needed to figure out a means by which to dissuade potential customers from bothering them. The plan they came up with actually helped distribute their remaining operatives.

Operatives, including Harvath and de Roon, were placed out of sight with each of the women. If a potential suitor approached and wanted to arrange for her services, each operative would say that he had bought her for the night and to take a hike. In addition, they would also be wearing the same soccer jerseys. If someone did hit up all five women, they'd be left thinking some soccer team or hooligan fan club had taken over the best talent in the district and hopefully move on.

With positioning out of the way, Harvath was left to reflect on the men they were looking for. Al-Yaqoubi had been quite ingenious. Instead of recruiting Arab Muslims for his attack, he had recruited Indonesians.

Indonesia was the most populous Muslim country in the world and had once been a Dutch colony. People of Indonesian descent could be found throughout the Netherlands. They had largely assimilated themselves into the culture and weren't considered threatening, unlike their Arab brethren. They also could move through the red-light district, even during a time of heightened anxiety and security, without drawing attention to themselves.

Al-Yaqoubi was in bad shape, and it was a fight to keep him conscious. He could only give rough descriptions of the men. They were of average height, with dark hair and eyes; all in their mid twenties. He had no idea how they would be dressed except to say that they would have to employ some means to cover their bomb vests.

The cell's controller was in his late thirties and also Indonesian. He had a thick, white scar behind his left ear from a motorcycle accident in his youth. The accountant only knew the bombers by their Muslim names and not their given names under which they lived their Dutch lives. He did, though, know the controller's given name, Joost Moerdani. It was all they got out of him before he slipped back into unconsciousness.

With that information, Martin had been able to pull the man's driver's license and passport photos. Everyone, including the plainclothes police that had been brought in to form a covert ring around the red-light district, knew what he looked like. If he was spotted, everyone had been given strict orders not to take him down. They were to report his location and attempt to keep him under surveillance.

It was a warm night and Harvath hoped that would help them spot their suicide bombers. Indonesian men wearing sweatshirts, sweaters, jackets, or bulky shirts would get very special attention.

Once a potential bomber was ID'd, the nearest team members would go to work. Posing as a tourist taking video of the red-light district with a camera phone, one member would try to get the man's picture while the other would track him.

The picture would be sent to de Roon's men on the *Sacleipea*. If al-Yaqoubi was awake, then he would be shown the picture to help confirm identification. If he wasn't awake, they were going to be in a lot of trouble.

Assuming al-Yaqoubi would be able to ID the bombers, the rules of engagement became very clear. The target needed to be taken out. The only question was how to do it without starting a panic that would send tourists screaming.

De Roon's men had come up with a solution that showed strong faith in their snipers. When the sniper was ready to take his shot, the AIVD team tailing the target would close ranks, come up right behind him, and catch him as he was being neutralized.

Harvath didn't like it. There was too much that could go wrong. If the bombers were walking around buttoned down with a dead-man switch, the minute they released their trigger their device would explode. There was still a chance that any interdiction could happen within sight of the controller, who would then activate the device remotely. According to al-Yaqoubi, the cell phone detonators were sewn into each vest in the back. It wouldn't be easy to get them out and deactivate them. Therefore, neutralizing the controller was an integral part of their plan.

Despite all of the risks, Martin's men wanted to go ahead with the operation. Harvath had a tremendous amount of respect for them. They were a tribute to law enforcement officers the world over.

The evening progressed, and the crowds of tourists in De Wallen grew heavier. Harvath had been paired with Nikki Rodriguez, who was wearing a lace bra, matching panties, a garter belt with stockings, and a pair of high heels.

'Are you getting a good eyeful from there?' she asked Harvath.

'I'm not looking at you,' he said. 'I'm watching the street.'

'Yeah, sure you are. How's my ass look?'

He was used to inappropriate banter in tense situations, but normally, it was with men, not a very attractive, half-naked woman. 'I've seen better,' he replied.

'You're a liar.'

'No offense, Rodriguez, but you're not my type.'

'What? A hot-looking woman in peak physical fitness turns you off?' she asked. 'Honey, you can come look, I don't have an Adam's apple.'

Harvath chuckled. 'I'm the Navy man, remember? I've been to some pretty interesting ports of call. If you had an Adam's apple, I guarantee you I would have spotted it from a mile away.'

'So we're agreed I'm all woman?'

'Absolutely,' said Harvath, 'just like my fiancée.'

Rodriguez shook her head. 'I knew it.'

'Sorry.'

'Just tell me she isn't a goat.'

'She's not a goat,' said Harvath with a smile, but the smile quickly faded from his face. 'Look. Do you see that guy out the window?'

'Where?'

'Ten o'clock.'

Rodriguez looked and when she did, Harvath could hear her draw in her breath. The man was going to pass right beneath her window.

Harvath activated his radio, identified himself, and said, 'Player one has entered the game.'

59

'I don't get it, Marwan. Are you trying to tell me that you trust him more than you trust me?' asked Abdul Rashid.

'It is not a question of trust, Shahab,' replied the older man. 'It is a question of loyalty.'

They were sitting in the lobby of the Chicago Marriott on Michigan Avenue. Rashid was drinking a coffee, Marwan a Diet Coke.

'So what are you saying? That I should swear allegiance to Aazim Aleem?'

'As long as you are loyal to me, that's all I care about.'

'How do we make sure we don't repeat the mistakes that the brothers in Europe have made?'

'That's not something you need to be concerned about,' said the older man.

Rashid set his coffee down and leaned forward. 'I don't even know what our plans are after Chicago.'

'And you're not supposed to know. It is — '

'For my own good and the good of the operation,' said Rashid, finishing the man's sentence for him.

'As long as you follow my orders, everything

408

will go according to plan.'

'And whose orders do you follow? Aleem's? I'm not exactly comfortable with the fact that he may be our supreme leader.'

'Don't concern yourself with matters beyond your control.'

Rashid glanced around to make sure no one was listening to them before continuing. 'Marwan, look at us. We've spent half the day surveilling hotel lobbies. Do you have any idea how crazy this is?'

'Circumstances have dictated that we change our methods.'

'*Circumstances?* What circumstances?'

Marwan took a sip of his Diet Coke and looked at his watch. 'You will know this afternoon.'

'What's happening this afternoon?'

'Insha'Allah, the final attack in Europe. Then it will be our turn.'

The young man lowered his voice. 'Can I speak honestly with you, Marwan?'

'I should hope you always do.'

Rashid smiled and bowed his head. 'Always. But I am concerned.'

'I've told you that you worry too much.'

'Maybe, but you made me operational director of the Chicago event. I helped train the recruits and do the planning. Now, you and Sheik Aleem want to throw all of our planning and all of our training out the window. That worries me.'

'It shouldn't,' replied Jarrah.

'But it does. We have this operation perfectly planned, everything. Then, all of a sudden, you want to switch us to a Mumbai-style event.'

'Straying from what is comfortable is often stressful.'

'Marwan, it would take us months to get our men properly trained.'

'We don't have months,' said the older man. 'We only have two days.'

'Excuse me?'

'You heard what I said.'

Rashid looked at him. 'It'll never work.'

'You must have faith. There is great wisdom in what Sheik Aleem has suggested.'

'I'm sorry, Marwan — '

The older man smiled and cut him off. 'Let me finish. I have decided that the original event will continue as planned.'

'But — '

Marwan raised his hand to quiet his protégé again. 'As a contingency, and hopefully to strike even greater terror into the hearts of our enemies, we will follow Sheik Aleem's suggestion.'

Rashid shook his head.

'Sheik Aleem wants you to be in charge of both.'

'I am honored.'

The older man looked at him. 'You should be.'

'But changing everything at the last minute will make success nearly impossible.'

'With faith in Allah, nothing is impossible.'

'Of course,' replied Rashid, 'but where am I supposed to find men in two days with weapons experience who are willing to be Shahid?'

'Do you have faith in Allah?'

'Of course I do.'

'Good, for He has already provided you with everything you need.'

Rashid's brow furrowed. 'I don't understand.'

'Allah has already given you six Iraqi National Guardsmen.'

'Your thugs at the mosque?'

'They are not thugs. They are exceptional instruments if wielded properly.'

'I thought they were just muscle you used for security.'

The older man shook his head.

'You should have told me about their backgrounds.'

'At the time, you did not need to know. Now that you do know, perhaps you will treat them with more respect.'

Rashid rubbed his mouth with the palm of his hand and said, 'While we're talking about respect, let's talk about where I fit into the bigger picture.'

'One step at a time,' he replied as he changed the subject and gestured toward the second story of the atrium that overlooked the lobby where they now sat. 'Aleem has suggested the men work in three teams of two. I think that is a good idea.'

'But two of your National Guardsmen were shot last night, remember?'

'They will be fine. One of them we will put up there, on the second floor, to act as a sniper.'

'That's not really the plan, is it? We're not just going to pick four hotels with the best fields of fire and turn the guardsmen loose, are we?'

411

'Why not? Anyone can walk into these hotels. There is no security whatsoever. Our men only need to make it as far as the lobby.'

Maybe it was the fatigue that caused him to take a moment to catch on. 'Mumbai was a combination of bombings *and* shootings. It turned the entire city upside down. Police, fire, ambulances; none of them knew where to go. It was mass chaos.'

Marwan smiled, 'Very good, Shahab.'

'I should have thought of that.'

'Yes, you should have. You have been focused on the success the brothers had in Bali and the 7/7 bombings in London. You must remember to always ask yourself, how can we do better. Mumbai was definitely better.'

Rashid nodded. 'So three teams means three hotels?'

'Come, Shahab. You're not thinking big enough. This is Chicago. The hotels sit side by side. The men will go from one hotel to another and then to another and another still. As our bombs rip through the city, the police will be overwhelmed.'

'And then what?'

Marwan removed a ten-dollar bill from his wallet and set it on the table. 'You concentrate on succeeding in Chicago. The rest of the plan will take care of itself.'

60

Three hours ago, Harvath and de Roon had almost come to blows in the infirmary of the *Sacleipea*. With al-Yaqoubi barely clinging to consciousness, he had given them everything he could about the Amsterdam bombing cell, but Harvath had wanted more. He had wanted to know who the overall architect of the plot was. What were the cities targeted for attack in the United States? When and by whom? How could they be stopped?

Al-Yaqoubi had lost consciousness twice and both times Harvath had brought him back around again with the salts. The third time he lost consciousness, though, de Roon had stepped in. If Harvath hadn't stopped, he would have killed the man. The accountant would have ceased being of use to anyone. De Roon needed him to be awake and alert enough to help ID the bombers if they were lucky enough to spot them.

Harvath had known his friend was right, but he also knew that he couldn't stop until al-Yaqoubi gave them everything. In the end, Casey's had been the voice of reason that had convinced Harvath to back down. The Amsterdam attack had to be neutralized first. The

413

red-light district would be packed with Americans. That's where Harvath's focus needed to be. The accountant was cuffed to the bed of an infirmary of a confiscated ship in the Dutch port, its crew cooling its heels in a Dutch jail cell. Al-Yaqoubi wasn't going anywhere. This was their chance to see if he was really telling the truth. If he was and they succeeded, then they could return to the ship and take the interrogation to the next level. She was right.

Harvath had apologized to de Roon, who called him a *klootzak* and suggested they formulate their plan and get their people into position. It had happened only three hours ago, but in the wake of the adrenaline dump it felt like three days.

But now, with fresh adrenaline pumping through his system, all Harvath could think about was taking out the bombers.

Back at the ship, al-Yaqoubi was awake and alert. He had ID'd 'player one,' the man spotted by Harvath, as one of the cell members. One of de Roon's teams was tracking him, but they were in a 'shadow,' an area where none of the snipers could get a clean shot.

Harvath had faith that the problem would soon remedy itself. What bothered him, though, was that no one had ID'd the controller yet. He was the wild card; the one who could detonate the explosives remotely. He needed to be found and neutralized immediately.

As Harvath was trying to put himself inside the controller's mind, his earpiece crackled with radio traffic. One of Martin's men had been speaking in Dutch, and de Roon quickly reminded him to speak English. The operative apologized and repeated his transmission. The 'soccer team' at one of the hash bars had just spotted 'player two.'

With that sighting, the floodgates opened. Back-to-back, three more sightings were registered — Indonesian men overdressed for the weather. Each one was confirmed. That made five. If al-Yaqoubi was telling the truth, there was only one more left. Once the sixth bomber had entered De Wallen, the countdown would accelerate.

Hidden from view in the back of the room, Harvath removed the map de Roon had given him and plotted where the men had been spotted and the direction they were all moving. He still had the same question: *Where's the controller?*

As the targets were confirmed via cell phone from the *Sacleipea*, the snipers locked in and held ready. They were all waiting for the final bomber to appear.

Harvath was tense. Sitting back with Rodriguez was driving him crazy. That sixth bomber was going to show up any minute, or worse, any second. They could no more wander around the red-light district aimlessly for hours without drawing attention to themselves than Harvath and de Roon's teams could.

Suddenly, the sixth potential bomber was sighted. Two minutes later, he was positively identified by al-Yaqoubi. They were in the final stretch, except for the controller.

Moments later, the snipers reported that the targets were all changing direction. As Harvath studied his map, de Roon's voice came over his radio. 'They're all converging toward the center. That's where the attack is going to happen.'

'Hold on,' cautioned Harvath as something Rodriguez had said played through his mind. 'We don't know that. Everyone stay calm.'

He then told Martin to meet him on the corner. The Athena Team members wanted to get into the fight, but Harvath wasn't exactly sure this was over and asked them to remain in place.

'What the hell's wrong with you?' asked de Roon when he met Harvath at the corner and they both headed for the center of the district.

'Why didn't any of your people spot the controller outside De Wallen?'

'Maybe they didn't see him,' replied the intelligence officer.

'Or maybe that's not where he is,' said Harvath. 'Maybe he's actually inside the district.'

'Then why didn't our teams spot him?'

'Because maybe they didn't know what they're looking for.'

De Roon stared at him, confused, but Harvath didn't have time to explain. Within seconds, one of the bombers walked right past them. The chill of death surrounding him was almost palpable.

'Did you see his hand?' asked Harvath.

De Roon nodded and radioed the others that the bomber they had just passed was holding a dead man's switch in his left hand.

'Okay,' said Martin when they arrived at the

center of the district, the only point the bombers' paths had intersected, 'what are we looking for?'

Harvath's eyes scanned the area until they fell on one particular window. 'Her,' he said.

The intelligence officer looked, but couldn't understand what Harvath was talking about. 'The ugly prostitute in the blue cover-up?'

Harvath kept moving. 'What do you think her nationality is?'

'Who knows? They all dye their hair blond.'

'Look at her face.'

He did, but he still couldn't figure it out. 'With all that makeup, she could be Palestinian, or she could even be Norwegian.'

'Look at the eyes,' said Harvath.

'Filipina?'

'How about Indonesian?'

De Roon saw it. 'You think that's the controller?'

'She, he, whatever, is the only hooker in De Wallen wearing a robe and a scarf in the middle of summer.'

De Roon understood that Harvath meant it was probably a man trying to disguise himself as a woman and watched as the American pulled his pistol.

Harvath kept the weapon hidden behind his leg as he approached the window. The man inside had been gyrating to music that couldn't be heard out on the street. He stopped as he noticed Harvath's approach.

The subtle change in the man's demeanor wasn't lost on Harvath. He kept walking forward and said to de Roon, 'Tell the snipers to get ready to fire.'

Either the man in the window was an incredible lip reader or he saw on Harvath's face that his cover had been blown.

Out of the blue, he lunged for his purse and that's when Harvath raised his pistol and fired.

The glass of the window erupted and people began screaming and running in every direction.

Harvath took the steps up to the little private room two at a time and kicked the door open. The figure with the scarf around its neck lay dead, a pool of blood rolling across the sloped wooden floor toward the front of the room.

Behind the man's left ear, Harvath saw a thick, ropey white scar. 'Take them down,' Harvath said over his radio. 'Take all of the bombers down now.'

He looked up to locate de Roon and as he did, a burst of traffic came over the radio. Less than a second later, an enormous detonation shook the entire red-light district as a roiling fireball exploded into the night sky.

61

Leaving de Roon's men to process the corpse and secure the scene, Harvath raced in the direction of the explosion.

'What the hell happened?' he screamed over his radio.

'One bomber detonated before we could take a shot,' a voice replied.

'What about the others?'

'All neutralized.'

Harvath ran against a sea of people who were all fleeing the bombing. Klaxons wailed in the distance and a heavy pall of dust and smoke hung in the air. It was like 9/11 in miniature. The force of the blast had shattered every window he passed. Shards of broken glass blanketed the street. As he got closer, he began to develop a sense of how bad the attack had been.

The walking wounded stumbled past him, unsure of where to go, knowing only that they had to get away, they had to get out of the area.

Then came the people who couldn't move. They sat or lay near walls, and despite the bravery of a few Good Samaritans, there weren't enough hands to administer aid, so the wounded stayed where they were, waiting for help. Many were crying and in extreme pain. There was blood everywhere. Then came the bodies.

Harvath had no idea how much explosive the bomber had been carrying, but its impact was unbelievable. It was one of the worst scenes of carnage Harvath had ever witnessed. The dead and dying were scattered everywhere. Some had even been tossed into the air and were hanging from signs or out of second- and third-story windows.

The buildings were charred and the stench of burnt human flesh was overwhelming. It took Harvath a moment to get his bearings and when he did, he was overcome with a sense of dread. The bombing had happened almost directly in front of the window Nikki Rodriguez had been in.

He attempted to hail her over the radio as he rushed into what remained of the building. Its entire façade had been sheared away.

Planting his feet, he tried to raise a section of collapsed wall, but it was too heavy. He radioed de Roon and told him to bring jacks and any earth-moving equipment he could get his hands on. Then, he began to dig.

There were severed electrical wires and the scent of gas from ruptured lines. Harvath ignored all of it.

He lifted piece after piece of heavy stone. Shrapnel and twisted metal tore at his hands until they began to bleed, but Harvath kept on.

At some point, Casey arrived; then Ericsson, Rhodes, and Cooper. De Roon and three of his men materialized with a long, iron pry bar. They used a piece of rubble for a fulcrum and managed to raise part of the wall.

Underneath, Harvath saw skin; Nikki's skin. Hitting the ground, he slid beneath the wall and crawled toward her. In the darkness, he couldn't tell if she was alive or dead. He had a flashlight in his pocket, but the space was so tight, he didn't have enough room to pull it out. The claustrophobic darkness reminded him of the pit full of children he had crawled into nine days ago in Iraq.

Behind him, Harvath could hear de Roon and his men grunting under the weight of the wall and yelling for Casey and her operators to find something to help prop it up before it fell.

As he got closer, Harvath tried to talk to Rodriguez, but she didn't reply. 'I need some light down here,' he shouted.

Someone cast a flashlight into the narrow confines. Harvath's body blocked most of the light, but he could just make out the side of Nikki's head. Her hair was matted and covered with blood. He strained his eyes to see if she was breathing, but he couldn't tell.

As he inched forward, the crawl space became smaller and smaller. His legs and arms burned and he realized that it wasn't from the exertion, but that he was worming his way across broken glass.

When he reached Rodriguez, he tried once more to get her to respond. 'Nikki?' he said. 'Can you hear me?'

She still didn't reply, and Harvath silenced his own breathing to listen for hers. De Roon yelled for him to get out, but Harvath told him to be quiet. He thought he'd heard something.

When the voices behind him fell silent, he cocked his head and didn't make a sound. That's when he heard her breathe. Rodriguez was still alive.

Ignoring the instability of the pile of debris he was crawling through, he muscled his way forward. When he got close enough, he reached out and touched the side of her face. He heard her groan in response.

'We need to get you out of here, Nikki. Can you move?'

Rodriguez didn't respond.

'Scot,' de Roon yelled. 'You need to get out now. We cannot hold the wall any longer. Leave her. We'll try again.'

'You hold that goddamn wall,' Harvath ordered as he reached for Nikki's shoulders. He had no idea what the extent of her injuries were, and moving her went against all rescue protocols except for one, saving someone's life.

Inching backward, he gave a tug and pulled her toward him. Rodriguez screamed in pain and the sound tore right through him.

He tried not to think about it as he backed up and gave her another tug forward. She screamed again, but this time she didn't move.

Please, no, thought Harvath. *She's pinned.*

They were close enough now that he could tell she was having trouble breathing. Her breath came in short, shallow gasps and was becoming more rapid.

'Nikki?' he said. 'Can you move your legs?'

The woman was unable to respond.

'Nikki, listen to me. I know it hurts, but we need to get you out of here. I'm going to count to three and when I do, I'm going to pull as hard as I can. If you have any ability to help me; if you can push with your legs, or twist your body in any way to get free, you need to do it. Do you understand me?'

Rodriguez said nothing. It didn't matter. Harvath knew what he had to do. With his hands beneath her arms, he inched his way back as far as he could without losing purchase and then, counting to three, he pulled.

There was a wrenching sound and then a snap, which he prayed was the crack of dried wood from somewhere behind her in the rubble and not bone.

De Roon yelled that they were losing the wall, but Harvath refused to let go of her. He had her now; they were moving. It was slow, inch by painful inch, as if she was dragging some sort of incredibly heavy weight.

'Hurry, damn it!' yelled de Roon. 'Hurry!'

Harvath's entire body burned from the strain, but they were almost free. He continued to slide back a foot and pull, slide back a foot and pull.

He had no idea how close he was to the end of the tunnel until he felt hands on his boots and then his legs, helping to pull him back. Then there were hands on his belt pulling him hard.

De Roon and his men grunted under the weight of the wall. They were yelling and cursing for the others to hurry. With Harvath out, there was only Rodriguez left. Already, the wall was beginning to fall.

Harvath rolled away from the rubble pile as Nikki's teammates reached in to pull her out. As they did, he saw a sharp piece of metal that had embedded itself in her right side. The realization that the metal protruding from her chest had caused all the drag on her body as he struggled to extract her made him almost want to throw up. Then there was a shout from one of the Athena Team members of 'Don't drop the wall!' and he realized how wrong he had been and how incredible Nikki Rodriguez was.

While Harvath was pulling her out, she was pulling out someone else; a young woman who had been in the room next to her. Despite her injuries, and the high probability that the rest of the building could have collapsed, Rodriguez had never let go.

With his last half-ounce of adrenaline, Harvath leapt to his feet and helped de Roon's team hold the wall. When the second woman was free, they attempted to lower the wall as gently as possible, but no one had the strength to see it all the way down.

It landed with a deafening crash, which hastened more structural failure and sent them all scrambling from the building. Casey and Cooper carried Rodriguez, while Ericsson and Rhodes helped the young prostitute from the room next door.

Out on the street, they began to administer first aid. Harvath's hands, elbows, and knees were bleeding, but he was in much better shape than most of the people around him.

Someone offered him a bottle of water. After dousing his wounds he drained what was left and surveyed the devastation around him. All of it from a single bomber. Though it would be no consolation to the families and loved ones of the dead, it could have been, *it was supposed to have been*, much, much worse.

He resolved to himself that no matter what he had to do, he would not let this scene repeat itself in America.

Calling de Roon over, he said, 'Give me your car keys.'

The intelligence officer looked at him. 'You can't drive like that.'

'I need to get back to al-Yaqoubi. I need to finish his interrogation.'

De Roon looked over Harvath's shoulder, saw the first waves of Dutch rescue personnel arriving on the scene and said, 'I'll drive and we'll finish it together.'

62

Khalil al-Yaqoubi asked to speak to his family when Harvath entered the *Sacleipea*'s infirmary. He wanted assurances that they were still alive and that they had not been harmed.

The DST operative in Rabat was Casey's contact, but Casey had gone to the hospital with Rodriguez while the other team members stayed at the scene to help treat the victims. Harvath couldn't have called the man if he wanted to. Not that it mattered. Al-Yaqoubi was in no position to ask for anything.

'The deal is off, Khalil,' said Harvath.

The Moroccan didn't understand. 'But I did everything you asked. I told you the truth.'

'One of the bombs went off,' said de Roon as he instructed his men to leave the infirmary.

You could have heard a pin drop as the heavy steel door slammed shut.

Harvath unwound the bandage from the man's left foot.

'What are you doing?' al-Yaqoubi demanded.

'I'm going to make you pay for all of the people who died tonight. Then I am going to make you pay for all the people who died in Paris. Then I am going to make you pay for Rome.'

Picking up a forceps and scalpel, he told de Roon, 'Hold down his legs,' and began probing for the sural nerve. It didn't take long to find it.

The terrorist screamed from the white-hot intensity of the pain.

'After I'm done making you pay, then we'll call your family and I'll let you listen to them pay.'

'No!' al-Yaqoubi shouted. 'I did everything you asked. I will continue to do everything you ask.'

Harvath dug the forceps in again. 'It's too late, Khalil,' he shouted so he could be heard above the man's screaming. 'I warned you what would happen if even one of those bombs went off.'

The man was crying and begged Harvath to stop. 'I will do anything. Anything. Please.'

De Roon looked at Harvath and he backed off. 'I want to know who you're working for.'

'I don't know,' he stammered and Harvath shoved the forceps back in.

Al-Yaqoubi's body went rigid and he arched his back so high it looked like his spine was about to snap. Tears were rolling down his face.

'Stop lying to me, Khalil.'

The man was hyperventilating. Harvath drew back the forceps and waited for him to catch his breath. 'Last chance, Khalil. Who are you working for?'

'I'm telling you the truth. I do not know.'

Harvath moved the forceps closer.

'Al-Qaeda!' the man yelled. 'Al-Qaeda. We swore our oath to Sheik Osama.'

'You only say that because that's what you think I want to hear,' said Harvath as he studied the man's face to discern whether or not he was telling the truth.

'It's true. I swear to you.'

'Tell me about site 243.'

'What?' replied al-Yaqoubi.

'*Site 243.*'

'I don't know what that is. I have never heard of it.'

'What about the Chinese?'

'I don't know any Chinese.'

Harvath sensed he was telling the truth. Whoever had put this network together, especially if it was the Chinese, would have used third-party nationals from top to bottom. Al-Yaqoubi probably believed he really was working for al-Qaeda. The idea that his network had been assembled by China only to be hijacked by someone else would have been utterly incomprehensible to him.

Harvath switched his line of questioning. 'Where did you train?'

'Yemen and Pakistan.'

'Who do you report to? Who gives you your orders?'

'I don't know his real name.'

Harvath noticed a slight change in the man's expression and rammed the forceps back into his foot. Once again, al-Yaqoubi's body rose off the bed and writhed as he tried to escape the pain.

'Aleem,' he yelled, 'Aazim Aleem.'

'I've never heard of him,' said Harvath as he twisted the tool inside the man's foot like a fork into a plate of spaghetti.

Al-Yaqoubi howled and had trouble catching his breath. 'He, he, he preaches on the Internet and on CDs and cassette tapes. They call him the Mufti . . . ' his voice trailed off.

'The *what?*' Harvath demanded.

'The Mufti of Jihad.'

That was a name Harvath had heard of. The man was a rock star to jihadists around the world. He kept a very low profile and as far as Harvath knew, no one had ever been able to identify him.

Harvath disengaged the forceps and slid them out of the man's foot. 'The Mufti of Jihad is a ghost,' he said. 'No one knows who he is. Why would he make his identity known to you?'

It took a moment for al-Yaqoubi to respond. 'Because he and I were in the camps together. He was my instructor. He recruited me.'

'Describe him to me.'

The accountant strained at the wrists and remembered that he was tied down. He was breathing heavily. 'Hands. He has no hands. Only hooks.'

'Why?'

'Jihad, Afghanistan.'

The man was slipping away again.

'Focus, Khalil,' Harvath ordered. 'Where is he from?'

'Don't know.'

'Saudi Arabia? Egypt? What languages does he speak?'

'Arabic and . . . ' he said, his voice trailing off.

'And *what?*'

When he didn't answer, Harvath slapped him. 'What other language does he speak?'

'English. Very good English. Like an Englishman.'

'Does he live in England? Is that where he's

429

based? Who else is involved?' Harvath demanded. 'Tell me about America. Who is in charge of
the attacks in America?'

The accountant didn't answer, and Harvath
knew he was on the verge of blacking out again.
He grabbed a package of smelling salts and
looked at de Roon.

The intelligence officer nodded. He had no
intention of getting in Harvath's way this time.

Harvath opened the salts and waved them
under the terrorist's nose.

Al-Yaqoubi began coughing and his eyes
started to normalize as he shook his head back
and forth. Harvath tossed the salts aside and
asked his question again. 'Who is in charge of
the American attacks?'

'There is an Iraqi,' sputtered al-Yaqoubi. 'He
is in charge of American operations.'

'What's his name? How do I find him?'

'I don't know his name. Aleem was the only
one I knew by name. The rest of us used code
names.'

Harvath doubted Aleem was his real name. He
would have used a pseudonym as well.

'The man in America,' said Harvath as he
raised the forceps again and hovered over the
accountant's foot, 'what's his code name?'

'Yusuf. We called him Yusuf.'

'What else do you know about him?'

'He is a businessman of some sort.'

'What kind of business?'

'I don't know.'

Harvath debated shoving the forceps back
inside the man's foot, but held back. 'You said he

was an Iraqi. How long has he been in the United States?'

'I don't know.'

'I am losing my patience, Khalil. You don't seem to know much at all. Where in Iraq is the man from?'

'Fallujah. He comes from a large family there.'

'How do you know?'

'Iraqis like to brag about their families. He had a cousin who was the local commander of the National Guard. He talked about him a lot. He said that was how he was introduced to al-Qaeda.'

Harvath lowered the forceps. 'What was his cousin's name?'

'I can't remember.'

'Try harder!' Harvath shouted. 'Your family's life depends on it.'

Al-Yaqoubi's pulse was pounding as he searched his brain for the name. 'Hadi? Halef? I can't remember.'

Harvath looked at de Roon. 'Call Rabat. Tell the DST that Khalil has been uncooperative and that they should begin.'

'Hakim!' the accountant yelled, the name rushing back to him. 'His cousin's name was Omar-Hakim.'

Omar-Hakim was the Iraqi National Guard commander Harvath had forced into helping him take down the al-Qaeda safe house outside Fallujah; the same safe house where the child hostages had been kept. Stunned, Harvath dropped the surgical instrument he was holding and ran from the infirmary.

431

Bursting through one of the exterior bulkheads, he began dialing the number for his contact in Fallujah before he even had a full-strength signal.

The call failed. Harvath cursed and dialed again. A few moments later, Mike Dent answered his phone.

'Mike, it's Scot,' said Harvath. 'Is Omar-Hakim still alive?'

'No,' replied the man from Fallujah. 'He was tortured to death a couple of days after you dropped him off. Are you having an attack of conscience or something?'

The Iraqi had gotten what he deserved. In fact, he probably deserved much worse, but that didn't matter now. 'Do you know any of his family members in Fallujah?'

'I don't know any of them, but everyone knows of them. Why?'

'He has a cousin. A businessman in America. I need you to find out everything you can about him.'

'How soon do you need it?' asked Dent.

'I need it immediately and I don't care what you have to do to get it. Do you understand?'

'Can I use local talent?'

'Use whoever you have to and agree to pay them whatever they want,' said Harvath, 'but you get me that information and you get it for me ASAP.'

432

63

CHICAGO

'I have already made provisions for weapons and ammunition,' said Marwan. 'Your trip is not necessary. Focus on the remaining elements which need to be accomplished.'

Rashid tried to explain. 'When we left the hotel, did you notice the two cops standing there?'

'Yes, I saw them, but I don't — '

'How about their vests?'

'Level-two soft body armor,' said the man. 'Level three if they have upgraded from what they were given at the police academy.'

'That's the armor. What about the carriers they use?'

'Carriers don't provide ballistic protection, Shahab.'

'No, they don't,' replied Rashid, 'but a lot of cops now have trauma plates in addition to their armor.'

Marwan Jarrah waved his hand dismissively as he liked to do when he felt a point was beneath his discussion. 'That's why our men have rifles. It will be like shooting through tissue paper. It won't be a problem.'

'But suppose it is? Suppose some young cop

doesn't mind the weight of hard plates.'

The older man laughed. 'Everyone minds the weight. You know this. You were a soldier. No one wears hard armor unless they expect an attack. This is going to be a surprise; something they will not see coming.'

'Maybe, Marwan. Maybe. In fact, let's say you're right. Let's say nobody expects this attack. But just for fun, let's also say that the two cops we saw at the Marriott *aren't* standing outside when our men arrive, but they show up one minute after.'

Jarrah exhaled. 'And?'

'How'd they get there?'

'This is foolish. Let's talk about something else.'

'It's not foolish,' insisted Rashid. 'Those cops came in a patrol car. Patrol officers are now being issued patrol rifles. So, firepower-wise they are equal to your men. And if they're smart, which many of them are, especially the younger, more aggressive cops, they are also going to have hard armor. It'll take them two seconds to get it out of the trunk and throw it on.

'Our men could have plowed through half the lobby, but they won't get to the other half, much less their next hotel. And what if it's not patrol officers, but one of the city's roving tactical teams that arrives?'

The man was silent as he pieced together what his protégé was saying.

'It will take me less than five hours to go and come back.'

'Why Wisconsin?'

434

'Because Illinois requires a firearms identification card to buy reloading supplies and Wisconsin doesn't.'

'It seems like a great risk to me this close to the attack.'

Rashid looked at him. 'I'm going to break up the purchases at three different locations. I'll get the reloading machine at one, powder and primers at another, and the rounds and jackets at the third.'

'What about video cameras?'

'I'll be careful.'

'What if you get stopped?'

'I'm not going to get stopped, Marwan. But even if I do, my driver's license has my Christian name on it.'

'I want Fadim and Uday to go with you.'

'That's a great idea. I think we should all wear turbans and *Islam is a dynamite religion* T-shirts. How about that?'

'I'm in no mood for disrespect,' Marwan snapped.

'Those two get enough looks here in Chicago. If I take them with me to Wisconsin we're going to raise a lot of eyebrows, or a lot of unibrows in Fadim and Uday's case.'

'This is why people in our organization are uncomfortable with you.'

Rashid raised his hands, palms up. 'Because of my sense of humor?'

'No. It is your belief that you know better than everyone else.'

'I do when everyone else is not using their heads. C'mon, Marwan. The first thing people

435

think of when they see Fadim and Uday is *terrorist*. You can't walk them into a store that sells guns and not expect to create a stir. I thought the idea was not to draw attention to ourselves.'

'That is the plan,' replied Jarrah. 'I am sending them along for your protection. They will ride in a separate vehicle and keep an eye on you. You will not go armed and I do not want you using your cell phone. Is that understood? You go buy the items you need and you return immediately.'

'You don't want me using my cell phone now?'

'Sheik Aleem is concerned that the network may have been penetrated.'

'Because of what happened in London?'

'Because of London *and* Amsterdam.'

'*Amsterdam?*' said Rashid. 'That's the site of the final European attack?'

The man nodded.

'What happened?'

'There were six bombers. Only one success-fully detonated. Sheik Aleem is correct to be concerned that the network may have been compromised.'

'Then all the more reason to put our plans on hold.'

'No,' replied the man. 'It is more important than ever that we succeed. That's why I agree with you about the ammunition and why I am letting you go get the things we need.'

'But without my cell phone and with Fadim and Uday keeping me company.'

'For once, Shahab, would you do something without arguing with me? That's all I ask.'

Rashid bowed his head. 'I'm sorry, Marwan. We'll do it your way.'

'Good. Thank you. Now we need to talk about the police officers we are holding. They're a liability and need to be dealt with.'

'I agree.'

Jarrah was taken aback. 'You do?'

'Yes. No good can come from holding on to them.'

'So then they should be disposed of.'

'Yes.'

The man smiled. 'This is very good, Shahab. I'm pleased that for once you see things my way. I'll let you, then, decide how to handle it.'

'I already know how I want to handle it,' said Rashid.

'How?'

'They are going to be martyrs for our cause, and they will take many of their fellow officers with them.'

64

It took Mike Dent about three hours to get Harvath the information he needed. Within forty-five minutes of Dent's call, he and the remaining Athena Team members were on a Citation X to Chicago.

It was a tough decision to leave their teammate behind in the hospital, but they knew Rodriguez would have wanted them to finish the job.

From that point forward, the Dutch took over the interrogation of al-Yaqoubi, though Harvath doubted they'd get much more out of him.

Meanwhile, Carlton's people were still working on Adda Sterk. She was producing only small amounts of intel, much of it not very useful. The same could be said of the controller for the London cell who had been broken by Ashford's team. Whoever had assembled this network had done a very good job. Everything was compartmentalized and cutouts had been used all along the way. It was only when you got closer to the top, as they had with al-Yaqoubi, that the payouts began to get bigger.

The last piece of information Harvath had harvested from the accountant had been the

438

most terrifying. Whatever 'Yusuf' had planned for America, it was set to begin in the next forty-eight hours.

Per Mike Dent, Yusuf was actually a furniture importer in Chicago named Marwan Jarrah. He had fled Iraq during the 1980s and eventually became a U.S. citizen. He was an influential member of the American branch of a Saudi Arabia-based charity. The charity was a member of the Conference of NGOs and had conducted multiple projects with the World Health Organization, the United Nations International Children's Emergency Fund, the United Nations High Commission for Refugees, and the World Food Program. Prominence in this organization had provided Jarrah cover to travel anywhere he wanted. It was no coincidence that the greatest hotbeds of terrorism and radical Islam were in the same parts of the Muslim world so keenly focused upon by his charity.

In order to prevent Jarrah's relatives from tipping him off, Dent had arranged for the ones he had questioned to be detained until Harvath okayed their release. For the first time since this operation had begun, Harvath felt that he had been able to take more than just one step forward before getting knocked on his ass.

He had to block the scenes from Amsterdam from his mind or he wouldn't be able to focus on what still needed to be done. Along with the pit of children from Fallujah and the little Iraqi boy who had died in his arms, he tucked them all into the iron box he kept for the unpleasantness of his job and shoved it back into the deepest

439

recesses of his mind.

He tried to think of something positive, something he could look forward to, and was surprised when Riley's image bubbled up in his mind. It made him feel disloyal to Tracy, and Tracy brought him back to the issue of having children; the exact thing he'd been sitting on his dock thinking about when all of this had begun.

As quickly as thoughts of Tracy and the hard decision he needed to make about his relationship with her came to mind, they were pushed aside by the work he had yet to do.

There had been some debate as to how the team should proceed once it landed in Chicago. They had no arrest or law enforcement powers. Acts of terror plotted and committed on American soil were treated as criminal acts, which Harvath had always thought a big mistake. By not treating them as acts of war, the United States government was only inviting escalation, greater bloodshed, and exponentially greater loss of life. The jihadists were at war with America, yet American politicians refused to go to war with them. They saw them as petty criminals to be tried and given all the benefits of the American legal system. The Department of Defense, though, saw it a different way.

The entire idea behind the Carlton Group was to protect America and her citizens, period. That was where things were now very sticky. Harvath and his organization had knowledge of pending terrorist attacks on U.S. soil. They also had intelligence regarding the man they believed to be in charge of those attacks inside the U.S. It could very well be argued that the information should have been shared with the FBI. But that was not how Reed Carlton or the small cadre of men to whom he answered inside the Pentagon saw it.

They wanted Marwan Jarrah all to themselves and they had no intention of sharing him. They also had no intention of reading him his Miranda rights or helping him secure an attorney. There was no telling how many cells he had within the United States. They needed to grab him, interrogate him, and neutralize his network as rapidly as possible. And if it meant violating a few terrorists' 'rights' along the way, then that was the way it was going to be.

With Carlton doing the groundwork for them, they used their time aboard the plane to eat, check on Nikki Rodriguez via the in-flight Sat-com system, and grab as much sleep as possible.

When they landed in Chicago, it was just after three in the morning. Two vehicles stuffed with gear were waiting for them; a windowless Chevy Astro van and a dented KIA Sportage with tinted glass. Harvath was anxious to set up surveillance and put together their plan for taking down Jarrah.

They divided up the equipment and broke into two teams. Once they had established a rendez-vous point, each team made a reconnaissance drive through Jarrah's residential neighborhood and the neighborhood where his furniture outlet and the American office of record for his charity was located. Two things immediately became clear.

The first was that surveilling Jarrah's house from a vehicle was going to be next to impossible. Street parking was by permit only and even if they had a permit, there wasn't a single space to be found. There were also *Neighborhood Watch. We call police* signs mounted everywhere, including in people's windows. Harvath had always hated doing residential surveillance and this was one of the biggest reasons. Neighbors tended to not only know and watch out for each other, but they also knew what everyone drove. Effectively, nonresidents stood out.

The second problem they faced was that there appeared to be multiple entrances and exits to Jarrah's furniture store. It was a large three-story commercial building with glass along the front and doors that opened onto the sidewalk. There was a fire escape and loading dock area in back that accessed the alley, a side door that allowed people to enter from the parking lot, and an exit on the far side of the structure that fed into a narrow gangway with the building next door. It was a lot to cover.

There was a third problem that Harvath didn't even want to think about. The fact that Jarrah's home and business were in Chicago didn't mean that he was. For all Harvath knew, he could be in New York City getting ready to oversee his first attack. Chicago had been their best and only lead.

Harvath would have given a year's salary to have placed drones overhead at the house and the business, or to have satellites retasked to help

442

give him extra sets of eyes, but that wasn't going to happen, not without setting off a bunch of alarm bells back in D.C. and getting them all in trouble. None of them were supposed to be here. Posse Comitatus notwithstanding, if anyone discovered that the DOD had created and was running its own covert, direct action network, there'd be absolute hell to pay. Harvath and his team were going to have to figure out how to get the job done while remaining under *everyone's* radar.

As they couldn't sit outside Jarrah's house, Megan Rhodes suggested they walk right up, ring the doorbell, and see who answered. As soon as the stores opened, she could buy an arrangement of flowers and pretend to be delivering them.

Harvath didn't like it, and Gretchen Casey immediately shot it down. 'Just like London and Amsterdam,' she said, 'this guy's paranoia level is going to be off the charts. An incorrect delivery is going to be highly suspect.'

'Who cares?' replied Rhodes. 'The door opens, my Glock goes in his face, everybody wins.'

'Not if he's got six other guys behind the door armed better than you are,' said Harvath.

'Six guys isn't even a fair fight. Now, if he had twelve, then maybe . . . '

'It's a nice idea, Megs, but keep thinking,' said Casey, who asked Harvath, 'What if there was another way we could get close to the house without arousing suspicion?'

'I'd be willing to entertain it. What are you thinking?'

'Do you think we could coopt one of the neighbors?'

Harvath shook his head. 'I doubt it. I saw two parked cars with Iraqi flag stickers. Either they both belong to Jarrah, or he and his neighbors share more than just the same zip code.'

'I'm with Scot,' said Cooper. 'I think we need to focus on the furniture store.'

Casey nodded. 'Okay, I agree. But I still want to see if we can't figure out some way to gain access to his house.'

'In the meantime,' replied Harvath, 'I want to get our surveillance network in place before it's light. If Jarrah is there, he's not only going to be expecting surveillance, he's going to be actively looking for it.'

65

'I don't know,' said Abdul Rashid as he pushed himself back from the table he was working at. 'You tell me. Would you want to already be shooting armor-piercing rounds, or swap out magazines once you finally come to the conclusion that you've got a problem? That's assuming you can remember which one of your mags is the one with the correct rounds to begin with.'

Jarrah looked at the reloading equipment and the piles of ammunition. 'Did you get any sleep at all last night?'

'No. And it's a good thing. You know what I found?' continued Rashid as he rolled his chair over to the adjoining table, picked up a cell phone, and tossed it to the man. 'This phone has something wrong with it.'

'We tested all the phones. What's the problem?'

'You tested to see if they'd vibrate and activate the detonators. I checked their electrical integrity. For some stupid reason, every once in a while this one pulses and gives off an electrical charge.'

'How strong?'

'Strong enough that I'd be worried about it prematurely setting off one of the explosives.'

Marwan walked over and kissed the younger man on the forehead.

'What was that for?' he asked.

Jarrah swept his arm around the room. 'For all of this. The improved ammunition. The double-checking of the explosives. All of it. You've done a very good job, Shahab. We are almost there.'

'So how do you want me to load the magazines for the shooters?'

The man thought about it for a moment. 'I'm apprehensive that we haven't had an opportunity to test the new ammunition you have fabricated.'

Rashid grabbed one of the rifles and a magazine he had loaded. 'Let's go try it in the parking lot right now.'

The Iraqi laughed at the young man's joke. 'You are as excited as I am, but we must be practical with our orchestration; cautious.'

'So no plinking in the lot?'

'Shahab, I believe that you know what you are doing. I also believe that Allah blessed your journey yesterday and that it adds a layer of security to what we are doing.'

'Good, so we'll use the new ammo.'

Jarrah waved his hand dismissively. 'We've already practiced with the other ammo.'

'The stuff you got from that gangbanging gunrunner? When?' asked Rashid.

'Weeks ago,' the older man replied.

Rashid looked at him. 'You've known all along that this was going to be a Mumbai-style attack.'

'I'm sorry I couldn't tell you, Shahab. The mission must always come first. You know that.'

The young man turned away and rolled his chair back to his reloading equipment.

The Iraqi smiled. 'You're tired. You should

rest. Tomorrow will be a glorious day, Insha'Allah.'

'I still have work to do. We're going to need to replace the bad cell phone and you haven't told me how you want the magazines loaded.'

'Relax. I have an extra cell phone up in the office,' he replied. 'And as for the armor-piercing rounds, load two of the thirty-round magazines for each man.'

'That's all?' Rashid asked.

'Yes, that's all. They will use the rounds we have tested as their primary ammunition. Your armor-piercing rounds will be a backup if they need them.'

'So you've got no problem, in the heat of battle, with them having to remember to transition to armor-piercing when the police show up.'

'Not at all. I have every faith and confidence. These men are well trained. They will remember.'

'It's your operation.'

'It is *our* operation, Shahab, and you have contributed many, many good things to it. Tomorrow, the infidels will be shaken. It will be the first blow of many that we will deliver on their own soil. After tomorrow, we will discuss the future and what Sheik Aleem and I have planned for you. But now, why don't you tell me what you are going to do with our guests; the police officers.'

The younger man reached for a piece of paper and a pen. He drew three squares whose tops came together to form a triangle. 'These will be the chairs that we duct tape together. Essentially, we'll be creating three separate blast directions like three claymores.'

'So each of the men will be wearing an explosive vest?'

'Yes, but it won't be obvious. As with our Shahid, their vests will be hidden by clothing.'

Marwan smiled. 'So you will place them in the center of the room and no matter how their colleagues gather around them, they will all be vulnerable?'

'Exactly. And along with duct-taping them to the chairs, they'll also have hoods and duct tape around their mouths so they can't speak or gesture.'

'Very good. How will you know the exact moment to detonate?'

'With this,' said Rashid as he reached over and picked up one of the remote camera balls John Vaughan and Paul Davidson had been caught placing in the alley behind the mosque.

The Iraqi brought his hands together in a clap. 'This is very good.'

'And it will be an excellent beginning to the chaos. It will draw tremendous resources to the exact opposite side of the city.'

'I'm proud of you, Shahab. You have indeed done a very good job. I just wonder if we should consider using another location.'

'No. Mohammed Nasiri's apartment is perfect.'

'How are we going to get the police officers in there without drawing attention?'

This time it was Abdul Rashid's turn to smile. 'Do you have faith in Allah, Marwan?'

66

As they had a very small surveillance team, Harvath decided that they could risk exposing only one of their operatives. Because she was biracial and Jarrah's furniture store catered to a largely ethnic clientele, Alex Cooper had nominated herself to go in and look around.

Armed with her camera phone and an exceptional *when-I-want-your-help-I'll-ask-for-it* attitude, she walked around inside ostensibly taking pictures of furniture while getting the most accurate lay of all three levels that she could.

She found the door to the basement, but it was locked. The door to the business office, on the other hand, was open and she walked right in. She was immediately confronted by two very large Middle Eastern men who told her in broken English that she was in an area off-limits to customers.

Feigning insult, Cooper scolded them for being rude and demanded to know where the ladies' room was.

One of the men directed her back into the showroom and pointed at a door on the far side. After she had washed her hands and come back out, the two men were talking to another, younger man who also appeared somewhat Middle Eastern.

As soon as he saw her, he headed straight for

her. Cooper pulled her camera phone back out and began taking pictures again.

'Can I help you, miss?' the man asked. He was tall and a bit skinny, but appeared quite fit.

'No, thank you,' she replied haughtily. 'I'm just browsing.'

'You've been taking a lot of pictures.'

Cooper turned to him with her camera in one hand and the other on her hip. 'Is there a problem with that?'

He put on a smile, spread his hands and replied, 'It's unusual.'

'It's *unusual?* Or it's unusual when a black woman does it?'

'It has nothing to do with the color of your skin.'

'Oh, *really?*'

His smile faded, and he glanced at a closed circuit camera as if someone else might be supervising their exchange and said, 'I just want to know why you're taking pictures.'

'You want to know why?' she said, turning the attitude knob all the way up. 'Because I'm tired of sending shit back. I'm tired of my boyfriend not liking a damn thing I buy. That's *why* I'm taking pictures.'

'We do have a Web site.'

'I know you've got a damn Web site.'

'I'd also be happy to get you a catalog.'

Cooper clicked her phone shut and got right in the young man's face. 'You know what? You can keep your damn catalog and your damn Web site. I'm going to find another store that isn't afraid of having black customers.'

450

The young man reached out. 'May I see your phone before you go?'

Cooper drew it to her chest. 'What the hell is wrong with you? No you may not. You people are crazy,' she said as she began walking toward the door.

The young man trotted alongside her and then stepped right into her path. 'You've been in here almost half an hour taking pictures.'

'I happen to be moving into a very big house.'

The young man was completely blocking her path now. He put his hand straight out. 'Give it to me.'

Cooper tapped her foot and then rolled her eyes before putting the phone into her purse. 'What are you going to do now?'

Rashid reached for the purse and before he knew what had happened, Cooper had kicked him right in the crotch.

'Never mess with a woman's purse,' she said as she stepped over him and quickly exited the store.

* * *

Cooper crossed the street, walked over two blocks, and turned the corner. Harvath was waiting in the Sportage. 'How'd it go?' he asked as she got in.

'You were right. They're beyond paranoid in there.'

'Did you learn anything?'

'From what I could see, they take their security very seriously. There were a couple of

Middle Easterners who got pretty upset when I stumbled into the office. The door to the basement was locked, which could mean anything or nothing, and their CCTV system looked like it came out of a Vegas casino. It was a little overkill, but what do I know? Maybe they have a problem with people shoplifting dressers and armoires.'

'Did you see anyone matching Jarrah's description?'

'No, but I did get pictures of his employees and a couple of the goons he's got working there,' said Cooper.

'So we have no idea if he's in the building or not.'

'No.'

'Do you think it's worth taking a look after dark?' asked Harvath.

'If we can get around their security system, I think it would be a great idea.'

★ ★ ★

The team spent the rest of the day and into the evening watching Jarrah's business. As darkness fell, the doors were locked and the lights dimmed. A handful of employees filed out, but missing from their ranks were the man Alex had kicked and the two goons who had chased her out of the office.

Shortly before eleven p.m., there was activity in the alley as a truck pulled up to the loading dock. A Pakistani-looking driver backed it in and one of the store's large, overhead doors was raised.

Casey looked at Harvath. 'Seems pretty late for a delivery.'

'Or a pickup,' he replied as he watched three medium-sized crates being wheeled on dollies into the truck.

'Those are the two goons I met earlier,' said Cooper over the encrypted radio as the men, dressed in matching delivery uniforms, placed the crates in the back of the truck and then were joined by the plain-clothes driver. 'And that's the man who tried to take my phone,' she said as a fourth man appeared. He was wearing a matching uniform.

Harvath and Casey watched from their vantage point in the KIA as the other team members held their positions.

The young man stepped out onto the loading dock and took a slow look around. Satisfied, he pulled down the truck's rear door, enclosing the two goons and the Pakistani man with the crates inside.

He said something over his shoulder and the furniture store's overhead door was closed. He then hopped off the loading dock, got inside the truck, and started it up.

'What the hell are they up to?' said Ericsson. 'Do we follow them?'

As the truck's engine rumbled to life and it began to pull away from the loading dock, Harvath had a decision to make.

'No, you stay here,' he replied. 'We'll go.'

Putting the KIA in gear, Harvath pulled out into traffic and kept as much distance as he could between themselves and the truck. As he drove, Casey reached into the backseat and flipped up the lid of one of the Storm cases. Removing a 4.6 mm Heckler & Koch MP7 submachine gun, she affixed its rectangular, Gem-Tech 'Brick' suppressor, inserted a fresh magazine, and chambered a round. 'Something tells me this is going to be a very long night.'

67

Marwan didn't need to tell him to drive carefully, but he did anyway. With two cops and a private eye boxed up in back, Rashid wasn't exactly anxious to get pulled over.

Traffic was light and the drive up to Nasiri's apartment took half an hour. The truck was large and difficult to maneuver, but he nevertheless conducted several SDRs to make sure he wasn't being followed.

In the alley behind Mohammed's building, he stopped and walked around to the back of the truck. The exterior stairwell was just as Nasiri had described. It was going to be a bitch carrying the three crates up to the apartment, but without an elevator, they had no other choice.

Rashid and Nasiri assisted, but Marwan's goons did the bulk of the work. They were sweating and cursing quietly even before they got halfway up with the second crate. This was probably not how they had envisioned spending their final night alive. And that went for Nasiri as well. They all knew what tomorrow would bring and they probably wished to already have ritually bathed and shaved themselves for their journey to Paradise.

Rashid had wondered if Aleem would lead the Shahid in prayers, but Marwan explained that the man had already left the city. It was important that he see to what was coming next. As usual, what that was, Marwan wasn't disposed to say.

When they got the third and final crate into the apartment, they closed the door and Rashid made sure the drapes were drawn as tight as possible. The odor in the kitchen was terrible. There was a plate of rotting food on the table, which Nasiri picked up and tossed into the garbage. He then pulled out some glasses and put on a pot of water for tea.

Rashid closed the blinds in the living room while the goons caught their breath and then set to work opening up the crates. The plan had worked perfectly. They hadn't seen any neighbors and even if one or two had been watching, it would have looked as if Mohammed Nasiri had purchased a three-piece bedroom set, as that's what was spray-painted on the side of the crates, and was having it delivered. Sure it was late at night, but with America's 24/7 culture, most of his immigrant neighbors wouldn't know to think anything of it.

Rashid arranged three chairs in the living room, just as he had diagrammed it for Marwan. They then tightly duct-taped the two cops and their detective colleague to them. The detective, whom he had shot at the mosque, had begun bleeding again.

Rashid checked their vests and dismissed the goons to join Nasiri in the kitchen for tea. He was almost finished.

After powering up the cell phone detonators, he adjusted their clothing to cover up the vests and then hid the camera ball between a couple of Nasiri's books in the corner of the room.

Satisfied that everything was exactly how he wanted it, Rashid joined the men for a fast cup of tea. Marwan would want them back as quickly as possible.

They gathered up the crating material and Rashid made sure to wipe down everything he touched so as not to leave any fingerprints. The other men didn't have to worry. Very soon, they wouldn't even have fingers.

As Nasiri and the goons threw the garbage in the back of the truck and climbed in, Rashid pulled down the door and checked his watch. It was after midnight. Wednesday had passed into Thursday. The day of the attack had come and now it was only hours away.

Rashid climbed back into truck and started it up. As he drove off down the alley, he had no idea that Harvath and Casey had been watching him the entire time.

68

As the truck exited the alley and disappeared from view, Harvath motioned to Casey and they stepped away from the Dumpster they'd been hiding behind.

'What do you think?' she asked.

Harvath looked up at the apartment. All of the lights had been turned out and the curtains were still drawn. 'I think that they've got something very bad in those crates.'

'That's what I'm thinking too. Whatever they're planning, it's big and they've got a lot of it.'

'Let's go take a look.'

She put her hand on Harvath's shoulder and said, 'Wait a second. Shouldn't we be sure there's nobody else up there?'

'Trust me,' he replied. 'There's nobody else up there.'

'How do you know?'

Harvath started down the alley. 'Because if they had more men, they would have gotten those crates up into the apartment a lot faster.'

Despite his confidence that the apartment was empty, Casey noticed that Harvath was still very careful about how he moved. He avoided motion lights and stayed close to large objects that could function as cover and concealment.

It had been hot and humid ever since they had landed in Chicago. There wasn't any breeze and the alley was thick with the odor of overripe garbage. Casey was sweating. Her shirt clung to her back as she followed him.

Their target was a four-story brick building with a wooden set of fire stairs behind it. A section of chain-link fencing with a broken gate separated the property from the alley.

They walked down the narrow gangway and were about to mount the stairs when Cooper's voice came over their earpieces. 'Two new trucks just pulled up to the loading dock.'

'What are they doing?' Harvath whispered.

'Bunch of Middle Eastern guys have come out of the store and are now loading cardboard boxes.'

That place was like a clown car. Just when you thought it was empty, more of them crawled out, Harvath thought.

'Do you want us to follow them?' she asked.

'Only if you see someone matching Jarrah's description. Other than that, hold your position and write down the license numbers, descriptions of the trucks, and anyone you see getting in.'

'Roger that,' said Cooper.

Looking at Casey, Harvath asked, 'Ready?'

She adjusted the laptop bag she was carrying and flashed him the thumbs-up.

Harvath opened his messenger-style bag the rest of the way and wrapped his hand around the grip of his suppressed MP7 and led the way up the stairs.

Though the weapon was extremely compact, it was difficult to conceal beneath casual, summer clothing so they carried their MP7s in bags that wouldn't look out of place in an urban environment. Beneath their shirts, each also carried a Glock 19 in a paddle holster.

All of the apartments they passed were dark. When they reached the third-floor landing, they could hear a television through an open window somewhere off in the distance, but nothing from inside the apartment itself.

They stepped carefully on the landing, just in case Harvath had been wrong about the unit being empty and a warped board gave them away. He moved to the door and pressed his ear against it while Casey covered him. He still heard nothing from inside.

He checked the door frame for any alarms or trip devices and when he didn't find any, he tried the knob. The door was locked.

Harvath removed one of the lockpick guns that had been included with their gear and went to work. When the dead bolt slid back, he returned the device to his pocket, removed his MP7 completely from his messenger bag, and stood back so that Casey could grip the doorknob.

He took a deep breath, then nodded, and Casey quietly pulled the door open. Harvath swept into the kitchen searching for hostile targets. Despite the drapes on the window being drawn, a certain amount of ambient light from the buildings on the other side of the alley illuminated the room. It also smelled like someone had forgotten to take out the garbage.

With Casey behind him, he moved past a card

table to the other side of the small kitchen. Across a narrow hallway, he could see through an open door into a bedroom. Next to that was a closed door, which he assumed led to the bathroom. To see any further, he needed to stick his head into the hallway, but suddenly the hairs on the back of his neck stood on end.

Harvath hated hallways. They had a bad habit of funneling the gunfire of even the worst shooter right at you. But that wasn't it; not completely at least.

His sixth sense was trying to tell him something. Someone else was in the apartment. He could feel it now. He didn't know if they were in the bedroom closet, behind the closed door to the bathroom, or at the end of the hallway where he couldn't see. Wherever it was, there was danger in this apartment and his body was tensing up in anticipation of engaging it.

He signaled Casey that he would cover the hallway while she crossed to clear the bedroom. When he was ready, he nodded and swung out into the hallway, and that's when he saw it.

In the eerie half-light of the living room was the outline of a hooded figure sitting in a chair. Harvath lit up the scene with a flash from his weapon light and saw that it wasn't just one figure, but three.

He held his position as Casey quickly exited the bedroom and cleared the bathroom, which was jammed with the shipping crates they had seen being carried upstairs.

Together they moved into the living room and secured it, making sure no one was lurking beyond the apartment's front door. Then and only then did they tend to the hostages.

Their chairs had been duct-taped in a sort of circle and the men to them. Harvath removed their hoods and the hostages wildly gestured with their chins at their chests.

He opened the shirt of the man nearest him and instantly understood. He didn't need to see vests on the other two to know that they had them as well.

'Everyone relax. We're going to get you out of here.'

Instead of calming down, the man who Harvath was standing in front of became even more agitated. He was gesturing even more urgently, but not at the vest anymore. He seemed to be nodding toward the corner of the room. Harvath turned and looked behind, but couldn't understand what the man was trying to tell him.

When Harvath couldn't figure it out, the man became even more impatient. His eyes were wide and he was yelling from behind the layers of duct tape that had been wrapped around his head and over his mouth.

'Don't move,' Harvath said as he pulled out his knife. The man didn't listen and Harvath had to sling his weapon and grab the man's face as he carefully made an incision along the left side of the tape.

Peeling enough of it away to get a good grip, he then pulled back — hard.

'The camera!' John Vaughan shouted as the tape came free. 'There's a camera between the books! The vests are triggered to remote detonate!'

It took Harvath a second but he found the camera and spun it so it faced the wall.

When he turned back around, Casey had opened the shirts of the other men, revealing their explosive vests.

'Get out of here, before they detonate!' said Vaughan.

'Easy,' replied Harvath. 'The men who brought you here drove off in their truck. That's a wireless camera with a limited range. If somebody was watching us, they would have already detonated.'

'I'm Sergeant John Vaughan with the Chicago Police. There's going to be a terrorist attack.'

'We know,' said Casey as she examined the man's vest with her flashlight, 'but I need you to be still for a minute. Don't talk, okay?'

Vaughan fell silent as she examined his vest and then looked under and behind his chair.

'Are you looking for the trigger?' he asked.

'Yes.'

'There's something in the small of my back. I think it's a cell phone.'

Casey put her flashlight between her teeth, bent down, and very carefully slid one of her hands behind the police officer. 'I feel it.'

'Can you disarm it?' Harvath asked.

'I won't know till we get him out of the chair and I see it.' Straightening back up, she looked at Vaughan and said, 'There's something called a mercury switch. The way it works is — '

'I'm a Marine. I was in Iraq,' interrupted the

policeman. 'I know what a mercury switch is.'

'I'm trying to figure out if moving you will trigger this vest.'

'We got the crap jostled out of us in those crates. Trust me, there's no mercury switch.'

'So all they did was tape you to the chairs?'

'Yes,' said Vaughan.

Casey took out her knife. 'Let's cut him loose.'

Once Vaughan was free, Harvath helped him stand, while Casey studied his vest. 'It's similar to the mechanism they used in London; probably how the vests in Amsterdam were set up.'

'Who are you?' asked Vaughan.

'That's not important,' said Harvath.

'Don't worry,' added Casey. 'I know what I'm doing.'

'Thank God, because — '

'Done,' she replied, having disconnected the cell phone trigger.

'What?'

Casey raised her finger to her lips for him to be quiet as she studied the buckles on the vest. She then put the flashlight back in her mouth and carefully unfastened them.

'Now very slowly,' she ordered, nodding at Harvath to grab the opposite side of the vest, 'we're going to lift up and I want you to slide out of it. If you feel even the slightest tug, a snag, even if you think you're imagining it, I want you to freeze. Okay?'

'Okay,' said Vaughan.

'Good. Now on three and remember, *slowly*. Here we go. One. Two. Three.'

The policeman slowly slid out of the vest and backed away from it. Harvath then took it from Casey and held it up for her to examine.

Her eyes narrowed as she moved in to look at something. 'What the heck is this?'

'What did you find?' asked Harvath.

'I'll tell you after we look at the other two vests. Let's hurry up.'

69

'Everything went okay?' asked Jarrah when Rashid returned.

'No problems,' he replied. 'Everything is in place.'

'And Mohammed Nasiri?'

'Mohammed is ready, as are the rest of our brothers. He told me to thank you and that he is sorry for any trouble he may have caused.'

Jarrah smiled and looked up at the two men behind Rashid. 'You have done very well. Go and prepare yourselves. We will pray together shortly.'

When the two men had left, Marwan motioned for his protégé to sit with him. 'Come and take tea with me.'

'I think caffeine is probably the last thing I need right now,' said Rashid as he sat down and dried his palms on his thighs. He looked at the empty tables where the suicide vests had been constructed and the reloading equipment he had used to build his special ammunition. 'Did you think about what I asked?'

'I did.'

'*And?*'

'And how are your testicles, from where the woman kicked you?'

'For the tenth time, Marwan, I'm fine. And in case I didn't make myself clear the other nine times I said it, if you ever want something that stupid done again, you can do it yourself.'

Jarrah pointed at the closed circuit television set near him. 'We have it recorded on video, if you would like to watch.'

'Have you been replaying it for everyone? Is that what you've been doing? You think that's funny?'

'She kicks hard, like a donkey,' the man said with a chuckle. It took him a minute to compose himself. When he had, he reached into his pocket and set a pill bottle on the table. 'Here.'

Rashid picked it up and read the label. 'Valium? You think I've got some sort of an anxiety disorder?'

'It has nothing to do with a *disorder*. It will help you to relax. Trust me, you need it.'

'The hell I do.'

'There's two left. Take them.'

'No. And what do you mean there's two *left?* What happened to the rest of them?'

'I gave them to the Shahid.'

'Without asking me?'

'I don't need your permission, Shahab.'

'What about your shooters? Did you give them Valium too?'

'Of course not. They've been given amphetamines.'

Rashid shook his head. 'Just like Mumbai.'

'Have faith in Allah, Shahab. Today we will strike a mighty blow for Islam, Insha'Allah.'

Rashid leaned forward and poured two glasses of tea. 'I guess you're right. We have worked very hard for this day.'

'Yes, we have,' said Jarrah, accepting his glass and setting it down to cool.

They were quiet for several moments, each man pondering what was soon to happen. It was Marwan who eventually broke the silence. 'I want you to know something.'

'What's that?'

'I want you to know that I believe in you.'

'Let's not go down this road again, Marwan. Okay?' said Rashid. 'I've got enough on my mind already.'

The man raised his hand. 'I'm telling you the truth. Sheik Aleem has gone to Los Angeles to prepare the next attack. He wants you to go to New York.'

'Are you serious?'

Marwan smiled. 'Yes.'

Rashid thought about that. 'You know after today, it's going to be nearly impossible to pull off the same kind of attack.'

'With Allah's help, nothing is impossible,' replied Jarrah, 'but Sheik Aleem and I agree with you, which is why the next attacks have been designed to be different.'

Rashid leaned forward. 'How different?'

'Airplanes will rain from the sky. Radiation and a plague will infect the infidel populations. They will know terror like they have never known before.'

'And what about the cells? Are they already in place?'

'Everything is ready and waiting. Sheik Aleem has prepared a communications protocol that — ' Jarrah's voice trailed off as his eyes shifted to his television monitor.

'What is it?' asked Rashid.

468

'Someone is in the store.'

The younger man pulled out his pistol. 'How many? Where did you see them?'

'On the first floor of the showroom. The west wall near the stairs to the — '

'Down here to the basement,' said Rashid as he leapt up. 'Stay right there. Don't move.'

As he stepped into the cinder block hallway, he heard a shout. Seconds later, automatic weapons fire began.

70

Vaughan, Davidson, and Levy had no idea where they'd been moved to after being captured and tortured — or in Levy's case shot — at the mosque. They knew it was a basement room somewhere, but that was it.

As far as why they had been placed at Mohammed Nasiri's apartment, Vaughan had only been able to pick up bits and pieces, but thought that maybe they were going to be used to draw in a bunch of police officers and then their vests would be detonated in hopes of killing as many as possible.

The only other information the men could contribute was in regard to the TATP they thought the terrorists were going to use and what Mohammed Nasiri and the other men they had seen looked like.

It wasn't a lot to go on, but it became a large part of Harvath's decision to hit Marwan Jarrah's place of business. With all of the activity, it was obvious that the attack was about to happen. But what had cinched it for Harvath was the camera at Nasiri's apartment. Even fully charged, it would run for only so long. Whatever the Chicago cell had planned, it was going to happen very soon. Harvath had decided they couldn't wait any longer.

Though Levy had taken two clean, in-and-out gunshot wounds to the shoulder and someone had done a fair job of patching him up, he was still going to need to see a doctor. Davidson and Vaughan had been roughed up pretty good as well. Vaughan had suffered a broken wrist, and both of Davidson's eyes were so swollen he could barely see out of them.

'You three need medical attention,' said Harvath.

'The hell with that,' said Davidson. 'We're going with you.'

'How many fingers am I holding up?'

When the Public Vehicles officer didn't answer, Harvath replied, 'I thought so.'

'How many fingers am I holding up?' Davidson replied as he flipped Harvath the bird.

'I agree,' said Vaughan. 'The hospital can wait. We want to help take these guys down.'

Harvath took the officer aside and quietly said, 'Listen, your team has done a great job, but you've got to let us finish it.'

'And if I say *no*?'

'Then I'm going to hold you in my custody until this is all over. And just so you know, my version of custody is duct-taping you back up, including the gags, and placing you in a Dumpster somewhere around here. If I get shot and don't come back, you'll be there till trash day, or till the rats gnaw through the restraints, whichever comes first.'

'What authority do you have to — ' said Vaughan, but Harvath interrupted him.

'Whether you think so or not, you guys need a doctor. All of you. You're only going to slow us down, or worse, get us killed.'

471

Vaughan knew Harvath was right. He didn't like it, but he understood it and consented to follow his plan.

He and Davidson would take Levy to Dennis Stern, the trauma surgeon, who would keep everything quiet. Not reporting the pending terrorist attack went against his instincts as a cop and his loyalty to his department, but Harvath had made it very clear that this was now a national security issue and needed to remain classified. The men were told they couldn't even contact their wives, who had probably already filed missing persons reports, until Harvath released them to do so. Vaughan agreed to hole up in Stern's office, gave Harvath the surgeon's cell and office numbers, and then Harvath handed over enough cash for them to get a taxi to the hospital.

When Harvath and Casey were back in their vehicle, they radioed the rest of the team to get ready to take down Jarrah's store.

★ ★ ★

Forty-five minutes later, when the team was regrouped and ready to take down the store, Harvath gave the 'go' command.

Ericsson disabled the alarm, but that was the extent of their prep work. There was no way they could shut down the power, which meant the closed circuit camera system would still be operational. Based on what Cooper had seen while inside the store, they had developed the best plan they could. Speed, surprise, and overwhelming violence of action would have to work.

They entered from two separate points and moved fast. Cooper and Rhodes took the first-floor office, while Harvath, Casey, and Ericsson headed for the basement. They had just made it to the bottom of the stairs when one of the delivery goons spotted them. He was completely naked, his skin damp as if he'd just stepped out of the shower.

Seeing the intruders, he yelled as he disappeared back into the room he'd just exited.

Harvath, Casey, and Ericsson advanced, only to be driven back by a heavy barrage of machine-gun fire. Several of the rounds ricocheted off the walls and ceiling as well as the pipes that surrounded them.

There was a grunt, followed by Ericsson saying, 'I'm hit.'

'How bad?' shouted Harvath as he returned fire and tried to keep their attackers pinned down.

Casey examined her teammate's wound. 'Upper thigh. It's starting to bleed pretty good.'

'Damn it,' Harvath replied as he fired another burst.

'Office is empty. We're on our way,' said Cooper over the radio.

'Hurry up,' ordered Casey.

Harvath noticed movement in the hallway and let loose another burst from his MP7. When he realized what had happened, he barely had time to yell, 'Flash bang!' as a concussion grenade was banked off the wall at them.

It went off immediately in a blinding flash of white light with a thunderous boom that overpressured the basement. Harvath had barely shut his eyes and his mouth was only partway open when it happened; not enough to fully mitigate the effects. He had no idea if the rest of his team had heard his warning or not.

His vision blurred from the flash, he thought he could see two forms coming right at him. He raised his weapon to fire, but someone beat him to it. There were two loud *booms* and both figures dropped to the ground. He didn't know who had fired and how he could have heard it over the ringing in his ears, as everyone on his team was using suppressed weapons. Then he realized the shots hadn't come from his team. They'd come from someone else; someone at the other end of the hallway.

71

'Drop your weapon!' Harvath yelled. 'Drop it now!'

Abdul Rashid straightened his trigger finger and allowed the pistol to roll upside down and hang from it.

Harvath repeated the command in Arabic.

'I'm going to bend down and set it on the ground,' Rashid replied in English.

'Slowly,' said Harvath, his vision and hearing coming back. 'Very, very slowly.'

'I'm setting it down.'

Once the weapon was on the ground, Harvath said, 'Back up five steps and kiss the ground.'

Rashid did as he was told, and while Rhodes helped tend to Ericsson, Harvath and the rest of the team cautiously advanced.

Harvath kept his weapon trained on Rashid while Casey and Cooper cleared the two rooms on either side of the hallway. Once they were done, he checked the two men Rashid had shot. They were both dead.

'Where's Jarrah?'

'There's another room at the far end of the basement. He's barricaded in there.'

'How many other people in the building?' demanded Harvath.

'There's nobody else. This is it. Listen, you can't shoot him. I need Jarrah alive.'

Harvath looked at Casey and Cooper. 'Go get

him.' Looking down at Rashid, he removed a pair of EZ Cuffs and said, 'Put your hands behind your back.'

'My name's Sean Chase. I'm with the CIA. Ground Branch.'

'Shut up and put your hands behind your back,' Harvath repeated.

Before Chase could respond, Alex Cooper yelled, 'Gun!' and all eyes turned to the end of the hallway where Marwan Jarrah had just stepped from around the corner with an AK47 and begun firing.

72

Marwan Jarrah never had a chance. As the bullets popped and zinged all around her, Alex Cooper stood her ground and returned fire.

Though she wanted to kill him on the spot by putting two rounds right into his head, she focused on his chest and didn't lay off of her trigger until he laid off of his.

The Iraqi fell back against the wall and left a trail of blood as he slid down into a sitting position. His AK clattered to the ground next to him and Cooper kicked it away.

Chase tried to get up, but Harvath kept his knee in his back as he zipped his cuffs.

'I don't know who the hell you are,' shouted Chase, 'but if he dies, you're in a lot of trouble.'

Harvath stood up, yanked Chase to his feet, and handed him to Casey. 'Let him ask any questions he wants, but watch him.' Harvath then took Cooper to clear the rest of the basement.

'You lied to me,' murmured Jarrah as Chase kneeled next to him.

'Tell me how I can reach Aleem,' he said, knowing full well it was pointless. Marwan wasn't going to give him up.

The Iraqi laughed and then produced a wet cough as he spat up blood.

'I treated you like a son.' His eyelids were

drooping and his breath was coming in sharp gasps.

He whispered something further but Chase couldn't hear it and so leaned in closer. 'What did you say?'

'I have something to tell you,' the Iraqi rasped, before his body was racked once more with bloody coughs.

'What is it?'

'I have a secret.'

Chase was inches away from his face. 'What is it, Marwan? Tell me.'

As his final breath escaped his body, Jarrah looked at his beloved protégé and said, 'I lied to you too.'

* * *

After clearing the basement, Harvath came back to interrogate the man claiming to be from the CIA.

'Listen, there's going to be an attack downtown in two hours.'

'Let's start with who the hell you are,' said Harvath.

'I told you, my name is Sean Chase. Call Langley and ask to be connected to Kip Houghton. He's my handler.'

Harvath nodded at Cooper, who removed her cell phone and headed for the stairs.

'Jarrah's got eight suicide bombers,' continued Chase, 'but you don't need to worry about them. What you need to be worried about — '

'Wait a second,' interrupted Harvath. 'Why

shouldn't we be worried about eight suicide bombers?'

'Because their vests don't work. I made sure.'

Casey looked at him. 'How?'

'The circuit's not complete. The detonators can't get any electricity.'

'Just like the vests in Nasiri's apartment.'

'Where are the bombers now?' asked Harvath.

'That's not important,' replied Chase. 'Jarrah has three two-man teams of Mumbai-style shooters that are going to hit a bunch of hotels unless we stop them. We need to get going.'

'Until we get confirmation on who you are, you're not going anywhere. Why was there a camera in Nasiri's apartment?'

'So I could have an excuse to get away from Jarrah. I wanted him to think I was going to detonate the vests on the hostages myself. If I could get away from him, then I could try to stop the shooters.'

'Why not call the cops? Why go to all this trouble?'

'Because this isn't the end of it. There's somebody else above Jarrah, a man named Aleem.'

'Aazim Aleem?' Harvath replied.

'That's him. The guy with the hooks. Jarrah told me that he has networks in at least two other cities. Supposedly, he's already left for Los Angeles and I was supposed to coordinate an attack in New York. But — ' Rashid's voice trailed off.

'*But* what?'

'I think he was lying to me.'

'About what?' asked Harvath. 'The location of the attacks or the fact that you were supposed to coordinate the one in New York?'

'I don't know. That's why I wanted Jarrah *alive*. He was the only one who knew how to get to Aleem.'

Harvath pressed him with more questions. 'Why'd you torture those cops?'

'You're wasting time,' said Chase.

'Answer me.'

'For fuck's sake. I'm the only reason they're still alive. Jarrah wanted to kill them.'

'But you shot one of them.'

'It was clean. Through and through. If I'd wanted to kill him, trust me, he'd be dead.'

Harvath was about to ask another question when Cooper hailed him over the radio and told him someone at Langley wanted to talk to him.

73

After Harvath had spoken to Kip Houghton, he hung up and called Reed Carlton, who contacted Bruce Selleck, director of the National Clandestine Service at CIA. Once they had both vouched for Chase and his deep-cover operation, Harvath had been instructed to remove his restraints and allow him to come along.

Chase was part of a small contingent of faux John Walker Lindhs whom the Agency had recruited from various walks of life, trained, and then set adrift in a handful of madrassas across the Islamic world hoping that they might get picked up by al-Qaeda. Several of them had, but no one had gotten as far as Sean Chase.

Trained to operate completely on his own, Chase went for long stretches without contact. The assignment and his cover always came first. His handler was used to the irregularity with which he reported in. But as well as the operation had worked, everyone was now extremely concerned that maybe they had let this go too far and that more innocent people were going to die.

Over two hours had passed and Harvath was developing a very bad feeling as Casey's voice came over his earpiece. 'Negative,' she replied to his request for a sitrep. 'There's no sign of any of them. We're still all clear at the InterContinental.'

Across the street at the Marriott hotel, Harvath looked at Chase. 'According to your timetable, they should have been here by now.'

'I don't know where the hell they are.'

'You're positive these were the hotels?'

'Yes,' replied the CIA operative, who was equally frustrated.

'I'm getting ready to pack it in,' said Harvath.

'I know. They should have been here by now. Give it a few more minutes. They'll come.'

'I don't think so.'

If the truth be told, Chase didn't know what to think either. *But why would Marwan have brought him here?* What was the point?

The last words the man uttered to him were that he had lied. *Was this what he had lied about?* It didn't make any sense. Marwan had six shooters. Minus the two Chase had shot in the basement of the store, there were four left, two of whom had been wounded by Levy's shotgun blast. Where were they? If the hotels weren't their target, what was?

All of a sudden, it hit him. 'The train station! That's the target.'

'How do you know?'

'Because I know him. He wanted this to be a dramatic attack. That's why all the bombers were supposed to detonate in the Loop, the city's central business district. Look at this lobby. It's half-empty. Where are you going to get the highest body count first thing in the morning? You go to where the commuters are.'

'I hope to God you're right,' said Harvath as

482

he radioed the other team members.

'So do I,' Chase replied under his breath.

* * *

Based on the CIA operative's guarantee that the suicide bombers wouldn't be able to detonate, they had decided to bring the Chicago Police Department into the plan. Plainclothes officers had been positioned where the bombers were supposed to appear and tactical teams were placed at the hotels.

With the morning rush in full swing, the streets were jammed with traffic. Even with lights and sirens, they'd never make it on time — unless they could avoid the traffic altogether.

Harvath radioed Casey and told her where to meet them. Next, he radioed the Chicago Police and then he and Chase exited the hotel and took off running faster than either of them had ever run before.

* * *

It was three long, hard blocks to the river. When they arrived, Casey and a Chicago Police boat were waiting for them. Harvath and Chase leapt in and the officer behind the wheel spun the craft into the river and put the throttle all the way down.

Casey yelled over the engine noise. 'We've got good news and bad news. What do you want first?'

Harvath's lungs were on fire and he could

barely breathe, much less speak. He held up two fingers.

'The bad news,' yelled Casey as she pointed at a map, 'is that there are basically five downtown commuter Metra stations and because of traffic, the tac teams can only get to two of them. It'll take them at least fifteen minutes to get to the others.'

Harvath then raised one finger.

'The good news is that the Millennium and Van Buren stations are near Cooper and Rhodes. They're the ones with tac teams who can make it, so they'll tackle those. Ogilvie and Union Station are pretty close to the river, but La Salle Street station is a few blocks inland.'

'I'll take La Salle,' said Chase, who was still panting.

'What's our first drop point?' asked Harvath as he tried to steady his breathing. Casey consulted the officer piloting the boat and then said, 'Ogilvie. Drop off at Madison Street and it's a block and a half west.'

Harvath raised himself to standing. 'I'll take that one.'

'Like hell you will,' replied Casey. 'I'm more rested. I'll take it. You take Union Station. It's the next drop and it's right at the river. I'm not taking no for an answer.'

Harvath bowed his head and kept sucking in air.

'It's going to be this bridge,' said the police officer as they approached. 'Starboard side. Coming up fast.'

As the boat slammed up against the landing,

Harvath looked at Casey and said, 'Mine.' Before she could respond, he had jumped out of the boat and was running up the stairs.

She yelled out, '*Klootzak*,' but had no idea if he heard.

74

Despite being winded, Harvath was ready to run when he got up to the street level. Then he realized how much attention he would be calling to himself and, instead, walked as quickly as he could toward the station.

Across the street, he waited for the light, sucked in as many deep breaths as he could, and fought to get his heartbeat under control.

Of all the places to try to apprehend a lone gunman, a crowded train station had to be one of the worst.

The Northeast Illinois Regional Commuter Railroad Corporation, known as Metra, served Chicago and six counties in a surrounding radius. The station was overflowing with commuters.

Harvath followed the signs and made his way to the escalators that led to the upper level where the train platforms were. He was only halfway up when the shooting began.

The people in front of him turned and began running down the up escalator. He tried to push through them, but they were panicked. Hopping over the rail onto the stairs, he fought through the masses of people and began running. The shooter was firing on full auto.

As he neared the top of the stairs, it suddenly stopped. *Magazine change*, thought Harvath, and he was right. Just as quickly as the shooting had stopped, it had started again.

The platforms fed out into a cavernous retail area several stories tall. With people running and screaming, it was hard to get an exact fix on where the shooter was. All he could tell was that the shooting was coming from the other side, away from where he now stood. He pulled out two spare mags for his MP7, tucked them in his waistband, and tossed away his bag.

Seconds later, the sounds of fully automatic fire were joined by the sound of something else — single-shot fire. There was another shooter and he was close.

Through the sea of people, Harvath caught a glimpse of a Metra police officer who had taken a knee out in the open and was engaging the attacker.

Passengers were running everywhere including back out on to the platforms and down onto the tracks. Harvath couldn't tell why the Metra officer hadn't sought cover. He was a sitting duck where he was. Then Harvath locked eyes on the attacker and saw what he was focused on. Pinned near one of the retail stores was a group of children. The Metra cop was not only engaging the shooter, he was trying to draw his fire — away from the children. They were very young, approximately six or seven years old, and were all sobbing. Two adults in matching T-shirts lay in pools of blood on the granite floor in front of them.

Harvath raised his MP7 to fire at the shooter, but as he did, he saw the Metra cop get shot in the chest and the throat. As he fell forward, his weapon clattered to the floor, its slide locked back, the pistol out of ammo.

With the cop out of the picture, the terrorist sprayed a bunch of fleeing passengers who had been running in the other direction. It caused a reverse stampede and any clear shot he could have had was now blocked. He needed to get to those children, but the only path available to him was through the shooter's wall of fire.

Running out onto the platform area, Harvath ran past three sets of tracks and then, using the closest entrance for cover, risked a peek back into the concourse. He was much closer and had a very good view of the shooter, a muscular Middle Easterner with a mustache and short hair.

The man was hyperalert and caught sight of Harvath immediately. He turned his weapon toward him and began firing.

Harvath ducked back behind the entrance as masonry, metal, and glass exploded all around him. When the firing stopped, he rolled back out to engage, but the man had disappeared.

In the concourse, the floor was slick with blood and covered with bodies that had been ripped to shreds.

It took Harvath a moment to realize where the shooter had disappeared to. He had leapt behind a concession-store counter. Harvath had no idea how thick it was, whether it was solid, or what was stacked behind it, but he knew there wasn't much a 4.6 mm round couldn't chew through. He also knew he had to keep the man's attention off those children, so he began firing.

His rounds tore good pieces out of the counter, but he spent his magazine quickly and had to roll back to his cover and reload. By the time he did, the shooter was up and firing again. He was firing at Harvath's position, which meant he wasn't targeting the children. That was good. The man, though, had also switched to three-round bursts, which meant he was not only being much more careful, but he also knew what he was doing.

The thing that didn't make any sense, though, was why he hadn't transitioned to the special armor-piercing ammunition Chase had fabricated and which he had explained to Harvath that all the shooters were carrying.

Harvath waited for another volley and when it subsided, he swung back out and did an entire magazine dump on the counter before ducking back. Through the smoke, he had seen that he had broken through in multiple places. It looked like metal canisters of some sort were stored underneath the counter. Nevertheless, the shooter had to know that Harvath was getting closer. What he didn't know was that Harvath only had one magazine for the MP7 left and had no idea if it would be enough.

When the man popped up this time to fire, he managed only two rounds before his magazine was empty and he was forced to drop back down and reload.

Harvath spun back around the entrance and, making sure to control his muzzle rise, focused on one particular area he had been tearing through the counter. He emptied the magazine as his rounds went clean through.

Ducking back behind the entrance, he dropped the MP7 and pulled out his Glock. He had fifteen rounds in the magazine, one in the chamber. It was make-or-break time. He needed to get to those children.

Crouching, he ran to the platform entrance nearest to where they were still paralyzed and crying on the concourse. Taking a deep breath, he counted to three, raised his Glock, and sped out from behind the door.

The shooter was already waiting for him. As Harvath appeared, he locked his sights on him and pulled his trigger.

The explosive round detonated inside the terrorist's chamber and blew up right in his face, just as Chase had planned.

As the man's scream filled the concourse, Harvath put two rounds into his head and killed him.

Epilogue

The end of August was not a good time to be in Yemen. In fact, as far as Harvath was concerned, there was never a good time to be in Yemen or anywhere else on the Arabian Peninsula.

He sat at one of the city's few halfway decent cafés, his chair propped up against the wall, an awning shielding him from the afternoon sun. As he took a sip of his chai, he thought about everything that had happened.

With visible tactical teams in plate armor at Chicago's Millennium and Van Buren stations, the shooters who had come there to cause maximum carnage had immediately switched out their magazines for the ones loaded with Chase's 'armor-piercing' rounds.

As their weapons exploded in their faces and civilians scattered, both men were gunned down. Credit was given to the quick-thinking CPD tac teams. The fallen Metra officer at the Ogilvie Transportation Center was rightly billed as a hero without whose actions many more innocent lives, including those of a small group of six-year-olds, would have been lost.

The slaughter at Union Station had been worse than Ogilvie because it had started three

491

minutes before Gretchen Casey got there. Positioned behind the shooter, she took a shot from over seventy yards and killed him instantly with one round through the back of his head. She then secreted her weapon and quietly left the station. While the police in general were given credit for fast action, no single officer or department had yet officially been credited for killing the shooter. A rumor that it had been done by an undercover U.S. marshal on his way to work had gained wide traction in the press.

All of the would-be suicide bombers were apprehended exactly where Sean Chase had said they would be. Neither Harvath nor any of the Athena Team members had seen him again after he had chosen to take the La Salle Street station.

According to Carlton's contacts at the CIA, Chase had been tasked with hunting down Aazim Aleem. Based on chatter the Agency had intercepted, Aleem was convinced that his entire network had been compromised and had fled the country for somewhere in the Middle East. Authorities so far had been unable to uncover any evidence of plots or Jarrah-Aleem cells in Los Angeles or New York. Their investigations were ongoing.

Once stabilized, Nikki Rodriguez was transferred stateside and was expected to make a full recovery. Julie Ericsson had been treated for her gunshot wound at Stroger Hospital in Chicago and released. She traveled back to Ft. Bragg with her teammates, Megan Rhodes, Alex Cooper, and Gretchen Casey. Casey had been keeping Harvath up to date on their progress and in her last e-mail informed him that, upon reflection, Rodriguez was convinced that he *had* been looking at her ass in Amsterdam. She wanted him to call her to discuss the matter further. In other words, they all sent their best wishes and looked forward to seeing him again soon.

Josh Levy, the owner of Surety Private Investigations, had been discharged from the hospital after being held overnight for observation and was expected to make a full recovery. Based on a couple of calls from Washington, John Vaughan and Paul Davidson both received commendations and promotions. While Davidson was happy where he was, Vaughan gladly accepted a newly created position with the Chicago Police Department's Intelligence unit. Davidson recruited the Pakistani mechanic, Javed Miraj, into his network and was using him to help build a case against the three stooges at the Crescent Garage.

Alison Taylor had begun making progress, and her family couldn't have been happier. Mr. Taylor had paid Vaughan the balance of his monies owed and realized that with all of the federal charges against Mohammed Nasiri, Alison would probably never get her day in court. Even so, knowing that she was getting better and that Nasiri would never walk free was justice enough for him.

In Switzerland, Adda Sterk had been remanded to a DOD black site for further interrogation, and Michael Lee was given immunity from prosecution, along with a small payment from the Carlton Group to guarantee his silence. He was reunited with his dog and also tracked down Sterk's contact, who had accepted the two decoy dogs that supposedly belonged to Nicholas. The Old Man had made it known to Harvath that he wanted the settlement money to Michael Lee to be reimbursed to the Carlton Group by the Troll, in person. Harvath had no idea where he was, but he assumed that he and Padre Peio had returned to the Basque country.

After Chicago, Harvath had intended to return to Virginia, but instead he had gone to Maine. He knew it wasn't going to be easy telling Tracy things were over. She was a beautiful woman and he loved her very much, more than he had ever loved anyone else. He wanted a family, though. He had come to the conclusion that he wanted that more than anything else, even more than his career. He had thought he could have both with her. He believed that at one point it had been possible, but not the way things were now.

They drank a lot and stayed in bed together for three entire days. When the Old Man called and Harvath told her he had to go, she told him she loved him and that she hoped he would keep in touch with her. She also told him that she understood and that he was doing the right thing.

As Harvath left, he consoled himself with the knowledge that if a great relationship had once been possible with Tracy, it could be possible with somebody else. Maybe even Riley, the doctor Carlton had sent to him in Geneva. For his part, though, the Old Man wasn't forthcoming with any further information about her. That was okay. When he was done in Yemen, he was seriously considering going to Paris to see if he could find her on his own.

Taking another sip of chai, he checked his watch and looked across the dusty street at the figure that was approaching.

'You're late,' he said as the man pulled out one of the rickety chairs and sat down.

'Fuck you.'

Harvath smiled. If he hadn't met Sean Chase in Chicago, he never would have been able to pick him out here in Yemen, or in any other Muslim country. He blended in perfectly. 'You still mad?'

Chase's eyes widened. 'Is that a serious fucking question? Because I spent *three years* of my life infiltrating Aleem's network only to have you cock it all up.'

'You're young, there'll be other assignments.'

'You're an idiot, you know that? How do you tell somebody to just walk away and forget something like that?'

'I didn't tell you to walk away and forget it,' said Harvath. 'I told you that there'd be other assignments.'

'Spoken like a true old-timer.'

'Forty makes me an old-timer?'

'It certainly doesn't make you a spring chicken.'

Harvath laughed. This kid was all mouth and balls. He liked him. Probably because that's exactly the way he had been. 'Hot enough for you?' he asked, changing the subject.

'We're going to talk about the fucking weather

now?' Chase asked. 'I thought you had something for me. Or did you fly halfway around the world just to pull on my dick?'

Harvath laughed again.

'What's so goddamn funny?'

'You've got an incredible mouth on you. If you don't get a handle on it, it's going to hold you back.'

'What the hell would you know about it?'

'I know,' said Harvath. 'Trust me.'

'So, are we going to cuddle up and read chapter two from Miss Manners or are you going to give me the intel you supposedly uncovered on Aleem?'

Harvath motioned for the waiter to bring another chai for his guest. Then, turning to Chase, he said, 'I've got good news for you, Sean.'

'I bet you do. What is it?'

'Aleem's close.'

'How close?'

Harvath pulled a set of car keys from his pocket and dropped them on the table. 'See that white Corolla over there?'

Chase looked at the car and then back at Harvath. 'You've got Aleem in there? In the trunk?'

Harvath nodded.

'Holy shit. Where'd you find him?'

'We followed the same leads you did here to Yemen.'

'Let me guess. Age and wisdom over youth and inexperience. Is that what you're going to tell me?'

'From what I understand,' said Harvath, 'you've already got more experience than a lot of people twice your age.'

'So what? You're trying to tell me you're just that good?'

Harvath smiled. 'You're going to learn, Sean, that it's often better to be lucky than good.'

Chase rolled his eyes. 'What's the catch? What do you want?'

'Personally, I'd like you to sit and have a glass of tea with me and then you can drive me to the airport.'

'That's it? That's all you want?'

'I said that's what I wanted personally. Professionally, we expect you to share everything with us you can download out of Aleem.'

'But you could do that yourself,' said Chase. 'Why give him to me?'

'Because we want to. You worked harder than anyone to get close to this guy and take his network apart. A lot of people have been killed because of him and it's going to make America look good that we captured him. My group doesn't want any publicity. The Agency on the other hand needs the good press. Just make sure management doesn't try to grab all the credit.'

'Thank you,' said Chase as the waiter set down his glass.

Harvath's phone vibrated. It was an unknown number and he was tempted not to answer it, but for some stupid reason he thought maybe Carlton had given in and passed his number along to Riley in Paris.

The moment he heard the modulated voice on

the other end, he knew he had made a mistake. 'You owe my boss some money, Nicholas. And he wants it from you in person,' said Harvath.

'I've got something else the Old Man's going to want a lot more,' replied the Troll.

'Then call him and tell him yourself,' he said as he reached for more chai. 'I'm going on vacation.'

'I found something on Adda Sterk's thumb drive.'

'What thumb drive?'

'The one I found in Geneva after you dumped her purse out looking for her inhaler.'

'That's U.S. government property, Nicholas.'

Wherever in the world he was, the Troll laughed. 'I'm doing you a favor. I really think you should see this.'

'Not interested,' said Harvath.

'Aazim Aleem has a nephew who works at Harrods.'

'So what?'

'So, his nephew was a digital courier for him. Real smart when it came to transmitting information without leaving a trail. Except he made one mistake, and I found it.'

'On the thumb drive.'

'Yes.'

Chase was listening intently. Harvath decided the conversation was over. Clinking the tiny spoon he had against his glass he said, 'You know what sound that is, Nicholas? That's the bell signaling the commencement of the local cocktail hour. I'm off the clock. I'm sure you can track down my boss if you try hard enough.'

That's when the Troll let the other shoe fall. 'A piece of data was transmitted to Sterk that never should have been. It was highly encrypted and even if she had noticed it buried in another file, I don't think she could have decrypted it. I think that's why it was left on her thumb drive, hidden in plain sight.'

'Okay, I give. What is it?'

The Troll took a deep breath and let it out. 'Site 243 wasn't just about a string of Islamic terrorist attacks. The attacks are a small wave preceding a giant tsunami meant to crush the United States.'

★ ★ ★

On a rooftop two blocks away, as a man listened to his employer, he could picture him sitting in his club's library, his liver-spotted hands holding his encrypted cell phone.

'You are positive Aleem is in the trunk of the car?'

'I am,' said the man on the rooftop.

'And nothing will be traced back to us?'

'Nothing at all.'

There was a pause before the man in London finally said, 'You have my permission to proceed.' With that, the line went dead.

The man on the rooftop plucked out his earbud, wrapped the cord around his cell phone, and replaced it in his pocket.

Bending over, he flipped open the lid of the hard plastic container at his feet and removed the rocket-propelled grenade.

He flipped up the sights and hoisted the weapon on his shoulder. It was heavier than he remembered. It took him a moment to focus on the white Corolla in the distance.

When he had his target perfectly aligned in his sights, Robert Ashford pulled the trigger.

Acknowledgments

Acknowledgments
The people who make my job so enjoyable are you, my terrific **readers.** Thank you for all your support and all the wonderful interaction we have on the BradThor.com forum. I also want to thank the best group of **forum moderators** the Internet has ever known.

My thanks go out to the marvelous **booksellers** around the world who have been so instrumental in turning new readers on to the Scot Harvath novels.

The idea for this novel came from time spent with my good friend **Barrett Moore.** He is an amazing warrior, patriot, and one of the wisest men I know. Thank you for all the help.

In addition to Barrett, **Mr. Red, Mr. White,** and **Mr. Blue** provided exceptional background for this story. I very much wanted to name them here, but they asked me not to, content to remain in the shadows where they so professionally ply their trade.

Keeping Scot Harvath on the cutting edge is a 24/7 job and I couldn't do it without **James Ryan** and **Rodney Cox.** I am much indebted to you for both your help with my novels and the service you have rendered our great nation.

Scott F. Hill, Ph.D., and **Ronald Moore** have given much to our country, and I can always count on them to provide invaluable assistance with my writing. Gentlemen, thank you.

Rob Pincus and **Carl Hospedales,** as usual, provided exceptional subject-matter expertise. Drinks are on me next time.

My core group of warriors: **Chad Norberg, Chuck Fretwell, Steve Hoffa, Jeff Chudwin, Mitch Shore, Gary Penrith,** and **Steven Bronson** were there for me once again with answers to all my questions. To them (and my other friends who asked to remain nameless) I want to say thank you for all you do for us. Stay safe.

I also want to thank **John Giduck** and **Joe Bail,** who gave me some very special assistance this year, as well as **Stephanie Dickerson.**

In Washington, **David Vennett** and **Patrick Doak** continue to be great resources and even better friends. Thank you.

Father C. John McCloskey, III, helped as I developed the life and background of Padre Peio. Thank you, Father CJ.

I am blessed to be on one of the best teams in the business and wish to thank everyone at Atria and Pocket Books: my wonderful editor, **Emily Bestler;** my fantastic publishers, **Carolyn Reidy, Judith Curr,** and **Louise Burke;** my remarkable publicist, **David Brown;** the incomparable **Atria/Pocket sales staff, art and production departments,** and **audio division,** as well as the invaluable **Michael Selleck, Laura Stern, Sarah Branham, Irene Lipsky, Esther Bochner,** and **Lisa Keim.**

I also wish to thank my outstanding literary

agent, **Heide Lange,** of Sanford J. Greenburger Associates, Inc., as well as the amazing **Jennifer Linnan, Rachael Dillon Fried,** and **Tara Singh** for all that they do for me.

Scott Schwimer continues to be not only a superb attorney, but also a very good friend. Thanks, Scottie.

Finally, every step of the way and every minute of the day I am able to do what I do because of the support of my beautiful wife, **Trish.** None of this would be possible without her. Thank you, honey. I love you.

VENOM

Joan Brady

Recently released from prison, David Marion didn't expect to find a hitman at his door. Warned that a powerful secret organisation is after him, David goes underground and off the radar — waiting for the perfect moment to wreak revenge . . . Physicist Helen Freyl has just accepted a job offer from a giant pharmaceutical company which is close to finding a cure for radiation poisoning. But when the mysteriously sudden death of a colleague is followed by another, Helen begins to doubt her employer's motives and realises that her own life is in danger, too.

THE ANATOMY OF GHOSTS

Andrew Taylor

1786, Jerusalem College, Cambridge. A disturbed fellow commoner, Frank Oldershaw, claims he's seen the ghost of murdered Sylvia Whichcote haunting Jerusalem. To salvage her son's reputation, Lady Anne Oldershaw employs John Holdsworth, author of *The Anatomy of Ghosts* — a stinging account of why ghosts are mere delusion — to investigate. But Holdsworth's presence in Cambridge disrupts an uneasy status quo in a world of privilege and abuse. And as for Holdsworth himself, haunted by the ghost of Maria, his dead wife — and Elinor, the very-much-alive Master's wife — his fate is sealed. He must find Sylvia's murderer or the hauntings will continue. And no one will leave Jerusalem's claustrophobic confines unchanged.

SISTER

Rosamund Lupton

When Beatrice hears that her little sister, Tess, is missing, she returns home to London on the first flight available. But Bee is unprepared for the terrifying truths she must face about her younger sibling when Tess' broken body is discovered in the snow. The police, Bee's friends, her fiance and even their mother accept the fact that Tess committed suicide. But Bee is convinced that something more sinister is responsible for Tess' untimely death. So she embarks on a dangerous journey to discover the truth, no matter the cost . . .

BREATHLESS

Dean Koontz

Alienated from the modern world, Grady Adams lives in the wilds of the Colorado mountains. And there, something miraculous comes into his life, and he knows that one of Nature's great mysteries has been revealed to him. He takes his friend, scientist Cammy Rivers, to bear witness to the phenomenal presence. She is stunned and awed, and emails photos to colleagues in far places to try and find a name for the wonderful beings. But soon Homeland Security has the wilderness around them quarantined, with scientists to track down and 'neutralize' the threat to the known world. Grady and Cammy, determined to prevent this atrocity, go on the run, and a pursuit of hair-raising suspense is under way, with no happy ending in prospect . . .

FEAR THE WORST

Linwood Barclay

It was the worst day of Tim Blake's life. His seventeen-year-old daughter, Sydney, was staying with him while she worked a summer job at the Just Inn Time hotel — father-daughter time to help with the after-effects of his divorce. Syd didn't arrive home at her usual time. Then, worryingly, she didn't answer her phone. And when the people at the Just Inn Time told him they'd no Sydney Blake working at the hotel, he was plunged into the abyss every parent dreads most. Where had she been every day, if not working at the Just Inn Time . . . ? To find his daughter Tim must discover who she really was, and what could have made her step out of her own life without leaving a trace.

THE MAGDALENA CURSE

F. G. Cottam

Two visits are enough to convince Dr Elizabeth Bancroft that Adam Hunter isn't just having bad dreams. He's a child possessed. His father is desperate: adamant that his son's affliction is the result of a curse he incurred in the depths of the Amazon, where a misguided military operation ended in a terrifying and macabre encounter. There he met two women — one more bad than good, who placed the curse — and the other more good than bad, with whom any hope of saving his son resides. Mark Hunter leaves the Scottish Highlands to beg help from the mysterious woman, leaving his son in the care of Elizabeth — who is about to discover there are equally dark secrets on their own doorstep. And in her blood . . .